The Prize

Part I: *The Quest for the Prize*

Keith Dyne

Raider Publishing International

New York   London

ISBN: 1-935383-04-3

Published By Raider Publishing International
www.RaiderPublishing.com
New York   London

Printed in the United States of America and the United Kingdom

By Lightning Source Ltd.

Acknowledgements

I would like to thank the gang of two: Jean and Romola, the teenage pensioners who regularly frighten the lives out of the Petts Wood hairdressers, each and every Friday.
I thank you for your support, guidance, and critique and I hope that others will benefit from your finding the Prize.
However, shush, do not tell: the old Queen Mary is watching.

I would also like to thank the team at Raider Publishing International for their help and support with bringing this story to you.

The Prize

Part I: *The Quest for the Prize*

Keith Dyne

To Thomas,

The first of three…

One Down

It was a warm July evening in the middle of London. There was a slight breeze blowing, each individual wisp bringing a temporary relief to the locals who had just survived one of the hottest summer days since records began over a hundred years ago. The sun was just beginning to say its daily goodbye, leaving a glowing reddish-orange fire spreading across the wide sky and reflecting off the many glistening glass windows and sides of buildings that was nowadays London.

It was Saturday and most of the local residents had spent the whole day hiding in their houses, behind closed windows and with air conditioners running full blast, each trying to bring an edge of sanity to the crazy temperatures of the day. Some were even now daring to venture outside, opening their windows and their patio doors, exhibiting their tropical wardrobes to their neighbours and anyone else who would look without sniggering.

Not a lot was stirring down on the streets, except in Cromwell Road SW7, close to the Natural History Museum. A shortish man in his early forties with neat well-trimmed dark brown hair, quite a little overweight, wearing thick black rimmed glasses and dressed in a chef's white apron, was running as fast as he could up the large bank of steep steps towards the museum doors. This would normally not be so strange, except that in this case the man was French, was muttering Gallic curses as he climbed the steps, and the museum was in fact closed. These things however did not seem to upset or deter the man from continuing along his chosen path; he seemed in a hurry, as if running scared from something. Had someone not liked the food he had just cooked and had refused to pay his or her bill? Or was this more serious?

Gavin, a quiet man, was the head chef (and a damn good one, at that) at a restaurant some miles away from the centre of London and was well-liked in his local neighbourhood. Gavin was now however, in the middle of a bitter struggle of life and death with the most sinister of evil forces that the planet Earth had seen in its short but violent history, and he now approached the museum as if it was his destiny.

As he reached the top of the steps, slightly out of breath, he found the doors locked shut. This did not bother him at all; he just held his hand over the electronic keypad and a thin, concentrated beam of white light shot from the palm of his hand and hit the keypad, causing the door latch to click open. Gavin pushed the door open and dashed inside, followed instantly by the very loud sound of highly agitated bells and sirens: his opening of the door had worked but it had not disabled the alarm system.

As he disappeared into the museum a sinister dark shape emerged from a street along the side of the building. It was the silhouette of a rather thin, middle-aged man, wearing a black cloak that covered his entire body. He had a hood over his head, obscuring his short blond hair, and as he passed a nearby street lamp, it lit up the central features of his face – pale white skin, blue eyes, a small nose, and a delicate mouth which, if not closed tight with anger, would have revealed a male model perfect set of teeth. But these facts should not mislead you, for this man, if it was correct to call him a man, was pure evil, and he was in hot pursuit of Gavin du Faire, his intentions far from pleasant.

Lord Dell was the name that this dark stranger used in his normal life. He was active in the highest of social circles within the United Kingdom. He was almost an untouchable, presenting on the outside a very handsome, respected, polite, and wealthy gentleman, who used these facets of himself as entry cards to get wherever he needed to. Once in he could turn to his darker side to unleash whatever evil and punishments he deemed fit.

Lord Dell dashed up the steep steps of the museum, followed by his two not-so-able-bodied sidekicks. The first one, Mike Johnson, was forty-five years old and slightly over weight. He had a very rough exterior, obviously someone whose trade entailed that he spent most of his life exposed to the outside elements. His companion in arms was Dave Smith, aged forty-three, who was in good-shape even if not gifted with looks like his master: Mr. Smith, it seemed, had had a nasty bout of chicken pox when he was younger, and looked as though he had ignored every mothers advice, proceeding to scratch each possible pox into non-existence, with the ultimate result that their scars would stay in existence until the end of his natural life.

As they all dashed up the steps, Lord Dell gave instructions to his two obedient sidekicks.

"Wait by the entrance" he shouted to them, trying to make himself heard above the noise of the sirens. "If I am not finished before the police get here then you must keep them busy until I return for you."

"Yes Boss" they both replied quickly, for they had learnt that to not follow their master's instructions to the exact letter would lead to the most awful punishments.

Gavin du Faire ran deep into the museum and headed straight for the Great Hall, which housed the main dinosaur displays. He was now clearly out of breath, for being a chef did not really go hand in hand with being the fittest individual in the country. A test of this and a taste of that all added up in the longer term to a bit too much of this and a bit too much of that, and quite a bit too much around his middle.

Gavin was crouching down and attempting to hide behind the solid underneath of a glass cabinet, one of many that were in the Great Hall, exhibiting different artefacts from the prehistoric age.

Lord Dell raced through the museum in hot pursuit of Gavin du Faire. He could sense where Gavin had gone, in the same way some could track their prey, and as he entered the

10

Great Hall he stopped running and looked around at the many exhibits that now stood in front of him.

The inside of the hall was quiet; there were no alarms going off inside the building. The quietness was eerie; the skeletons of the huge monsters of the planet from a previous era, lit up by the lights of the modern age, were all looking down onto the single, most evil monster ever to have roamed the planet.

"Ah, my pets" muttered Lord Dell, as he looked up longingly and fondly at the skeletons that stood high above him. "It seems like only yesterday when we were having such fun together." Then a grim expression came across his face, an expression of such anger, mixed with a tinge of fright and maybe the glistening of a tear in one eye. "Not even I could stop that bloody rock" he said quietly, as if talking, almost apologising, to the dinosaurs.

It was a strange and timeless scene; it was as if different eras from the history of the planet Earth had been brought together under the roof of the Great Hall, brought together by the single entity that had seen and lived throughout them all: the Evil Lord himself, masquerading as Lord Dell.

Lord Dell leant back, stretched his arms wide open, and sniffed in a big lung full of air, as if trying to smell his potential victim.

"I know you are here, Guardian" he called out in his dark voice, a voice that sent shivers of fear running down the spines of mere mortals.

However, Gavin du Faire was also no mere mortal; while not as powerful as the Evil Lord he was a Guardian, and as a Guardian he could definitely look after himself, as well as the object he had been entrusted to guard.

"I can smell your fear, Guardian" he called out, taunting Gavin du Faire. "The Evil Lord wants you to bow before him. Come to me Guardian, I grow weary of this pursuit and I want what you protect."

Gavin du Faire looked out from the cabinet under which he was hiding. He could see the back of the Evil Lord from where he was crouching, but the Evil Lord could not see him.

'Now is my opportunity' he thought to himself and, in an instant, he stretched out his right hand and raised his palm towards the Evil Lord.

"NEVER!" he shouted.

The Evil Lord turned to face him and as he did a concentrated jet of brilliant white light, just like a strong laser beam of pure and raw energy, left Gavin du Fair's palm and headed straight towards the Evil Lord, where it hit him on his left side, knocking him several metres backwards, and forcing him downwards, causing him to fall and land on his back, on the cold museum floor.

"You fool" cursed the Evil Lord. "Your pitiful strength is no match for me, Guardian" and he pointed his right forefinger towards Gavin, releasing another concentrated beam, but this time of red light, and so powerful that it screeched as it left his finger and shot straight towards where Gavin du Faire was still crouching, straight towards its target.

Gavin however had already been expecting this and had started to move away before the words had even left the Evil Lord's mouth. He had dived over to his right just in time as the ray of power shot passed and hit a glass cabinet behind him, which subsequently exploded, sending shattered glass and dinosaur bone all over the place.

"You will never succeed" shouted Gavin, in a defiant voice. The situation may well have been hopeless for him, but he knew that he would fulfil his task to the best of his ability, to the very end.

"There are five of us, and we will protect the clues to the location of the Prize, even if it means our own deaths" he bellowed, mocking the Evil Lord.

"Then you will die" spoke the Evil Lord, in his cold cruel voice, and he pointed his right forefinger again towards where Gavin was now lying. Gavin however had again rolled out of the way just in time and there now appeared a small crater in the floor where he had been lying but a few moments ago.

Gavin was worried. He knew that he was no match for the Evil Lord himself. He wondered how the Evil Lord had found him for he had been so well protected, he thought.

Now it was Gavin's turn to miss: he sent a bolt of white power heading straight for the Evil Lord, who moved out of the way, just in time – causing the beam to hit another cabinet, which subsequently exploded into a thousand pieces.

"We are running out of cabinets for you to hide behind, Guardian" called the Evil Lord, mockingly. "I will soon catch up with you."

The battle continued for several minutes more; at least twenty cabinets now lay shattered, wrecked ruins lay all around the hall, and the air inside was full of the smell of smoke from the residue of the battle. As the Evil Lord had predicted there were now not many cabinets left intact and only one was close to where Gavin du Faire was now hiding. The Evil Lord on the other hand was openly walking in the hall, not feeling the need to hide. He knew that he was winning and very soon the victory would be his.

"It is time" called out the Evil Lord, and he pointed his finger at the last cabinet that Gavin was hiding behind and it promptly exploded, leaving Gavin lying spread-eagled on the floor, looking up at the Evil Lord as he slowly but steadily approached him.

"I am not completely without mercy" said the Evil Lord, as he looked at Gavin with a strange expression on his face. "Tell me where the clue is that you protect, and I will spare you."

"Never" replied Gavin as he looked up into the cruel face of the Evil Lord, refusing to give him the pleasure of victory. "You will never succeed. A new one has been selected and he is being groomed to succeed and to defeat you, as before, and as ever more" continued Gavin, with a tinge of defiance in his voice.

"Your leader is growing weak" replied the Evil Lord. "His time is running out, just like yours is about to as well, Guardian. One last chance, where is the clue?"

Gavin however was not saying anything, he was preparing for his death. He was remembering the times he had enjoyed during his life before becoming a Guardian and the fun he'd had since that delightful day some six hundred years ago when he joined the ranks of the Guardians and pledged to serve the Good Lord.

'These six hundred years have been wondrous' he thought silently to himself. 'It is time for me to go on now, for I have done my task and I have had enough, it is now time for someone else. To want more is to be greedy'. And with those last words he smiled to himself and looked defiantly into the eyes of the Evil Lord.

"Kill me then, for you will get nothing from me" he stated.

"Then so be it" replied the Evil Lord in his cold, cruel, merciless voice.

He then raised his right forefinger towards Gavin, who remained where he lay, looking up at the Evil Lord with his arms by his side and a smile across his face. His whole being was content with its imminent destruction.

"Your leader is growing weak, Guardian, and his time is running out" continued the Evil Lord. "Your death will make him even weaker."

Within a millisecond of finishing his words, another jet of pure violent red energy left his right forefinger, screeching as it flew towards, and hit, Gavin, straight in the chest.

The result of this was immediate. Gavin, with a smile still on his face, became frozen stiff and all life was instantaneously gone from his body. His stiff torso lifted slowly off the ground to about one metre high and then hovered there for a few seconds. Then a thick beam of brilliant white light shot out from the now dead body and made its way up to the top most parts of the Great Hall, where it formed itself into a sort of cloud, which just floated high in the ceiling, as if waiting for something to happen.

"COME TO ME" called out the Evil Lord as he leant back with his arms wide open and his chest held as far out forward as it could possibly go.

The white cloud of light, as if responding to its new master, reformed itself into a beam, and then shot down from the ceiling and hit him straight in the chest, causing him to scream with delight, as if consuming the best meal he had ever tasted. This lasted for around five seconds, after which he collapsed to the floor on his knees, at the same time as the lifeless body of Gavin du Faire also fell to the ground, twisting as it did to land face down on the cold museum floor.

The Evil Lord was out of breath; he was exhilarated and he was stronger. He jumped to his feet, stretched out his arms, raised his head and shouted out "YES!"

The power emanating from his body became so immense, so bright and so strong that everything, including all of the not yet destroyed cabinets and displays, were shattered instantly into pieces.

The only thing remaining intact in the Great Hall, apart from the Evil Lord himself, was the lifeless body of Gavin du Faire, lying in the middle of the wreckage, facing downwards into the dust. The Evil Lord walked over to him, and kicked him over onto his back so that he could look deep into his still-opened eyes.

"One down, four to go, and then I will reach you" he said directly into the dead man's face. He then smiled, turned slightly on the spot, and vanished.

Meanwhile in a grassy field many miles away, an old horse was looking deep into his water trough. It was as if he had been watching the whole sad, sorry tale unfold. Tears were falling from the eyes of the old horse and anger was raging in his face. He lifted his head away from the trough and made a loud and long "neeeiiigh." He then turned around and galloped away into the distance, jumping over a small riding fence as he went.

Back at the museum, the police had started to arrive outside of the main entrance. Someone named Williams was shouting instructions to his team as he led them up the steep steps. Johnson and Smith were still hiding just inside the main entrance and were about to start firing on the police when their master suddenly appeared beside them.

"Quick, come, it's done" he said to them. "We must leave here now; we do not want to be seen. Quick, grab hold of my shoulders."

Smith immediately grabbed hold of his master's shoulders, followed by Johnson, who inadvertently knocked his hand against the side of Lord Dell's head. Nevertheless, Lord Dell turned slightly on the spot and all three of them vanished without a trace, just as the police were running up the final steps into the entrance of the museum.

"Did you see?" asked the officer leading the charge to his colleague behind him.

"See what, Sir?" he replied.

"Err, nothing" said the officer, looking, and feeling, a tad confused. "I thought I saw three people here, just behind the doors, as we were coming up the steps."

"Well there's no one here now Sir" said the second officer, as he looked down onto the bright red carpet, and then rushed passed him into the main building.

It did not take the police long to find the place where all of the evening's action had taken place, for these were London's finest, headed by Inspector T Jones (and yes the 'T' stood for Tom, and he had heard all the jokes before).

When the police entered the Great Hall, they were immediately met with a sight of total devastation. There was broken glass, smashed cabinets and the powder of pulverised dinosaur bones lying all over the floor of the Great Hall. In fact, the only thing not literally broken was the body of the dead man lying in the middle of the building. Apart from the fact that he was totally and utterly dead, his body showed no signs of any foul play.

The museum was a secure establishment, full of the latest security systems to help the police in the rare event that someone would actually break in. Even the video surveillance system was state-of-the-art and had been working the whole evening. The strange thing about it though, was that it had not recorded anything happening in the Great Hall that evening, just a series of blank screens.

The police were baffled, to say the least. All they knew was what the contents of the dead man's wallet told them: that he was a Mr Gavin du Faire who owned a restaurant in Cambridge. Apart from that, it was almost as if he did not really exist: the local police had no information on him, not even a parking ticket. Inspector Jones knew from the very first moment he saw the crime scene that this was going to be a long and difficult investigation. He doubted if he would actually solve this one before he retired, which was due in five years time.

Nevertheless, he was a professional who knew what he needed to do. He would pursue and follow-up on the leads and take the case as far as it could possibly go. He owed the family of the victim that much.

A Nerd, a Fib and a Centre Forward

It was now Sunday afternoon, and the temperature was just slight lower than the previous day, an almost bearable 30°C. Earlier that morning, Jeremy Dumbarton, or Jerry to his friends, had received his Sunday newspaper, which he was now reading in the living room of his apartment: Number 14, Windgrove Crescent in Cambridge.

Jerry was a 32-year-old bachelor who was in what is nowadays termed his second youth, although he would be the first to admit that finding the points in time when the first youth ended and the second began, and if indeed there had been any noticeable period in between, would be a very hard challenge indeed.

Jerry had enjoyed several serious relationships when he was younger, but he currently felt that he did not want the hassle associated with having to keep a relationship going for years and years. The company of women was readily available nowadays, so his view, as he often explained to those who asked, was that the only real consequences of his current style of life, was the need to have a regular supply of condoms and the inability to raise his own child. The first of these did not bother him that much- it was normal practice nowadays anyway, and the second he felt was not so bad either, for he did not really want to bring a child into such a brutal and loveless world, like the one he lived in today. His mother, of course, did not really share his view on this subject, but had long since given up trying to discuss it with him, for fear of starting a family feud. She had lost her nerve after her husband, Jerry's father, had died three years before.

The newspaper was naturally full of speculation about the previous evening's events at the Natural History Museum, as was the television news and the media web sites all over the internet. The police were baffled and no one could really explain how Gavin du Faire had been killed. There was even some speculation about a suicide bomb attack which had gone wrong. Most successful suicide bombers didn't really leave much of their bodies behind for formal identification, and although Gavin du Faire was dead, his body was still intact. In this case the police had found his wallet in his back pocket, complete with his driving licence, bank and credit cards, and membership card for the UK-Chefs Association.

Jerry read the different articles on the subject; it rather fascinated him. Here was a real mystery, and he fancied himself as a private investigator, even though he never normally solved any of the murder mysteries he watched on the television. Jerry usually played football on Sundays. He was a 1.92 metre tall, well built, good looking guy who played centre forward in his local team. This meant that he should be the one to score the goals and then run around the pitch waving his arms in the air, or do some kind of crowd pleasing celebratory stunt, such as trying to dance like a robot. He was also, of course, the captain. However, it was now the middle of July and football was in its temporary break between seasons. He missed it. Until the new season started, he would have to make do with beating his best mate Pete Potts on the squash court and on the golf course and at whatever other sport Pete challenged Jerry, for Jerry was just one of those gifted people who were good at any sport, and Pete was not. Pete would be coming round later in the afternoon; they had agreed yesterday to go out for a Sunday afternoon drink together with Julia Evans (Jules to her friends).

Jules was a great girl, who was described by Jerry as one of those rare commodities, an I.B, an Intelligent Blond. To be more precise she was a FIB, a Female Intelligent Blond, which, as Jerry continually reminded people whenever the chance arose, was a contradiction in terms, and did not actually exist. "This is, in fact" he would say, "as all good dictionaries will tell you, the origin of the word fib, which means a lie."

Jules, Pete, and Jerry were the best of friends; they had all met at university when they were younger and continued their friendship after graduation. All three of them were currently single, although Jules had been in one serious relationship since leaving university. They all three now lived in apartments in Cambridge and had never really left the university scene. They lived in close proximity to each other, but all had their own space, which was just as well, since they each enjoyed different hobbies.

Pete was a computer freak, he loved anything and everything to do with computers; he had even built his own. He was a genius in this field and had graduated with a first class honours from Cambridge. Jules was into alternative medicines, faith healing, making contact with dead spirits and that sort of thing. She had long since given up trying to talk to Jerry and Pete about it for they formed the combination of a football player and a computer nerd- no match for a fib.

Jerry was reading through his newspaper. The articles on the museum had lasted six pages. 'Not bad' he thought, considering that they had no idea what had actually happened. Most of the articles were about the priceless relics that had been lost, and referred of course to the loss of the dinosaur bones. This made absolutely no sense to Jerry; 'how can bones be worth anything?' he thought to himself.

As he read further in the newspaper, he came to a strange advert. This advert caught his attention. It was right in the middle of page nine and it read:

DO YOU SEEK THE PRIZE?
A hunt for the Prize is being arranged for all those who are interested to take part. The winner will receive the Prize. Those who are invited to join will receive an email.

Jerry read it a few times. "What is the Prize?" he thought to himself, "I wonder how much?"

Jerry was fascinated by the advert, and as he thought about it the doorbell rang, so he put the newspaper down and got up to answer the door. It was Jules, and she had brought some of her homemade vegetable curry with her. This was great, for Jules was a great cook; everyone enjoyed her curries. She came in, kissed Jerry gently on the cheek, and then headed straight for the kitchen.

"Shall we have this now?" she asked, and then immediately continued before Jerry had a chance to reply. "Or shall we wait until Pete arrives? Do you know if he is coming here today? What time will he be here?"

This was normal for Jules- she often held several different conversations at the same time with her girl friends. Pete and Jerry were convinced that all girls learnt this talent at school while everyone else, meaning all the boys, believed that they were studying needlework.

"Yes, no, yes, about 10 minutes" replied Jerry.

Jules looked at him with a scowl on her face. "Ok, ok" she said, "I get it" and she immediately put on a pan, muttering something about football players, as she started heating up the curry.

At three o'clock, as predicted, which was just ten minutes later, the doorbell rang again. Jerry put the newspaper back down on the coffee table and got up to answer the door, still wondering as he went what the Prize could be.

"It's Pete" he called out, as he walked towards the door, and yes, it was.

Pete came into the apartment, high-fived Jerry, and then went into the kitchen where he greeted Jules and kissed her on the cheek. Pete was the same age as Jerry, but had a pale skin complexion, which merely reflected the amount of time he had spent indoors behind a computer screen, rather than outside in the fresh air. Pete's hair was dark brown in colour, not too long, but not to short either, and it looked as though it had never been combed in its entire life. Pete himself gave the impression that he was never likely to put a comb to his hair in the future either, but Jerry didn't mind, for he and Pete were best friends, and neither would tolerate hearing a bad word said by anyone else about the other.

"Lovely, curry" said Pete. "Always puts a good lining into the stomach before going out for a drink" and he rubbed his stomach in eager anticipation of both.

Several minutes later the curry was ready, and the three of them were sitting at the kitchen table happily eating away and drinking a glass of cheap white plonk, courtesy of Jerry's last shopping expedition to his local supermarket.

"Did you see the articles in the newspaper about the museum last night?" Jerry asked them both.

"Yes" they immediately replied.

"Really weird" added Jules, "what was that guy doing in the museum when it was closed?"

"Well that's the sixty-four million dollar question" answered Pete. "If we knew that we would know a lot more than the police."

"He was a chef" continued Jules, ignoring Pete's comment. "He owned that restaurant around the corner- 'The Grid' I think it is called?"

"Did he?" said Pete; he had not read that in any of the articles. "Wow – that's a bit close to home" he added, looking slightly surprised.

"Exactly what I thought" remarked Jules. "I wonder if it's open tonight. Maybe we could go and take a look around?"

"That's a bit bad taste, isn't it?" said Jerry, who was looking at Jules with a 'you-sad-girl' look on his face. "Let's go next week some time; otherwise everyone will think we just want to see where the dead guy worked."

"Maybe you're right" Jules replied, looking slightly embarrassed at having suggested it in the first place. "Anyway, we have eaten now – let's just go down to the local pub and have a few drinks."

"Sounds good to me" said Jerry, and he got up from the table and went back into the living room where he saw the newspaper on the coffee table.

"Hey, you two" he called out, turning back to face the kitchen. "Did you see the advert in the paper informing people about the hunt for a Prize?"

"No" said Pete, as he came running out of the kitchen, jumped over the back of the sofa, and landed sitting on it, right in front of the coffee table. "Is it here?" he asked, as he grabbed the paper from Jerry's outstretched arms.

"Yes, it's open at the page" replied Jerry, who had hastily removed his hands for fear of getting them broken- Pete's legs had only narrowly missed the table when he landed on the sofa.

"That's weird" said Pete as he read the advert. "I don't remember seeing this in my newspaper when it was delivered this morning?"

"What kind of Prize is it?" asked Jules as she walked towards them from the kitchen.

"That's exactly what I would like to know as well!" exclaimed Jerry. "The advert didn't mention anything about what it actually is."

"What do you mean?" queried Pete. "It's here in black and white," and he read the advert out loud to Jerry and Jules.

DO YOU SEEK THE PRIZE?
A hunt for the Prize is being arranged for all those who are interested in taking part. The Prize is an object that will bring love and happiness to the Race of Man. The winner will receive the Prize and be able to use it for the benefit of all. Those who are invited to join will receive an email.

"WHAT!" shouted Jerry, and he immediately snatched the newspaper out of Pete's hands and re-read the passage out aloud. It was correct, exactly as Pete had read it. However, this was not what he had read. He was sure of that.

"This is different." he muttered. "It was not like this before we had the curry."

Both Jules and Pete looked at him in a strange way.

"What did you put in the curry?" asked Pete, turning to Jules and laughing slightly as he said it. He was not used to Jerry acting this strangely. Jerry was a straightforward kind of person – to be more precise, he was a centre forward.

"Nothing" said Jules, not quite sure whether to laugh or not. "It was just curry. Honest! Just curry."

"I don't understand this" mumbled Jerry, with a total look of incomprehension written all over his face. "I must be going crazy; I am sure it didn't say that earlier."

"I think you need a drink mate" suggested Pete, not quite knowing whether to believe what Jerry was saying.

"Good idea" remarked Jules. "Let's go down to the Dog and Bone and we can grab a few beers, then you can check it again when you get back."

"Yeah, and I'll check my copy when I get home tonight" added Pete, laughing.

Several minutes later, they had all left the apartment and were walking towards the pub. Jerry was in a strange sort of mood, but not quite strange enough to take the newspaper with him. The Dog and Bone public house was just around the corner on Castle Street. It was one of those 'modern' pubs, based on an American style sports bar that targeted the younger generation. It had countless numbers of video screens hanging from the ceiling, large extractor fans for the smoke (from the times when it was legal to smoke in pubs), and bright lights and signposts hanging from every possible vantage point. And, of course, there was lager, lager, and more lager – for this was one of the main hangouts of the students from the university. There was also a strange story connected with this pub, and it concerned a jet-back raven. The raven was always to be seen perched on the street sign attached to the lamppost outside the entrance, and it seemed to spend its entire life watching people going in and coming out of the pub. It was no different this afternoon; as Jerry, Jules, and Pete reached the door, there it was, sitting on the street sign, watching them enter the pub.

Inside there were three 8-ball pool tables and once Jerry saw that one was empty he immediately headed for it, ready to challenge Pete.

Two hours and several pints later, both Pete and Jules looked depressed: Pete because he had lost heavily to Jerry, and Jules because she had spent the whole time staring at two young 25'ish well-proportioned male student studs, who both seemed immune to the longing desire that was emanating from every square-inch of her body. They all therefore agreed that it was now time to call it a day and go back to their homes. As they were about to leave Jerry saw a copy of the newspaper he had in his apartment, on one of the empty tables. He picked it up and immediately turned to page nine, to where the advert about the hunt for the Prize should be. It was not there.

"Look at this" he said quietly, as he turned to Pete and Jules. "It's not there, it's empty."

They both looked at the page and then at each other. They could not explain it.

"Maybe it's an early edition" suggested Pete. "I'll check mine this evening and call you tomorrow."

"Good idea" replied Jerry, but he noted that this time Pete was not laughing, as he had been earlier in the evening when he had made the exact same suggestion.

Dark Stock

Later that same evening, sitting in his study in his Mansion, Lord Dell was also reading the Sunday newspapers and taking stock of the events of the previous day. As normal his two sidekicks, Mike Johnson and Dave Smith, accompanied him. Lord Dell was deep in thought, and both Johnson and Smith knew not to make a sound for fear of interrupting him.

Lord Dell's mansion, which was situated in a remote part of south-eastern England, was built originally in the sixteenth century and considered a jewel in the crown of old English properties. It was one of the very few such properties that were still in private ownership and Lord Dell made sure that his privacy was total: there was an elaborate security system installed all around the estate. Not only was the building huge and the grounds massive, but it was also surrounded by several very deep and very old forests.

Lord Dell's study was a large rectangular room that spanned the rear of the mansion. In keeping with the mansion itself, the study was massive, almost like a long, wide corridor. The wall running along the outside of the study was full of large windows, each looking out onto the immaculately kept gardens and allowing the light from outside to brilliantly illuminate the study. At the far end of the study there was a very large mahogany desk, which looked as though it was several hundreds of years old, behind which there stood a wall of shelves, each shelf packed with very old and very dusty books. In front of the desk were two dark yellow chintz armchairs.

There was a knock at the door of the study.

"Yes" said Lord Dell as he looked up to see the door open and an elderly man in an immaculate dress suit and tails appear. "Yes Jensen, what is it?"

"Sir Ivor" replied Jensen, who was the butler of the house. "Shall I serve dinner in the study or do you wish to eat in the dining room?" he enquired.

"The dining room is fine, Jensen" replied Lord Dell, who then went on to add "I will be there shortly. Please proceed and start serving the soup."

"Yes my Lord" replied Jensen, who then bowed and exited backwards from the study, closing the door in front of him as he left.

"Humph" mumbled Johnson, in a discontented fashion.

"What is it?" snapped Lord Dell, as he looked at Johnson with a hard penetrating stare.

"Well" he replied, starting to regret that he had made any sound at all. "It's just that if we had spoken, you would have cursed us, yet you do nothing to him."

"That" said Lord Dell, with a tired expression in his voice, "is because he is someone who I trust and appreciate, and if he interrupts me then it is because he has been trained to do so. While you on the other hand only interrupt me when there is something that fails to make sense to your pitiful brain, which unfortunately occurs all too frequently."

Johnson bowed to Lord Dell. "Yes my Lord" he said, content with the fact that he had only been verbally and not physically punished.

As they walked together to the dining room, Johnson and Smith walking several paces behind of course, Lord Dell continued thinking about the previous day's events.

The dining room was a splendid room with a bright white ceiling that was at least five metres high. It arched down towards royal red striped wallpaper, which was lined with what seemed to be large gold-framed paintings of Lord Dell in different period costume, each one reflecting a different era of English history. The furniture was magnificent: there were ten solid black wooden cabinets distributed around the room, each filled with silver and gold ornaments of all different shapes and sizes. The floor was a deep dark brown wood, its shine reflecting the large quantities of tender love and care it had obviously received from its polisher- you could see your face in it, almost as clearly as in a mirror. On one side of the room there was a massive open fireplace, in which a bright fire was burning away, and a table of mahogany, standing on eight handcrafted legs, surrounded by fourteen wooden hand carved chairs, each with red velvet cushions for the seats and backs. Covering the table was a clear white tablecloth, gleaming silver cutlery, serving dishes, ornaments, and places set for three. It was a truly wonderful sight.

They all sat down at the table. Lord Dell was sitting at the head, of course, and Johnson and Smith were sitting opposite each other, fairly close to Lord Dell but not right next to him. It seemed they were sitting just out of arms reach, maybe something they had learnt over the years.

Lord Dell was still in deep thought as he sipped his soup. 'Gavin du Faire' he thought to himself. 'He was the first Guardian that I have been able to track down in the last thousand years. It had been a tough period. The combined strength of the Guardians and their leader had so far been much too great for me to be able to sense any of them, anywhere, but it was now obviously weakening. The period of the current Good Lord is coming to an end; he is growing weaker and can no longer protect the Guardians'.

'Who are the other Guardians?' he continued thinking. 'And how can I find them? I must use all my cunning in order to trap and kill them one by one, and then until I get to their leader and watch him die. Yes, and then the Prize will be at my mercy'.

Jensen came back in to clear away the soup and to bring through the main course. It was roast beef, the traditional Sunday dinner, which Johnson especially enjoyed and started tucking into with great gusto.

"Please Sir" enquired Smith, looking slightly revolted at the way his colleague was eating. "What are you thinking? What are you planning? And how can we help?"

"I am deciding how I can capture the remaining Guardians" replied Lord Dell, "and I am not sure how you can help me at the moment. But don't worry; your time will come…" He paused slightly; he was now also looking in disgust at Johnson gobbling down his food. He then continued "… your time will come when I will call upon you to make your contribution."

"Yes Sir" said Smith. "Do you know how you will capture them?"

"Their leader is getting weak" he replied, "which means that he can no longer hide their powers from me. I can sense them when they are close to me and far from him."

"Is that how you tracked down Mr du Faire?" asked Johnson, who had just taken a short break from eating to slurp down some wine.

"Mr du Faire was a lucky accident" answered Lord Dell. "I just happened to be attending an event in London which he was catering for. When I arrived, I sensed something. It is a strange feeling, sensing a Guardian, and one that I have not experienced for so long, but one I must get used to again if I am to secure the Prize."

"It took me some time to narrow down where the source of the power was coming from. After the main course I sneaked into the kitchen. He saw me and started to run. That is when I called the two of you and we chased him to the museum."

"Yes Boss" said Johnson again, maybe relaxing just a little bit too much. "You had some fun there didn't you boss?"

"FUN?" screamed Lord Dell back to him. "This is a deadly serious business, Johnson. I do not have fun – although I must admit I enjoyed killing him in the end."

"Sorry Boss, that's what I meant to say" replied Johnson, wiping the sweat off his forehead.

"But he told me something" continued Lord Dell, thinking aloud. "What was it he said to me?" he muttered, as he sunk deeper into his thoughts, trying to recollect the exact order of events.

"Yes, that was it," he declared several moments later. "He told me that a new one had been selected and that he was being groomed to defeat me."

Johnson and Smith looked towards each other, horrified at what they heard.

"Defeat you Boss?" asked Johnson. "Is that possible?"

"Unfortunately…" replied Lord Dell, who then paused as he looked at Johnson with a touch of pity in his face, as he watched him wipe up the last remains of his plate with his bread.

"Unfortunately it is possible" he continued, "however, as the days pass and as the Guardians become fewer and fewer, it becomes less and less probable. It will be our job to track down this new Chosen One before he can take over as the leader of the Guardians. We must follow him to the clues, or even better, get to them before him, so that I can find the Prize. If we fail I will be subject to another thousand years of not being in control."

"But what of the police, Sir?" enquired Smith. "Do they not suspect you? I mean all the video cameras and surveillance in the streets around the museum and in the museum itself. Do they not know that you, or rather we, were there?"

"No, of course not" replied Lord Dell, with a sense of urgency in his voice. "Video cameras cannot film me, for I emanate such power that these feeble machines only record blank images whenever I am around."

"Wow" said Johnson in an awed voice.

"Wow indeed" mumbled Lord Dell, observing how easily impressed Johnson was. "The police have nothing on me; I am far too clever and powerful for them to bother me, and if they come too close, I just stamp on them like little ants. But I do not want the attention in the first place, so keep away from the police!" he barked, as Johnson and Smith both looked as though Christmas had come early, hearing their boss speak in these tones.

"What will happen, Sir," asked Smith as he settled himself, "when you do get hold of the Prize?"

"Ah, a good question" said Lord Dell, as he delved deep into his own thoughts again, and a wide and wicked smile broke across his face. "Man will come under my total control for at least a thousand years. There will be bloodshed, carnage, terror, and evil throughout the globe. All love and happiness will be banished, and I will rule men's hearts and minds." With these words he let out a long and loud laugh, stood up from the dining table, and exited the room, leaving Johnson and Smith to finish their deserts alone.

The Invitation

When Jerry returned to his apartment, he went straight back to re-read the advert in his newspaper. Had it changed again? He picked it up and read it.

DO YOU SEEK THE PRIZE?
A hunt for the Prize is being arranged for all those who are interested to take part. The Prize is an object that will bring love and happiness to the race of man. The winner will receive the Prize and be able to use it for the benefit of all. Those who are invited to join will receive an email.

It was the same as last time, although he still believed it was different to what he had first read. Had it really changed at all, or had he just imagined it? Anyway, something strange was clearly happening since it definitely was not in the copy in the newspaper at the pub. He knew exactly what he would do. He would wait for Pete to phone and tell him what was in his version of the newspaper. So that is precisely what he did. He turned on the television, sat down in his favourite armchair and immediately fell into a deep sleep.

Jerry did not generally have dreams while he slept. Well, at least he could not remember them in the morning so he assumed that he did not have any. He had, however, occasionally had the type of dreams that caused him to wake up in the middle of the night, drenched in sweat, and with his arms wrapped tightly around his pillow, but these kind of dreams were normally the result of a dry period (a common term for far too long a period without the sensual company of a woman). In Jerry's case the measurement unit was days. Some men however could last weeks, but at least it was not hours like the goalkeeper in Jerry's football team.

This night however Jerry did have a dream, and it was not about a sensual encounter with a woman, although it did involve a woman. In his dream he was drifting back into his schooldays, when he was at his final year in primary school. He was eleven and sitting in a classroom, receiving his marks from the test he had done the day before. It was a mathematics test, and the teacher, a Miss Jones, was furious with him for only scoring four out of ten but he was sure that he had correctly answered all of the questions. He was in tears. All of his friends were staring at him with somewhat embarrassed looks on their faces. Jerry was never the brightest student- he preferred to kick a ball about in the playground rather than to sit down and do work. However, this test was different. He had rushed through all the questions. The first four were the easiest but then came the last one, which he thought he had done correctly, but was not completely sure. He had checked with Geoffrey Perkins, his best friend of the time, who also had the same answer to the last question. But Geoffrey had received eight out of ten as his score. Something was wrong, he was sure of it. He was just about to go up to the teacher to shout and rave at her, so that she would go through the paper with him, when the school bell went. That would not stop him though, he would still go to the teacher anyway, she was only a short distance away, but that bloody bell would not stop ringing and ringing and ringing. Then, after a few moments, the teacher and the classroom slowly drifted away and vanished, and the only thing remaining in his head was the sound of the bell. It was, however, not the school bell: it was his front door bell, and someone wanted to see him.

He woke abruptly from his awkward sleep in the armchair. It had been ages, at least several years, since he had last fallen asleep in his chair but he would worry about that later. For now he was concerned with how late it was, or rather how early it was, for outside the sun was clearly shining and threatening to light up his living room as if it was midday. One thing was for sure though: it was Monday and he had to go to work.

The bell rang again and so he stood up and made his way to the door.

"Who is it" he called, to the other side of the door.

"It's me" replied Pete. However, it was far too early in the morning for Jerry to determine who the owner of the voice was.

"Me who?" he answered back at the stranger, as he stretched and yawned, trying to fully awaken himself.

"Me, Pete" replied Pete, who was sounding very eager to get in. "Come on, open up, quickly."

"Ok, ok," said Jerry, "hold your horses" and he bent down to unlock the bolt at the bottom of the door. Before he knew it, Pete had rushed in, almost knocking him over as he dashed through the hallway and into the living room.

"What time is it?" asked Jerry, starting to look a bit agitated as he closed the door and followed Pete into the living room.

"Time?" muttered Pete, "I don't know. It must be about seven o'clock."

"In the evening?" replied Jerry, astonished.

"No, seven am" answered Pete, "and you look in a real bad way. "What happened to you" he asked as he looked at Jerry, who was fully dressed in clothes that looked as though they had been crushed under several tons of rocks.

"Oh, I just failed my maths test" replied Jerry, not really knowing what he was saying. Then he realised.

"Seven am?" he called out. "Seven o'clock in the morning? Are you mad?"

"What do you mean failed your Maths test?" asked Pete, now feeling as confused as Jerry looked.

"Oh, nothing" replied Jerry, "it was just a dream I had. What do you mean by coming here at seven am? What's happened?"

34

This snapped Pete out of his confusion and he immediately walked over to Jerry with his copy of yesterday's newspaper.

"It's not here in mine either" said Pete. "Look, it's blank, just like the copy in the Dog and Bone, no advert."

Jerry grabbed the paper from Pete and walked over to the coffee table where his copy was still lying. He compared the two of them and it was as clear as it could be; they were both the same. Blank.

Jerry looked at Pete. Pete looked at Jerry. They both looked at the two newspapers.

"What the hell is going on?" said Jerry, in total disbelief.

"What the hell, indeed..." repeated Pete, as he scanned both of the newspaper pages for a third time, just to make sure.

"It was there yesterday, you saw it, didn't you?" asked Jerry, with tears now almost in his eyes, as if he was starting to understand that he was going senile.

"I saw it mate" replied Pete. "This is weird."

"What can this mean?" asked Jerry, as he felt completely at a loss to explain what was going on. Here was a newspaper advert that was in some newspapers and not in others, and in the one it was- the text changed, and then vanished. This did not make any sense at all.

"I have to go to work" said Pete. "Anyway, I need some time to think about this. This is weird. Man, this is really weird."

Pete started walking towards the front door. "I wonder what Jules will make of all this?" he muttered.

"Let's meet this evening" suggested Jerry. "I'll call Jules later today and get her to come over as well, after work, and we can sit down and discuss it together and see if we can make any sense of it."

"Sounds great" answered Pete as he waved goodbye and left for work.

Jerry closed the door behind him and went back into the living room. This was strange, very strange, and he had no idea how to explain any of it. Jerry looked over at the clock. It was now a quarter past seven and he had no time now to think about it– he also had to get to work. Ok, he did not have to start until ten o'clock because he was still at the University, although nowadays he worked there– which, truth be told was not much different from being a student. Anyway, Jerry put the two newspapers down onto the table and then went to have a shower.

Jerry returned home at 4 p.m. that afternoon, after a long and hard day's work at the University, and immediately went over to the coffee table to check the two newspapers again. He turned to page nine, where the advert should be, and yes, they were both still blank – at least he was not going completely mad, not yet anyway.

He had arranged with Jules and Pete that they would come over around six o'clock. Pete was going to pick up their regular order from the local Fish and Chips take-away, just around the corner, and they would then eat, drink (Jerry was providing the plonk) and discuss the newspaper advert.

At a quarter to six Jules arrived - an early fib, nevertheless in this case true. She explained to Jerry that she had been asking different people at work for copies of their Sunday newspapers and none of them had the advert on page nine.

This, as Jerry was quick to point out, did not really help clarify the situation, but just made it a bit more mysterious.

Pete arrived at ten past six.

"What, Jules already here?" he asked, looking slightly amazed and puzzled at the same time as he walked into the kitchen. Then, rather too quickly, he added. "There was a long queue at the Chippy" as his face did an impression of the tomato sauce that Jules was rather menacingly holding in her hand.

They sat down together at the kitchen table. Jerry fetched the glasses and the plonk, while Jules updated Pete on what she had already told Jerry.

"Yes, I did the same" replied Pete, after listening to every word. "They all said the same to me as well. Not a single one saw any advert, and none of them even noticed that the space was blank either" he continued. "Not until I pointed it out to them."

"But what does all this mean?" asked Jerry.

"Well" said Pete, standing up to walk around the table. "I put it to you, members of the Jury, this case…"

But before he could finish Jules was snapping at him. "Oh be serious Pete Potts, for once in your life. This is real; this is not some TV play."

"Yes, of course" replied Pete. "Sorry Jerry."

"Do we know anyone else who has actually seen and read the advert?" Jerry asked them both.

"Not that I know" replied Jules.

"Me neither" added Pete.

"How many have we asked?"

"Well, I asked twelve" said Jules.

"And me, seven" said Pete. "That makes nineteen. Hardly a national sample size" he added.

Jerry was thinking. Pete and Jules could tell this because it was so unusual for him to be silent for so long.

"What are you thinking?" asked Jules – leaving a slightly too long pause after her first word.

"Of course I am thinking" barked Jerry, feeling a little hurt by the question.

"No, I meant, what are you thinking about?" Jules replied hastily, as Pete sniggered.

"Oh, sorry" said Jerry. "I was thinking, what if I was the only one to get the advert. What would that mean?"

"Good question" replied Pete, an impressed expression on his face as he looked at Jerry as if to say– he might not think much, but when he does, wow!

"What was in the advert again?" asked Jules

"It was about a hunt being arranged to find a Prize" replied Jerry, who appeared to be trying to remember word for word, and with some difficulty, what was in the advert. "The Prize was some kind of object that would bring love and happiness to man."

"So it obviously isn't a woman" sneaked in Pete.

"Oh, ha, ha" said Jules. "No, go on Jerry."

"And the winner can use the Prize..."

"What can it mean? Bring love and happiness to man" interrupted Jules.

"Well, I think that Pete has a good point" said Jerry. "I mean, it couldn't possibly be a woman could it. How could we use a woman for the benefit of all?"

"Yes, it can't be a woman," agreed Jules "or a man either. So it must be something else."

"An animal" suggested Pete, but as he said it he thought about it and added, "but how can an animal be used for the benefit of all, and bring love and happiness to man?"

"No, I don't think it is anything living" said Jerry. "It must be some kind of thing. Anyway, whatever it is, it must have some great power if it can be used for the benefit of all."

"What about a crystal ball which can predict the winning lottery numbers?" suggested Pete. "That could be used for the benefit of man, and would bring love and happiness to whoever won."

"Oh, you are so shallow Pete" said Jules, as she glared at him. "Money can't buy love."

"Oh, let's not argue about that now" Jerry interrupted quickly.

Looking slightly relieved, Pete turned to Jerry. "Didn't it say something about an email being sent to those who are invited to join the hunt?"

"Yes, you're right" said Jules.

"Yes, that was it" confirmed Jerry. "Those who are invited to join will receive an email, that's what it said."

"Well" said Jules.

"Well what?" replied Jerry.

"Well" she continued. "Did you get an email today inviting you to join?"

"No, not today" said Jerry, sounding disappointed.

"Me neither" added Pete, with a sense of dejection also in his voice.

"Nor me" said Jules optimistically, "but it didn't say today, it just said that an email would be received, it did not say when."

"Oh, this is going nowhere" said Jerry, starting to get frustrated.

"What about your question Jerry?" asked Pete. "You were saying. What if you were the only one to get the advert? What would that mean?"

"Good question" said Jerry, laughing slightly as he said it. "I have no bloody idea" was the answer he added back to Pete.

"I do" said Jules as the boys both turned to look at her. "It might mean that since you were one of the only people to see the advert in the newspaper, that you might be one of the people to receive an email."

Pete and Jerry were both silent, thinking.

"She might have a point," remarked Pete.

"I have already told you" began Jerry, "I didn't get any email today... at work" he said, as he paused slightly and then looked across at Pete, who at the exact same time looked towards him.

Suddenly, they both sprang up and dashed over to Jerry's PC.

"My private account" shouted Jerry all excited, as Jules followed them both into the Den. "I haven't checked this one yet today. Come on, come on, start-up you bloody slow machine."

It was always the same with his PC. It was fairly-modern yet the amount of software that he had running on it far exceeded the hardware capabilities of the machine – at least that is what the company that provided the software would say.

"I told you to upgrade it" said Pete, who was also getting anxious as things were not going fast enough.

Finally, they were there. He had logged on and was starting up his email application. Then he saw his inbox. Ten emails were waiting for him. Two from his mother (leave those for later, he thought), three from colleagues in his football team, some spam emails offering him an erection to match the porn stars (as if he needed that). Then there was one, received today, which he did not recognise. It was entitled: "Verse Three". It was from someone called "The White Horse."

They all started to read the email as it appeared on the screen.

"What the hell is that supposed to mean?" asked Jerry.

"Well" said Jules, as if she was about to explain that one plus one equals two to a toddler. "I have no idea."

From: The White Horse
Sent: Monday July 16th
To: Jeremy Dumbarton
Subject: Verse Three

Location of Verse Three

Dear Jeremy,

Welcome to the Quest for the Prize; I hope that you are the worthy one, for only the worthy can inherit the Prize. This first clue is a test, it is very simple, but most will fail even at this first simple hurdle.

In order to find Verse Three, you will need to find me.
But I am not so simple to find, because I might just be in your mind.
When it's fine I am clear to see, the White Horse is next door to me.
Drinks and Rugby go hand in hand, and come together where I stand.
Let the crowd through, but not that pig, then you can find me, I am not that big.
And now I've told you all you need, its down to you to come here full-speed.

Best Regards

The White Horse

"Well" said Pete, just succeeding to hold back a snigger. "It at least means that your assumption was correct. You have received an invitation to take part in the Quest for the Prize" and he slapped Jerry hard on the back. "Well done mate."

"Yes, well done" added Jules, although not really understanding at all what Jerry had done to warrant such an invitation.

"But as for the rest of it" continued Pete. "I am afraid I haven't got the faintest clue what the rest is about."

The Email

Jerry immediately printed out three copies of the email. They all then went into the living room and sat around the coffee table.

"Any ideas?" he asked.

"Not straight up" replied Pete, "but I think if we go through it line by line then maybe we can start to make some sense out of it."

"Ok, good idea" said Jerry, and he went and picked up a red pen from the cupboard.

"*From the White Horse*" read Pete out aloud. "How can a horse write an email?"

"Well it's obviously not a real horse" said Jules.

"Yes, I agree" concluded Jerry, with a look of certainty across his face. "It's obviously some organisation, nickname, or maybe some kind of alias."

"It could be a pub" said Pete.

"Oh, be serious" remarked Jules, who was starting to lose her patience a bit. "A pub could no more write an email than a horse could."

Pete felt a bit put out by this verbal abuse from Jules, after all he thought that it was a good idea, but she did have a point; a pub could no more write an email than a horse.

"*Subject: Verse Three*" read out Jerry. "What is Verse Three, and where are Verses One and Two?"

"We'll have to come back to that one" said Jules.

"*Location of Verse Three*" read out Pete. "That's the second time Verse Three is mentioned."

"*Dear Jeremy*" said Jerry. "Well at least that's clear."

"Welcome to the Quest for the Prize; I hope that you are the worthy one, for only the worthy can inherit the Prize" read Pete out aloud. "Well, 'welcome to the Quest for the Prize' sounds simple enough. 'I hope you are the worthy one', worthy for what I wonder? For only the worthy can inherit the Prize. There is that word worthy again. Inherit the Prize; I thought that you had to find it, not inherit it. What does all this mean?"

"Thanks for clearing that one up mate" said Jerry, rather sarcastically to Pete before continuing to read the email. *"This first clue is a test, it is very simple, but most will fail even at this first simple hurdle.* Therefore, this is the first clue, even though it is Verse Three, hmm. It is very simple."

"Well that's good isn't it?" said Jules, disbelievingly. "I mean if this was difficult then we would be in deep trouble wouldn't we?"

"Steady girl" replied Jerry, in his calming, reassuring voice – the one that he normally used to referees when they were about to show him a card. "We'll get through this – let's just concentrate. We are not going to fail at any hurdle."

"In order to find Verse Three, you will need to find me" read out Jules, feeling now slightly better after the encouragement from Jerry. "You will need to find me. Who is this 'me'? It must be the White Horse, whatever that is. *'But I am not so simple to find, because I might just be in your mind'.* What does that mean? Is it all an illusion?"

"When its fine I am clear to see, the White Horse is next door to me" read Pete. "Aha! The White Horse is next door to 'me', and 'me' is who we will need to find. So we don't need to find the White Horse we need to find who is next door to the White Horse" summarised Pete triumphantly, as if he has just solved the whole thing.

"Drinks and Rugby go hand in hand, and come together where I stand" Pete continued to read, feeling that he was on a hot streak now. "What have drinks and rugby got to do with it?"

"Well rugby players are well renowned for large drinking appetites" said Jerry. "If they were to come together then that would be in a bar."

"Or a pub" shouted Pete, "just like I said earlier" as he turned and smiled at Jules. "If I was a rugby player and having drinks then I would be standing at a bar in a pub" he declared.

"*Let the crowd through, but not that pig, then you can find me, I am not that big*" said Jerry. "Let the crowd through. What can that mean? I am not that big. So it's most likely a small person we are looking for."

"*And now I've told you all you need, it's down to you to come here full-speed*" said Jules, "the last line."

"No" remarked Pete. "The last line is *Best Regards, the White Horse.*"

"Oh yes, you're right" replied Jules. "But what has he told us?"

"He?" questioned Pete. "Is it a 'he' we are looking for?"

"Ok, 'it'" clarified Jules, "what has it told us?"

"All we need" said Jerry. "It has told us all we need, so we must go there full speed, wherever the hell there is."

It was getting late, and they all had to go to work tomorrow, so they agreed to call it a night for now and resume the Quest the next evening. They also agreed not to mention this Quest to any other living soul since this was their secret and their Quest – at least as far as they knew.

The next evening the three of them were running through their latest theories in Jerry's apartment.

"I searched the internet for 'The White Horse'" said Pete.

"Any luck?" asked Jules.

"Oh yes" said Pete. "Well, it first asked me if I meant *The White House*, obviously written by an American, but I did eventually find something".

"What, what, do tell!" said Jules, sounding very excited, as if the whole riddle was about to be solved right in front of her eyes. Jerry however did not look that confident.

"It came up with over 40 million hits" announced Pete.

"40 Million" said Jules, letting out a somewhat exasperated sigh and allowing her whole body to sink a few centimetres.

"40 Million, 700 thousand actually" added Jerry. "I checked also this morning. All that came up were millions of references to Pubs and Inns and local councils. There is no way we can go through all of those. We will have to narrow down the search criteria if we are going to get something manageable to work with."

They continued to discuss the different lines of the text, over, and over, but did not really make any further progress that night. After three hours, Jerry decided that they should stop for the day.

"If we are going to succeed with this then we will have to tackle this like a football team" he said, to an astonished looking Pete and Jules.

"You mean we have to kick a ball about?" asked Jules, looking thoroughly confused.

"No, absolutely not" replied Jerry with a slight laughter in his voice. "We will each have to play a special role and look after a part of the clue. Let us assume the main six lines of the clue are the pitch. I will be the centre forward and take the front part, like the first two lines, and work on those. Jules you can be midfield and look at the middle two lines, and Pete…"

"Yeah, I got it" interrupted Pete "I'll take the last two lines."

"But aren't they all sort of connected?" asked Jules.

Jerry was stumped. It was as if he had scored an own goal. Luckily for him however, Pete came to the rescue.

"They might well be" said Pete, "but if we each focus on the main part we have been given, then it doesn't stop us from using the other parts of the clue to make sense of our section."

"Brilliant" said Jerry, rather a bit too quickly. "I mean, yes of course. Ok everyone, now let's go and each focus on our own little pieces. We'll meet back here on Thursday evening and present our theories to each other."

They all agreed, and then Jules and Pete left Jerry's apartment to walk home. Jerry felt elated: he had managed to get the others to focus on the clue and present their theories to him. However, he then realised, he would have to present his theories to them as well.

"Oh, shit" he mumbled to himself as he turned off the lights and went into his bedroom.

The next day Jules woke up, thoroughly dreading having to tackle her part of the clue. She had the midfield, as Jerry had put it, and so she had to focus on the middle two lines:

When it's fine I am clear to see, the White Horse is next door to me. Drinks and Rugby go hand in hand, and come together where I stand.

They had already concluded that this meant the person lived in a bar next to a white horse. Jules started applying her own logic to the clue.

'*Drinks and Rugby*' she thought to herself. 'Well, the obvious link is what we already discussed, but what if it is something else?'

Then it came to her. Rugby is also a place in England, near Coventry, and it was a well-known fact that people from the midlands were rumoured also to have large drinking appetites. Drinks and Rugby could also be referring to the place Rugby and not the game. Now she was getting somewhere, although she did not really know where.

'Hang on' she thought. 'If it is next door and it is quite far away, then the only possible place that it could be is in the countryside'

"Wait a minute" she said aloud to herself, as no one else was with her. "There is a white horse carved into the chalk on a hill somewhere in England, I think. Now where was that?"

She dived onto her computer, brought up her favourite search engine and typed in the search criteria "The White Horse." Not surprisingly, she came up with over 40 million hits.

"Ok" she mumbled, "now I need to think about this for a bit."

She gradually refined her search criteria until she came to the town of Uffington, in Oxfordshire. That however was around 85 miles away from Rugby, so you could not see that, even on a fine day. She therefore concluded that the riddle must be referring to something else, or some other place.

'Hold on,' she again thought. 'Was there a rugby club close to the village of Uffington? Or, on the other hand, was there a white horse close to the town of Rugby?' She dived back onto the web again, convinced that she was on the right track.

Jerry meanwhile had decided to skip work in order to focus on his part of the clue. He was the centre forward so, naturally, he got the front two lines.

In order to find Verse Three, you will need to find me. But I am not so simple to find, because I might just be in your mind.

This was confusing for Jerry. His first thoughts were 'Why do I want to find Verse Three or find you?' but it was obvious this was a test – he had to find Verse Three and before that, he had to find 'me', and 'me' was the person who called himself 'the White Horse'.

Who could that be? Why would anyone refer to himself or herself as a White Horse? Then he remembered that the old Indians in the American Wild West used to call themselves after animals. There was Running Bear and Crazy Horse and a Buffalo Bill – American history was not one of Jerry's strong points.

'Was there ever a White Horse?' he wondered to himself.

Jerry started typing into his search engine to look for Indians called 'White Horse' but he could not find any. 'Another avenue closed' he thought and then satisfied himself with another sip of his milky white tea. He was thinking as hard as he had done in many a year now; his mind was racing around in circles. 'My mind, your mind, in your mind,' how was he going to solve this? Then another thought came to him.

'What if this is like one of those cryptic crosswords?' he thought to himself. '*In your mind* would mean in 'your mind'. Is there a place called 'Yourmind'?" He hardly thought so, but it might be a part of it. He again searched the web. There was a place called Urmin in California and a river in Russia called the river Urmi, but these two didn't really sound as if they were linked to a White Horse. He was not getting anywhere with his part of the clue and he hoped the Pete and Jules were having more success.

Pete was relishing the opportunity to demonstrate his superior intellect and highly developed logical brain. He was a real nerd. His two lines were the last of the riddle and he was confident that he could develop at least three theories.

> *Let the crowd through, but not that pig, then you can find me, I am not that big. And now I've told you all you need, it's down to you to come here full-speed.*

'What has that pig got to do with letting a crowd through?' he thought to himself. 'If I am going to crack this part of the clue then I have to look earlier at the other lines' he decided, otherwise he would get nowhere with his part.

When the team met up again it was Thursday, and they discovered that none of them had made any real significant progress since receiving the email on Monday. Nevertheless, they felt that they were at least moving forward.

Jerry went first and concluded that he had not really made any progress at all, and felt that he had let the team down. It was clear from the expressions on the faces of Jules and Pete that they felt something similar.

Jules, the most impressive of the bunch, presented what she had discovered. They spent at least two hours discussing her different theories. This was possible because Pete had already told them that his part made no sense without looking into the midfield, and they all agreed that the midfield section seemed to be the key, "as in any great football team" Jerry was heard to say.

During the discussion they also looked into the possibility of how to link 'Drinks' and the town of 'Rugby' a bit closer together, and Pete discovered on the internet that there was a soft drinks factory in Rugby. As it approached eleven o'clock, they again decided to call it a night, and agreed to all meet up the next evening.

Friday evening came and the trio were again sitting in Jerry's apartment scanning the email. They were no further forward when Jerry slammed his pen down on the table, looked at the others and announced "we should go and get a drink."

"Best idea you've had all week" said Pete, as he shuffled his notes together into a pile on the kitchen table and stood up.

Jules followed and all three of them then walked out of the apartment and down towards the Dog and Bone.

"I don't fancy the Dog and Bone" said Jerry, "let's go somewhere quieter this evening."

The others agreed and they followed Jerry down to the local Equestrian Club where they entered the bar and sat at a table near the back. It was a large bar with the entrance on one side, opposite the windows looking out onto the indoor practice arena. The front was where the bar was, and the back was just a wall filled with pictures of horses, each famous for a particular steeplechase or derby victory. The tables and chairs were all of dark wood and the whole atmosphere of the place mimicked an old country pub. All that was missing was the sawdust on the floor.

Neither Pete nor Jules had spent any time in here in the past. Jerry however had spent quite some time here, some ten years ago, when he was dating a girl called Anne, who had loved horse riding and even had had her own horse, and she was fairly-good. Jerry went up to the bar to get the drinks.

"Hi there Jerry" said Bill, the old barman. "Long time no see. What have you been up to these past years?"

"Oh, this and that" replied Jerry. He had liked Bill, and had often spent an evening talking with him while waiting for Anne to finish her lessons or practice sessions. "Three lagers please, Bill."

Bill pulled the pints and passed them over to Jerry.

"What's new in the club, Bill?" asked Jerry as he handed over the money to pay for the drinks.

"Oh, not much" replied Bill. "Just got in a new collection of photos over there on the wall" and he pointed to the wall opposite the windows overlooking the practice arena. "All pubs named after horses; thought it would be amusing."

"Any called the White Horse?" asked Jerry, in a kind of non-interested and casual manner.

"Oh yes, a few" said Bill, "somewhere over there, take a look, they all look nice. Why, you thinking of going away for a dirty weekend?" he whispered, winking his eye and looking over at Jules.

"No, nothing like that" replied Jerry, laughing. "Just something I'm working on at the moment".

Jules and Pete were already discussing their lack of progress again, when Jerry returned with the drinks.

"Oh no, give it a rest for a few moments" said Jerry "it's already driving me mad that we can't work it out."

Jules looked disappointed and turned to look out of the windows into the practice arena to see who was riding the horses. There were a few; two men and a woman, and one of the men did not look too bad, thought Jules to herself – and she was not commenting on his riding ability, or maybe she was?

Jules got up and walked over to the windows with her drink in her hand. She found it quite pleasant and relaxing in the bar; it was a nice atmosphere. She looked around to her left, back towards the table and noticed all the different pictures of the famous horses. She walked along them. Red Rum, Desert Orchid, both of those she knew from the past, but most of the others she had never heard of.

She walked further around to the wall opposite the windows, and then she saw all the photos of the pubs whose names had links to horses. There were many.

"I wonder" she mumbled to herself, and started looking for the White Horse. She was not disappointed for there were at least five different 'White Horse Pubs' or 'White Horse Inns'.

"Hey Pete, Jerry!" she called. "Come over here and take a look at these."

Jerry and Pete both stood up and walked over to where she was standing, and joined her looking at the pictures.

"Oh no" said Jerry as she pointed out the pubs which mentioned the White Horse. "I thought we were giving it a rest for a bit."

Pete however was not having any of it, for he had seen something; he was staring, almost in a gaze, eyes fixed on one of the photos, the one of a pub in Sutton Coldfield, called "The White Horse."

"What's the barman's name?" he asked Jerry.

"Bill" he replied, "why?"

"Call him over" said Pete. "I want to ask him something."

"Hey Bill" called Jerry, wondering what Pete was up to. "Can you spare a moment?"

Bill had no major rush of clients on, so he came over to where the three of them were standing.

"This is Bill" said Jerry, as he introduced him to Pete and Jules.

"Do you know what's over here?" asked Pete, pointing to the area next to the picture of the pub.

"Oh, I know it well" said Bill. "I stayed there myself several months ago. That's a great pub, just off the Kingsbury Road in Curdworth. There's a field next to it. Quite strange

50

actually, there's a great old White Horse that lives there, really nice old stallion."

Jules and Jerry looked at each other. Pete however, was staring hard at the picture.

"*Drinks and Rugby*" muttered Pete to himself. "*Drinks and Rugby, Drinks and Rug...*" Pete suddenly stopped, looked up from the picture, and stared straight at Jerry. His eyes were bulging; it was as if he was in a trance. "Oh my God" he mumbled, as he grabbed tightly onto Jerry's arm. "Quick!" he spurted, now almost trembling. "We have to go, quickly you two, come on, let's run!"

Pete let go of Jerry's arm and moved towards the door.

"What? What is it?" said Jerry and Jules together.

"I'll tell you when we get back home" said Pete, starting to get agitated that they were both standing quite still. "Quick now hurry!" and he started running towards the door, followed very shortly by Jerry and Jules, who were both looking a tad concerned that Pete might have finally flipped.

The three of them left the bar, leaving a thoroughly confused and dejected looking Bill standing alone, next to the photograph.

"Say hello to Jose for me" he called out, as they disappeared through the bar entrance. "Well, I thought it was a nice place" he muttered to himself, as he cleared up their unfinished drinks, smiling a wicked smile as if something strange had just entered his mind as he walked back behind the bar.

Jerry, Pete, and Jules ran back to the apartment and straight to the kitchen table.

"Drinks and Rugby, Drinks and Rugby" was all that Pete kept repeating to himself, over and over again, as he sat down at the table and started scribbling on his notes.

Jules and Jerry were just watching him.

"What are you doing?" asked Jerry. "What's up?"

"YES!" screamed out Pete aloud, and he threw his clenched fist up in the air. "I knew it! Oh, you sneaky git!"

"Knew what? Knew what?" yelled Jerry back to him, and Pete turned around his notes and showed them both. On the paper he had written:

DRINKS RUGBY - KINGSBURY RD

It was an anagram. *'Drinks and Rugby go hand in hand and come together where I stand'*, the Kingsbury Rd. Jerry and Jules were speechless and that was not a normal state for either of them to be in.

"You clever son of a bitch Pete" said Jules, "but what about the rest?"

"Let's run through it" stated Pete, quickly turning to his original printout, wanting to make sure he avoided misquoting anything.

"In order to find Verse Three, you will need to find me" he said. "If it is the White Horse Pub, then we need to find either the Pub or the owner. *'But I am not so simple to find, because I might just be in your mind.'* That could mean anything. It could just be here to confuse us. *'When its fine I am clear to see, the White Horse is next door to me'*. This part works. The real White Horse, the old stallion, is next door to the pub. But, on a rainy day, you might not be able to see him. *'Drinks and Rugby go hand in hand, and come together where I stand'*. That bit we got already, the anagram linking to the Kingsbury road. *'Let the crowd through, but not that pig, then you can find me, I am not that big'*. Now what does that mean?"

Pete had stopped. This part did not make sense.

"Where was the Pub?" asked Jules.

"Kingsbury Road" said Pete, "but we already know that."

"No, I mean what town" she asked, starting to look excited.

"Curdish or something" said Pete. "What did he say Jerry?"

"Oh, I have no idea" replied Jerry, "but we can check on the web, it's bound to be there. Quick Jules, get it up."

Jules typed in 'the White Horse' and 'Kingsbury Rd' into Jerry's search engine. She then pressed enter, and there it was. Number one hit, out of sixty-six: The White Horse, in Curdworth.

"Curdworth" called out Jules, as she ran back into the Kitchen. "Curdworth" she repeated, as she got to the table. Then, like a bolt of lightning, it suddenly came to her. "What is another name for a pig?" she asked.

"Hog" replied Pete, as he stared at Jules, who was grinning like a Cheshire cat. "Oh, not again" he added, as he scribbled down the words:

CROWDTHROUGH

"And now we have to remove the Pig" said Jules, and Pete crossed out the letters 'H', 'O' and 'G'. That left them:

CROWDTHRU

Pete then rearranged the letters, and the word became:

CURDWORTH

"Oh, this is clever" he said to the other two, who were both nodding in agreement. "*Let the crowd through, but not that pig, then you can find me, I am not that big,* means that you can find me, I am a small pub in Curdworth."

"Then, finally" he continued, "*and now I've told you all you need, it's down to you to come here full-speed.* This obviously means that we have the full address, now come and meet me."

"Wow" said Jerry, as he leant back on his chair. "Shall we go first thing in the morning? Be here no later than ten."

"Great" chimed Jules and Pete in a sort of induced euphoria.

"We'll be here, wouldn't miss this for the world" added Pete, and with that they opened another bottle of white plonk from Jerry's cupboard to start toasting their brilliance.

The White Horse

After several hours, and bottles of wine, later, Jerry stood at his front door saying goodbye to Jules and Pete. In the end they had all had a most enjoyable evening and were each still in a heightened state of elation- the solving of the email had been the result of a whole weeks struggle. They had turned this way and that, gone down blind alleys and eventually, due only to pure chance, arrived at a conclusion that made total and utter sense.

"And this was supposed to be an easy one" he muttered to himself, as he waved farewell to his brothers-in-arms and closed the door behind them.

Jerry then tidied up the last of the glasses, putting them into the dishwasher which, truth be told, had not really washed many dishes since Jerry had become its owner. He put the empty wine bottles beside the bin, switched out the lights, and walked into the bathroom.

After brushing his teeth and washing his face, he got undressed and climbed into bed. He was still so excited; he felt that he could not wait for tomorrow to arrive and their journey to the pub to begin. He looked at his watch- it was already tomorrow as it was 1:30 am, but he still needed to get some sleep. Jerry had been sleeping uneasily this past week, his mind disturbed by the email and his repeated dream of failing his mathematics test which had reoccurred virtually every night.

His initial dream of failing the maths test was bad enough, but now it had become even worse. Each night as he slept, he had to take the test again, and again, and each time he never scored more than four. The day after the newspaper advert disappeared he began to dream that the questions on the test paper were also disappearing, which eventually led to the whole test disappearing.

That night he dreamt again of being back in school. This time however, his teacher, the very pretty but highly strung Miss Jones, was not scolding but praising him, for he had now passed his test and scored eight out of ten.

"See what you can do when you put your mind to it Jeremy" she was preaching to him, in front of the whole class.

"Which one did I get wrong Miss?" he asked, as he raised his hand.

Then he didn't know how it happened, but the nice and pretty Miss Jones suddenly began to grow to an enormous size, sprouted two horns, one either side of her head, and her whole body turned a bright, crimson red. She slowly turned her horned head and stared straight down at him, her eyes bulging out from their sockets, each of them now matching the bright burning red colour of her body. She opened her mouth, spat out a huge flame of fire towards him, and screamed in a dark and threatening voice "ALL OF THEM, YOU FOOL!" She then let out a slow and merciless laugh that was so loud and so scary that it caused Jerry to wake up from his sleep, sweating and shaking from head to toe.

He jumped straight out of bed and ran into the kitchen to get a drink of water. It was not yet 2 am so he had not even been asleep for half an hour. He did not understand what the dream meant, but he knew that he did not like it, not one bit. Maybe he would talk to Jules about it since she was supposed to be good at trying to make sense out of dreams. He finished his drink and went back to bed, where he slept like a log for the rest of the night, without dreaming anything.

Jerry awoke the next morning around 9 am, still excited about making the trip to Sutton Coldfield and visiting the pub. Jules and Pete would be at his place at ten, so he had just enough time to shower and breakfast.

Ten o'clock came and right on cue the doorbell rang. Jerry opened the door to find both Jules and Pete standing there, as if they had been waiting there all night.

"Are you ready?" asked Pete, intimating that he had been ready ages ago and had been waiting all this time for Jerry.

"Yup" replied Jerry. "Do you guys want any breakfast or a drink before we go?"

"No thanks" they both replied.

"So what are we waiting for?" asked Jules, "can we go now?"

"Ok, ok" replied Jerry, grabbing his printout of the email and cramming it into his pocket as he dashed out of the apartment, closing the door behind him.

Jerry's car was his pride and joy. It was one of those old Ford Capri's that they do not make any more, not an expensive car by any stretch of the imagination, but it had a fond place in Jerry's heart.

"When are you going to get a decent car then?" asked Jules, because she always liked winding him up about his 'pride-and-joy'.

"When hell freezes over" answered Jerry, smiling at her.

Even though it was an old car, Jerry had fitted many modern extras to it in his spare time, including one of the newer satellite assisted navigation systems, which he promptly switched out of stand-by mode and entered their destination 'Curdworth', and then 'Kingsbury Road'.

"Should take us around two hours" he stated.

They set off heading westward out of Cambridge, all excited. The journey as such was not so challenging, up the A14, over onto the M6, then M42, and finally A4097 to Sutton Coldfield. There was one bright moment when, driving along the M6, they passed the turn-off to Rugby.

"Hey, did you see that" remarked Jules. "Rugby, I wonder?"

"No, give it a rest Jules" answered Pete, "we have solved that part – it had nothing to do in the end with the place called Rugby."

"Yes, I know" she answered, "but don't you think it's a little bit fishy that we have to go past Rugby to get there?"

"Maybe" answered Jerry, "but it could also just be a coincidence. I mean our journey does not take us past the River Urmi in Russia does it?"

They all laughed, but they were also starting to get some doubts. Whether they liked to admit it or not, it did seem a bit 'fishy' as Jules had put it, that Rugby was indeed very close to their destination.

Eventually they came to the A4097 exit to Sutton Coldfield and then at Lichfield Road they took the first exit onto the Kingsbury Road. They were so close now they could all feel it.

"First one to see it buys the first round" shouted out Jerry. But even that would not stop them. They each wanted to be the first to see it as Jerry drove further along the road.

"It should be on the left side" he said, as Pete hurriedly moved over to the other side of the rear seat, almost causing Jerry to steer off the road.

"Steady mate" he called out towards the back of the car, "we want to get there in one piece you know."

"THERE IT IS!" shrieked Jules, pointing her hand into the distance.

"Yup, there it is" grumbled Pete, "and mines a Lager" he added in a bitter sort of tone.

As they passed the field the White Horse Pub stood before them in all its glory. It was a wonderful old Tudor period building. The brickwork was all-white and interspersed with four solid, well-manicured, green climbing ivy plants. On the side of the building they could see a sign stating that there was 'Great British Food' available all day, every day. A small pathway, bordered with vibrant coloured flowers, led down a few steps to the front entrance. The Pub's sign, hanging from a tall wooden pole on the grass verge, was a picture of the head and neck of a beautiful white horse, painted against a bright light blue background. They had arrived.

Jerry parked in the car park, which was between the pub and the adjacent field, and they all got out and looked around.

There was not much to see. At the far end of the field was a barn of sorts, but they could not see any White Horse. In the middle of the field, close by, was an old riding fence, obviously used to train horses for show jumping, but this one looked very easy, not very high at all; even Jerry thought that he could jump it himself.

"Shall we go in then?" suggested Pete, as he started walking towards the entrance. "Come on you two!"

They both nodded and followed him into the bar.

The inside of the pub was exactly as Jules had expected it to be, with pictures of horses and ponies hanging on all of the walls. The tables and chairs looked as old as the building itself, steeped in history. The bar housed a collection of different pumps; beers, ales and spirits, all huddled together in a tiny space that offered not even enough room to swing a cat. Nevertheless, it was great, and all three of them instantly fell in love with it.

"My round" said Jules, and she turned to whisper to Jerry and Pete, "I don't think we should ask for lager here. What do you guys fancy?"

"Hmm" mumbled Jerry as he looked around the bar, "I think I'll have one of those Bishops Fingers" he concluded, licking his lips in anticipation.

"Me to" added Pete, hoping that Jerry knew what he was talking about. Jerry however was a semi-expert on beers and ales. Forget the wine, that he had no idea on, but the beers; he had tasted a few of those in his younger years.

"Is it nice, this Bishops Finger" asked Jules, feeling slightly embarrassed and not really looking forward to having to go up to the barman and ask for three Bishops Fingers; she could imagine what snide remarks she would get thrown back at her, I mean; they were in the countryside now, none of this sexual discrimination stuff here.

Sensing her unease, Jerry offered to get the drinks (she could pay him back later), and so, feeling much relieved, she sat down next to Pete and watched Jerry go up to the bar and order her round.

Their presence had drawn a few looks from the locals, but absolutely no hostility, just some enquiring glances as they sat in the corner, lapping up the atmosphere of the pub, and of course their drinks. They each enjoyed themselves so much that they almost forgot why they were there in the first place.

"So what do we do now?" asked Jules as she refocused the team onto their Quest. "I mean, what are we looking for? And how do we ask without making ourselves out to be complete loonies?"

Jerry got out his copy of the email and started reading it. Nothing came to his mind.

By this time, a smallish, well-dressed man of Mediterranean appearance was now serving the drinks. Above the bar was a small brass plate, stating that the licensee was a 'Senor Jose Garudo'. Jerry's brain was now running at full speed: analysing inputs, making connections, and concluding, quite rightly as it turned out, that this was in fact Senor Garudo himself.

The name 'Jose' rang a bell with him as well. 'Yes' he thought to himself as his mind drifted back to their recent trip to the Equestrian Club, 'Hadn't Bill said to him, as they dashed out: 'Say hello to Jose from me?' Yes, he had – and this might be the perfect way in'.

He stood up from the table and leant back down to Pete and Jules. "Leave it to me" he whispered to them, after which he straightened up and walked over to the bar to talk to Senor Garudo.

Jose looked up at him as Jerry approached, and gave him the customary welcome smile that he gave to all his tenants. He was indeed a smallish man, couldn't be more than 1 metre 70 tall, and he looked a youngish middle age, but you couldn't really tell with these Mediterranean types, their tanned skin appearance often gave them a few years advantage on the younger looking side.

"Good afternoon Sir" he said, in his best English, which was not bad; there was a hint of a Spanish accent, but not nearly as much as Jerry was expecting. Jerry suspected however that the locals might think differently as this was definitely not a midlands countryside accent.

"Hello" said Jerry politely, and held out his hand to shake that of Jose's. "I believe that we have a friend in common."

"Oh yes?" enquired Jose, shaking Jerry's hand. "And who might that be?" he asked, in an interested fashion.

"Bill from the Equestrian Club, in Cambridge" replied Jerry, closely watching Jose's face to see if he was getting anywhere, which he did not seem to be, for Jose was scratching his head and muttering.

Starting to panic Jerry added. "Elderly guy who loves horses and serves behind the bar at the club. He stayed here a few months ago."

"Si, si" said Jose, falling back into his mother tongue. "I mean, yes of course. Bill from the bar, nice chap, actually helped me out a bit while he was here, what did he call it 'Bus conductors holiday' or something?"

"Busman's holiday" said Jerry smiling. "It means that you do the same thing you do at work when you go on holiday, like a busman always used to catch a bus when he went on holiday, although I don't really know why" he added looking also a bit confused. "Maybe in those days they weren't paid enough to be able to afford their own cars, I guess."

"Ah yes, Busman's holiday" replied Jose, "yes, that was it. Welcome to the White Horse Public House" he went on. "My name is Jose Garudo, and I am the patron here. And you are?"

"Hi, I am Jerry" he replied, shaking his hand again, "Jerry Dumbarton, and these are my friends Jules and Pete" he added as he escorted Jose over to the table to meet them.

"Ah, nice to meet you all" said Jose, "and what brings you to these parts?"

"Well" said Jerry, after a slight uncomfortable pause as none of them really knew what exactly to say. "We are on a sort of treasure hunt, and we were wondering if we could look around your pub for a bit?"

"A treasure hunt" replied Jose, "now that is exciting isn't it. But I don't expect you'll find any treasure here" he added.

"I mean, this public house is old, yes it is, but I have looked in all nooks and crannies since I have been here the last five years, and my wife has been here since she was a child- this used to be her parents pub. I am sure that we would have found anything of worth by now if it existed" he concluded.

The others had gone quiet, and Jose was looking at their crest-fallen faces. He could see that they were a little disappointed, so he continued. "But, of course, you are welcome to have a look around, just please don't break or damage anything eh?"

"Of course we won't" said Jules, looking suddenly much happier.

At that moment, a very pretty woman walked out from behind the bar.

"Ah, Annie" called Jose over to her. "Please, come here my dear and meet our guests. This is Jules, and Pete and Jerry. They are all friends of old Bill who was here a few months ago, from Cambridge – you remember: the horse fanatic?"

"Ah yes" she said, "I remember. He was a lovely man."

"They are all on a treasure hunt" added Jose. "How exciting, eh dear?"

"Oh, yes" she said, "what fun indeed! Hello there Jules, Pete and hello, we meet again Jerry."

Jules and Pete both looked at Jerry, at the same time that Jose looked into the eyes of his beloved wife. "You know this man my dear?" he asked her.

"Anne" said Jerry, astonished, "Is it really you? You don't look a day older."

"Oh that's so sweet of you Jerry" she said as she blushed. "You always were the charmer, and such a tease with the girls."

"Jules, Pete, this is Anne, the girl I used to go out with around ten years ago. The one who used to go riding at the club, the one we were at yesterday" said Jerry, still in a state of shock as he sat down into the vacant chair.

"Well this is a wonderful coincidence" remarked Jose, in a sincere way, "how does that saying go my dear, 'in all the bars, in all the world, you have to walk in to mine'."

They all burst out laughing, even Jerry, who was looking very pleased to see Anne again, even if she was now called 'Annie' by her husband.

"Shall I take you on a tour of our pub?" asked Annie, to the three treasure hunters.

"Oh yes, please" answered Jules, "that would be most fascinating."

The group of them then spent the next hour walking around the pub with Annie showing them all the different rooms, and the nooks and crannies as her husband had called them. Jerry at first found it a bit difficult to call her Annie, but after a few times he got used to it. After the hour was up they were all feeling a bit tired, but most of all rather peckish.

"Would you each like one of our excellent Ploughman's lunches?" asked Annie.

That sounded great and they all three thought that it was an excellent idea and said yes please.

"Why don't you guys go and sit outside in the sunshine" she suggested "and we will bring out the lunches to you when they are ready."

"Fine" said Jerry, "thanks" and they all walked outside into the bright sunny day.

It was wonderful weather again. The temperature was up in the early thirties centigrade, but the accompanying soft breeze meant that sitting in the shade was a very nice experience. The three of them went over to the table closest to a nearby tree, such that the shadow of the tree protected them from the harsh direct rays of the scorching sun, and sat down.

"Well it is a lovely place" said Jules, "but we have not really found out anything yet, have we?"

"Not a sausage" added Pete, who was starting to get a bit disgruntled. "I mean, they are either very good actors, or they know absolutely nothing about it."

"Well I know Annie" said Jerry, "and if she is one thing, it is not a good actor. She was always giving away secrets when we were together, giggling at the wrong times and blushing like you saw her earlier, so I am sure that she knows nothing about any of this."

"What about him" said Jules, "I mean he seems very suave, maybe a bit too so" she added, "and what about that accent of his, where did he buy that from?"

"Oh, you are getting paranoid" said Pete, "I think he sounds quite sincere."

"Sincere?" remarked Jules, who obviously could not believe what Pete had just said. "I think he is up to something. You heard him. He said he had also been searching the house for the last five years."

"Could be" added Jerry. "I mean you never know nowadays do you?"

At that moment, Annie came out of the rear door of the pub accompanied by one of the pub waitresses, and carrying between them four pints of ale and four wonderful plates full of the most delicious Ploughman's Lunch that any of them had ever seen or tasted before. It was a feast beyond feasts; Great British food indeed, without doubt.

After they had finished, and their plates were completely empty; they had eaten everything, Annie called the waitress back, who then took the empties and left them alone at the table.

"That was really delicious" said Jules as she looked at Annie, "you are a really good chef."

"Yes, great" added both Jerry and Pete.

"Why thank you" she replied, in a kind of school girlish embarrassed fashion. "I've lived in this pub for quite a few years, and I learnt from my mother." She then stood up from the table and turned to Jerry.

"Let's all go for a short walk; there is something that I want to show you all" she said.

They all got up and walked around 50 metres away from the pub into the middle of the field. Annie let out a strong loud whistle and within a few moments a large, handsome, elderly, White Horse, came galloping into view towards her.

"This is the real White Horse" said Annie, "and I love him like no other."

"He is beautiful" remarked Jules. Girls could obviously appreciate such things, for Pete and Jerry just looked at each other and thought to themselves, 'well he looked ok'.

"I have looked after this horse since I was a girl" she added. "He is a part of me."

"You mentioned you had a horse when we went out together" said Jerry. "Was this him? I never saw him at the club."

"Yes, this was him, but I would never take him to the big city; he likes his freedom here and all the grass. It was torture for me to be away from him for so long. That is why we could never have lasted Jerry. You loved your University scene and I loved my countryside."

"Yeah, I guess so" mumbled Jerry, in a somewhat reluctant agreement.

"This is a quiet little place" added Annie. "Nothing ever happens here, it's like we have been here for 400 years. When I was young, I hated it. That is why I went away to the city. However, when I got there I hated that even more. It made me appreciate what I had here. This used to be my father's pub you know, and his father's before him. When I returned, I met Jose and we soon got married. He is a very caring man."

Annie turned to the horse and started stroking the side of its head and talking to it. The others felt slightly embarrassed to be there, as if they were intruding on a private moment.

"Have a nice day you three" said Annie, as she grabbed hold of the horse and climbed onto his bare back. "It's now time for me to take him on his daily ride across the fields and back."

"Ok" said Jerry. "Thanks for the food and everything. Maybe we will see you again sometime, you never know."

"Yes, maybe" she replied, waving to them as the horse galloped off, jumping over the small riding fence that they had seen earlier, and then off into the distance.

"Well, what do you make of that" said Pete, in a strangely inquisitorial manner.

Jerry was thinking again. He took the printout of the email out from his pocket and looked at it again.

He read the first part out again. "*Location of Verse Three,* and, *In order to find Verse Three, you will need to find me.* What can they mean?"

"Well obviously" said Pete who, with Jules, had moved closer to Jerry to form a small group, "we need to find a Verse Three."

From:	The White Horse
Sent:	Monday July 16th
To:	Jeremy Dumbarton
Subject:	Verse Three

Location of Verse Three

Dear Jeremy,

Welcome to the Quest for the Prize; I hope that you are the worthy one, for only the worthy can inherit the Prize. This first clue is a test, it is very simple, but most will fail even at this first simple hurdle.

In order to find Verse Three, you will need to find me.
But I am not so simple to find, because I might just be in your mind.
When it's fine I am clear to see, the White Horse is next door to me.
Drinks and Rugby go hand in hand, and come together where I stand.
Let the crowd through, but not that pig, then you can find me, I am not that big.
And now I've told you all you need, its down to you to come here full-speed.

Best Regards

The White Horse

"ME!" shouted Jules. "It's me."

"What do you mean?" replied Pete.

"It's 'me' that we have to find" said Jules. "Verse Three is the 'me'. Look it says it in the first line '*In order to find Verse Three, you will need to find me'.*"

"Yes" said Jerry rather slowly, as if he did not understand a word that Jules was saying. "But so what, how does that help?"

"Well read further" said Jules. "*When its fine I'm clear to see, the White Horse is next door to me.* That does not mean that the White Horse is next door to the pub, it means that the White Horse pub is next door to Verse Three, next door to me. That could mean that the Verse Three is here in this field."

"Clever" said Pete, in an impressive and slightly awestruck tone.

Jules grabbed hold of the email, obviously feeling that she was now on a hot streak. "Yes, of course" she said out aloud.

"What, What!" cried out both Jerry and Pete together.

"Read the second line" she said, as Jerry snatched the paper from her.

"What, '*but I am not so simple to find because I might just be in your mind*' replied Jerry.

"No" said Jules, "the second line" as she snatched back the printout of the email from him. "*This first clue is a test, it is very simple, but most will fail even at this first simple hurdle.* Don't you see" she cried, almost pulling her hair out. "The first clue is not the text we were looking at, that must be the second clue. The first clue is a test. It is a very simple test. It is a simple hurdle. The hurdle is a test for the horse; he has to jump it. Even we said when we first saw it that it was a simple one. The Verse must be over there by the jumping fence, the hurdle" she explained.

"Jules" began Pete. "Forget what I have ever said about blondes in the past; that was inspired" and with that they all ran over to the hurdle and started to examine it, looking for markings or anything that was out of place in any way. They looked all over the hurdle but could not see anything. Then Pete took off the highest pole, which was only half a metre off the ground, and looked inside.

"There's something in here" he said, and he squeezed his fore and middle finger of his right hand into the inside of the pole and pulled out a small piece of paper, enclosed in plastic to protect it from the rain. They had found it, for the top of the piece of paper stated without any doubt that this was 'Verse Three'.

```
Verse Three
    3.1     This verse is what contains a clue,
    3.2     without the 4S's, just for you.
    3.3     Will you stop here on what is best,
    3.4     or will you miss it, like all the rest.
    3.5     Keep in mind that its clear to see,
    3.6     the number's here it's in verse three.
    3.7     Your mission exists to find that clue,
    3.8     but if I've hidden it, what can you do?
    3.9     But hang around there's more to know
    3.10    like where this number's got to go?
    3.11    Never mind you know, it's there to see,
    3.12    that answer's also in verse three.
    3.13    So which is which? and what is what?
    3.14    their very close, around a spot.
    3.15    It's not so difficult a thing to hide,
    3.16    place and number are side by side.
    3.17    Were getting close, no time to waste,
    3.18    one is code, and one is place.
```

Jerry turned over the piece of paper, and there was some more on the other side.

```
    3.19    But hold on there is more to know,
    3.20    like what comes next and where to go.
    3.21    To find the first you must talk to,
    3.22    a mystic of a nearby zoo.
    3.23    But where to go one shall not say,
    3.24    but look for her where kings can play.
```

"Well what do we make of that?" asked Jerry to his two colleagues.

"Well I think that we have found all we can here" said Jules. "I think it's time we went home and then we can start to work on understanding this Verse. And if it's anything like the email then we are in for a long night."

They all agreed and walked back to the car. As they passed the side window of the pub they could see that Jose was looking out at them. Had he been watching them all the time? Did he know that they had found something? Whatever, it made Jerry slightly uneasy. Deciding not to show it, he stretched out his hand and waved good-bye to Jose, indicating that they were going to drive home now. Jose nodded his head and waved good-bye to them as well.

When they arrived back at Jerry's apartment they were all feeling rather tired. They were not hungry at all; the late lunch had been spectacular. Despite their tiredness however, they decided to have a quick chat about the new challenge that was ahead of them, understanding Verse Three.

They each read the passage a few times.

"Any ideas?" asked Jerry, looking at both of them in turn.

"Well" started Pete, "it seems that we have to find two numbers, and the numbers are hidden within the Verse. The two numbers tell us a code and a place, which I think means a position. This is apparently the third Verse, which means that there are, at least, two others that we will also have to find. If each one gives us a number and a position then we will most likely get some kind of code number resulting out of it."

"Like a combination to a safe?" suggested Jules.

"Yes, exactly" replied Pete. "I think we should all make a copy of the Verse, take it home with us, and then see how many different numbers we can find within it, to see if any make specific sense when trying to solve the riddle."

"That sounds a great idea" said Jerry, and he immediately got out his mobile phone, took a picture of the Verse and then radioed it over to his printer to print out copies for Jules and Pete to take home with them.

"Let's meet tomorrow evening" suggested Pete. "Why not come to my place for a change; then we can have some decent wine."

They all agreed and then Jerry walked with them to the door, where they all then went their separate ways.

The next evening, Jerry and Jules both turned-up at Pete's place, a penthouse in the top floor of a three-year-old apartment block in the centre of Cambridge. It was a bit more up-market than Jerry's; it had its own balcony overlooking the River Cam. Today had been another fine day, yet in the apartment it was still cool, and sitting outside with a chilled good quality white wine in the hand, was a pure delight.

Pete had set up a table on the balcony for them to work on, and after they had all greeted each other they sat down to get on with the task for the evening; the solving of Verse Three.

"Well" said Jerry, "how many numbers have we found?"

"Fifty-six" said Pete, wearing a proud sort of 'beat that if you dare' expression.

"Fifty-six" repeated Jules, looking absolutely amazed; "I only found seven."

"Seven" mumbled Jerry in a very dejected tone. "I only found six."

"Well Pete, I guess we should start with you then" declared Jules.

"Ok" he replied, "here we go then. The first forty-eight are obvious; they are the numbers to the left of each row. Each row has two numbers, the first being always three, I guess to signify Verse Three, and then the line number. It is sort of like what you see in the bible."

"Oh, yes" said Jules, "I missed those. I was only looking at the text."

Pete continued. "Then we have 'Three' in the title, 'Three' on line 3.6, 'one' on line 3.7, and 'five' on line 3.8."

"Where is that?" said Jerry.

"Oh, it's hidden" said Pete. "It states *'what if I've hidden it'* and in fact the word 'five' is hidden; see starting with the 'f' of 'if'."

"I missed that" said Jerry, "yes, I see it now."

Pete continued again, feeling quite happy with himself. "There is both "three" and "seven" on line 3.12."

Pete paused for he was sure that both Jerry and Jules would have missed that one, but it seemed he was wrong for they had both crossed it off their lists, so he continued, a little crest-fallen, "and there is 'one' on line 17."

"What, Where?" said Jules.

"It's spelt backwards" said Pete, "here look" and he pointed to the end of the word 'close', followed by 'no', which forms the word 'one' backwards."

"Sneaky" said Jules, looking impressed.

"And there is 'one' twice in line 3.18" he concluded.

"Yes, we all got that one" said Jerry. "Well you got all mine" he continued, not looking too surprised. They both then looked at Jules who was smiling.

"What?" said Pete.

"You missed one" she said.

"Where?" replied Pete in his disbelieving voice, "show me."

"The very first lines 3.1 and 3.2" said Jules, and she repeated the lines "*this Verse is what contains a clue, without the 4S's, just for you.* Now there are four S's in the first line, but removing them makes no sense. However" she continued. "If you rewrite 4S's you can state it as 'IV' 'SS' i.e. replace the number 4, with the roman numeral for 4, which is 'IV'." She was now smiling and enjoying every second. "Then, if you now take the letters 'I, V, S, and S' away from 'This Verse' then you are left with the letters 'There', which can be rearranged into 'Three'."

"Wow" said Jerry.

"Well done" said Pete.

"Thanks Guys" she said, muttering, "Fib indeed" under her breath.

"So" said Jerry, "that means we have in total fifty-seven numbers" smiling towards Pete who despite missing one was still feeling pleased with himself. "What do we do now?"

This question brought Pete down to earth with a bump. Jules did not look so pleased either anymore.

"Well" began Pete. "Before Jules came up with her masterstroke, I was going to say that the two numbers we were looking for were both the same number three, although I was not completely sure. After Jules' brilliant find, I am at least more certain that the first number is three."

"Yes, I agree" replied Jules. "And, if we take it a bit further, Line 14 says that both numbers are around a spot. All the numbers on the left are separated by a 'spot', i.e. a dot" she added, pointing to the dots on the papers between all of the two numbers. "Line 16" she continued, "says that place and number are side by side, and line 18 says 'one is code and one is place', which could mean the first one is the code and the second one is the place, but that is not conclusive" she concluded.

"Yes, but hold on" said Jerry; "if both numbers are the same, like Pete suggests, then it would not matter which was what."

"And look at line 3" said Pete, with a tinge of excitement in his voice. "*Will you stop here on what is best.*"

"*Or will you miss it like all the rest*" added Jules, smiling.

"What?" said Jerry.

"The number is here in line three" said Pete. "It's 3.3, the number to the left of the line, side by side, separated by a spot, and we did not miss it."

"Yup, I agree" said Jules, "it has to be; nothing else makes sense."

Jerry however was not sure. "It can't be that easy" he said. "I mean look how long it took us to work out the email."

"But didn't the email talk about the first clue being easy" said Pete, "maybe it was referring to this and not the email. I mean that was definitely not easy was it?"

"Maybe you're right" said Jerry, "I mean they can't all be that difficult can they?"

"So" concluded Jules. "If the number and place are both three, then what comes next?"

"Oh that's easy" said Pete, and he turned over the paper Jerry had put on the table to reveal lines nineteen to twenty-four of the Verse. "Well, at least part of it is" he added.

They read the lines in the text. Jerry looked stumped.

"Which part is easy?" he asked.

"Well" said Pete, "the first two lines tell us that if we want to know what comes next then we have to go and talk to someone at a certain place. The next two lines tell us that the person is a 'mystic' of sorts, meaning I guess that she can look into the future, and the second part tells us that it is in a zoo somewhere. The last two tell us where to look for the 'Mystic' in a place where kings can play."

"Yes" said Jerry, not trying to interrupt Pete but more to push him on.

"Well we already know that the 'mystic' is to be found in a zoo, and therefore the zoo must be where 'kings can play'" he concluded. "The mystic must be in London Zoo."

"London Zoo?" replied Jerry, with a confused expression all over his face "How did you work that one out?"

"Yes" said Jules. "I agree; London Zoo is in Regents Park, where kings can play. Oh very good" she added.

"But" said Pete, "I have absolutely no idea as to what this mystic is, that we have to look for in London Zoo."

"We need to think about this" said Jules, "and it's getting late now and I am exhausted. Why don't we look into this on another day?"

"Ok" said Jerry, as he laid back, filled his glass with more white wine, and tried to soak up the last minutes of warmth that were being offered by the setting sun.

Mystic

When Jerry arrived home later that evening, he decided to put the original Verse Three text into the top draw of his desk for safekeeping. Tomorrow was Monday and he, like the others, had to go to work, but very soon now he would be on vacation.

That night he slept very well, no weird dreams or anything strange at all. The next day at work went fine as well, and in addition, he also managed to sneak some time looking at the London Zoo web site, but he could not find anything that mentioned a 'Mystic' of sorts. There was a Zoo Guide, but you could not get to that on line; you could of course buy it on line with your tickets and then pick it up when you got there, so that did not help him much.

Pete and Jules were not coming around this evening; they had both decided to give it a rest for a day, since they had both fallen behind with their own housework and had some catching up to do. The "Quest" had occupied almost all of their spare time this last week, and the need to do washing and cleaning had become greater and greater, such that urgent action was now called for. Pete had already declared DefCon 2 at his apartment, as old socks and underwear were mounting up and about to cause a health hazard. The threshold for DefCon 1 would be breached when his neighbours actually started complaining, which Pete estimated was only a few days away, unless he did something about it.

Jerry felt that he could also do with an evening alone. As he sat in his favourite armchair, thinking about how to find this 'Mystic', and what she even was, he decided that

Wednesday would be a good day to go to the zoo, as it was bound to be another fine day. He now knew that Mystic, whatever she was, was in London Zoo, so all he needed to do was get a train down to Kings Cross, jump on the underground over to Regents Park, and then visit the zoo. Going to London Zoo would also be a good excuse to reminisce; the last time that he had been to a zoo was when he was a ten-year-old child; his school had arranged a science day trip to a local zoo. Yes, Jerry had decided. He would take a day off from work on Wednesday and go to London Zoo, and he would give Pete and Jules a call tomorrow to ask if they wanted to join him.

Wednesday came around very quickly. Jules had said yes, but Pete could not join them as he had several meetings at work that he could not miss, but he wished them success.

As the zoo did not open until 10a.m, Jules and Jerry did not have to catch the early train, but set out for the local station around eight thirty, and caught the next train down to Kings Cross in London, where they then jumped into a taxi which took them the short distance to London Zoo. They had until 5.30 p.m., which was seven full hours away, but they still had no idea where to start looking or what to look for. Jerry finally bought one of the Guide Books, but that also did not help much with their particular Quest.

"Let's just walk around a bit" suggested Jules, "and see what we can see."

Jerry agreed and they set off towards the Birds, where they found nothing to do with 'a Mystic' or a 'mystical being' or anything like it. Then they walked further into the Lions and Tigers enclosure and again nothing, which at this point was quite a relief since neither of them really fancied trying to talk to a big wild cat.

Just close by however, Jules was very touched by the seven baby lion cubs that were there; it seemed that several of the lionesses had given birth earlier in the spring. It was quite funny for several minutes, as the keepers were trying to weigh the cubs to make sure that they were properly nourished.

There were several television cameras also capturing these moments on film, obviously for some local news programme that was covering the event.

After three hours they had been nearly everywhere, and found nothing. At two o'clock, Pete called Jerry on his mobile phone and asked how it was going. He had hoped to hear all the good news, but there was none, not yet anyway.

At five o'clock, both Jerry and Jules were feeling very disappointed. They still had the Reptile House to visit, but neither of them felt that would have anything to do with their Quest. As they walked in, they immediately saw all the snakes on display. Pythons, Adders, Boa Constrictors and many more, were all there to see, but none of them looked mystical and none of them could talk. Jerry suddenly remembered the Harry Potter story, and wondered if he, Jerry, could talk to snakes as well, but that did not work either, although it did cause Jules to burst out laughing when he tried. The whole day was turning out to be a fiasco, and the sooner they got back home the better.

They left the zoo just after a quarter past five in the evening and, as their train was not leaving until half past seven, Jerry suggested that they went and got something to eat and drink at a nearby pub, one that he had been to several times when he was younger. He had though only been there on a Friday, and they were great nights with karaoke competitions. The Pub was the Thornbury Castle, in Enford Street, Marylebone, and it was a real cosy atmosphere inside, and had some excellent food on offer.

They arrived at the Pub, sat down, and ordered their meals and drinks. Wednesday night was much more civilised than what Jerry remembered of the Fridays, and it was a perfect place for a good meal, especially after a hard day walking around the zoo. Jerry really enjoyed being in the pub, it brought back such good memories of his young adulthood.

"What made you come here?" asked Jules, after she had been listening to one of Jerry's more riotous memories of a Friday some ten years ago.

"I just felt like it" he replied. "I had passed it several times, and I always had a kind of attraction to it, you know when you get a good feeling about something. Many of my friends also recommended the place. Then, when I finally went in, it was great, and we had such wonderful evenings."

Jerry recanted a few more tales to Jules, who was also thoroughly enjoying the cosy atmosphere of the pub.

At around half past six they grabbed a taxi back to Kings Cross station, where they arrived with about forty minutes still to wait before their train departed. They made their way over to one of the waiting rooms. It was quite handy anyway since their train was leaving from the platform right opposite.

They went into the waiting room and sat down on one of the benches. The waiting room itself looked, and felt, old; it had obviously not received much attention, or budget, over the last years. Over on one side stood the latest timetable, which was not so strange to see in a waiting room in a train station. Then, however, hanging in the middle of one of the walls, there was an old clock. It was a strange clock, sort of a mixture between a tourist map and a normal clock; with each number on the clock face pointing to a specific castle in England, Scotland, or Wales. Dead smack in the middle was Nottingham Castle, and dotted all around it, as if extracted directly from a map, were all of the others. Jerry had of course been to the Castle at eleven o'clock (that was Edinburgh Castle) when he was younger, and the one at five o'clock, that one everyone new, the Tower of London, but he did not immediately recognise any of the others, although they all looked to be in good condition.

There was also an old picture on the wall hanging to the left of the clock. Jerry found it quite amusing since the person hanging it had obviously not done a good job as it was hanging much below the centre line of the clock. The picture was also a bit faded, but they could still make out the subject; it was a picture of the old Queen Mary.

The picture, the timetable, and the clock however, were of absolutely no interest to Jerry and Jules; they just wanted to get home and try to forget the whole day. The train journey would only take an hour as it was one of the fast trains and they could not wait to get on it and get home. They were of course feeling disappointed as they had not found the 'Mystic' at London Zoo, and that they would now have to go back, retrace their steps, and find out where they went wrong.

Finally the train arrived and they made their way to their reserved seats ready for the journey home. Pete called during the journey and agreed to meet them at Jerry's around nine o'clock.

When Jerry and Jules got home they were both exhausted and feeling depressed as they had not found what they had been looking for. Jules did not really know why she was sitting in Jerry's apartment waiting for Pete; she was in no mood for this. Nevertheless, she was there, she was after all, one of the team.

Pete arrived and they told him the whole sorry saga. They spoke about all the animals they had seen and tried to speak to, and Jules relished telling Pete how Jerry had tried to speak Parsel-Tongue when he was in the Reptile House. They mentioned also the nice food and drinks they had consumed at the pub and concluded that the meal was actually the best part of the whole day. The zoo had been nice, and they had done a real good job of making it interesting for visitors; Jules remembered how it was when she went there as a child with her parents, nowadays it was much better.

"Did we get it wrong?" asked Pete. "Or did we just not find her?"

Neither Jerry nor Jules knew the answer to those questions. Pete even asked at one point if they wanted to go back tomorrow and he would go with them, but neither of them could face that. Pete was welcome to go on his own of course, but he decided against it.

Pete asked Jerry to go and get the text that they had found in the field next to the White Horse pub, and so Jerry went to his Den and fetched it from the top drawer of his desk. Pete was convinced that they had translated it correctly, but he wanted to double check it again, just to be on the safe side. Jules and Jerry did not have any energy left to go through all that again.

Pete studied the text as he sat on the sofa. He was focussing on the backside of the message, the part that spoke about what to do next.

3.19	But hold on there is more to know,
3.20	like what comes next and where to go.
3.21	To find the first you must talk to,
3.22	a mystic of a nearby zoo.
3.23	But where to go one shall not say,
3.24	but look for her where kings can play.

Pete was deep in thought, but he was not really getting anywhere.

"I'm thirsty" said Jerry, "all that walking has really taken it out of me. Fancy some wine anyone?"

"Yeah that's a good idea" replied Jules, who was also feeling the same.

Jerry went it into the Kitchen, but very quickly came back empty handed.

"All the wine has gone" he grumbled. "Do you fancy coming down to the Dog and Bone?"

"The Dog and Bone" replied Jules, "on a Wednesday. Are you mad?"

"Why?" he replied.

"Well, we have just been to one zoo" she stated, "and you know what that place is like on a Wednesday with the Uni crowd; it's just like another zoo."

"It's not a zoo" said Jerry, sounding a little bit offended. "It's a Boo...."

However, before he could finish his word, Pete had interrupted him and yelled out "Boozer!"

Jerry and Jules both looked at him.

"What do you mean?" said Jerry, as he walked over and sat down on the sofa, next to Pete, who was still staring at the text.

"It's another of those bloody anagrams" said Pete, and he grabbed a piece of paper from the coffee table and wrote down the words.

NEARBY ZOO - ANY BOOZER

"Any Boozer" said Jerry. "How are we going to find a Mystic in any Boozer? I mean, are we going to have to go and check every Boozer in the country?" he asked, as if it sounded ridiculous, although there was a tiny part of his brain that was imagining that that sort of Quest might not be such a bad idea.

Jules meanwhile was now leaning forward from her armchair and looking at the words Pete had written, still thinking about the Dog and Bone pub that they were just discussing.

"That's not 'Any Boozer'" she said, "that's" and she took the pen from Pete and put a line between the 'A' and the 'N' of 'ANY' and it now read:

A NY BOOZER

"A New York Boozer" she said triumphantly, "an American Bar."

"The Dog and Bone" said Jerry.

"Whoa, whoa" said Pete, "we have absolutely no evidence that it could be the Dog and Bone."

"Well it's a sort of a zoo, isn't it?" said Jules.

"And it's nearby" added Jerry.

"But what about the last part?" said Pete, obviously trying to make sure it was correct this time; he felt a bit guilty already for the others maybe wasting a whole day at the zoo, let alone the train fare. "*Look for her where King's can play.*"

"Well that just confirms it" said Jerry to the other two, who were now looking at him in a strange way. He continued. "Where do Kings play? They play in their Castles. And, the Dog and Bone is in Castle Street" he announced triumphantly.

"Wow" said Pete, who looked like he was starting to be convinced. "Let's double check first" and they all immediately started reading the last part of the text again.

"Well, it could be" said Jules, "I mean there is nothing there that contradicts it."

"True" Pete replied "but we still have no idea what the 'Mystic' is though do we?"

"Well we're not going to find out sitting here are we" said Jerry. "And I for one am quite happy to go down there even if there is no bloody Mystic; I need a drink!" and with that they all agreed and immediately set off for the pub.

Five minutes later they arrived at the pub and all went straight in, not hanging around outside at all. Jules was correct; it was really like a zoo inside with all the young students cheering and throwing things at each other; almost a Chimps Tea Party.

Jerry got the beers and they all sat together at one of the tables that was free, and, quite luckily, was the furthest away from all the animals.

"So, where is the Mystic?" asked Pete, as he eagerly looked around the pub. "Could be anyone of these guys; I mean they all fancy themselves and think that they know everything don't they?"

"We're looking for a 'she'" said Jules, trying to remind them of the text in the Verse; "Look for her" and she stressed the 'her'.

"Ok, ok" said Pete, thinking at the same time that he hoped it was not another fib. One in the team was enough!

No one stood out from the crowd. There was no one sitting at a table with a Crystal Ball, or with any Tarot Cards, so they were again at a loss. It was now half past ten and was almost closing time. Were they going to be frustrated twice in one day? They obviously hoped not.

Eleven came and went, followed quite quickly by eleven thirty. The pub was starting to empty out now, as only the hard core of the students remained, which was still quite a few, and they were all looking slightly worse for ware.

"Shall we go?" asked Jerry.

The others agreed, and they all three got up, feeling well watered, but also slightly depressed as they were now sure that they were actually going to be frustrated for the second time, and in the same day.

It had been a warm evening and as they walked through the still-opened doorway to the pub, Jerry noticed that the jet-black raven was there again, sitting on the street sign. Not paying any attention to it, he started walking back up the street with his two colleagues following him, when a voice from behind him called out, "did you have a nice time at the zoo, Jerry?"

"Oh, it was ok" he replied, as he stopped dead in his tracks, turned around and looked at Pete and Jules. Was Pete trying to wind him up?

"What did you say?" he asked Pete.

"I said nothing" replied Pete, who was also looking puzzled.

Jules looked around, for there was no one else visibly close to them.

"Someone just asked me if I had a nice time at the Zoo" said Jerry. "Didn't you hear it?"

"I heard nothing mate" replied Pete.

"I heard it" said Jules, "it came from behind us."

"You heard it Jules?" repeated Jerry, trying to tell himself that he was not going mad.

Pete looked furious. "Be quiet" he said. "Maybe we can here it again."

"Over here" said the mysterious voice.

"There! Did you hear it Pete?" asked Jules

"NO!" cried Pete, "I heard nothing."

"It said 'over here'" said Jerry, as he walked back towards the entrance of the pub.

"What?" said Pete, starting to think that this was one of Jerry's wind-up's and that Jules was in it as well because he had sent them both on a wild-goose-chase down to London Zoo. "Are you two winding me up?"

"No mate, this is honest" said Jerry, and he meant it as well.

"Up here" said the voice, and both Jerry and Jules looked straight up at the jet-black raven.

"Did you enjoy your trip to the zoo?" it repeated, in a voice that was a bit squawky, although sweet, feminine, and quite mature at the same time.

Jerry and Jules looked at the raven that was perched where she was normally perched, right above the word 'Castle', on the 'Castle St' signpost.

"*Look for her where Kings can play*" whispered Jules, "castle" she muttered, and then both Jules and Jerry looked at each other; each trying to check that they were both still completely awake and not dreaming.

Pete on the other hand was looking at both of them furiously, as if he was following a tennis rally, thinking that they were both going mad.

"Is that bird talking to you?" he asked, not really believing that he could be asking such a stupid question.

"Of course I am" replied the raven, but not to Pete, for Pete could still not hear it. Jules and Jerry however could hear it perfectly.

"What's your name?" said Jules to the bird, completely fascinated by it and captured by its voice, which sounded a bit like her mothers.

"I am Mystic" it replied, and then continued saying, "and are you going to stand here all night and talk to me, or shall we go somewhere more private?"

Jerry and Jules were a bit taken-aback by the question. After all, they were not used to meeting talking ravens outside pubs, or anywhere else to be more precise. Jerry still had a slight suspicion that he might have drunk the last beer a fraction too quickly, but anyway he did not even have a chance to think up an answer to the question, for Mystic had already started to answer the question herself.

"Never mind" she said. "I will be waiting for you at your window Jerry" and with that, she stretched out her wings and flew off in the direction of Jerry's apartment.

"I guess she knows where my apartment is" said Jerry, as he turned to face Jules.

Pete on the other hand was now almost on the floor laughing. "What, you've been picked up by a real bird?" he cried, and even Jules had to laugh at that one.

"Serious mate" said Jerry, "it was actually talking to me."

"Yeah, yeah, and I bet you got her phone number as well, didn't you" laughed Pete. "Fine, fine, I am sorry that I didn't come with you to London, I'll go alone tomorrow if you want me to" he stated.

Jerry finally understood what was getting to Pete. "No it's not that" he replied, "it's really true; you tell him Jules."

"Yes, Pete" she added, "I mean I couldn't believe it, but it told us that her name was Mystic and that she would be waiting for us by Jerry's window."

"Oh come of it" said Pete, "are you in on it as well?"

"Look" said Jerry, starting to get a little bothered. "Let's go back to the apartment and if the bird is there we'll let it in and hear what it's got to say, and if it's not there, well, then we'll know that both Jules and I are drunk. How's that then?"

"Fine" chuckled Pete, "let's go now, I don't want to miss this for the world" and with that they all three set off at a brisk pace back to Jerry's apartment.

They got back to Jerry's apartment block as quickly as they possibly could, without running or drawing too much attention to themselves. Once inside they dashed up the stairs and into his apartment, where waiting at the window was, nothing.

Pete started laughing. "Sussed!" he shouted out, in his triumphant voice.

Jules and Jerry just looked at each other. Jerry went into the kitchen, followed by Jules and Pete, and there, with her head staring in through the kitchen window, was Mystic.

"Ha!" said Jerry, "who's sussed now then?" as he looked at Pete.

Pete had stopped dead in his tracks. All sounds from his mouth had ceased the moment he saw the two small eyes looking through the window. He could not believe it. He did not want to believe it; this meant that Jules and Jerry could hear something that he could not, and it meant that they had not been winding him up. Pete was gob-smacked.

Jerry opened the window and let Mystic fly in and onto the kitchen table. Jules and Jerry sat down on the chairs, and Pete just stood watching. Mystic continued as if nothing strange was going on at all; she knew Pete could not hear her, so she was well prepared to answer the question that she also knew Jerry was now going to ask."

"Why can only Jules and me hear you and not Pete?" asked Jerry.

"Jules and I" replied Mystic, correcting his English.

For Jerry this was a first, a raven correcting his English. However, even for Jerry's centre forward brain, he knew that this was no ordinary raven, although he still did not have any vague idea of what it really was.

Mystic continued. "It is not yet time for Pete to hear me, but for the two of you it is important that you listen; I am not allowed to help you with your Quest; I can only give you the clue. However, I am watching you, and I will be following you to make sure that you do not wander into any danger. For there is great peril in this Quest, and great reward when you succeed."

"Will I succeed?" asked Jerry.

"Only the worthy can inherit the Prize" replied Mystic, in a pondering manner as if this statement was bringing her many sad memories. "We shall see. You, Jerry, are on a Quest, and your colleagues here are vital if you are to succeed. Now listen carefully."

Jerry and Jules both sat up straight, paying close attention to what Mystic was saying. Pete was listening hard as well, but could still not hear anything. He knew though that he should not say anything or interrupt them, since whatever it was saying was obviously very important, as both Jules and Jerry looked riveted. They would tell him afterwards, he was sure of that.

Mystic continued, and both Jerry and Jules started writing down exactly what she said. After she had finished, Mystic looked at what they had written and then lifted her head and looked hard into Jerry's eyes.

"I must go now" she said to him. "Good luck you three" and with that she flew out of the still opened window and onwards and upwards into the clear night sky.

Jules and Jerry both looked at each other, and then at Pete.

"What did it say?" he asked them both, still not really believing it.

Jerry and Jules then both looked at their notes and compared them. They had each written the exact same, and so they showed their papers to Pete.

Twenty-eight feet measured today, will mature to the singular yard you need to go to. The first Verse is in there; it is a new angry text that hides in the injections our children dare to take as a challenge.

"What does that mean I wonder?" asked Pete. However, before anyone could answer, he quickly added. "And what did she answer when you asked her why I can't hear her?"

"Well" started Jules.

"She said you were too much of an idiot, Pete" finished Jerry, who could not prevent himself from smiling as he said it, so Pete knew instantly that he was joking.

"No, she didn't" said Jules, also laughing slightly. "She said that it was not yet time Pete, and she didn't say anything more about it, she went straight on to tell us about the clue."

Pete believed what Jules was saying, because she was normally sincere when it was an important time, like now. "So, how do we solve this one?" Pete added.

"Well, we aren't solving anything tonight" said Jerry rather forcibly. "I am knackered and I am going to bed, so I suggest the two of you go home as well and we can tackle it tomorrow evening."

They both agreed and also decided that they would leave Jerry to do the tidying up, especially as they had both been busy tidying up their own apartments the last few days. Jerry showed them both out and then went back to his living room, collected all the paper notes that were still on the coffee table, threw them into his empty waste paper basket, and placed the plastic coated Verse Three text, that they had received last weekend, back into its place in the top drawer of his desk. Tomorrow they would look at the next clue and see what adventure that would lead to.

As he got into bed, he laid there wondering how he would tell his children when he was older that he had had a conversation with a raven called Mystic, and that it had given him a clue to a magical Quest. Little did he know; at this particular point in time having children was not in his destiny, not in any way, shape, or form.

Meeting of the Guardians

July was coming to a close, and in the field next to the White Horse pub, the White Horse himself was getting restless, waiting for Annie to come and give him his daily afternoon exercise. He looked forward to this as it was really the only time of the day that he could have a decent conversation, and it was not fun just roaming about in a field all day.

Of course, he did not stay in the field every day; for he had his work and his message to spread as well, which he would normally do through his spiritual form. However, the time of the replenishment was now approaching and he was growing weaker as each day passed, and he could sense it.

Guardian Five was now dead; he had seen it all happen, and the only reason that Gavin had died was because he had not been able to shield him from the Evil Lord. The only good thing to come out of this was that the clue that Gavin had protected all these years was still safe and the Evil Lord was nowhere near finding it. That was a relief, but he had known Gavin for six hundred years now, and to lose someone you have known for that long was a deep loss.

At that moment, Annie strolled into the field and walked up to him. She had a big wide smile on her face, beaming almost from ear to ear.

"He has found Mystic" she said, "I knew he had it in him."

"Yes" replied the White Horse, as he looked up into her face.

"Why so sad, my Lord?" she asked him, as her expression turned from happiness to concern. "Are you not pleased that he is making progress."

"Oh yes, of course" he replied, "don't get me wrong, I am delighted about that. However, there are other things going on, evil things, and it is these things that are worrying me; my influence is weakening and evil is spreading, we must act quickly."

"Yes, my Lord" she replied. "What do you require of me?"

"We must summon the other Guardians, for it is time for us to meet" he muttered, lifting his head and stretching his neck as if to reach up towards something.

"Do you not wish to ride today?" Annie asked.

"Of course I do" he answered, turning to Annie and smiling at her, "but first I must talk with Mystic."

He then closed his eyes, moved his head down towards the grass, and within his mind he called out, "Mystic, oh Mystic, hear me."

His mind stretched out across the boundaries of space and time and came to the jet-black raven, sitting as normal on the street sign outside the Dog and Bone pub.

"Yes, my Lord" came the reply straight into his mind. It was the voice of Mystic, the same sweet voice Jerry and Jules heard that previous evening.

"Well done Mystic" he said to her.

"Thank you my Lord" she replied, with her head bowing as she said it.

"We must all now meet" he added. "The time is approaching; we must make sure that we all know what to do. And I have some sad news for us all."

"Yes my Lord" she replied, "when?"

"Tonight" he said. "At seven, we meet in the old barn."

"I shall summon them" replied Mystic, "does one know already my Lord?"

"One and Five" replied the White Horse, "so you have a smaller task than normal, my wise Mystic."

"Yes, my Lord" she replied, again bowing her head, and with that she flew off her signpost and up into the afternoon sky.

The White Horse lifted his head towards Annie. "We will meet tonight, at seven" he said.

"Yes" she replied, "but now we ride into the distance" and with that she jumped onto his back and they rode off together, first jumping over the small hurdle as they went.

This was a great feeling for both of them. To feel the wind rush across their faces as they sped over the ground and jumped over hedges and fences was exhilarating, as if all their troubles were left lying far, far, behind them. Today was a long ride, for they went deep into the countryside, over fields, streams and roads, and even past the famous Belfry golf course, site of some really famous and memorable Ryder Cup battles.

Jerry meanwhile was at work, for even though the term had now officially ended, there was still work to do in the university. He had not forgotten his meeting yesterday with Mystic, how could he have done; it is not every day you have a conversation with a bird, at least one of the feathered variety.

Jerry's mind was not really on his work, which was also to be expected; he had not understood at all why Pete could not hear Mystic, and why Jules could. He knew however that Pete would not mind that so much, and after all Mystic had indicated that Pete would be able to hear her later; she had said, 'it was not yet time for Pete to hear her', which surely meant to Jerry that at some point in the future he, Pete, would be able to hear her. However, he, Jerry, had no idea when, or what had to occur, in order for that point in time to be reached.

Jerry was also struggling over the latest clue left behind by Mystic. This was much shorter than the previous clue, but even so he had still not fathomed it out yet. There was one thing however that he was sure of, and that was the next time Pete came up with a dead certain interpretation, then Pete was going to go with them, especially after he had wasted a whole day at the zoo. Although, thinking about it, Jerry did

90

have to admit that it was nice to spend some time alone with Jules, they had not done that for over ten years.

Twenty-eight feet measured today, will mature to the singular yard you need to go to.

This was the first line of the text that puzzled him. How can twenty-eight feet mature to a single yard? Everyone knew that there were three feet in one yard, (which was almost one metre) and twenty-eight feet was in fact 9 yards and twelve inches, or nine yards and one foot, but definitely not one yard. And, why was it so important to measure the twenty-eight feet today, which was of course yesterday, since it was now tomorrow, which of course is now really today. He was getting confused.

Jerry was also fascinated by the use of the word 'singular', for that had many connotations with time travel and the link towards the word 'today' and the maturing of the day into the next day, and so on. It was also however, linked to the technological singularity, which predicted the point at which artificial intelligence would outstrip that of man, 'although in his case that point had already been reached several years ago', was the retort he felt sure would have come from Pete's mouth had he stated that question out aloud.

Jerry got home from work around five o'clock and made himself something to eat. Both Jules and Pete were coming around later, so he would have to go down to the local supermarket to get some more vintage wine, or 'plonk' as Pete called it, before they arrived. He looked around the windows and could not see Mystic anywhere. He wondered if she was sitting on her normal perch outside the Dog and Bone pub.

Mystic in fact was not sitting on her perch, for she was off to each of the Guardians to inform them about the meeting that evening. The first on her round lived close by, and she was the Guardian of Verse One. Mystic caught up with her fairly-quickly, and passed on the message. Next, it was off to Guardian Four who lived in Birmingham and then the long flight south to London where the last remaining Guardian resided, protecting the last Verse.

When Annie and the White Horse returned from their ride in the countryside, it was already late afternoon, and the other Guardians would be arriving within a couple of hours. They had stopped at a pub they came across on their journey to get something to eat and drink, so they were not thirsty or hungry. Nevertheless, Annie made sure the trough was full of water and then went back indoors to her husband Jose, who was waiting for her.

"How was it my dear?" he asked; "you were away for a long time. I was starting to get worried."

"Oh, he is a bit restless" she replied, and then after giving Jose a long kiss on the lips she continued. "Do not worry, my dear; we will soon be alone together."

"Yes, my darling" he replied to her, with a big smile spreading across his face. "I look forward to that day" and with that he grabbed her around her middle, pulled her towards him, and kissed her again, although this time slightly longer and with an amount of passion that even Jerry's goalkeeper would have been proud.

At ten to seven in the evening, Annie left the pub and walked over to the old barn at the far end of the field. The White Horse was already there, standing alone on the loose hay on the ground.

"Hello again Annie" he said, "twice in one day. Today is a good day."

"Hello my Lord" she replied, bowing her head slightly.

"How is Jose?" he asked her.

"Oh, he is fine" she replied again. "He cannot wait. He is so excited. It must be all that Spanish blood in him."

"You must control him, Annie" replied the White Horse, "for there is too much at stake for us to allow him to spoil anything."

"Yes, my Lord" she replied. "He will be ok, I am sure of it."

As she finished she heard the fluttering of wings as two white doves flew into the Barn and landed beside the White Horse. The White Horse looked at them, nodded his head, and both of them transformed before his eyes into young middle aged women, wearing what could only be described as average businesslike clothes for women of their ages in today's modern times. They were of course however both wearing a black cloak over their clothes, and a hood, which covered their head and hung sufficiently over their faces as if to cover their identities from anyone who could be watching.

"Welcome Two and Four" he said to them, as they both bowed and took their places next to Annie, starting to form a circle with some empty spaces, as if waiting for others to arrive and fill them.

The next to arrive was Mystic, who landed on top of the White Horse's head, gave him a short affectionate peck, and then flew down to the ground and immediately transformed into a late middle aged woman, wearing a long dark cloak covering a tatty old dress and short ankle length boots. She also was wearing a hood, which was covering most of her face, and had with her a small black handbag, which she was holding onto as if it contained the most valuable possessions of her life. This person looked much more like what you would expect a magical female person to look like, although no one around the circle would have dared call her a Witch.

The last to arrive was a dark handsome majestic black Swift, who glided into the barn, landed in the middle of the circle, bowed his head and then transformed into a middle-aged man, around thirty-six, and immaculately dressed in a perfectly pressed black suit. He was clearly someone who would easily fit into the upper-class scene if he wanted. The man walked to one side, took his position in the circle, bowed again, and swished his cloak and hood to make sure that it was completely covering his body.

"Good" said the White Horse to them all; "We are now all here" and then paused slightly, for there was one empty space in the circle and he could see that the others had noticed that as well.

"Where is Five?" asked Guardian Four, as she looked around to the others.

Mystic immediately pulled out a tissue from her handbag.

"No" said Two, as she looked in horror at Mystic who was now wiping tears away from her eyes.

"I am afraid so" said the White Horse. "Gavin has been killed by the Evil Lord, who now grows in strength every day. We must all be extra careful, because my abilities to protect you all are starting to decline; the time of the replenishment is approaching."

"Yes, my Lord" they all replied, as if in unison.

"Is the clue safe?" asked Two.

"Yes" replied the White Horse, who then added, "for now" which caused the relief expressed by the others to be quickly curtailed.

"But what of the Chosen One?" asked Three, in his deep, almost sexy, voice.

"He is making good progress" replied Mystic. "He has already found Verse Three and he has found me. He is now working on solving the location of Verse One."

There were some general murmurs of content in the circle as they all nodded and agreed that this was good progress indeed.

"He still has a long way to go" added the White Horse, "and I sense that he is starting to doubt himself."

The crowd went cold again, as if an icy breeze had filled the old barn.

"Can we help him My Lord" asked Two, who was the youngest of the Guardians.

"No we cannot" snapped back Mystic. "You should all remember that."

"Oh" said Two, looking a little upset at the verbal scolding she had just received from Mystic.

"Sorry" stuttered Mystic, "I am a little upset. I should not have jumped at you D…."

"ENOUGH!" said the White Horse rather forcibly, and cut-off Mystic in the last part of her sentence. "We never mention our names, Mystic" he added staring at her in complete disbelief. "We never know when the Evil Lord is watching or listening to us. And with my strength weakening our anonymity is to be highly guarded."

"Sorry my Lord, Sorry Two" she said. "I am all a flutter at the moment" and proceeded again to wipe away even more tears from her eyes.

"Why have you called us here?" asked Three, quickly adding afterwards, "my Lord."

"It is important that you all understand" said the White Horse. "My powers are weakening and I cannot protect you all as I would like, especially those who are far away from me" and he particularly looked into the face of Three. "Five lived close, but he ventured astray, and was plucked from us by the Evil Lord. You must all be very careful now."

"Yes, my Lord" they all replied, again in unison.

"As Mystic said" he added, "you are not allowed to help the Chosen One; he must find the pathway himself. However, we can and must protect him from evil. The Evil Lord does not yet know who he is, but Gavin, in a weak moment, told him that there is a new one chosen, and that he is now in training. So it is only a matter of time before he finds out who he is."

There was silence amongst the Guardians. No one spoke; they all listened intently.

"One" said the White Horse. "You have spent time with the Chosen One several years ago. Tell us all about him."

Annie took a step forward, but was careful not to lower her hood. She told them all about Jerry and the two years they had spent together. She told them how, despite being a rough footballer on the exterior, he was a kind and gentle man, who did not like evil and was not happy to see the world fall into the hands of evil villains and tyrants. She described Jerry's appearance to them all, so that they could each recognise him if they ever met, and she spent some time also telling them about his two colleagues, Pete and Jules. She concluded by saying that she was sure that Jerry was worthy, and that he would be able to inherit the Prize, and that he just needed some time to solve the clues.

At the end of her talk, Two asked a question.

"Are we to let him know that we are Guardians?" she asked the White Horse, hoping that she would not get another scolding from Mystic. However, Mystic remained silent as the White Horse answered.

"It is best that he does not know, until he needs to know" was his considered response. "So I suggest that we don't tell him yet, unless his life is in danger. Mystic will prepare him, and let him know that Guardians exist, but not for the moment, whom they are. Remember" he continued, "the Evil Lord can not kill me, nor can he kill the Chosen One. But he can kill all of you, and without you we cannot protect the Prize."

"Yes, my Lord" they all replied, and with that the meeting was over.

Three then transformed back into the swift, bade everyone good night, and flew off back to his home. Similarly two and four did the same, although turning back into white doves of course. That just left Mystic, Annie, and the White Horse, who stayed a little longer and talked together, before Annie left them to walk back to the pub.

As Annie walked out of the barn, she heard Mystic crying again, and the White Horse trying to calm her. Something about, "still having time" was all she could make out, as she became too far away to hear anything else. Mystic however was clearly upset about something, and Annie did not fully understand what all that was about.

Two Down

It was eight o'clock in the evening and Jules, Pete, and Jerry were sitting around the kitchen table, glasses of wine in one hand and pens poised in the other; ready to make notes on the blank pages now lying before them. The last clue from Mystic was not what you could call long, but it was still a challenge. Jerry read it out again.

> *Twenty-eight feet measured today, will mature to the singular yard you need to go to. The first Verse is in there; it is a new angry text that hides in the injections our children dare to take as a challenge.*

They were all at a loss; even Pete did not have a solid theory. The first line did not make any sense, so they decided to start with the second line.

"*The first Verse is in there*" read Pete. "Well that is either referring to the line before or what comes after" he concluded, not really adding any value to the conversation.

"What does a '*new angry text*' mean?" asked Jules, "and *linked to Injections our children take as a challenge*" she added, looking even more confused as she said it.

"Is it referring to drugs do you think?" asked Jerry.

"Maybe" replied Pete, although he did not seem too sure.

"Well they definitely take drugs as a challenge nowadays" said Jules, "some of them are so high they don't know what they are doing half the time" she added, sounding as though she thoroughly disapproved of the practice with every part of her being.

"They are bullied into it" mumbled Jerry, "those evil Drug Lords or Barons, whatever they call themselves. We never had that temptation when we were at school, I mean a cigarette or a glass of beer were the worst we ever had."

"Yeah" added Pete, as though in the middle of a pleasant reminiscence, "the occasional joint as well though" he added, with a dreamlike smile across his face.

"Oh yeah" whispered Jerry, "that as well of course, but nothing pumped into our blood via injections."

"Never" seconded Pete.

"We're getting off the point a bit, aren't we?" asked Jules, trying to snap the two boys out of their dreamlike state.

"Oh yeah, absolutely" replied Jerry, suddenly snapping to, as if he was in the army and the General had just walked by. "Let's put the telly on, the news is on in a moment and I need a break" he suggested as he walked over to fetch the remote control. He then sat in his favourite armchair, the other two joining him, sitting on the sofa.

The news was a boring affair, as normal; more gloom and depression read out by a news reader who thought it, and he, were the most important things those poor old viewers would encounter that whole day. The police were no further with solving the homicide at the Natural History Museum and the museum had calculated the value of the damages and, apart from the priceless antiques which could never be replaced, they estimated several tens of millions of pounds of damage had been caused that night. There was also some problems in the Airports in London, Vandals in Rome, Drug Wars in Los Angeles, and now came that ridiculous story at the end of the bulletin which was meant to make us all cheer up and forget everything that we had just been told.

"Hey Jerry, it's those lion cubs we saw yesterday" said Jules, as she immediately stared at the television trying to see if she could see herself there.

"Lion cubs" said Pete, "you never told me anything about that."

"Oh it wasn't important" added Jerry, "just some lion cubs that had recently been born and four keepers trying to chase them to get them weighed. It was quite funny actually."

They listened further to the 'Lions being weighed at the zoo correspondent'; they seemed to have a correspondent for everything nowadays, and some senior ones as well.

"And the darling little cubs, all seven males" said the reporter, "are running all over the place. Those poor keepers, they just can't keep up" was the last punch line that was supposed to make everyone cheerful.

She handed back to the presenter who, looking like he was in his first time talent show and trying to audition as a comedian then said, "and it looks like 28 feet are faster than eight" and the entire country groaned in unison with those in the backstage of the studio. That was, everyone in the country except the three of our heroes sitting around the television; they were staring hard and fast at the television, each one of them thinking the exact same thing: "*The twenty-eight feet measured today.* They were measuring the lion cubs today; they were weighing them, and they had in total twenty-eight feet between them."

Jerry dashed over to the table, followed instantaneously by Jules and Pete.

"Twenty-eight feet" he muttered, "twenty-eight feet will mature to the singular yard."

"How does that fit in?" wondered Pete, aloud.

"Well it certainly gives us a different angle" said Jules, "let's play with it a bit."

They all sat down and thought. They had seen seven lion cubs and they were all males. What would the seven lion cubs mature in to? Well, they would mature into seven fully-grown Lions.

"But how does that match into the 'singular yard'?" asked Jules.

"I wonder" said Pete, as if a distant light was flickering on inside his brain. "Remember, we are looking for where the Verse One is, so it could be an address we are looking for. *Twenty-eight feet measured today, will mature to the singular yard you need to go to'*, could mean" and he started writing on his piece of paper.

"The twenty-eight feet come from seven lion cubs. They will grow into seven lions. If we then take the singular of 'lions', then that becomes 'lion' and then add the word 'Yard', then we get the address 'Seven, Lion Yard'."

> *28 Feet*
> *7 Lion Cubs*
> *7 Lions*
> *Singular = 7 Lion*
> *Then add Yard = 7 Lion Yard*

"And I know exactly what is at '7 Lion Yard', don't you Jules?"

"Absolutely" she said, with a smile on her face, "the Cambridge Central Library."

"So, it's the library that we have to go to" said Jerry, feeling really pleased with his two accomplices, "but what that's got to do with the next part of the text?" he then asked.

"That's tomorrow nights work" said Jules, as it was now almost eleven o'clock and she needed to go to work tomorrow.

The others reluctantly agreed, and Jerry showed them out of the apartment and then went to bed himself.

Jerry was feeling really excited all through the next day at work; he could not wait for the evening to come. He decided that he would nip down to the Library during his lunch break and see if he could find out anything of use for the upcoming evening session. He arrived there about ten minutes past twelve and had a quick look around.

'Good' he thought to himself, 'no sign of Jules or Pete' and he went on to spend several hours at the library, which was just a tad longer than his normal lunch break would allow.

He had not found anything about angry texts concerned about drugs abuse for children. He had even gone to the children's section, called the junior section in the actual library, but found nothing. He was about to give up when he decided that he would ask for some help and he strolled over to the main desk, where an official, smartly dressed middle aged woman was sitting, with a gold embossed name plate on her desk reading...

LIBRARIAN – Miss Tugrow

"Eh, excuse me, Miss Tugrow" said Jerry. "I am looking for information about drug abuse by children, and any angry letters than have been written on the subject. I wonder if you can help me as I am not having much success."

The librarian looked at him in a strange way. 'Drug abuse by children was not an every day subject that people asked for in the library' she thought to herself, 'and angry letters indeed. I wonder what he really wants'.

Jerry was also doing some thinking. 'Miss Tugrow was actually quite a good looking woman' he thought to himself. 'She must be just under thirty, and is very well proportioned' and after all he was currently in the middle of a dry-period, maybe not one of the longest periods he had endured, but still he wondered if the day might after all turn out to be good.

From the way Miss Tugrow was eyeing Jerry, it seemed to any casual onlooker that she was having very similar thoughts, but about Jerry of course.

"Derek" she called to a young spotty faced lad who, upon hearing his name being called, came out from the back office. He could not have been more than sixteen, and he immediately walked over to her side.

"This gentleman" she said, moving her eyes up and then down Jerry's body, momentarily stopping at specific points of interest. "Hem, hem" she coughed, "this man is looking for some angry letters about drug abuse by children. Do you know if we have any Derek?"

Derek lifted his finger to his mouth and started pondering. "I don't think so" he replied, "I mean I have never seen any such thing since I have been here."

"No, me neither" she added, "but you never know, I might have missed something."

The young lad laughed slightly. "You miss something Di" he said, watching her eyes scanning again over Jerry's body, "I don't think so" and he walked back into the office, smiling as he went.

"I am sorry Mr?" she paused, waiting for Jerry to give her his name.

"Dumbarton" replied Jerry, who was also now making sure that his radar was on and fully scanning the landscape standing in front of him.

"Oh, Mr Dumbarton" she replied. "Well you heard Derek; we don't seem to have any such thing. Sorry about that" and then she turned and did a little skip, quickly tried to recover, and then walked as normally as she could back into the office.

At this point Jerry decided that his time here had run out, at least for the moment. In addition, he now had to dash back to his office, which he did, while on the way trying to think how he was going to explain to his boss where he had been the extra half hour.

Later that evening, Jerry was at home in his kitchen, making himself a cup of tea, when he heard a tapping on the window. It was Mystic, so he opened it and let her in.

"How are you doing?" she asked.

"Oh fairly ok" replied Jerry, trying to keep his spirits up. "We have worked out that it is in the library, but we don't know what exactly it is that we are supposed to be looking for. I went in today but I could not find anything. Can you help me a bit?" he asked her, with almost a pleading look in his face.

Mystic looked at him. "I cannot help you I am afraid; only the worthy can inherit the Prize."

"Oh, ok" replied Jerry. "Thought I'd ask, you know."

"I have come to tell you some more general information" she continued, "information about the Quest, and what is going on."

"Ah great" replied Jerry, and he sat down at the kitchen table and looked eagerly at Mystic.

"There are five Guardians that exist to protect the clues to the Prize" started Mystic. "And these Guardians will also try and protect you if you fall too close to the Evil Lord."

"The Evil Lord" interrupted Jerry, "who is that?"

"I am afraid that I cannot tell you much about who he is" said Mystic, "but suffice to say that he is the force that puts evil into peoples hearts. He is the opposite in every way to the 'Good Lord', the lord I, and all good people, serve."

"Oh."

"The Evil Lord knows now that you exist, but he does not know who you are" she continued. "If he finds out that it is you, then we, that is to say the Guardians and I, will protect you, so you do not need to worry."

"Oh, right" said Jerry.

"The Evil Lord" continued Mystic, "cannot kill you, but he can use you to get to the Prize, and if that happens, then it will be a disaster" she concluded.

"Oh" said Jerry again, who seemed to be demonstrating his wide use of the English language in this conversation with Mystic.

"We need to move quickly" she continued, wondering if Jerry was actually understanding anything that she was saying to him.

"Yes" he said, sitting up quickly as if being reprimanded by a teacher.

"I am here to help you find Verse Five" she said.

"But I haven't found Verse One yet" he stated. "Does that matter?"

"Of course not" answered Mystic, "otherwise I would not be giving you these instructions would I?"

Jerry did not say anything; he just picked up his pen and held it ready just above a blank piece of paper.

Mystic began. "Verse Five is what you'll find in one of the best establishments. Stored, in what is a fertile place, in a street, a lane, and a park. You'll need a key to get in, and that you'll find begins with ninety-two, which you will get from the second Guardian."

"Is that it?" asked Jerry. Mystic however had not listened. She had seen that he had written it down correctly and then she made ready to depart by stretching out her wings and preparing to fly off.

"Remember the Guardians, Jerry" she said, as she lifted herself off the table. "They are here to protect the clues and to protect you" she called out, as she flew towards, and out of, the still opened window.

'I must remember to close the window next time she comes in' thought Jerry to himself, as the doorbell rang.

It was Jules. Jerry let her in and went back into the kitchen to make some more tea.

Pete arrived soon after and then Jerry updated them both on what Mystic had told him, except for some reason, known only to Jerry, he did not tell them the part about the Evil Lord.

"So now we have two clues to solve" said Pete, "which one shall we work on first?"

Jerry then told them about his trip to the library and about how he could not find anything about angry letters and drug abuse with children.

"No that's obviously some sort of code" said Jules, "I mean, look how the first part of the text was changed. I guess we have to do something similar with the second part as well."

"So that means" began Pete, as they both turned to him, "that we're going to work on the clue to Verse One first then."

They all had a small chuckle and then got down to it again.

"Where did you go while you were there?" asked Pete.

"Oh, I looked all over" said Jerry, "but most of the time I was in the children's section" he added, "which, by the way, is called the Junior Section."

"Of course" said Jules, "'Junior Section', 'injections our', it's an anagram again, don't you see?" and they both looked, and saw instantly, albeit rather too late to actually contribute.

Pete wrote down the second line of the text.

The first Verse is in there; it is a new angry text that hides in the injections our children dare to take as a challenge.

"Let's assume" he started, "that the first part, is just referring to the fact that the first Verse is in the library we uncovered in the first line of the text. That means that the main text we need to worry about starts after the semi-colon."

They all agreed.

"If we replace 'Injections our' with 'Junior Section'" he said.

"And 'dare' with 'read'" added Jules.

"Then we get" said Pete, and he wrote down the words.

it is a new angry text that hides in the Junior Section children read to take as a challenge.

"It still doesn't make sense" said Jerry. "Does anyone have any idea what could be an anagram of 'new angry text'?" he asked.

"No idea" said Jules, but Pete was smiling, which could mean only one thing and that was that he had an idea.

"It's not an anagram" he said. "It's a play on words."

"What do you mean?" replied Jerry.

"Angry Text" said Pete, "is the same as, Cross Word. It's a crossword" and he updated the text.

*it is a new Crossword that hides in the Junior Section
children read to take as a challenge..*

"It's nothing to do with Drug Abuse or Angry Letters"
concluded Pete, "no wonder that Librarian was looking at
you in a strange way."

"That wasn't the reason" said Jerry, looking at Pete with
an 'I'll tell you later – boys stuff' type look on his face.

Jules also instantly recognised that look in Jerry's face and
laughed a bit to herself. "Let's all go down there tomorrow
lunchtime" she suggested, and they all agreed.

"Now what about this Verse Five clue from Mystic?" said
Pete. "What can that mean?"

Jerry read it out again.

*"Verse Five is what you'll find in one of the best
establishments. Stored, in what is a fertile place, in a street, a
lane, and a park. You'll need a key to get in, and that you'll
find begins with ninety-two, which you will get from the second
Guardian."*

"Didn't she say anything else?" asked Jules.

"Well not about this, she flew straight away once I had
written it down. Didn't say another word" Jerry said, looking
slightly disappointed.

"Look" said Pete, "tomorrow's Saturday. Lets all go
down to the library just before lunch and see what we can
find. Let's meet there at 11 am, then, when we come back, we
can work on this new clue."

They all agreed, and then Jules suggested that they each
get an early night for a change, especially early for a Friday.
Pete instantly agreed, but Jerry pondered for a few moments
before finally agreeing; they had been out boozing earlier in

the week, so he felt that he would still be able to show his face in public, even if his football team found out. He then tidied up his papers, put the clue for Verse Five from Mystic into the top draw of his desk, together with the plastic coated text that was Verse Three, and said goodbye to his two friends before going to bed.

Saturday arrived in another blaze of sunshine. They all met at 11 am outside the Cambridge Central Library and went straight to the Junior Section. Jerry noticed that Miss Tugrow was again on duty and their eyes met for a brief fraction of a second, but it was enough to tell an experienced womaniser like Jerry that she was definitely still interested.

"Crosswords, crosswords" said Pete to himself, as he looked through the library catalogue on the computer. There were many, but he refined the search to focus on crosswords for children and that reduced it down to five. He showed the list to Jerry and Jules

Arthur S Johnson	*Crosswords for Children, Vol. 3*
Arthur S Johnson	*Crosswords for Children, Vol. 4*
Harry Williams	*Crossword Annual, Children's Edition*
John Coward	*Children's First Crosswords, new edition*
Jonathan Marks	*Crossword made easy, even for Children*

"Which one?" asked Jules.

Jerry got out the text they had received from Mystic, looked it over before stating "the fourth one."

"Why?" said Jules.

"Because in the text" said Jerry, "it says 'new' and this is a new edition. In addition, it says that 'it hides in the junior section' and 'J Coward' has written the book, and cowards are people who hide. So I guess it's the fourth one."

They both agreed with him and then went to try and find it, which turned out to be not so easy. Jules watched on, thinking that Jerry was just trying to make it difficult so that he could ask the librarian to help them, which he of course did, with Pete playing along like a good supporting actor.

"Here it is Mr Dumbarton" said the librarian, as she stood on a stool reaching up, while Jerry was holding on to her around the waist, to prevent her from falling of course. Jules could not stop herself from laughing, and even Pete looked a bit embarrassed.

'Children's First Crosswords' it said on the front cover, and underneath it had printed in bold black letters '83 crossword puzzles for children'. It was just a normal crossword puzzle book, with a bright glossy yellow (almost plastic) cover with text all over the front, an empty crossword on the rear cover, and in each of the puzzles inside, one of the answers was filled-in.

"I guess that's just to make it easier for the children" suggested Jerry, as he handed it to Jules and Pete so they could each look.

"We'll take it" he said. "I think I still have my library card from my student days" and he delved into his wallet, picking out a plastic card with an old picture of him on it, which he handed to the librarian.

"Yes, you're still in our computer" she said to Jerry, "Mr Dumbarton, Jerry" and she flushed immediately that she said his first name.

Jules and Pete drifted away, for they did not want to cramp Jerry's style – if you could call it style. But anyway, it appeared to be working in this case; for when he returned he winked at Pete and whispered that he had got her phone number, and, while making sure that Jules was not watching, showed Pete a slip of paper with the initials 'DT' written on it, and next to it a phone number '555-924-2417'.

"She wants me to call her next weekend" he whispered, also making sure that Jules could not hear. He folded it up, put it into his wallet for safe- keeping, and they all three strolled out of the library, back into the brilliant sunlight and back to Jerry's apartment.

Cross Words

"Let's split up" said Jules, as she sat in Jerry's favourite armchair.

"I didn't know we were going together" replied Jerry, who was obviously still in his romantic mood after his short encounter with the librarian.

"Ha, ha" retorted Jules, "you know exactly what I meant."

"Good idea" said Pete, trying to raise the level of the conversation. "Jerry, you can play with the crosswords for *Children*" he said, making sure that he stressed the word 'children' just enough to completely fail on his goal to raise the level of the conversation.

"Hooray" cheered Jules, as she picked up the glossy covered puzzle book and threw it at Jerry, hitting him lightly on the chest.

"Ok, ok" replied Jerry as he opened up the puzzle book.

The first thing he saw was that he was the only person so far to have actually checked out the book, since the lending list, where peoples library id's are entered each time they lent the book, only had his id in it. He also noticed that he only had two weeks, after which time he must return the book. Jerry quickly decided that he would fill in the answers with a very soft pencil so that he could rub them all out before taking the book back; otherwise they might charge him for defacing library property. Here therefore got up and went over to his Den to get a soft pencil, before returning and sitting back down in his other armchair (Jules was still sitting in his favourite one) to start looking through the book.

Jules and Pete started working on the clue from Mystic for Verse Five.

"This is easy" called out Jerry some fifteen minutes later. "I've nearly finished the first one." He was really pleased with himself, since this was the first time in his life that he was actually going to complete, without cheating, a full crossword. He did have a slight moment with number seven down, but finally managed that after he had discovered that he had spelt 'tail' as 'tale' on ten across. Jules and Pete felt that it was best not to wind him up by pointing out that it was for eight year olds, and at his age of 32, he should not have much difficulty.

Jules and Pete were not making such good progress with deciphering their clue; the text was not making any sense.

"What did it mean *'best establishment'?*" asked Jules, thoroughly confused.

"*A fertile place, in a street, a lane, and a park*" said Pete, also confused.

"FINISHED!" shouted Jerry, standing up in triumph.

"What, all of them?" replied Jules, looking thoroughly impressed towards Jerry.

"No, the first one" he replied, not quite sure if she was joking or not.

"Oh" said Jules, turning her head away so she could smile without upsetting him.

"Has it told you anything?" asked Pete.

Jerry looked at the crossword. He looked over at Pete. He looked again at the crossword, turned it 90 degrees to the left, then 180 degrees to the right, then even upside down, and turned back to Pete and answered "no."

Pete could not help but laugh. "Give it here" he said, "let me have a look" and Jerry proceeded to throw the book over to Pete, slightly harder than he would have done if it had been to Jules.

Pete looked at the completed crossword, but very soon he also concluded that it did not tell him anything either, and so Jerry felt a bit more relaxed.

"Fancy some tea or wine?" he asked them both, and they both fancied tea, so Jerry went into the kitchen to put the kettle on and make a big pot of Earl Grey tea, his favourite.

Five minutes later, he came back into the living room and put three steaming hot mugs of tea onto the coffee table, and then sat down with Pete and Jules to hear what they had learnt so far about the clue to Verse Five. That process did not actually take very long; in fact, by the time Pete had concluded that they had learnt absolutely nothing, they had not even drank any of their tea, primarily because it was so hot. Jerry smiled as he leant back in his 'other' armchair with his tea on the coffee table still giving off steam. Luckily, he had already of course made some progress by solving the first crossword, and now it was time to continue. He picked up the crossword book, ready to check again if he could see any patterns in his answers. He opened the book, turned to the crossword he had just completed, and let out a big gasp.

"What the hell…" he started to say.

"What is it?" asked Jules, who had been watching him out of the corner of her eye.

"They're gone" he said, as if he was about to lose his voice and burst out crying. "All of them, they are gone."

"What's gone?" asked Pete, as he got up and walked over to Jerry.

"All my answers" replied Jerry. "All my answers" he repeated again, not quite wanting to believe that all his hard work had been in vain.

Pete took the book and looked at it. Jerry was right; there were no answers.

"Hold on" said Jules, "did you actually see him write any answers in there Pete?"

"No" replied Pete, "but he said he did, and he did look really excited when he'd finished."

"Will you two stop talking about me as if I am not here" said Jerry starting to get angry. "Of course I wrote the answers in. I did it in this soft pencil so I could rub them out later."

"Well you won't need to do that now, will you" laughed Pete.

"What does it mean?" mumbled Jules, to herself.

"It means I wasted my time" said Jerry.

"Exactly" said Pete. "That was obviously not the right crossword. I mean there are 83 crosswords in there, and only one will make sense to solve the Verse. You will just have to do them all, or at least continue until you find the one that doesn't disappear."

"All of them?" said Jerry, clearly in a state of advance shock.

"Yup" said Jules, trying to prevent herself from laughing, but her insides were bursting with laughter just watching the expression on his face.

Jerry sat down. He needed to. He flipped all through the book. "All 83 of them" he mumbled to himself, and immediately tried to drown his sorrows in his, now warm, cup of Earl Grey. "But this will take forever" he continued to grumble, as he started on crossword two.

Jules and Pete went back to their clue, trying to ignore Jerry's mutterings.

"I KNOW!" Jerry suddenly shouted out a minute or so later. "I'll do one answer in each crossword and see which answer doesn't disappear" he declared, throwing his fist up in the air and making a manly "YES" shout as he did.

"Good thinking Jerry" said Jules, as she then went on to suggest that she and Pete each make a copy of the Verse Five clue, so that they could take it home with them, and then meet back together tomorrow afternoon to see how they got on.

They all agreed, and re-wrote the text from Mystic onto their own pieces of paper, and then Pete and Jules left.

Jerry was now all alone in his apartment. He had very quickly found an answer in each of the first twenty puzzles, meaning he now had only sixty-two crosswords to go. So far, however, nothing had disappeared, so he was feeling a little bit nervous.

Finally, after a couple of hours passed, he had answered one clue in each of the crossword puzzles, except the first one of course, and he looked through them all. Nothing had disappeared. Jerry sat on his armchair, thinking to himself; the last time his answers disappeared was when he went to make a cup of tea, so he decided he would try that again. He therefore left the puzzle book on the table, and went into the kitchen to make yet another cup of tea.

A few minutes later he returned, put the teacup on the table, and picked up the puzzle book. Not a single answer had disappeared. Jerry was angry; he threw the book down on the table, left his tea and went to bed thoroughly annoyed with life, the universe, and that bloody puzzle book.

Jerry awoke early on Sunday morning, well early for a Sunday anyway; it was around ten o'clock, and he immediately jumped out of bed and ran to the coffee table in the living room. He opened the book and looked straight at crossword number 2, and his answer had disappeared. He was thrilled, he looked further into the book: three gone, four gone, five gone, six gone, seven gone, in fact he went all the way through the book until he got to the very last crossword and his answer to that one was…

"Gone" he shouted out to himself, "the whole bloody book is blank." He was furious with it. He had had it. This whole Quest was driving him mad. How many Verses were there? Why was he collecting all these numbers? He had found Verse Three, which was in a field of a White Horse next to a pub called the White Horse. This gave him the number three in a position three and sent him to meet a bird called Mystic which he thought was in London Zoo, but which was really outside a pub, just down the street, and whom could talk and tell the future.

She then told him about Verse One, which he had absolutely no idea how to find in a crossword book, and Verse Five. He was going crazy and he did not even know why. Thoroughly frustrated he went and had a shower so that he would be more relaxed when Jules came over later.

Jules turned up about 1 p.m. just after Pete had called saying that he could not come round; had to go and see his parents (birthday duty) and would not be back until Monday afternoon. Jules however found Jerry in a slightly better mood than the evening before, and much better than earlier in the morning, although she of course had no knowledge of that. Jerry had let out some of his frustrations in the hot steamy shower and now felt a little better with himself. He explained to Jules about the answers to the puzzle, but she was not annoyed or frustrated; she was more puzzled and pondering why.

"Maybe you are not supposed to write in it at all" she said, thinking aloud.

"But why wouldn't you write in a crossword puzzle book?" asked Jerry, not following her train of thought at all.

"Because it just wants you to read it" she suggested, still in her thinking mode.

"Just read it" he repeated, his frustration starting to boil over again. "But I've read all the clues, they don't make any sense."

Jules started reading through the book. There was nothing strange in the titles of the crosswords; they were just numerically numbered: one, two, three and so on. Each clue had one answer in it and it was not the same number, or the same word size. Then she started reading the single answers that were on each of the crossword puzzles. "What" she said, reading puzzle one, then, "is" from puzzle two, followed by, "not, here, is" from puzzles three, four and five.

"Jerry" she said, "it's the clues, look" and she showed him the answers, and that reading them sequentially made some sense. They both sat down together and as she read out in turn each of the answers, Jerry wrote them down onto a piece of paper. When they were finished, they sat back and looked at what he had written.

*What is not here is plain to see, take two away and add
i.e. That leaves you with the magic code, one step further along*

the road. But where to place it we hear you ask, and so you get another task. In the crossword you will find, one clue to keep in your mind. The length of which is equal to, the position of the crossword clue. Now if you have both values found, it must be time to move aground.

They were both feeling elated. They had cracked it, and without Pete. However, what did it mean?

"What is not here?" asked Jules, as she sat pondering the problem in front of her. "That must be the answers since they are not here" she quickly added, after experiencing one of her eureka moments.

"But, none of the crosswords allow you to write anything in them" added Jerry. "I've tried. All eighty-two of them; remember. Of course the answers are not there."

"How many did you say?" she asked, as she was looking at the front cover of the book.

"Eighty-two" he repeated.

"So why does it say eighty-three crossword puzzles?"

"Give it here" said Jerry, as he reached out his hand and grabbed the book back from Jules.

They both then started together at the beginning of the book and counted one-by-one the crosswords. When they got to the last one, they had reached eighty-two.

"One is missing" said Jules.

"Our one" added Jerry in complete frustration. "Oh this is driving me mad" he shouted, and he threw the book across the room.

They both watched as the book flew towards the cupboard, doing a double back somersault as it went, and then landed on the floor, on its front. As it landed, both Jerry and Jules immediately looked straight back at each other; there it was, lying in front of them, the empty crossword puzzle, the one on the back cover, the eighty-third crossword, complete with clues, and with no answers filled in.

116

The crossword on the back cover of the book

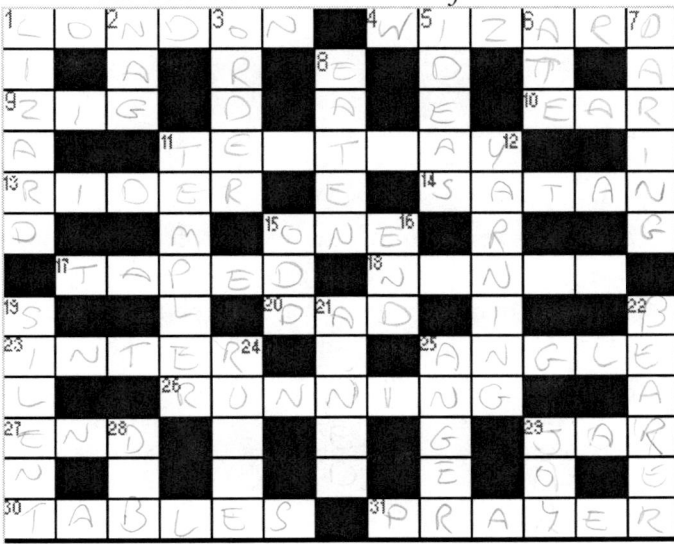

CLUES

Jerry sprang up and went over to the cupboard, picked up the book, and placed it again on its front, but this time on the coffee table in front of them.

They both bent down to study the puzzle, and began filling it in.

"One across, London" said Jules.

"Yes I know; that was easy" said Jerry. "Two across: Merlin, 6 letters?"

"Wizard" answered Jules, and Jerry wrote down 'wizard'.

They had a little bit of trouble with fourteen across, until Jules recognised that the answer was a bit cryptic. "Satan" she said, Lucifes planet. Lucifer without the 'r', Saturn without the 'r' gives Satan. Quite sneaky" she added.

The storyline was the 'angle', also a bit tricky, and the stretching sound was something Jerry had been doing a lot lately, 'yawning'.

Overall, they finished it together in about twenty minutes, which was not bad.

"This one was not for children" concluded Jerry. "It was much harder than the ones I did yesterday" he added, wiping his brow. "So what next?" he then asked, as they both sat, staring at the now completed crossword on the back cover.

"Let's first wait and see if anything disappears" suggested Jules, who promised to sit and watch the puzzle and to scream out to Jerry if anything started disappearing, while he went and made them some tea. The fact that he returned several minutes later in a peaceful environment meant that nothing had indeed disappeared when he gave a mug of hot milky tea to Jules.

Jules read the clue again.

What is not here is plain to see, take two away and add i.e. That leaves you with the magic code, one step further along the road. But where to place it we hear you ask, and so you get another task. In the crossword you will find, one clue to keep in your mind. The length of which is equal to, the position of the crossword clue. Now if you have both values found, it must be time to move aground.

"The middle bit" said Jerry eagerly. "That's easy; look" and he pointed to the clue for five down, 'Things you thought of'."

"Yes" said Jules, "and the answer was 'Ideas' and ideas are what you keep in your mind. In addition, the length of it is five letters, and that is equal to the position of the crossword clue. But we know that already, it's five down" she repeated, looking a bit confused.

"No" said Jerry, "not the clue in the crossword, but the whole crossword is the clue. The position of the number from the crossword is position five."

"Oh well done!" said Jules, "yes, of course."

"But what is the number?" said Jerry, thinking hard.

"*What is not there is plain to see*" repeated Jules. "Everything is there" she said, "all the words are filled in."

"The letter X is not there" said Jerry.

"Oh yeah" she replied, in a sort of dreamy voice. "Are there any other letters not there?"

They ran through the crossword, and it turned out there were five letters not anywhere in the solved puzzle.

"Five" said Jerry, the number is, five.

"Hold on, wait a moment" said Jules, "it can't be that simple. The letters 'F', 'K', 'Q', 'V' and 'X' are not there."

"*Take two away and add i.e.*" repeated Jerry, "i.e. what?"

"*That leaves you with the magic code*" added Jules. "Jerry, your right, its five; look" and she immediately wrote down the two letters 'F' and 'V'. "Take two away" she added, "away from the five that were not in the code" and then she proceeded to add the letters 'I' and 'E' and had made the word 'FIVE'.

"Brilliant" said Jerry, and he kissed her hard and firm on the lips. "The number is five and it is in position five" and he proceeded to write that down with his other number that he had from Verse Three.

Now he had two numbers and two positions.

Verse	Position	Number
3	THREE	THREE
1	FIVE	FIVE

They were so happy that they tightly hugged each other while Jerry gave Jules a tender kiss on her lips. As their warm, dry bodies embraced, the tender kiss led into a much longer and less tender but more passionate kiss, a short snog, a rather longer grope, all of which eventually led to what the Weather Man would have summarised as "an end to the dry period that we have recently been experiencing."

"Damn that shower" muttered Jerry to himself, as he ripped of his clothes and chased Jules into the bedroom.

A Mystic Update

Jerry awoke the next morning with a warm feeling all over his body. He moved slightly and then realised that it was Jules, who was still asleep, cuddling him. 'It was great last night' he thought to himself; he had not had sex that good for quite some time. Even when he was with Jules some ten years ago, it had not been that good. Maybe it just felt good due to the long dry period that he had recently endured, but he did not think so. Jules had also enjoyed it, he was sure of that due to the noises that they had been making together. The downstairs occupants knocking on their ceiling at 1:30 in the morning was sufficient evidence of that.

Jerry watched her as she silently slept; she looked beautiful. Had he just forgotten how good it was with her? Or, on the other hand, had she, and maybe he, just both matured over the years, like a fine wine?

It was Monday morning and Jerry was now officially on vacation for two whole, wonderful weeks, so he had no need to get up and go to work. He did not know if Jules was free, he suspected not, so he could not let her sleep for too long, just in case. It was now eight o'clock, and as he gently slid out of bed, his movement woke her. Jules rolled away from him, rubbed her eyes, and then turned back to face him.

"Hi" she said, in what Jerry remembered was her early morning voice. "What time is it?"

"I was just going to make us some breakfast" he said, thinking that up, right on the spot.

"How late is it?" she asked, stretching and then turning to look at the small clock on his bedside table. "Eight o'clock" she mumbled to herself, answering her own question as she snuggled back down into the middle of the bed, pulling the still warm duvet cover back over her.

"Don't you have to go to work?" asked Jerry.

"Oh SHIT!" she suddenly screamed, and immediately sat up, jumped out of bed, grabbed her clothes, and dashed out of the bedroom, past the opened kitchen door and into the bathroom, not noticing that Mystic was sitting on the kitchen window ledge looking in.

Jerry put on his shorts and then walked into the kitchen, where he instantly saw Mystic. He paused for a moment as he turned around and looked back along the hallway between his bedroom and the bathroom, instantly twigging that Mystic would only have missed Jules if she was blind, and he knew without a shadow of a doubt, that she was not. He turned back and walked over to the window, opened it, and she flew in.

"Sorry about that" he said as he began to fill the kettle, "I am not used to having visitors so early in the morning, and coming in through the kitchen window."

"Never mind" replied Mystic, "I am glad to see that you two are getting along so well; you will be seeing a lot of each other in the coming years" she added, in her all-knowing voice.

"Do you need to speak with Jules as well?" he asked. "Or is it enough, with just me?"

"You'll do" she replied, in a rather sharp, but dreamy fashion. However, as it turned out it did not matter anyway, because the moment she finished, Jules emerged from the bathroom fully clothed, rather luckily, and ready for a cup of tea before she had to dash to work.

"Ah, great, tea" she muttered as she walked into the Kitchen. She then looked down at the table and noticed Mystic. "Oh hello Mystic" she then added, as she sat down to join her.

The kettle was now boiling, so Jerry made two mugs of tea and brought them over to the table. "Would you like anything Mystic?" he asked as an after thought; he was still not quite used to having a raven as a houseguest.

"No thank you, Jerry" she replied in her most civilised of voices, "but it was nice of you to ask."

"What did you want to tell us?" he replied.

Mystic started talking as Jerry and Jules just sat riveted to their spots, eagerly listening to what she had to say.

"In men's long and distant past" she began, "there have been many wars. Men have fought each other countless numbers of times, and due to many different reasons. Most of the wars were not however fought for religious beliefs, even if that is what most believed at the time, but they were fought due to the pursuit of power, driven mainly by men dominated by evil. There was much evil in men's hearts, and so to bring balance, to bring love and happiness into their evil minds, a Good Lord was created, and to help him there were his Guardians."

"The Guardians, born of man, hide themselves well, and guard the eternal Prize, the object that gives the Good Lord his powers, for if that ever fell into the hands of the dark side, man would be lost to eternal misery. The Prize is hidden well, and each of the five Guardians guard a specific part of a puzzle, which when put together and correctly solved will show the pathway to the Prize."

"Every thousand years the Good Lord has to be replenished, and a new Good Lord selected. The Chosen One, if he is worthy, will inherit the Prize, and take the place of the Good Lord at the time of the replenishment, but only if he has found the Prize."

"You Jerry" she said, turning to him and looking at him straight in the eyes. "You are the Chosen One."

Jerry and Jules just looked at each other. They were both speechless.

Mystic continued. "There are five clues that you need to correctly solve if you are to succeed. Each clue will give you a number and a position. You will need these numbers, in their correct order, to be able to find the pathway to the Prize. Solve them wrong and the pathway will not make any sense."

"Five numbers, five positions" repeated Jerry.

"Solve them wrong, and the pathway will not make any sense" repeated Mystic.

There was a pause for some moments.

"Can I ask you some questions?" Jerry then asked; trying to make sure that he at least got this question in before she flew off again.

"Certainly" replied Mystic, who then added, "but remember, I am not able to help you with your Quest, I can only protect you."

"Are you a Guardian, Mystic?" he asked.

Mystic was already expecting this question, although it still took her some time to prepare herself to answer it, as if actually answering it was painful for her.

"I am not a Guardian" she replied, "I am a mere servant, but an important one nonetheless" she quickly added. "My function is to act as the oracle for the Good Lord; to advise him and to help him communicate with his Guardians. I am much older than the Guardians" she concluded "and I shall still be here when they are long gone."

"May I ask something?" said Jules, breaking her silence for the first time since Mystic had begun speaking.

"Certainly, my Dear" replied Mystic.

Jules felt a little bit patronised, but ignored it nevertheless. "What is?"

"Ah" said Mystic, interrupting her. "You want to know what your role is in all of this" she concluded, smiling, as much as ravens can smile. "This, my child, depends upon where your heart truly lies" she continued to say as she stared deep into Jules' eyes. "I see for you two futures, and it is not yet decided which future you shall serve. But beware, for both futures will end in sorrow, the only difference will be for how long you are happy" and she sort of sniffed a little herself, as if trying to hold back a tear.

Jules suddenly understood. She was not being patronised at all; instead, someone who was full with the wisdom of the world was acting as if they were her great grandmother and trying to pass that wisdom on.

"Me" she murmured.

"Yes, my dear" replied Mystic, as if she understood what Jules had suddenly understood. "It is unfortunately the same the world over, and it is also unfortunately your destiny, should you be brave enough to take it."

Jerry was puzzled; he did not know what they were really talking about, but he had not interrupted for two reasons: One, it looked very serious, and two, he couldn't really think of anything further to ask Mystic anyway, so the extra time came in quite handy.

Mystic then turned to Jerry. "No more questions then at the moment Jerry?" she said to him, and prepared to fly off the table.

"No wait" said Jerry quickly, remembering that he had still not shut the window.

"That does not matter" said Mystic, for I can open it again if I need to."

"What?" said Jerry, obviously confused for a few moments before he suddenly realised what she was talking about. "Oh, ok," he replied, "but that was not what I was going to ask."

"I know" answered Mystic. "You want to know how you can get in touch with me if you need to" she added, and of course, she was right. "All you need to do is close your eyes and extend your mind to find me. Call out my name from deep within your mind and I will answer you. If we cannot communicate through your mind, then I will come to you."

With that, Mystic called out, "see you all later" and then flew off and out of the still opened window.

Jerry and Jules just sat in silence for several moments. They were numbed and really had no idea what to do next. Finally, Jules started to speak.

"What did you make of all that?" she asked, and in an awestruck tone of voice.

"I don't know really" replied Jerry, which was the honest truth. Anyone suddenly hit with that kind of a bombshell, could not really know what to do next.

"You are the Chosen One" she said, still not quite believing it. "Destined to become the next Good Lord and live for a thousand years."

"With five Guardians" added Jerry, in a terrified voice, "but only if I am worthy, and if I find and inherit the Prize."

"We will have to work harder at the clues" concluded Jules. "I am late for work anyway, so I will call in and take a day off, and we can try and get further with Verse Five."

"Fine, thanks" mumbled Jerry still, kind of dumbfounded.

"Oh my God, Jerry" shrieked Jules, suddenly in a state of panic.

"What, what!" he replied, wondering what the hell had happened.

"I've just had sex with the Good Lord" she said.

"Was I worthy?" he asked as a large smile broke out across his face.

"Very worthy" she softly replied, her panic attack suddenly cured and a similar wide smile to Jerry's now developing across her face.

They sat there looking at each other for several moments longer, got up, held each other's hands, and walked slowly back into the bedroom.

After lunch, Pete phoned to say that he was now home, and asked Jerry how far they had progressed on Sunday. As Jerry had so much to tell him, he suggested that he came over straight away. Jules went back home directly after Pete's phone call in order to shower and get some fresh clothes. She also did not want to be there when Jerry told Pete about their night together. She knew how boys behaved about that sort of thing, and it only infuriated her, so best let them do it while she was not around.

The short period between Jules leaving and Pete arriving gave Jerry just enough time to clear up the living room. He had been so busy recently that he had not had any time to do his normal chores. He therefore quickly collected all the scrap pieces of paper that they had been using and threw them into his waste paper basket, half filling it, and then put the yellow glossy covered crossword book on a shelf in his cupboard next to a few other books that he had collected over the years.

Pete set out from his apartment straight after he had called Jerry; so when he arrived Jerry immediately updated him on all of the events of the last twenty-four hours.

"You and Jules" he said, clearly demonstrating to Jerry that he also had his life priorities correct. "Was it as good as before?"

"Much better" replied Jerry, "I guess we are both a bit more practiced nowadays."

"And you the Chosen One" said Pete. "Is the Good Lord supposed to do that sort of thing?"

"Well I am not the Good Lord yet" mumbled Jerry, "and even when, or if, I become him, then I will; I mean, if I am going to be around for a thousand years, then that wouldn't be a dry period; it would be a bloody drought of biblical proportions."

"Absolutely" said Pete, laughing slightly as he said it. "But seriously, I mean all those church vicars and priests, don't they have to have some kind of vow of chastity, or something?" he asked.

Jerry suddenly understood what Pete was talking about; he had never attached what Mystic had said to anything to do with religion. However, maybe Pete was right; the Good Lord, as opposed to the Evil Lord, God as opposed to the Devil, it was very similar.

"Jesus, I hadn't thought of it like that" said Jerry, starting to be scared and not realising that he had said the name 'Jesus'.

"Oh very funny" smirked Pete.

"No, I didn't mean it like that" Jerry said quickly. "I mean, the Good Lord today, he doesn't have people praying to him does he? At least I don't think he does. I mean, everyone prays to the God they choose to believe in. No one would ever pray to me" he concluded, trying more to reassure himself than to convince anyone else.

Pete felt it was best to change the subject. "Did you ask her how long you had to find this Prize?" he asked.

"No, I didn't think of that" muttered Jerry, feeling slightly stupid. "I must remember that for next time."

"Well at least we now know why we are doing this Quest" said Pete, "and that you have to get five numbers and five positions."

"Yes" agreed Jerry.

"And so far" added Pete, "we have got two numbers and two positions solved."

"Yes."

"And you and Jules solved the Crossword puzzle on Sunday. Well done!" exclaimed Pete.

"Yes, once we found the right crossword it was not that difficult really."

"And now we are working on Verse Five. So shall we get on with that, and see what we can work out, oh wise one?"

"Yeah, and cut the wise one crap" said Jerry, as he moved to slap the side of Pete's face. Pete however was used to Jerry and had already guessed, before he had made the comment, that some sort of mock-physical retribution would be heading its way towards him the moment Jerry had realised what he had said, and so he had already leant to one side to avoid any contact whatsoever.

"Hey, hey" said Pete, smirking as Jerry's hand flashed past his face. "Chosen One or not, you'll have to be a bit quicker than that to get to Potts."

Jerry stood up, causing Pete to wonder what was about to happen, but Jerry just picked up the piece of paper that Pete had placed on the table when he arrived. It was Pete's handwritten copy of Mystic's text; the copy he had made last Saturday.

Pete relaxed slightly as Jerry came around the table and sat next to him. They both then settled down to their main task of the afternoon, solving the clue to the location of Verse Five.

"Where's your copy?" asked Pete.

"Oh, it's in my desk drawer in the Den. Do we need it as well?"

"Well, it would be best" replied Pete, and so Jerry stood up again and went to walk out of the kitchen, but this time he made sure that he made a gentle contact with Pete's head, just before he turned around and sat down again.

"Fooled you" he said laughingly to Pete. "Let's use your copy; I can get mine later if needed".

Verse Five

"Verse Five is what you'll find in one of the best establishments. Stored, in what is a fertile place, in a street, a lane, and a park. You'll need a key to get in, and that you'll find begins with 92, which you will get from the second Guardian."

"I have been thinking about this a bit" said Pete, rubbing the side of his head as he and Jerry sat at the kitchen table.

"Did you get anywhere?" asked Jerry

"Well" he replied, not wanting to sound too negative, "I haven't solved it, if that's what you meant. But I think that I now understand it a bit more."

"Go on" said Jerry, trying to encourage him.

"Have you met the Second Guardian?" he asked Jerry.

"No" Jerry replied, looking a bit dejected. "No one has come to me and said they are a Guardian. I mean I only found out about them on Friday."

"Well, then it only leaves the part about a fertile place, in a street, a lane and a park" concluded Pete. "The only thing that I can think of that is fertile, and which exists in a street a lane and a park, is a 'tree' or some kind of 'flower-bed'" he added. "I mean, it's not such a clear clue, is it?"

"So you basically mean" said Jerry, trying to sum-up what Pete had told him. "That you are not really any further."

"I guess so" was the answer he got back.

They decided to go over to the PC in Jerry's Den, and try and do some searches on the web to see if that came up with anything interesting. The first thing they tried was to search on 'A Street A Lane A Park', but that did not come up with anything conclusive.

"Wait a minute" said Pete, after slowly sipping his tea that Jerry had just brought into the Den. "*Stored in, what is a fertile place*" he repeated.

"Yes" said Jerry.

However, Pete was ignoring him and was scanning through the words with his eyes very close to the paper on the desk.

"It's a safe place" said Pete. "Look" and he underlined the word 'safe' made up from the letters 's', in 'is', the 'a', and the 'fe' from 'fertile'.

"Oh yeah" mumbled Jerry, "I didn't spot that. You're getting good at this mate."

"Let's add that to the search" suggested Pete, and he typed in 'Street Lane Park Safe' into the search engine, and something very interesting came up.

Park Lane Safe Deposit,
Park Street,
Mayfair,
London

"It's a safety deposit centre" said Pete, feeling proud that he had sussed it. 'All we need now is the key from the second Guardian."

"But what does the first line mean?" asked Jerry, "I mean it must mean something?" he added, looking baffled.

At that point Jules arrived at the front door and rang the doorbell. Pete let her in, and she greeted him with a kiss on the cheek. She then walked over to the Den, where Jerry was sitting at his desk, and gave him a long 'hello' kiss on the lips. Pete, who had of course followed her into the Den, smiled to himself, but for a bit too long, as Jules noticed him.

"So he told you then, did he?" she chirped as she scowled at Pete.

"Told me what?" he replied, rapidly developing sunburn all over his cheeks.

Jules just smiled; she had had her revenge, so she said no more.

"Pete has just deciphered part of the clue to Verse Five" declared Jerry in a proud voice, trying to raise the tone of the conversation, and he proceeded to show Jules.

"That's good" she said, "but what about the first line, what does that mean?"

Then Jerry spotted it. "It's a test" he said, "look" and he proceeded to do virtually the same thing that Pete had done just before, and underlined the 't' from the word 'best' and the letters 'est' from the word 'establishment'. "You'll find it in one of the best establishments" he said again, "meaning a test."

"Well spotted" said Jules, who then paused for a moment, before asking: "but why would someone store a test in a safety deposit box?"

"Why not?" replied Pete. "I guess it depends what type of test it is."

"Well we can go there tomorrow" suggested Jules, "and find out. We like going to London don't we Jerry" she added, sarcastically.

Pete got the message, but he did not say anything.

"I thought you had to go to work" said Jerry, looking up at Jules.

"Well, after this morning, I decided to take the whole week off. My boss did not mind as it was kind of quiet anyway" she answered as she winked at Jerry.

"Well I can't come tomorrow" grumbled Pete, "as I have some more meetings at work which I can't miss."

Pete was now experiencing some mixed feelings. On the one hand he felt a bit peeved since it was he who had solved that part of the clue and he really wanted to know what it meant. On the other hand however, he was also feeling a bit relieved as he would now not have to sit next to Jerry and Jules and watch them making eyes at each other every minute.

"Well, it doesn't really matter" concluded Jerry, "I mean we can't go anyway since we haven't got the key from the second Guardian. And without the key we can't open the deposit box, or even know which deposit box it is."

This was the brutal and honest truth.

"How on earth do we find the second Guardian?" asked Jerry aloud, as if asking the others for help. They however, had absolutely no ideas.

It was now approaching teatime, and Jerry was getting hungry. "Shall I order some take-away?" he asked.

Jules and Pete both agreed and so Jerry opened the top drawer of his desk and started searching for the local Chinese takeaway menu. He first took out his copy of the clue for Verse Five, putting it on the desk, and then slid the plastic coated text that was Verse Three to one side to pull out the Chinese menu. Jerry and Pete started looking at the menu, but Jules had spotted something.

"That's strange" she said as she looked at his hand written clue to the location of Verse Five, the text Mystic had dictated to him. "Your text is different."

"What" he replied, as he looked at his text.

Jerry picked it up and read it. She was right. His text now read:

"Verse Five is what you'll find in one of the best establishments. Stored, in what is a fertile place, in a street, a lane, and a park. You'll need a key to get in, and that you'll find begins with 92, which you got from the second Guardian."

"It says that I 'got it from the second Guardian'. However, Pete's version says that I 'will get it from the second Guardian'. What's going on?"

"Well we know that texts sometimes change" said Jules, thinking out aloud. "I mean, remember the advert in the newspaper, and also the clues in the crossword puzzle. It seems pretty normal practice for texts to change."

"But then why didn't mine change?" asked Pete.

"Well" said Jules, thinking about it. "The only reason I can guess is that yours was not an original. You wrote it yourself from Jerry's original version. I guess the magic does not transfer when someone else just writes it down themselves."

"But this" said Jerry, completely forgetting about the Chinese meal that he was supposed to be ordering, "means that I have already got the key from the second Guardian. It means that I have already met the second Guardian."

"Well who have you met?" asked Pete, "since Friday."

"Mystic" said Jerry.

"Yes, but she has already told us that she is not a Guardian" said Jules.

"What did you do after we left on Saturday evening?" asked Pete.

"Nothing" Jerry replied. "I mean, I didn't meet anyone; I just wasted my time doing those stupid crosswords."

"Then it can only be one place" said Pete, "the Library."

"Who did you meet at the Library Jerry?" asked Jules, knowing full well what answer she was going to hear.

"The librarian" said Jerry, with a smile on his face, which he quickly removed the moment he saw that Jules was watching him. "Could she be the second Guardian?" he quickly asked, trying to pretend that he was not embarrassed.

"She might well be" said Pete. "She gave you that crossword book. Was there anything in there beginning with 92?"

"Not that I remember" said Jerry, as he immediately went over to the living room cupboard and pulled out the puzzle book from the bookshelf. "No, look there are only 83 crosswords, remember; it doesn't go up to ninety-two."

"Then it can't have been her then" said Jules.

"Didn't she give you something else, Jerry?" asked Pete, with a snide wink as he said it.

"Oh yeah" said Jerry, "I had forgotten about that. She gave me her phone number" and he immediately pulled out his wallet, realising as he did that Jules was watching him and steam was starting to come out of her ears.

'Oh shit' he thought to himself.

"SHE GAVE YOU WHAT?" shouted Jules, just slightly louder than the laughter that was emanating from Pete. "And you had it in your wallet. After everything we did last night, and this morning."

"And this morning" added Pete, in hysterics. "You didn't tell me about that Jerry."

"I am sorry Jules, babe" said Jerry. "I hadn't had time to throw it away. I would never have called her babe. Honest!"

Jules was calming down. After all, it was true what he had said; he had not had any time to throw it away, she had seen to that. Moreover, he did really seem to be sorry. "Ok," she said, "I forgive you this time. Let's see it then."

That gave Jerry a new lease of life, so he unfolded the phone number and showed it to them both:

DT: 555 – 924 – 2417

There it was, clear and plain: 92 42417. The key; it began with ninety-two.

"Lucky I didn't throw it away eh?" said Jerry, in an attempt to try to justify his holding on to it.

"Very lucky" said Jules, with a kind of 'don't you dare do that again' look on her face.

"Shall we go tomorrow then Jules, you and I" suggested Jerry, "and we can see if we can find this test?"

"Ok" she agreed. "Now what about this Chinese meal you were supposed to be ordering?"

Jules stayed at Jerry's place that night, as they would travel the next morning on the train down to London. Before going to bed, Jerry was careful to make sure that he closed the kitchen door leading into the hall, and it was a good thing he did, for when he walked into the kitchen the next morning, there was Mystic waiting at the window.

"Morning Mystic" he called out as he opened the window, allowing her to fly in and land on the kitchen table.

Jerry then put the kettle on and went over to the table and sat down opposite her.

"Good morning Jerry" she replied, as she bobbed over to him. "I have come to warn you about your upcoming visit to London."

"Oh, what's the problem?" asked Jules, as she joined them in the kitchen, trying to dry her hair with a towel as she was walking.

"Good morning, Julia" was the rather formal reply she got from Mystic.

"You can call me Jules" she said back to her, "all other people who know me by my first name call me Jules; it's more informal."

"Oh, all right then, Jules" said Mystic, who then started to continue her previous message to Jerry. "When you are in London you will be on the outskirts of the Good Lord's protection. He will not be able to cover your presence all the time, and this may give the Evil Lord an advantage. He asked me to warn you about this, and suggested that I come along with you."

"A chaperone" whispered Jules, as she cuddled up to Jerry and sat on his lap, "how sweet."

"No, not as a chaperone; you two are quite capable of looking after yourselves in that department" replied Mystic, sounding a little shirty, agitated, and maybe even slightly jealous. "There are however" she continued, "many forces in this world that you two know absolutely nothing about. You would both be easy prey for the Evil Lord."

"Sorry" said Jules, "I was only joking."

"This is deadly serious" replied Mystic. "Many people's lives depend upon a successful replenishment, and before this week is out, some will even die trying to ensure that it actually happens" she snapped, almost looking as if she was in tears again.

"I am really sorry" said Jules, "I didn't mean to..." However, she did not actually get to the point of saying what she had not meant, because she actually did burst into tears and then ran into the bedroom.

"Go easy a bit Mystic" said Jerry, "she didn't mean any harm."

"I know she didn't" replied Mystic, maybe feeling a touch guilty. "But it's better she gets a bit upset from a few of my harsh words, than falls prey to the Evil Lord" she added as she flew onto the floor, landed, shook her body from head to tail, and then transformed into a late middle-aged woman, holding a black handbag and wearing a long dark cloak with a hood covering most of her face.

"Whoa!" called out Jerry, who nearly fell backwards off his chair in complete and utter amazement. "Who are you?"

"I am Mystic" replied Mystic, who seemed to think that the question was a complete waste of time. "Who did you think I was?"

"Well I didn't really know" he replied. "I mean, I had just assumed that you were a bird that could talk."

"Not gone out with many birds that could actually talk then have you Jerry?" she said, with a rare smile across her face.

Jerry looked at her, and suddenly understood. "Oh, very good" he mumbled and smiled at her in return.

Mystic then looked at him. "Excuse me a moment, Jerry" she said, and she walked out of the Kitchen and into the bedroom to go and comfort Jules.

Jerry knew that this would not be a good time for him to go and join them, so he stayed in the kitchen and made some toast and a pot of tea, secretly hoping that the two girls would quite soon emerge as best of friends.

And, he was not disappointed, for within five minutes they both did reappear; Mystic holding her arms around Jules, and Jules displaying her bright red eyes, clearly indicating that she had been heavily crying, although Jerry did not really have any idea what she had been crying about for so long.

"Are you going to come with us, dressed like that?" he asked, pointing to Mystic's black coat and what appeared to be a tatty old dress underneath. Of course, he was trying to remain as polite as possible.

Mystic walked into the hall where a long mirror was hanging on the wall.

"Oh dear" she muttered. "I do seem to have let my appearance sag a bit recently, haven't I? It has been such a long time since I was in the presence of mortals that I had forgotten. Never mind" she added, and with a click of her fingers she had transformed again; gone was the cloak, dress, boots and hood, replaced by a much trendier, well at least for a mature woman in her late fifties, full length dress, shoes, hat and a three quarter length jacket. Her handbag remained of course. "Now that's better isn't it?" she declared, studying herself in the mirror.

Jules just looked at her and stared in disbelief.

Jerry asked Mystic if she wanted anything to eat, and she was very keen to try some of the toast and jam; she had not eaten like this for quite some time. After they had finished, Jerry went to get dressed while Jules and Mystic gossiped and tidied-up.

They arrived at the station around nine o'clock, ready to catch the train down to London. Jerry bought the tickets. It seemed that Mystic had never actually travelled in a train before, and had only seen them whilst flying high above.

Nevertheless, the journey to Kings Cross was most uneventful and the time really flew quickly by. Mystic had given them some instructions whilst they were on the train. If there was any trouble then she would be there to protect them and to keep the attacker at bay, while they should try and dash back to Cambridge as fast as they could. They should go to Jerry's apartment and wait for her or Diana, the librarian- who they now of course knew was a Guardian, to make contact with them. Jules was careful not to make any remarks when Mystic had finished.

When they arrived at Kings Cross, they got into a taxi and headed over to the Park Lane Safe Deposit centre in Park Street, Mayfair. It was a very secluded building, not heavily advertised; it looked as though it contained many secrets and it was a secret itself. There was a lot of security in evidence around the building; many cameras were visible.

They rang the bell at the entrance and were greeted by a very large security guard who escorted them into what can only be described as an inside of a palace. It was a massive reception area, decorated all over in marble. The ceilings were huge and spotless, and pieces of artwork were strategically positioned all over the place. In the middle, sitting behind a perfect marble desk, was a receptionist who was eyeing them very suspiciously. Jerry suddenly realised that he did not know what to ask for, and he turned to Mystic.

Mystic whispered to him. "The key Jerry, what does it begin with?"

Jerry understood immediately, and put his hand into his back pocket to take out his wallet, to check the phone number he had received from Diana. At that point, someone who looked very official walked over to greet them.

"Good morning, Madam" said the very elegant and well-dressed man, as he bowed slightly and kissed Mystic's hand. "And Miss" he went on to say as he turned to face Jules, bowed slightly again, and kissed her hand.

He then turned to Jerry and held out his hand. Jerry put his wallet back in his pocket and shook his hand with a firm grasp.

"Good morning, Sir" the man went on to say. "Welcome to my depository. My name is Meneer de Gaunt; I am of Dutch origin, just in case you wondered, and I am the Manager here of the depository. Now how can I help you, Mr?"

"Dumbarton" added Jerry, quite pleased that he had at least answered the first question correctly. Jerry felt a tad intimidated by Mr de Gaunt; he was a real classy gent, as Jerry would have described him, 'a real banker'.

"And what can I do for you Mr Dumbarton?" he said, as he shook Jerry's hand again. He looked as though he was deep in thought, trying to remember something. "Have we met before?" he asked.

"No, I don't think so" replied Jerry.

"We have come to look at a safe deposit box" added Mystic, as she looked hard into Mr de Gaunt's eyes.

Mr de Gaunt looked straight back at her. "Ah" he said, as if something was slowly dawning upon him. "Yes, you will need first to sign in; all visitors have to sign in to the visitors log" he added, and so they all duly signed in.

"Will you come this way please" said Mr de Gaunt, and he walked off towards a smaller corridor that led off, away from the main entrance. This corridor was also full of marble, with artwork hanging on the walls, interspersed with the odd tropical plant here and there. There were many doors along the corridor and again, many cameras as well.

"Security, you know" continued Mr de Gaunt, as he saw Jerry looking at all the cameras, "we can never be too careful, you know."

"Yes indeed" replied Jerry, wondering what he was now getting into.

Jules had kept quiet the whole time, but she was feeling a little afraid; she had Goosebumps forming on her back, and she felt very uneasy, as if someone was watching her. Mystic was also acting very cagy.

"In here Sir, Miss" said Mr de Gaunt, as he opened a door for them.

Mystic waited outside. Mr de Gaunt went into the room with Jerry and Jules. It was a small room, which had a solid table on one side, fairly close to the door, which had a curtain rail around it and a curtain hanging from one end, so that the occupants could have even more privacy if they wanted it. On the far side of the room was an electronic key pad, with a special flat-screen display attached to it.

"Here" said Mr de Gaunt, pointing to the electronic keypad, "is where you enter the key to open your box. When you have selected your box, you will enter the five-digit pin code, which the computer will then verify. If correct, then our guards will bring the box to you in this room and you can look into it and make whatever changes you like. When you are ready you can press the red call button here" and he pointed to a large red circular knob on the side of the wall. "You will see" he continued, "that there are no cameras inside the room, Sir. This is because what is in your box is private and for your eyes only."

Jerry and Jules both thanked the man, and he then left them to get on with entering their code. Jules looked over at the keypad and the display panel. The display panel had two rows of identical blank boxes and an area for messages. Each row required two letters and two numbers to identify the box, and it required a five-digit pin code to confirm that they were the owner.

Jerry again put his hand into his back pocket to get out his wallet and read the phone number he had received. He carefully unfolded the piece of paper and showed it to Jules.

DT: 555 – 924 – 2417

"It said it began with 92" said Jules as she tried to remember the clue that they had received from Mystic some time ago now.

"Yes" said Jerry. "But the first two letters; they must be the 'D' and the 'T'."

"Yeah, I agree" she said, "and the PIN number must be the '42417' which means that the box number must be 'DT92'."

"Why do you say that?" asked Jerry, "what about the three fives?"

"Oh that" replied Jules. "In the movies they always use a phone number beginning with '555' because they don't actually exist. That way no one can get any crank calls and no one can sue the movie producer. Didn't you know that?"

"No" replied Jerry, for he had honestly never heard of that before.

"Had you shown me the phone number when you got it" she added, "I would have told you instantly that it was a fake number. But you didn't" she smirked, a big smile across her face.

Jerry ignored her gloating, and started to enter the code into the keypad. 'D', 'T', '9', '2' for the box-id, and '4', '2', '4', '1' and '7' for the PIN code. As he keyed them in, they appeared, one by one, in the first line of the empty boxes in the display panel. He then pressed the 'ENTER' button. The computer then copied the nine-digit code to the second row of nine boxes and the message: 'CONFIRM Y/N?' came up flashing, together with a recurring beeping sound.

"Are you sure?" queried Jerry, as he looked deep into Jules' eyes, in which he could see the reflection of the flashing message from the display panel.

"Yes" she said, "it has to be."

Jerry pressed the 'Y' button and the machine froze, at least the beeping stopped sounding and the flashing message stopped flashing. Jerry and Jules both looked at each other and wondered if it was going to work. Then, after a few moments, a small 'ting' sound came from the display panel, and a new flashing green message was displayed which stated 'CORRECT'.

After a few seconds, the message field on the keypad then gave the message: "Please wait, your box is being collected and will be brought to you."

Jerry and Jules held hands as she kissed him on the side of the face. So far, it was going well.

"AAAARRRRGH" cried Lord Dell, from his bathroom, deep within his Mansion. "Jensen, quickly come here, NOW!"

Johnson and Smith looked at each other and could not make out what was going on. What was wrong with their Master? He had never screamed like that before.

Jensen came running as fast as he could, which was not very fast for a sixty year old man. "Yes my Lord" he called, gasping for air as he entered the bathroom.

"Quick Jensen" said Lord Dell, "bring me my robes. Something is happening; I can sense it. They are close, quickly now, quickly!"

Jensen was doing things as quickly as he could. However, his training was to be correct, not to be quick, and now his master was getting all in a fuss.

Jerry and Jules looked around as the door opened. Four guards came in carrying what could only be described as a normal size safety deposit box. It could not have been more than 20 cm deep and no more than 30cm wide by 50cm in length. However, what was inside the box seemed to be very, very, heavy, for it needed four guards to carry it, and they were all struggling with its weight.

The Guards put the box down onto the solid table that was inside the room and immediately proceeded to wipe the sweat off their foreheads. They all then bowed, turned around, and left the room, quietly closing the door behind them.

Jerry and Jules walked over to the box and pulled the curtain closed behind them. Jerry opened the lid and they both peered in. Jerry was amazed; all that seemed to be in there was a normal page of A4 paper.

"How can that be so heavy?" asked Jules as she looked at the piece of paper, obviously expecting some large precious stone, or gem, or something heavy to be inside, but not a single page of paper.

"I have no idea" Jerry replied as he bent down to pick up the page. He took hold of it and went to lift it out of the box, but it would not move. "I can't move it" he said, looking confused.

Jules put her hand into the box and tried to remove it together with Jerry, but neither of them could shift it. "This is really strange" she said to him, looking thoroughly bewildered. "Can you read it?"

"Yes, no problem" said Jerry, "it's as clear as day what is written on it."

"Well we're never going to remember all those words are we?" said Jules, who had started also to read the text. It seemed to be like some kind of test paper, with several questions on it, and they did not look very easy.

"No, I agree" said Jerry, who then proceeded to get out his mobile phone and take a series of pictures of the paper.

"Did they come out ok?" she asked.

Jerry checked his phone and looked at the images. They were pretty-small on the phone's screen, but he knew that when they were sent to the printer that they would come out ok, and that they would be able to read them.

"Yes, fine" he replied.

"Is there anything else in the box?"

Jerry felt around inside the box, but there was nothing behind, below, or on either side of the piece of paper. "Well that's that then" he said. "Shall we go now?"

"I guess so" she replied, "I mean, we have a copy of the test, we cannot take it out of the box, what else can we do but send the box back, and go back home with Mystic. Anyway" she added, "I am feeling a bit strange. Something is not right, and I feel like someone is continually watching me. Let's go."

Jerry closed the lid of the box, put his phone back in his trouser pocket, pulled back the curtain, and pressed the red call button. The four guards came back in. They each had a glimmer of hope in their eyes, but when they lifted the box, the hope vanished as they struggled again with its weight, lifting it between the four of them, ready to take it back into the depths of the depository. Jerry and Jules walked outside of the room where Mystic was still waiting for them in the corridor.

"Quickly" she said, "we must move quickly. He has detected our presence. The longer we stay here the more danger we are in" and with that they walked as fast as they could, back to the reception area where Mr de Gaunt was waiting for them.

"Was everything to your satisfaction Sir, Miss, Madam?" he asked.

"Yes, everything was fine" replied Mystic. "Thank you very much Harrie" and with that they shook hands and departed.

When they got outside Jerry hailed a cab and they went straight back to Kings Cross Station.

Meanwhile in his Mansion, Lord Dell was holding his hand over his special map of the United Kingdom. "Where are they? Where are they?" he was repeating aloud, as he scanned his hand over different parts of the country. Nothing was registering in Wales, nor in Scotland and not in Ireland. He moved his hand towards the different parts of England, starting with the midlands. His hands were still feeling nothing, as they had done for the last thousand years, but as he came closer and closer to London he started to sense something.

"They are in London" he said to Johnson and Smith, "London, again."

The cab carrying Mystic, Jules, and Jerry arrived at Kings Cross and they got out. Jerry paid the cabbie, and they walked into the station. As they walked towards the waiting room Jerry noticed a plaque on the wall. It was a plaque marking the location of the make believe Platform nine-and-three-quarters from the Harry Potter novels by J. K. Rowling. Jerry stopped and stared at the plaque.

"Humph" he muttered to himself, comparing his own situation to that of the books. "This is real magic, none of that make believe stuff."

He then turned to Jules who was also looking at the plaque.

"Wingardium Leviosa, my arse!" he muttered to her, and at that very same instant a strange feeling started coming over him, as his bottom started lifting from the ground and pulling his legs and feet up with it.

"What?" said Jerry, suddenly looking rather scared, feeling a bit stupid, and not knowing at all what was happening?

"Well" said Mystic, as she clicked her fingers, causing Jerry's bottom, legs, and feet to resume their normal positions below his stomach. "She was bound to get one right, wasn't she" added Mystic as she turned away and stormed off into the waiting room with Jerry trailing in her wake, and Jules in an advanced state of the giggles.

The Test

Mystic instructed Jerry and Jules to stay and wait for her in the waiting room whilst she went outside; she had to check on something and would be back in a few minutes. Inside the waiting room Jules and Jerry sat on one of the old benches, cuddling each other and thoroughly enjoying their own company, but also eagerly waiting for Mystic to return. They had sat together in the very same waiting room after their last trip to London, when they visited the zoo trying to locate Mystic for the first time. Jerry looked around; nothing had really changed, except, perhaps it had been cleaned since they were last there.

Mystic returned within a few minutes, exactly as she had stated. She seemed fascinated by the waiting room; she had never been inside it before even though she had heard of it. Mystic walked slowly around the room, looking at the ornaments and objects scattered all over the place. She was most interested in the old faded picture hanging on the wall. She even remarked to Jerry, when she returned to sit next to them, that she did not look too bad for her age, but she could not quite make out the artists name, something like Leonard, Everard Bon, but that also was very faded. She thought that there was some letters afterwards as well, but she could not quite make them out. Jerry, on the other hand, was not at all interested in the picture; he was still smarting from his recent lifting experience.

They all sat together on the bench waiting for their train to arrive. Luckily they did not have to wait long, and within ten minutes they were walking the short distance to their platform and boarding the train. Mystic was relieved that no danger had befallen them on the trip. She knew that the Evil

Lord had detected their presence whilst they were at the depositary, but now they were on the train and they were safe. As Jerry had shown with his inappropriate use of words by the plaque, he was already starting to develop powers, and these powers would eventually attract the Evil Lord to his presence.

"We are safe for now" she assured Jerry and Jules. "For with every minute that now passes we are getting closer and closer to the Good Lord, and more and more under his protection."

Jerry and Jules looked relieved and hugged each other.

"However" continued Mystic, "just to be on the safe side, I will stay with you until we reach Jerry's apartment" she informed them.

The three of them sat together in the train as it raced along the tracks and the changing scenery sped past their window. Mystic was sitting opposite Jerry and Jules, watching them as they sat cuddled together. They really did look good together as a couple, she thought to herself, and they would also be good for each other, which was just as well for they would need each other if they were to succeed, Pete as well.

The journey, as Mystic had predicted, went off without any further incidents. They arrived safely at Jerry's apartment, where Mystic said her farewells, transformed back into her raven form, and then flew off into the clear blue sky.

Jerry and Jules did not quite know what to make of the day, but one thing was certain; they had now found Verse Five, and all they had to do now was solve it. Jerry immediately sent the images to his pc and selected the best shot to be printed. After printing, he showed the result to Jules.

Jules and Jerry just looked at each other with blank expressions on their faces.

Around four o'clock, Pete phoned Jerry to see how they had got on, and to check if it was all right to come over. He had started doing that now, just in case he called at an inopportune moment. Pete came straight over to meet with them both, and to start working on solving the new Verse.

They sat together around the kitchen table and started with question 1.

> *1. John lived alone with his 12 Rabbits. These were his family, and he loved them all. The house was small, so space was fairly cramped. On Monday however, when John returned home from work, he found that all but four of his Rabbits had died. How many Rabbits did he not bury?*

"Well that one and the next one are not so difficult" said Jerry, who had after all spent quite some time earlier in the afternoon studying the questions. "I mean, even I can answer those" he continued, and then immediately started explaining to them that if all but four had died, then that meant that eight had survived, meaning that he had not buried eight of them. He then went on to Question 2, pointing out that if eight had survived, then dividing them in half would give four. That meant that the answers to Questions one and two were eight and four respectively. Mathematics was not one of Jerry's strong points.

Jules looked at him with an 'oh dear, you poor thing' look on her face.

"I am afraid you are wrong" she said to him, and immediately started utilising her fib logic to explain that he had misread the question, in as much that if 'all but four' had died, then it meant that all of them had died, except four, meaning four had survived, and eight had died, and that then meant that he did not bury four of them, the ones that were still alive.

"Oh yeah" mumbled Jerry, looking thoroughly embarrassed.

Jules continued. "If you then divide four in half" she said, "then you end up with the answer two, and that means that the answers to Questions one and two are four and two respectively" she concluded, smiling at Jerry.

Jerry looked depressed. Pete however had remained quite silent during the two outbursts and now it was his turn to look at Jules with an 'oh dear, you poor fib' look on his face.

"What?" said Jules.

"I am afraid" began Pete, "that you're wrong as well" and he immediately continued to explain. "You answered question one correctly, that is to say if all but four died, then in reality eight had died and four survived, meaning that he did not bury four of them." He smiled at Jules. "But then you did not read the second question properly. If four survived, and you divide that by half, then the answer is not two, but is eight, since a half goes into four, eight times." He smiled at Jules again, before continuing. "That means that the answers to Questions one and two were four and eight respectively."

Now it was Jules' turn to look depressed and she did a good job of it; she had missed the trick in the question. To divide something by a half was different to dividing something in half.

"What about the next two questions?" asked Jerry, who had decided to keep quiet and not make any more smart comments after having got both the first two question wrong, and in the process demonstrating that maybe he did have something in common with the rabbits after all, his I.Q.

"Well they are slightly trickier" said Pete, and proceeded to read out the next question:

3. On Wednesday, John decided that he needed some more Rabbits. Since of those that had not died, 75% were male, he needed some more females. If the ratio of males to females for a rapid expansion required 3 females to every male, then how many females did John buy on Thursday?

Pete continued. "We know from question one that there were four rabbits that survived. Question three tells us that 75% were male, so that means that there were three males and one female, so far so good. For rapid expansion, he required three females to every male, then that meant, if he had three males, that he required in total, nine females. But since he had one female already, then he would have to buy eight more."

"Wow" said Jerry, "that was good work mate" and he slapped him hard on the shoulder.

"What about the last one then brain of Britain?" asked Jules, still sulking a bit.

Pete read out the question:

4. On Friday, in order to speed up the process and make sure his new family would grow very quickly, he decided to feed them with the stew he had just prepared. It was of course his favourite Rabbit stew. And there were no leftovers, even the Rabbits loved it. They each looked very nourished; after all they would be, because they had eaten one Rabbit. What John needed to do now, was to count how many Rabbits he had remaining. How many live Rabbits did John now have on Saturday?

Pete had to stop and think about this one a bit. "I have no idea" he finally admitted after a few minutes silence.

"But surely" remarked Jules, "you just said that he bought eight new rabbits, so that would mean that he had eight plus the four who had survived, meaning that he had twelve again. Doesn't it?"

Pete however was keeping quiet. He was not sure. He also did not believe that it could be that simple. On the other hand, maybe it was supposed to be that simple and the whole question four was a trick. "Hold on" he muttered. "The answer is not twelve, but it is eleven."

"Why?" asked Jules, not really understanding.

Pete licked his lips; he was giving them a kind of clue. Jerry looked at the text again, banged his palm of his hand to his forehead.

"You sick bastard."

"What?" said Jules.

"He had put one of the rabbits into the stew on Friday" said Jerry, "that means that on Saturday he had eleven live ones left."

Jules pulled a face of extreme revulsion, but could not help admire Pete's logic. "So what does that mean for the total answers?" she asked.

"Well" said Pete. We now have the answers: Four, Eight, Eight, and Eleven, and if we follow the instruction, we have to add those numbers and we get the answer thirty-one. But I still don't like it."

"Why not?" asked Jerry.

"Well it was too easy for one" said Pete, "and there is a hell of a lot of information in the questions that we have not yet used at all in coming to our answers."

"Yes" said Jules, "but so what though, I mean, it could just be there to misguide us."

"You may well be right" he added, "but if we look at the previous clues then they were much more detailed. I am sure we are missing something. I suggest I take a copy of this with me and think about it in some peace and quiet. Is that ok Jerry?"

"Sure mate" he replied, "how about some wine, and we can tell you about that guy we met at the Depository."

"Ok" replied Pete, and he leant back in his chair listening to Jerry and Jules recount their adventure from earlier in the day.

The next day Jerry woke again in Jules' arms. This was getting to be a habit, although one he felt he both needed and enjoyed at the same time. After a few hours of playing around together, Jerry suggested that they should go out for the day and proposed that they drive up to the White Horse Pub. Jules thought that this was a great idea, but she first had to go home and get a change of clothes. Jerry agreed to pick her up at one o'clock, at her place, and then they would go and have a nice romantic afternoon together.

Jerry did not know why he felt like going back to the pub. He doubted if it was the attraction of Annie, as he had not really looked at another woman since he had been with Jules those magical few days ago. He even felt like he was now in the middle of a monsoon period, even though outside it was the middle of summer, and one of the hottest summers on record. Jerry just felt that it was a good idea to go back to the pub; this had been where his whole journey had really started, and it was the first place they had found once they had successfully deciphered the email. Even so, travelling over ninety miles for a romantic drink and a meal in a pub was a bit eccentric, even for Jerry, but he was now falling head-over-heels in love with Jules, and that explained everything.

Jerry picked her up at one o'clock exactly, right outside her apartment. She was ready on time, which was unusual, but definitely a good sign. She also looked radiant; her bright blond hair, her lovely eyes and beautiful smile, each leading down to her wonderfully proportioned body, was enough to get any red-blooded centre forward's motor running full speed.

The journey to Curdworth was non-eventful, except for a few strange looks from lorry drivers as they passed them by on the motorway, obviously admiring Jerry's wonderful car. When they arrived at the pub it was not very busy, which was fine for them as they liked the peace and tranquillity of the area. The pub was still the same in all its splendour, and had not lost any of its magical appeal. Jose was serving behind the bar and he warmly welcomed them back.

Jose was an observant sort of chap, and he immediately noticed that they were much closer to each other than the previous time they had been to his bar. This warmed his heart, and he quietly called his wife to come over and look at them in the corner, cuddling each other. Annie was also delighted, and walked over to greet them.

"Hello Jerry, Hello Jules" she said to them, as they separated from each other and, in a slightly embarrassed manner, said hello back to her. "Lovely weather again isn't it" she remarked. "Longest dry period we have had in years."

"Yes, Great" said Jerry, chuckling to himself.

"Wonderful" added Jules, not really understanding what had caused Jerry to laugh.

"Can I get you guys anything to eat?" Annie asked them. "Would you like to see our menu?"

"Yes, that would be great" replied Jules, "and can you get us two more of those Bishops Fingers please."

"Oh, not for me" said Jerry, "I am driving and one is enough. Just get me an Orange Juice please."

Annie was very impressed, for when she last knew Jerry, such a thing like having too much to drink and then driving home afterwards was never an issue. Of course, he was never drunk, but if the police had stopped him, then he would have been in trouble. 'He is finally growing up, taking on more responsibility', she thought to herself, 'yes he really could be a good Chosen One'.

Jose brought them their drinks, and asked what they were going to have to eat. Jerry had selected the Ploughman's lunch again, but Jules was going for a Lasagne. The food was, as expected, excellent, and they really enjoyed the afternoon talking to Jose and Annie.

Around three o'clock, Annie suggested that they went for a walk into the field, which they thought was a great idea. Jose stayed behind to look after the bar.

As they walked into the field, the old White Horse strolled up to them. Obviously, thought Jules and Jerry, he thought it was time for his afternoon ride with Annie.

"Are you going to ride him today?" asked Jules, looking at Annie.

"Oh later on" she replied, as she watched Jerry stroking the horse's mane. "Hey, Jules" she said, continuing to look at Jerry, "come, let's go over here; I want to show you something."

The two girls then walked away, hand in hand to the side of the hedge, leaving Jerry stroking the White Horse.

"You're a handsome old beast, aren't you" muttered Jerry as he continued stroking the horse's mane and trying to see where the girls had gone.

"Why, thank you very much" replied the White Horse.

You could have knocked Jerry down with a feather. He stopped stroking him, took a step back, and turned his head and looked straight into the horse's eyes.

"What did you say?" he asked him, not really knowing whether he had imagined it or not, and definitely not realising that he was now speaking to a horse.

"I said, thank you very much, Jerry" repeated the White Horse, who then added, "I meant for the compliment."

"You as well?" mumbled Jerry, looking dumbstruck. "I am never going to be able to look another bird or animal in the face without expecting it to start talking to me; first a raven and now a horse."

"Well I believe that we are the only two of a kind" he said to Jerry, and he immediately proceeded with introducing himself. "Jerry, I am the White Horse, the one who sent you the original email. I am the leader of the Guardians and the current Good Lord, the one whom you have been chosen to replenish and I trust, the one who will continue the good work that has been done by the five who came before me."

The White Horse then went on to tell Jerry about all the different things he had done. Jerry was speechless; here he was talking to the Good Lord, and being explained things that he had never even dreamed of.

"You are doing well Jerry, so far" continued the White Horse. "However, you must speed-up if we are to avoid that the Evil Lord shall find and steal the Prize. The Evil Lord is looking for you. He has not found you yet, but he sensed you the other day in London, and I fear that great danger lies ahead. If we do not secure the succession then the Prize will become unprotected, and at the mercy of the dark side. We must fight to prevent that from happening."

Jerry listened intently to what the White Horse was telling him.

"Jerry, please look down on the ground" directed the White Horse.

Jerry immediately looked down and saw an old book appear just in front of where he was standing. It was a very old book; it looked like one of those ancient texts you see in old libraries or museums.

"This is the Book of Gred" said the White Horse, "and you must read it to understand your destiny, and that of the race of man."

"I have so many questions" said Jerry, "like why me?"

"Why not?" replied the White Horse, "for there is greatness in everyone, if they only decide how to use it."

"But I don't know all the answers" said Jerry, "I have no idea…"

"Being a leader" interrupted the White Horse, while looking deep into Jerry's eyes, "is not about knowing all the answers; it is about being able to get the best from your group, so that the group can get all the answers and then decide how to move forward."

Jerry felt that he understood it a bit better, but he did not really; this would only come in time.

"You are going through the same doubts that I went through when I found out that I was the Chosen One" continued the White Horse, "but I have belief in you Jerry, and your partners Jules and Pete also believe in you."

They stood together and spoke for quite some time. Eventually the two girls came back. Jules looked excited about something.

"Are you ok?" Jerry asked her.

"I am great" she replied.

"Aren't you going to introduce us Jerry?" asked the White Horse.

Jules did not seem to be bothered at all by the fact that the horse was talking, it was as if she was almost expecting it. Jerry had given up trying to guess anything that was going to happen any more.

"Jules" he said, "this is" as he turned to the horse and stroked him, "the White Horse, leader of the Guardians and the current Good Lord."

Jules bowed to him.

Jerry looked at her and thought to himself that he had not bowed to the White Horse. Had he been disrespectful?

"It is alright Jerry" said the White Horse, turning his head to look at him. "You have had an enormous shock this last week; it has turned your whole mind, and your whole world, completely upside down."

He then turned to face Jules. "Hello my dear" he said to her, bowing his head in return. "It is very nice to meet you."

"It is an honour to meet you" replied Jules, as she straightened up. However, something else was pressing on her mind. "Jerry" she said.

Jerry turned away from the White Horse and looked at her.

"And now let me introduce you to someone" she continued as she turned to face Annie. "Jerry, this is Annie Garrudo, and she is Guardian One, protector of Verse Three, and the keeper of the White Horse."

"You're a Guardian?" replied Jerry, slightly startled. "For how long have you been a Guardian?" he asked.

"I have already answered that one" replied Annie, "when we met the other week. I told you that I felt like I had been here for four hundred years, and that is exactly how long I have been here."

"So you were a Guardian when we were, err.." he sort of looked a bit lost; trying to search in his mind for the right word to use in front of Jules and the White Horse. "Together?" he added.

"Yes" she replied. "It was important for us to see how you were doing, and that you were guided and protected in the event that the Evil Lord should find you out."

"Oh" said Jerry, his ego being hurt a little; he was sure that she had fancied him half rotten.

"And yes I did fancy you as well" said Annie, understanding exactly what he was thinking.

Jules was hiding her face again; she did not want to be seen giggling in front of the Good Lord.

"Jerry" said the White Horse, who was also wearing an expression that looked as though it had been an effort to refrain from laughing. "As I was telling you, time is not on our side. The time of the replenishment approaches and you still have a lot to do. Now" he continued, "I have just sent the clue to Verse Four to your email address. Work quickly with it."

"Yes, I shall" replied Jerry, who was paying absolute attention to everything the White Horse was telling him.

"This is the last time that you will see me in this form, Jerry" continued the White Horse. "The next time you will see me is when you will have found the Prize and have proven that you are the worthy one."

"Yes" said Jerry, gulping as he said it.

"Come Annie" said the White Horse; "it is time for our ride. Good Luck to you Jerry, and to you as well Jules."

"Good Luck you two" said Annie, as she climbed onto the White Horse's back.

Jerry and Jules both stood together watching Annie wave to them as she and the White Horse sped away into the distance.

"Wow" said Jerry, as he turned towards his still radiant Jules.

"Wow indeed" she replied.

This had been a wonderful afternoon, but time was now pressing on and Jerry still had the warning from the White Horse ringing in his ears.

"Shall we go home now?" he asked.

"That sounds good, my Lord" she said to him smiling, as if she was starting to get used to the idea of addressing him like royalty.

"And you can cut that crap out" he replied as he bent down and picked-up the book of Gred which was still on the ground.

They then grasped each other's hands tightly and set off walking back to the car, making sure to wave good-bye to Jose at the window as they went.

The Book of Gred

In the beginning, before the rule of man was fully established, his dominating characteristic was evil; long and bloody conflicts were continually raging throughout the planet as other beasts challenged him for the right to rule the planet Earth. The force that was driving man during this period came from the Evil Lord. As his evil influence spread across the globe, man entered into ever more bloodier conflicts. Once however the age of man was established, the force of Evil was to reduce. Man though was not satisfied; his thirst for evil was still strong, and man then turned upon man, leading to the start of many new conflicts. These conflicts escalated until they reached a point where man was killing man, and thus slowly killing himself.

One day, around 6000 years ago, a young boy named Gred, one who had not yet come under the evil influences, but one who had seen and experienced them via others in his village, was wandering in the forest close to his home. He had never been so deep into the forest before, but he had promised his mother to find mushrooms for their evening meal.

Gred lived in the local village with his mother and father. It was a small village in the southern part of what is nowadays England. His mother was sweet and lovely and his father was a man, and like all men of the village he had no time to be either sweet or lovely, for he had to work in the fields every day with the other men so that they would have enough food for the village during the upcoming winter.

The summer so far had been bad; it was raining that day, just as it had been continually for the last weeks. The general feeling in the village was of sorrow and despair, for the autumn and then winter would soon be upon them, and if they did not harvest enough crops then it would be a hard winter, and some would no doubt perish.

There were only twenty or so families in the village, each with their own hut, similar to the hut owned by Gred's family. The huts were close together, close enough so that their occupiers could protect each other if called upon, as happened when other nearby villages raided them. Gred's hut was small and constructed mainly from wood from the forest. They had no openings to see out of, only a gap for a door, which they covered with the skin of a dead cow, to keep out the wind and rain. The family ate and slept in the one room, on the floor, together with the small insects that were too quick to catch or too small to eat.

The forest next to the village was old. The trees were very tall and so close together that they hid the sky. It was early afternoon that day, when Gred was wandering in the forest, searching for mushrooms for their evening meal. What little sunlight that existed above the trees, became mere beams of light here and there as they penetrated and bounced off the leaves and branches of the trees. For outside the forest it was still raining, but inside the forest it was only damp; no raindrops penetrated the canopy of the trees, yet still the air was wet.

As Gred walked deeper and deeper into the forest, he came across an opening in the side of a steep cliff. It looked as though the opening led into a cave. The entrance was thin, like Gred, and the rocks were old and had sharp ragged edges. 'The cave looked like a good dark and damp place for mushrooms' he thought, so he decided to go in. Gred very carefully slid between the rocks forming the opening and moved into the cave. Inside the air was very stale, old like the cave itself, which had probably been there since the mountain formed, since the

161

beginning of time. Slowly and carefully, Gred walked further in. The light in the cave came from holes in the ceiling, each one strangely somehow trapping the sunlight and forming an almost uniform strip of lights leading off into the distance, showing him the way. This however was not the only strange thing, for Gred felt something, a kind of longing that was pulling him deeper and deeper into the cave, willing him to go further, to follow the light.

He walked over smoothed rocks on the ground and came across a small stream, which he crossed. Then, after several minutes of walking, over rock, over water and over earth, he saw a distant gleam of light emanating from under a small pile of rocks. He approached it, driven by curiosity mostly, but he also sensed a feeling that had not been rife in his village for some time. It was the feeling of love and hope.

He lifted away the small rocks that were covering the object until it lay bare on the ground, nothing between him and it.

"What are you?" said Gred, which was a strange question, since the object had no body, no mouth, and no voice to speak back to him. Nevertheless, it answered; the answer came back straight into his mind.

"I am the Prize" it said, "claim me and we will become one, and together bring this evil tyranny to an end."

Gred leaned forward and touched the object. Initially it was wondrous beyond belief, truly amazing, he was numb with excitement, in such a state of delight that he did not want it to end. It was as if all the troubles of the world seemed to vanish from his shoulders; he felt lighter than air. The object had become a part of him; it saw what he saw, and felt what he felt at that moment. Then, suddenly, it stopped. The period of wonder, amazement, numbness, and delight had finished, and now became replaced with thoughts and visions of evil, of killings, of slaughter, of pain, hate, and suffering. Gred felt misled, abused even; he had trusted the object, it had shown him love and happiness, but then it went on to evil and hate.

"Let us go forth together" it said, straight into his mind. "Together with me, we will set right this place and we will drive the Evil Lord from the hearts and minds of your people. And you shall be known as the Good Lord, the one who brings love and understanding to the race of man."

Gred suddenly understood. In order to appreciate love and happiness, he had also to experience the opposite. There was too much evil and hate in his world today, and he was going to correct it. He, the Good Lord, was now to steer the race of man, for the race of man was not certain to survive, it needed guidance; it needed balance.

Gred decided to keep hold of the object and turned to go back the way he had come. He started running. He ran out of the cave and back through the forest towards his home. As he approached the edge of the forest, he stopped dead in his tracks; he had no mushrooms with him. Whilst his mother would not scold him, the tolerance of his father would not be so gracious.

'I need mushrooms' he thought to himself, and as he thought it, he turned to his left and saw a field of mushrooms. He stood amazed, looking at the field; not only was there enough for his family this mealtime, but enough for the entire village for a year.

'How come he had never seen this field before?' he wondered, 'and so close to his village. Anyway, no time to wonder about that now' he thought, and he immediately started picking some for their evening meal, and then ran straight back home and into the arms of his waiting mother.

As he passed through the edge of the forest, he felt the rain falling again on his head. It had been raining for so long now. The earth had turned to mud, and the seeds they had planted were not growing. As he got home, he showed his mother and his father the mushrooms and they were both delighted. He did not however mention about the object he had found.

At dinner that evening, his father spoke about the failing crops and his worries about the lack of food for the upcoming winter. "Do not worry father so" said Gred, "for it will stop." He did not know why he had said this, but he had a certain feeling that it would be so.

"What do you know?" replied his father, starting to get angry, but as he said it, the silence was deafening. They all looked at each other and then ran to the opening of their hut, pulled aside the old cow skin that was their door and looked outside. The rain had stopped. "Humph" grunted his father, "let us see how long this lasts."

That night Gred went to sleep as normal, but with the object held close to his chest. He felt a kind of strength emanating from the object, going straight into his own body, giving him extra belief, extra warmth, and a sort of loving energy.

The next morning they awoke and it was still silent outside. The sun was shining and the mud all over the village was slowly drying back into earth. Within a few days of this new wonderful weather, the crops were starting to grow, as was the influence of the object on Gred.

The only good thing about the wet had been that it had also prevented raiding parties from the adjacent villages coming in and stealing their crops, for there were no crops to steal. Now, after several weeks of good weather, there were plenty. Low and behold, one sunny morning, when the men of the village were working hard in the field to harvest their crops, a raiding party on horseback rode into their village and started threatening the women. On seeing and hearing this, the men of the village immediately ran down from the fields and gathered *around their women, forming a human shield to protect them. The raiders got down from their horses and raising their wooden clubs and shields they started to move towards them.*

Gred had been watching the events unfold from within his family's hut. Upset by what he had seen, and by what he sensed was going to happen, he walked out of his hut towards the two groups. On seeing this, Gred's mother nearly fainted. "Go back, hide" she screamed to him, but it was too late for the advancing raiders were now standing between Gred and his mother. They turned to look at the young boy. "No" screamed his mother, but it was again too late, for one of the biggest and most brutal of all the attackers walked towards Gred and raised his club as though to strike him down.

As he did this Gred looked up at him and smiled. His innocence was total and so pure. How could anyone want to cause any pain to such a harmless and pure child? However, the Raiders were evil, and they neither knew nor cared for love. The attacker raised his club higher and he laughed an evil laugh. Then, just as he was starting to bring down his club with a force sufficient to smash the child's skull into pieces, Gred quickly stretched out his arm, raising the palm of his hand upwards towards the attacker as if to stop him. The attacker was immediately lifted into the air and thrown about ten metres backwards, where he then fell with a great thud to the ground, landing on his back in a small pool of water which the horses used for drinking.

The other attackers looked on in shock. One of them immediately started running towards the child, ready to attack him, but again Gred stretched his arm out towards the attacker and he was repelled. Again, and again, they tried to attack him, and each attack was repelled. The villagers were stunned, but not as much as the raiders were for they ran to their horses and rode off as fast as they could, and without any crops. As they left the village, Gred's mother ran towards him, just as he collapsed to the ground. He was weak. The rest of the villagers watched. They did not understand what had just happened; for they were happy, but they were also scared at the same time. How can such a child repel grown men, and so many of them? This however was not their main concern; their harvest was safe and they could now get it into the village and store it in their huts so that they could eat this winter.

After a day of rest and tender care from his mother, Gred had recovered and was up and walking around again. People however were avoiding him, especially the other children.

At dinner that evening, his father asked him, "what did you do to those attackers, and how did you do it?" Gred merely looked at him and said, "I did not want them to hurt you, I wanted them to leave, and they did."

That night as Gred lay asleep, he heard the object talking to him again, not through his ears, but straight into his mind. "You are the first of the Chosen Ones Gred" it said to him. "You have been chosen to be the balance against evil. To make sure that the race of man will survive, it needs to find love and goodness in its hearts, and you will bring this."

'But how' thought Gred, for he did not want to speak with his parents sleeping just a few steps away.

"The Evil Lord has had his way with man for too long now" it continued. "You must fight evil in order for man to see that evil is not the answer. When they see that you can overcome their evil, they will listen to you and follow your words."

Gred lay covered by his cow skin and thought about these words. He was the first of the Chosen Ones, what did that mean? He fell asleep and in his sleep, the object continued to talk to him….

"The Evil Lord was to ensure that the race could protect itself and bring order and control, for evil was needed if the race of man was to secure its foothold on the planet. The Evil Lord has been eternal, surviving forever, and always adapting to find

166

new ways to be more evil. Now that man has succeeded in establishing his age, the Evil Lord was supposed to leave, but he did not - he remained in their hearts and in their minds. The creation of the Good Lord will balance the evil, and ensure that love survives and that the race of man does not destroy itself. The Good Lord will be chosen from the race of man, he will be made from one of them, and so the Prize was created and hidden on the Earth, awaiting the Chosen One to seek it out, and through it become the Good Lord. To ensure that good will ultimately survive, and maybe become the predominant force, the Good Lord would be able to create Guardians to help him."

"The role of the Guardians is to protect the Good Lord from evil, and to guard over the clues to the location of the hidden Prize, for to ensure that love is continually renewed and refreshed, the Good Lord must be replenished every 1000 years. For this to occur, a new Chosen One has to first discover and find the Prize."

"The Guardians protect the clues that can be used to find the pathway to the Prize. The Good Lord draws his strength from the combined power of the Guardians and the Prize. He cannot be killed while a Guardian lives, but if the Guardians are destroyed, he has only the power of the Prize."

"Once a Guardian they become, their life is put on hold; they will never age but will live forever at the same age until they are replaced, where after they shall continue to live their life as before, but in a new time of course, and aging again as normal."

"The good Lord weakens towards the end of his 1000 year tenure, he is then at his weakest and most vulnerable. The Chosen One must first find the Prize before he can take his place as the new Good Lord. To find the pathway to the Prize, he must find and correctly solve the five clues that lead to the location of the Prize. Consult this sacred text to find enlightenment and the pathway to the Prize. Once the Prize is *found, and the Good Lord replenished, then new clues and the Prize must be hidden anew."*

"The Guardians are anointed by the Good Lord, and are replenished when needed. Together the Guardians and the Good Lord protect the Prize from falling into the hands of the Evil Lord, for if this was to happen then man himself would be faced with a period of total evil, cruelty, and hate, such that he has never known."

"Every so often, and normally when the influence of the Good Lord is weakening, evil influences spread throughout the race, culminating in evil wars and periods of excessive hate and vengeance."

Gred listened and learned as he slept in his bed, and went on to serve his thousand-year tenure as the first Good Lord. Love and happiness was spread throughout the globe, but evil was also never far away, for it had not been eradicated, it had just been balanced.

During his thousand-year tenure, Gred anointed the first five Guardians and became a truly powerful force for good in the world. The power of the object which he had hidden in the forest near his home and which was protected by the five clues, each guarded by one of the Guardians, flowed through him at all times, and allowed him to do wondrous things for the benefit of all mankind. He helped man survive and build on its foothold that it had established on this wonderful planet.

Towards the end of his thousand-year tenure, Gred started to weaken. He had to prepare for his succession, prepare for his replenishment, and then finish his mortal life. He had selected his Guardians well; his most trusted was of course his mother. She had survived with him and they lived very close together for the thousand years.

When the new Chosen One emerged, he found the clues and beat the Evil Lord to the Prize. With the replenishment secured, Gred was now free with his mother to live out the remainder of their mortal lives. They returned to their original village. There was not much there anymore, all people had left and gone to larger settlements, but this did not deter them, for Gred and his mother were now used to living without help. Gred however was now severely weaker after his period as the Good Lord; he had been just eleven years old when he became him, which meant he was now still eleven years old and had the body and strength to match. Gred however was not a strong boy and he looked even younger than he really was.

The next Good Lord wrote this Book of Gred at the start of his thousand-year tenure, as a tribute to him, and so the facts would live on and so preserve the legend of Gred. This has since become a tradition; after the replenishment, the Good Lord's first task is to update the Book of Gred.

As Gred approached the final days of his life, he was very weak and almost incoherent. The Good Lord brought the book to him and asked him to leave a message in it for the next Chosen One. This message, although not making much sense in parts, became the 'Testament of Gred', for after completing it he closed his eyes and moved on.

As a tribute to Gred, the Good Lord commissioned a tomb, a wondrous monument, to be built in the forest where Gred had first found the Prize. The Good Lord walked into the forest, thumped his staff down firmly on the ground, and the forest cleared. It was not one of the highest points around, but the area he had cleared meant that people could see the tribute from far away. People came to the site from all over the country. They helped to erect the wooden supports into a big circle surrounded by a bank and a ditch. Gred's body was buried in the middle facing the rising sun.

People came from all around to pray at the monument and it soon was in danger of collapsing. The new Good Lord had also wanted a more lasting tribute for Gred, and he was not satisfied that the current monument would last, so around halfway into his thousand year tenure he decreed that the monument should be re-made from stone, and he had seen the very stones to use when he was recently travelling to Carreg Samson. Stones from the Prescelli mountains were transported and set-up to form the new lasting monument to Gred. However, the Good Lord became disturbed; he was thinking that Gred would not like this, for Gred had loved the forest so, and now to surround him in stone would be like putting him in a prison. He therefore ordered that a new, smaller, and more private monument to Gred should be built in an area just under two miles away to the north east, and there, in the shadow of the forest, would Gred's body finally be laid to rest.

And so it was to be, a smaller monument of only six wooden posts was erected, with a roof made from the forest, like his previous home. This area become known as the private Henge of Wood, as opposed to the more public monument, still visible today at the Henge of Stone. The new Good Lord then decided to make the Henge of Stone even more splendid, with even larger stones of sand from the Downs. The design of the monument was such that no man would ever need to go anywhere else to look, for surely the first Good Lord was resting here.

Since this day there have been six replenishments of the Good Lord, and never so far has the Evil Lord succeeded in securing the Prize, although he gets closer every time.

Man has survived, and man has flourished under the guidance of the Good Lord, but always there is evil at his doorstep, for evil is the easy way to get what is wanted, but it is never the right way to completely rule ones life.

The Testament of Gred:

If it is the Quest of the Prize that drives you then it is important to seek answers in your life. The clue to the place is important.

Beware a stranger causing illness. Keep fit, train hard.

Evil draws closer, taking you where you must not go to. But, it is you that evil must follow. You will therefore not go alone.

Go with stealth to the place where the Prize hides a king's reward. The end cometh; don't cross the old central park!

Terminal illness waits where you and the Prize shall be. Stay waiting for none. In a safe room the Prize or the number must be. Eight different places to look and thus find where, but remain patient for the time cometh.

Beneath lies the seven clues, each shows you in which direction you must go to.

Don't look back for the final battle approaches.

Under final clue you'll see where and how to find last part of Prize.

For the blood of the Royal is without stain.

The seat of kings marks the spot, the place to seek.

Ask where is the Quest for the Prize? for it ends somewhere, buried in time.

Only the worthy can inherit the Prize.

For when he shall find the words saying what is missing, then the order the words are read is good.

Praise the Good Lord, he who serves you and I, to suffer for, and replenish, me and you.

Amen.

Three Down

Jerry and Jules arrived back at Jerry's apartment around six o'clock in the evening. The weather that day, like the previous weeks, had been great and it was still very warm as the Sun still had a few hours left before it would disappear for the night. Jerry however, had no time to enjoy the weather as he had already called Pete when they were getting close to home, and asked him to be at his apartment around a quarter past six. Jerry was all flustered; he now had at least three things to do, and all had to be done very quickly. He was not used to having three balls in the air at once; one was enough. He now had the Verse Five test, which he was partly sure that Pete had solved yesterday, he had the Book of Gred to read, the book that he had received from the White Horse, and he had to check his email for the clue to Verse Four. Jules could sense his mood was not good, and that he was getting flustered.

"Let's split the tasks amongst us" she suggested to him. "Why don't you, after we have made a cup of tea and printed out the next clue, sit and read the book, and then Pete and I will continue to work on the clues. It's not a large book" she continued, trying to offer him some support and encouragement, "and you will soon be finished. Then you can tell us all about it."

"Yeah, that sounds great babe" he said to her, pulling her closer to him and kissing her on the cheek. "Thanks."

Jules went into the kitchen and put the kettle on while Jerry went into his Den to start-up his PC, and began to print out the email for Verse Four. Pete arrived as he was printing it out.

"Hi Pete" called Jules from the kitchen, as Jerry opened the door and let him into the apartment, "had a good day?"

"Oh fine" he replied, "what about you two?"

Jules brought the tea into the living room just as Jerry picked up the printout from the printer. It seemed to be some sort of code. He showed it to Pete.

"Wow, another clue" he said looking pleased, "you two have been busy. Where did you get this one from?"

Verse Four

A used computer is what you need in order for this code to read.

Key in the letters on the board, and work it out for your reward.

But one decipher does not do, a chinese rule is needed to.

And then add on the four answers from five, repeating to keep your quest alive.

But then again to keep your quest alive, the rule is back to Jackson Five.

So now I've told you a bit too much, but this is how I made it such.

H	T	A	L	D	W	A
U	N	C	D	J	J	F
V	V	Y	A	W	D	B
K	Q	Z	H	U	U	E
A	B	E	X	D	X	V
C	E	A	E	C	K	A

Jerry and Jules then spent about 10 minutes drinking their tea and telling Pete about their day. Pete listened, fascinated.

"That old horse could talk" he said, "and that was him, the Good Lord?" Pete's mind drifted back to the original email. "So the email did come from the White Horse, and it was 'him' that we had to find."

They told him about the book of Gred, the new Verse Four and about the fact that Annie was a Guardian. Jules also looked rather excited, but she did not say anything specific, and left most of the story telling to Jerry.

"Let's see the Verse Four then" said Pete.

Jerry handed it over to Pete, saying as he did, "this one looks definitely up your street; you need a used computer for it, and you have loads of them, eh?"

"Yeah" said Pete as he studied the printout closely.

"It's a code" he said, "and I am guessing that we have to decipher it using a computer."

"Why a computer?" asked Jules.

"Well it's just quicker" said Pete, "I mean most codes have several million combinations, and computers can work those out very quickly."

"Yes, I know that, of course" she replied, "but why not a new one, why a second hand one?"

"Well I don't really know" he surmised, as he pondered the question. "If it can have millions of different possible outcomes, then this could take a very long time. Maybe a used computer is just cheaper."

"Well we don't have a long time" said Jerry; stating the obvious would have also been one of his best subjects had he stayed on even longer at University.

"I suggested" began Jules, who was trying to prevent Jerry from getting too flustered, "that we let him read the book" as she slanted her head in the direction of Jerry, "and you and I can get on with solving the clues. What do you think Pete?"

"Sounds fine to me" he replied.

"Did you get any further with the one from yesterday?" asked Jerry.

"Oh yes" he said. "I think that I have got it now, but I need to run the logic through with you guys. But" he added smiling as he began, "I think that I was right; there was much more to it than what we thought yesterday."

"Ok" said Jules eagerly, "let's start with that then, and you can get on and read the book Jerry."

They all agreed. Jerry sat in his favourite armchair in the living room and started to read the Book of Gred, whilst Pete picked up the printout of the test that was Verse Five, and went with Jules to sit together at the kitchen table.

"Right" said Jules, eagerly looking at Pete, "what did you discover?"

"Well" he began. "The first thing is that we basically got all the answers wrong when we did it last time."

"What?" replied Jules in astonishment, "all of them?"

"Yes" he replied, "all of them" and went on to explain. "In order to answer the questions correctly you must first of all understand that all the questions are connected in some way or another, and you cannot answer one alone; you have to understand the whole story."

Jules was riveted as she listened to Pete explaining what he believed was the solution.

"Firstly" said Pete, "let us read all the questions again":

1. John lived alone with his 12 Rabbits. These were his family, and he loved them all. The house was small, so space was fairly cramped. On Monday however, when John returned home from work, he found that all but four of his Rabbits had died. How many Rabbits did he not bury?

2. On Tuesday, if the number of Rabbits alive is divided by half then how many would they be?

3. On Wednesday, John decided that he needed some more Rabbits. Since of those that had not died, 75% were male he needed some more females. If the ratio of males to females for a rapid expansion required 3 females to every male, then how many females did John buy on Thursday?

4. On Friday, in order to speed up the process and make sure his new family would grow very quickly, he decided to feed them with the stew he had just prepared. It was of course his favourite Rabbit stew. And there were no leftovers, even the Rabbits loved it. They each looked very nourished; after all they would be, because they had eaten one Rabbit. What John needed to do now, was to count how many Rabbits he had remaining. How many live Rabbits did John now have on Saturday?

"Lets start with Question one" he said. "Question one is pure misdirection. I mean how many did he not bury? We naturally assumed that he did not bury the ones that were alive, or more precisely he buried the ones that had died. However, that was not necessarily the case; for question four states that on Friday he made some Rabbit Stew. Since he loved Rabbits, he would hardly have killed any of them to make a stew, so it is most likely that he made the Rabbit stew using one or more of the Rabbits that had died on the Monday. Therefore" he concluded, "the trick to this whole Verse is to work out in which order you have to answer the questions, so that you can come to the correct answer."

Jules was fascinated and sat very quietly listening intently.

Pete continued.

"Question two is really the only one we can answer straight away, on its own" he said, "but even that one is tied to question one. We said yesterday the answer was eight, but that is not correct as the question includes two tricks. The first trick we understood, that was to divide by 'a half' and not to divide 'in half'. That meant that four rabbits divided by 'a half' gives the answer eight. However, the question says, how many would they be? The word 'they' is the second trick. For in question one it talks about John and his family, and that 'these' Rabbits were his family, which means that 'they' i.e. John and his Rabbits, is referring to the whole family. Therefore, the answer to question two is not eight, but it is eight plus one; eight Rabbits plus John, which equals nine."

"Wow" said Jules, "and that was the easiest part?"

"Absolutely, it only gets trickier from then onwards" he said, smiling at her. "Question three was also a trick, because it talks about a formula for calculating the ratios of male and female Rabbits. It then concludes with the question how many females did John buy on Thursday? In order to answer that, we first need to know how many Rabbits he actually had on Sunday, which means that we first have to answer question four."

"Question four" repeated Jules.

"Yes" said Pete. "Question four is the key to answering the whole Verse, and naturally the question is last in the list. If we have already answered questions one to three, then it is totally obvious that we will get question four completely wrong" he continued. "The part we have to understand is how many Rabbits are there in the stew and how many Rabbits are there in total. The question tells us that there were no leftovers. We can read this in two ways, one way is that there was nothing left from the soup after they had eaten it, but it can also mean that there was nothing leftover after preparing the soup, i.e. when John made it. Reading it the first way adds no extra value to the question, so it is therefore most likely that the second way is the correct one. If we know that on Monday eight Rabbits had died, then if there were no leftovers then that would mean that there were eight Rabbits in the stew. We also know from the question that the Rabbits *'each looked very nourished; after all they would be, because they had eaten one Rabbit'*. The key here is to understand the use of the word 'each', the position of the semicolon, and the use of the word 'they'. Semicolons can imply the same as the word 'because', and the word 'they' coming after the semicolon indicates the subject to the left of the semicolon, which is 'each Rabbit'. Therefore this last sentence, when read literally means that each Rabbit looked nourished because each of them had eaten one Rabbit each, whereas the text is clearly intended to misdirect the reader to think that they had all eaten one Rabbit in total. Therefore" he concluded, "if each Rabbit had eaten one Rabbit, and eight Rabbits were in the stew, then the total number of Rabbits that John had on Sunday would be eight!"

"Can you say that again Pete" said Jules, scratching her head.

"Ah" said Pete, "but I haven't finished yet" he added. "If you look further into question four then there is yet more misdirection. One line reads 'And there were no leftovers, even the Rabbits loved it'. This is clearly implying that it was not only the Rabbits that ate the stew, but it must have been also John, and that he also, if you follow the same logic I just stated, was one of the 'they' that was nourished because he had eaten one Rabbit. Therefore, this means, as there were eight Rabbits in the stew, then for 'they', meaning the family again, to all eat one Rabbit, then John on Sunday must have had SEVEN Rabbits, plus himself."

Jules was gob-smacked, and could hardly believe it. Pete had to go through it several times, but the logic made sense, and was really the only logic that made sense, when you applied all the parts of the questions.

Pete then continued. "Now that we know the answer to question four, we can now go back and answer questions one and three correctly. For question one" he said pausing to let Jules catch up. "If we now know that he put all eight Rabbits into the stew on Friday, then the answer to the question 'how many did he not bury', must be twelve. This is since he obviously did not bury the four that were alive, and he used the other eight in the stew, so he buried none of them, so he did not bury twelve."

Jules dared not interrupt as Pete was now in full flow.

"And finally" said Pete, "if we know that he had seven Rabbits on Saturday, and we know that he only had four rabbits after Monday the week earlier. Then on Thursday, he must have bought an extra three. We can only assume that they were all females due to the intention of the question, but there is no evidence in either way that the Rabbits were male or female."

"So" said Jules, "the answers are?"

"The answers are" said Pete, "twelve, nine, three, and seven."

"Are you sure?" she asked him, because she had been completely lost and needed to go through it later at her own pace.

"Yes, I am 100% sure" said Pete.

"But what do we do with four numbers?" asked Jules; "we were supposed to end up with a value and a position?"

"Well" said Pete, "that's the first part of the clue" and he read the first part out again for Jules.

Add up the numbers that make the sum of the answers one to four then you will find the number you are looking for. Then take one step back and on the right you'll see, the position of which it has to be.

Pete continued. "If we add up the answers: twelve, nine, three and seven" he said, "then we get the value thirty-one."

"But that's the answer we got yesterday" said Jules.

"Yes, I know" he replied, "strange isn't it. I mean, we get the answers to the questions completely wrong, so completely wrong that it is clearly so obvious the answer is wrong, but it is correct. That got me for some time, because I was convinced that it was a sign that my answer was wrong. But the more I read it the more I was convinced that I was right."

"So thirty-one is the answer then?" asked Jules.

"No" said Pete. "Because we have not done what we were told. We were told to add the numbers that make the sum of the answers" he added. "The sum of the answers is thirty-one, but the numbers that make the 'sum of the answers', i.e. the numbers that make thirty-one, are three and one" he said, "and if we add those, we get the answer 'four'."

"So the answer is four" said Jules.

"Yes" said Pete, "at least for the first part. The clue then tells us to take one-step back and look to the right to see the position. Well, physically taking one-step back and looking to the right makes absolutely no sense. But in mathematics, to take one step back is to look at the result to the step you had taken previously to getting your answer. This means that we got the answer four from adding the numbers three and one from the value thirty-one. Thirty-one was the result to the previous step, which was to add the four individual numbers from each of the four questions. Looking to the right of thirty-one we see..."

"One" said Jules who had understood this part completely.

"Yes, absolutely" said Pete, again smiling at her.

"This means that the answer to Verse Five is number four and position one" she concluded, and sat back to applaud Pete.

Jerry, having heard the applause, put down the Book of Gred and walked into the kitchen. "What's up?" he asked them.

"Pete has solved it" said Jules, "and he was brilliant!"

"Ah, it was nothing" he said modestly, and he went on to repeat the whole story to Jerry, several times.

One hour and two mugs of Earl Grey tea later, Jerry was so impressed that he actually kissed Pete on the side of the face, much to Pete's embarrassment. He then went over to his piece of paper and updated his latest status:

Verse	Position	Number
5	ONE	FOUR
3	THREE	THREE
1	FIVE	FIVE

Jerry was so ecstatic he broke open a bottle of his most expensive white plonk from the local supermarket, and they toasted their success.

"How is the book coming along, Jerry?" asked Jules.

"Oh it's fine so far" he replied, "I have learned loads about the origin of the Good Lord and the Guardians, but I still have a long way to go. Plus" he added looking at Jules and Pete, "you know that sitting and reading is not one of my strongest talents; I find it difficult to concentrate and my mind wonders off, so I have to keep coming back and re-reading."

"I know exactly how you feel" said Jules, smiling at Jerry; after listening to Pete explain that last Verse her head was spinning in all directions.

It was now however getting late in the evening. Pete suggested to Jerry that he forward the email to his private email account and then he would look at it tomorrow and see if he could crack it for them.

Jules also suggested that she slept at home tonight, as Jerry needed to concentrate and read his book, and she had some tidying up at home to do. She would come over in the morning and Jerry could tell her all about the book.

They all agreed. Pete would come over tomorrow evening, and Jules would come over around half past ten in the morning. Jerry said goodbye to them both, gave Pete a hearty handshake and thanked him again, and then gave Jules a long kiss goodnight.

After they had gone, Jerry decided that he would read the rest of his book in bed. First, however, he would need to tidy up again, as his apartment was a mess; there were papers and bits of clues all over the place. He had forwarded the email that was Verse Four to Pete, so he collected all the scraps of paper they had used to solve Verse Five and put them all into the wastepaper basket in his Den, which was already half full before he even added these papers to it. He decided that he would keep the original picture that he had printed of the Verse Five test, and hang it up on the wall in his Den, as a memento, but he could not find any drawing pins, so he left it on his desk; he would handle that tomorrow.

All he needed to do now was to get undressed and clean his teeth, get into bed, settle down, and read the remaining three-quarters of the Book of Gred.

Withdrawal

It was early Thursday morning. Lord Dell was sitting in his spacious study in his Mansion, furious with the lack of progress that he had made so far in tracking down the Chosen One, or the remainder of any of the Guardians. It was now almost two full days since he had sensed the presence of 'someone', which he assumed was a Guardian, in London. As with all situations like this, the trail went cold fairly-quickly. However, a residue of power, a sort of shadow, always remained behind at the place where a Guardian, or someone with special magical powers, had been. The moment that Lord Dell sensed the presence of someone with magical powers in London, he had spent every moment he could trying to further sense where in London the person, or persons, had actually been. Of course Johnson and Smith, who had not an ounce of magical powers between them, were of no use whatsoever in this exercise. However, once the magical Being had been detected, then he would be able to go to the scene and deal with the individual, and use the talents of Johnson and Smith to keep away any interfering mortals, like the police.

Lord Dell had sensed that the Being was in London and he had managed, while in his mansion, to isolate the presence to the north of the river Thames. While this was a big help, it still meant that the area they had to actually search, remained massive.

While the Good Lord was still powerful and could still hide the presence of a Guardian's magical powers, the closer the Evil Lord got to the Guardian, then the easier it became for the Evil Lord to actually sense him. This was how it had worked with Gavin du Faire; Gavin had wandered far from the Good Lord, at the time when the Good Lord's powers were weakening. At a certain point in time, Gavin ended up really close to the Evil Lord, such that he was only a few metres away from him, whereas he was over a hundred kilometres away from the Good Lord. This meant that the weakened powers of the Good Lord were then not sufficient to hide the Guardian's presence, and so the Evil Lord could sense him, track him down, and ultimately destroy him.

Lord Dell was angry because he had not yet found out where the Guardian was actually hiding. He knew that he had been in London and there was a strong possibility that he was still there. He knew this because the residual shadow of his magical powers was still strong. The moment he had sensed a presence, that other day, he immediately got dressed, and then tried to isolate where the presence was in London by passing his hand close to his special map of the UK in his study. Upon narrowing the search area to above the river Thames, he had ordered his car to take him to London, where he had spent the rest of the day, and the entire next day, driving and walking around London trying to narrow down the search area.

However, now it was Thursday, almost two days later, and he could still sense something. This puzzled him slightly. If it was a Guardian who resided in London, then why had he only just now sensed him? Were the Good Lord's powers rapidly degenerating? If it was a Guardian who had just travelled to London, just as the first Guardian had, then his residual power shadow should have disappeared by now. Something was strange, and this intrigued Lord Dell even more than usual.

'It had been so easy to kill the first Guardian' he recounted to himself. Nevertheless, he had been making progress, and his trip to London yesterday meant that he had now managed to track the residual shadow down to an area in London, known as Mayfair.

'One last try' he thought to himself, and he immediately ordered his car to take him, Johnson, and Smith to Mayfair.

All through the journey, Lord Dell was excited; he could not wait to get there.

Meanwhile at the Safety Depository, Mr de Gaunt was going about his normal daily business, unsuspecting that he was close to being 'identified' as a Guardian. The Depository was not a busy place; clients came and went, but in the most cases, clients were very secretive and did not regularly come to the centre, for fear of the police or the relevant tax authorities.

This Thursday however, Mr de Gaunt was expecting one of his most important, and most wealthy of clients. This was a client of such importance that he alone dealt with him, and he had informed the staff that at just before eleven o'clock that morning, they should all go off to lunch, and just one guard would remain. The staff had of course not at all questioned their instructions; it did not do to ask too many questions when working in such an establishment.

Lord Dell and his sidekicks arrived in Mayfair just before ten o'clock. They all got out of their car and started walking down Park Lane. Lord Dell could sense what he was sure was a Guardian, even stronger now. He was continually standing up very tall and, it seemed, sniffing as if to sense in which direction to go to track his prey. Johnson and Smith were merely following in their masters footsteps, making sure that he was not interrupted by anyone.

There was much traffic on the streets, for this was London in the morning and it did not make any major difference that it was July; the roads were still busy. Lord Dell would have to proceed with caution, as he did not want to draw any attention to himself. They continued to walk in the direction of the depository, although they had, at this moment in time, no knowledge of their final destination.

As eleven o'clock approached, the staff at the depository followed Mr de Gaunt's instructions, and all went and had their extended lunch break. Just after eleven o'clock, a spotless black 2006 Rolls-Royce, pulled up outside the depository and a tall, middle-aged, silvery-haired, slightly overweight gentleman stepped out, and walked quickly towards the entrance. Mr de Gaunt opened the door for him, and let him in.

Mr de Gaunt welcomed the man as if he was an old friend, and immediately showed him into one of the small rooms where, shortly afterwards, the one remaining guard brought to him a sealed black metal box.

This box was not as heavy as the one which had been brought to Jerry that other day; in fact it could be said that this appeared to be a normal box with a normal content, if anyone knew what a 'normal content' actually meant in such a place like this.

The gentleman was only in the room for a few minutes, when the guard returned to collect the box. He then shook Mr de Gaunt's hand and left into his waiting car. It was a very mysterious visit, but Mr de Gaunt appeared neither to be bothered, excited, or unduly concerned, in any way.

Meanwhile Lord Dell was closing in on the depository; he had already crossed into Park Street and was now standing outside the main building. He had also noticed the silver haired gentleman leave the depository and get into his car. Lord Dell felt that this definitely had to be the place, so he primed Smith to go into the building and say that Lord Dell wanted to open an account and would be arriving in a few minutes time. Mr de Gaunt was always happy to get new clients, and he had of course heard of Lord Dell, as had everyone else who walked in the same social circles as Mr de Gaunt.

Lord Dell in the mean time had walked back to his car and told his driver to drive him and Johnson up to the entrance of the depository, and then to wait for them until they came back out.

The car pulled-up outside, and Lord Dell and Johnson got out and went in. As he walked through the door into the reception area, he immediately sensed the Guardian. He looked around to see who was in the reception area, to try to see which one was the Guardian. It was obviously not the guard, but who was it?

Mr de Gaunt now knew that he was in big trouble, for he had also sensed something when Lord Dell had reached the entrance. Fearing the worst, he had immediately dashed behind a secret panel just to the left of the reception, in order to take some time to think about what to do and how to tackle the person he now knew to be the Evil Lord.

Lord Dell walked around the reception area. The guard approached him.

"I am sure that Mr de Gaunt will be straight along Sir" said the guard, and he showed Lord Dell to an immaculate red cushioned settee, and invited him to sit and wait. Lord Dell and Johnson duly obliged, followed by Smith who had been waiting in the reception area for Lord Dell to arrive.

As the guard turned to go back to his post, Johnson struck him from behind, and he immediately fell to the ground.

"Where are all the guards?" asked Smith. "Surely a place like this would have more guards, more security?"

"Did you not see who had just left?" asked Lord Dell, knowing already the answer that was about to come from both the lips of Johnson and Smith. Of course, they did not know. "The previous gentleman" Lord Dell continued, with a tinge of distain to his voice, "would not have wanted anyone to see him. The place is almost empty, but will not be for long. Now lock the doors and move the guard out of sight."

They obeyed his commands instantly. Lord Dell then continued to walk around the reception area. Mr de Gaunt however had already started to make his escape; he would follow the secret tunnel into the storage room and then leave via one of the back exits.

Lord Dell looked around the reception area, sniffing as he did. He very soon found the panel, opened it, and immediately told Johnson and Smith to run down it.

"We must get to the Guardian before he escapes" shouted Lord Dell, and they started running as fast as they could.

Mr de Gaunt had heard them coming; you would have had to have been deaf not to hear them. The tunnel was not long, but it had several corners in it, as if it was following the contours of the rooms outside. Clearly it was a tunnel within the walls of the building. Mr de Gaunt stopped and hid just around one of the corners. The noise of Johnson and Smith running towards him was getting louder and louder the closer and closer they got. Then, suddenly, he saw Smith; he was in front, obviously the fitter of the two.

De Gaunt stretched out his right arm and lifted the palm of his hand up towards the oncoming Smith. He then released a brilliant beam of pure white power from his palm which shot towards Smith, hitting him straight in the chest. The force of the beam lifted Smith clearly off the ground and threw his now spinning body about three metres backwards before it landed with a loud thud on the ground, right in front of the oncoming Johnson.

Johnson stopped and bent down to feel if Smith was ok. He was still breathing. Lord Dell arrived behind him.

"He'll be ok" he said. "He's just stunned. Quick, we must prevent him from escaping" referring obviously to the Guardian.

Johnson ran on ahead of Lord Dell, who also picked up his speed. He had not planned to lose Smith, and he did not want to lose Johnson either. He would sort out Smith later, before they had to leave, but now he had to get to the Guardian before he fled into the outside streets.

De Gaunt was feeling pleased with himself; he had reduced his pursuers down to two, but he had not yet tackled the most dangerous one, the Evil Lord himself. He had not previously known that the Evil Lord was in fact Lord Dell and he was sure that the other Guardians did not know either, so if he could only get that information to them then it might give them an advantage.

De Gaunt came to the end of the passage and opened the secret door that led into the storage room. It was a big room in the basement of the depository and it was filled with many large crates, mostly stacked on top of each other several crates high, but not, it appeared, in any structured way. He looked around, and then ran inside, trying to hide between some of the crates that were on the side of the room furthest away from the secret door he had just exited.

Johnson burst through the door, maybe rather to hastily.

"Wait" screamed Lord Dell, but it was too late. De Gaunt had levitated one of the large crates and hurled it across the room towards them. Lord Dell arrived just in time, and diverted it at the last moment, leaving a cowering Johnson kneeling on the ground with his arms over his head.

"Thank you my Lord" he said gratefully.

"Quick, Get up" demanded Lord Dell. "Let's split up and search the room; he is still here, I can feel it."

"Yes Sir" he replied, and immediately went looking in the opposite direction to his master.

De Gaunt thought to himself. 'First I must get rid of the mortal. Then I might be able to make my escape while he is trying to protect him'.

Lord Dell however had other ideas. He was not hiding behind the crates as Johnson and de Gaunt were; he was not afraid, for he knew that he had the superior powers and he could handle anything that the Guardian could throw at him. His only challenge would be to make sure that the Guardian could not escape; he had to capture him and destroy him, and now.

De Gaunt made another crate fly through the air towards Johnson. Lord Dell stopped it again, just in time, but this time he had seen where it had come from. He dashed over to the spot, but it was empty. 'Clever' he thought to himself. 'This Guardian will not be as easy at the last one' and he immediately called over to Johnson who joined him at his side.

"Stay by me" he said to him, and of course Johnson obeyed, thinking anyway that this was also the safest place to be.

For the next few minutes they both very slowly and very carefully walked around the storage room looking for De Gaunt.

"Enough of this stupidity" suddenly called out Lord Dell, who had clearly lost patience and began blasting crates into pieces. "I will find you Guardian" he yelled. "Your previous colleague ran out of places to hide from me and so will you" and with maniacal laughter he continued blasting crates, to Johnson's great amusement.

De Gaunt knew that he was in trouble. While the Evil Lord was, at this particular moment, blasting crates in the wrong part of the room, he would eventually get to him. He therefore had to get to the second secret door, the one that led into the security room, which was sadly empty of guards, but full of technical equipment that safeguarded the depository. Alas however, this was only capable of safeguarding the depositary from mortal attack, and not from the most evil force that the planet had ever known.

De Gaunt edged around the sides of the crates. There were however still about ten crates that were between him and the second door, and that door appeared to have a crate right in front of it. He had no choice; he would also have to start destroying crates if he wanted to escape. Maybe he could get away with it as the Evil Lord was destroying crates one by one, would he notice a few more?

He raised his hand. Several crates exploded, but the timing had not been his best. Johnson had detected something was not right, but Lord Dell was so engrossed in destroying his crates that he had not noticed. Johnson looked around. He could not see de Gaunt and he was not sure. De Gaunt decided that he must continue, so he sent a bolt of power directly into the remaining six crates and they exploded, flying through the air. This time Johnson saw them and they were in a completely different place to where his master had been aiming. He then saw de Gaunt running towards the door.

"SIR!" he shouted, pointing over to the figure of de Gaunt, who was now at the door and opening it.

"What you…" shrieked Lord Dell, who was about to lambaste Johnson for interrupting his enjoyment, when he saw Johnson pointing. He looked in the direction and saw the figure of de Gaunt disappearing behind the door.

"Good work" he shouted, as he set off towards the door, calling out "follow me" to the already pursuing Johnson.

De Gaunt reached the security office and closed the door behind him. He tried to put things against it, but he could hear Lord Dell and his sidekick approaching. What could he do? He could not telephone the White Horse or Mystic for neither of them had a mobile phone. He could not speak to them via his mind either, because the presence of the Evil Lord so close to him was blocking any attempt to communicate with them via telepathy. He would have to call Annie or Diana using the phone. Annie would be in the pub and Diana in the library and he did not have much time. He picked up the phone and started to dial.

Meanwhile Lord Dell had reached the door and felt that it was sealed.

"Stand back" he said to Johnson, who duly obliged. Lord Dell then proceeded to send a power bolt toward the door, a bolt of such intensity that the whole door and everything wedged against it the other side, immediately exploded into smithereens. The debris from the exploding door went flying all over the security room and towards de Gaunt, hitting him, and knocking him to the ground, before he had time to finish dialling the phone number.

De Gaunt laid there on the floor, helpless, as the Evil Lord walked over to him.

"Well Guardian" he said, in his cruel merciless voice. "Your race is run." He then called over to Johnson who immediately ran behind de Gaunt and tied his hands together.

"No more magic from you for the moment" said Lord Dell to the tied de Gaunt, who Johnson then lifted onto the chair, where he sat, staring at the Evil Lord, Lord Dell.

"So it was you" said de Gaunt, as he stared at him.

"You had no idea?" he replied. "You and your pathetic leader will never defeat me" and he laughed, joined rather pathetically by Johnson.

"Now Guardian" he continued, "tell me where it is. Tell me where you have stored what you protect."

"You are too late" replied de Gaunt, "for the Chosen One has already seen it."

"Ah" said Lord Dell, "that is excellent, for now I will see what he looks like, and then I can find him to."

"Damn" muttered de Gaunt, for he had not thought of that. Here they were in the middle of the security room, with all the security tapes of the last week, and he had led them both straight to them. He had failed; he had let down the other Guardians, and more importantly, he had let down the Good Lord, both current and future.

"Yes indeed" said Lord Dell, who appeared to have been reading his very thoughts. "Quick Johnson" he added, as he scanned the banks of tapes around him. "Look for the tapes for last Tuesday and we shall see who has been here."

Johnson obeyed immediately, looked through the logs, and found the relevant tape. He placed it into the nearby video tape machine which immediately started playing pictures from all of the cameras in the building.

"Select the main entrance camera" said Lord Dell, "he must have come in through the front door like everyone else."

"Good thinking, my Lord" replied Johnson, and immediately started pressing buttons until the picture of the entrance area came up on the main screen.

Several people walked in and out of the reception area. De Gaunt was also watching, for he knew that Mr Dumbarton would be next, accompanied by...

"WHAT!" screamed Lord Dell in frustration, "how can that be?" There was one elderly woman in the middle of the screen, accompanied by two vague shadows, but he could not make out who they were, or even whether they were men or women.

"Zoom in on the old woman" commanded Lord Dell. Johnson immediately obeyed and started twiddling a knob which then focussed and repositioned the picture so that everyone in the room could see an enlarged face of an elderly woman. Lord Dell walked towards the main screen and studied the picture.

"Fortune Teller" he muttered in a frustrated, but also slightly impressed, voice. "You shielded them from me. Clever, but maybe not clever enough" he continued. "Follow them Johnson; let's see what they do, where they go, and what they get."

Johnson wound the tape forward and they watched them going into the corridor. He switched camera and then watched them walking into the small room.

"There is no camera in there my Lord" said Johnson.

"Never mind" replied Lord Dell. "Let's watch and see what is brought to them."

The tape went on further and the next sight they saw were the four guards carrying the heavy box into the small room.

"That's it" screamed Lord Dell, "it has to be. Quick Johnson, find out what box it is."

De Gaunt was devastated. While temporarily relieved that Mystic had protected the identity of the Chosen One, he was now sure that Lord Dell would find out the box number, for it was in the security guards logs, and he duly did.

"Its box DT92" he said, "but I don't know the pin number, that is not recorded."

"Never mind" said Lord Dell. "We don't need that, I have other means of opening the box" and he stood up and switched the camera to the vault area where the deposit boxes are stored.

"Make sure that nothing is recording" he said to Johnson, who immediately removed the tapes and made sure that all recorders were unplugged. Come, we go" he said to Johnson. "Leave him here; I will reduce my power omissions so that he can watch me make his failure complete on television" he concluded, laughing as he and Johnson left the room, picking up a map that was conveniently on the wall showing which cameras viewed which area.

The way to the vault was easy to follow, and in only five minutes, Lord Dell had blasted his way into the safety deposit area. They searched high and low for box DT92.

"Over here" called Johnson who had found it, immediately pulled it out, and carried it over to the table, right in front of the camera that was covering the vault area, right in front of Mr de Gaunt's view.

Harrie de Gaunt was watching on the television screen. He was gutted; his whole world was about to be destroyed and the clue that he had successfully protected for the last seven hundred years was about to be handed over to the Evil Lord himself. Then he noticed something; Johnson had carried the box all by himself to the table. It had taken four security guards to carry it from the vault area to the viewing room when the Chosen One had viewed it, and the same four guards had been required to carry it back. He was positive that no one else had been to the box in the mean time. Johnson did not look as strong as the combined strength of four guards, so how had Johnson carried it alone?

Lord Dell was also wondering the same thing, and looked strangely at Johnson, but then turned his eyes away and focussed on the box. He directed a jet of red energy from his right fore finger directly onto the lock on the box and the lid sprang open.

"AARGH!" he cried out, in a piercing scream of anger. "I am too late" he shrieked, picking the box up and throwing it across the room, just like a young child having a tantrum. Lord Dell turned his head and looked up towards the camera. "You knew Guardian, didn't you?"

"What's up Boss?" asked Johnson, who had clearly lost the plot.

"The clue has been solved" said Lord Dell, as he continued to stare into the camera. "It has vanished. A clue can only be solved once, after that it has to be replaced with a new and different clue."

Harrie de Gaunt was ecstatic. The clue had gone. He had done his job properly; he had not failed and the Chosen One must have correctly solved the clue and was now on the way to find the Prize.

"Quick" said Lord Dell, as he looked back to Johnson, "we must get back to the Guardian before the others return."

De Gaunt knew that he was now in deep trouble. However, his time was now finished, his job was done, meaning that he could now move on; the last seven hundred years had been great, but now he was tired and he could finally finish, and with that thought in his mind, he leant back in his chair, closed his eyes, and finished his life.

Lord Dell and Johnson arrived back in the security room to find the lifeless body of de Gaunt sitting in the chair. Johnson had also spotted from the security screens that there were now people arriving outside the main entrance and were looking worried that they could not get in.

"Sir" he said, pointing to the security monitor.

Lord Dell looked over and quickly thought what to do next.

"Go back and get Smith" he said to Johnson. "Bring him to me. I have some unfinished business here."

"Yes my Lord" replied Johnson, who then ran off back up the secret tunnel.

"Now then Guardian" said Lord Dell, towards the dead body of Harrie de Gaunt. "You still have something for me" and he raised his right forefinger towards him and a jet of pure red energy left his finger and hit the lifeless body of Harrie de Gaunt straight in the chest.

The result of this was again immediate. De Gaunt's dead body rose slowly off the chair to about one metre high and hovered there for a few seconds. Then a thick beam of brilliant white light left his body and made its way up to the top most parts of the security room, where it formed itself into a brilliant white cloud.

"Come to me!" called out the Evil Lord, as he leant back with his arms wide open and his chest held as far out forward as it could possibly go. The white light reformed itself into a beam and shot down from the ceiling, hitting him straight in the chest. Lord Dell again, just like in the museum, screamed with delight, as if he had just consumed the best meal he had ever tasted. After this, he collapsed to the floor on his knees together with the lifeless body of Harrie de Gaunt, which also fell down with a large thud as it hit the ground.

Lord Dell was out of breath, exhilarated, but again he was now stronger; nourished by the magical force that had left the body of the Guardian, and which now supplemented his own powers. He jumped to his feet, stretched out his arms, and shouted, "YES!" The power emanating from his body became so immense that everything in the security room was shattered instantly into tiny pieces. Flames lapped around everything that was plastic or metal, melting it completely, and especially destroying all of the video evidence that was stored in the room.

Johnson arrived back in the room with Smith's arms over his shoulders, dragging him along. Smith was now starting to stir and recover some consciousness.

"Quick, hold on to my shoulders" Lord Dell commanded.

They immediately obeyed and as their hands touched his shoulders, Lord Dell turned slightly on the spot and all three of them vanished, instantly reappearing inside Lord Dell's car, which was still waiting for them parked outside the depository. As they appeared, Jensen slowly pulled away and drove off, back towards Lord Dell's mansion.

Outside the depositary, the police had started to arrive.

Decode

It had taken Jerry quite some time to read the Book of Gred, but like a true sportsman he had seen it through to the very end, and finished reading it around two o'clock in the morning. Later on that same morning, around eleven o'clock, he was rudely awoken by someone ringing his front door bell, which he went to answer without bothering to get any further dressed; for whom else could it have been on a Thursday morning?

"I hope you don't answer your door to everyone, just wearing your underwear?" remarked Jules who then, as a kind of punishment, grabbed hold of his boxer shorts and yanked them hard, pulling them down to the ground, such that they were now covering his feet. Smiling, she then walked passed him and went into the kitchen, leaving Jerry exposed to the elements, or was it Jerry's elements, exposed.

Jerry quickly closed the door; he did of course have neighbours who, he felt, would not be so keen to see him wearing his boxer shorts as ankle warmers, especially in the middle of summer.

"Did you sleep well?" he called out to Jules, as he started pulling back up his boxers and walking into the kitchen, but not necessarily in that order.

"Hello Mystic" called out Jules, smirking as she did so.

Jerry rapidly finished the last part of repositioning his boxer shorts and then turned to face the window, in exactly that order. However, and luckily for him, Mystic was not waiting by the window, but Jules was having a good laugh to herself by the kettle.

"Tea darling?" she said to him, trying without much success, not to lose control.

"Yes please dearest" replied Jerry, who was now desperately thinking of some awful revenge he could wreak on her, much later of course; once she had forgotten and would not be as prepared as she undoubtedly was now.

Jules turned around and fetched the cups from the cupboard, still not quite able to look at Jerry without giggling. Jerry on the other hand was now sitting at the table watching Jules trying to control herself, and thinking how much he had missed her the previous night.

"Tell me about the book, did you finish it yet? Did you learn anything?"

"It was really interesting, and yes I have finished it, and yes I have learned loads" he replied. "I'll go and get it" and he went into the bedroom to fetch the book, boxers still firmly secured in their correct place.

Jules did not follow him into the bedroom, although she had a very strong urge to do so. She felt that he might be preparing a trap for her, so she put the cups of tea on the kitchen table and sat down waiting for him to return, which he did within a minute, wearing a t-shirt and a pair of shorts.

"It was really interesting" began Jerry, "all about this young lad called Gred who was the first Chosen One around six thousand years ago."

He continued for about fifteen minutes recapping the entire story, as Jules sat listening, riveted to her chair. Jerry finally concluded his recap with the testament of Gred, and commented about the two blank pages at the end, which he assumed were for making notes, although nobody had dared deface the book as it was still in, what he assumed was, its original condition.

"Wow, I always wondered what Stonehenge was used for" said Jules. "Am I allowed to read it as well?"

"I don't see why not" he replied, pondering slightly, "I mean it doesn't say it's only for me, and I trust you anyway" he added, smirking as he said so.

"I should hope so to" she replied to him; if he could not trust her then whom could he trust?

"I have to shower" continued Jerry, making sure that he quickly changed the topic of conversation. "Then I have to go and get some shopping, so if you want to read it now?"

"I'll read it later" she replied rather furtively, "after I have scrubbed your back" and with that they went together into the bathroom.

Some time later, but still before breakfast in America, they both emerged, fully refreshed from the shower. Jerry went and got dressed while Jules opened the window to let out some of the hot steam. She then went into the living room, turned on the television and snuggled into the settee, exhausted, but feeling quite content.

It had just passed two o'clock and the news had started. Something was going on in London. Jules turned up the volume and immediately heard a reporter telling her story to the nation.

"Police were called to the depository on Park Street around twelve thirty today, as staff could not get back into the building."

"JERRY!" she called out frantically.

Jerry came running into the room, not quite fully dressed, and sat next to her. Both of their eyes were now staring, as if glued to the television screen.

"It is not clear what has happened here" continued the news reporter, "but there are several police cars here, and about five minutes ago we saw an ambulance carry away a body from the scene. The body appeared to be dead as it was fully covered."

"What's happened?" asked Jerry.

"Don't know" replied a concerned looking Jules. "Jerry, we were there only the other day."

"I know" he added, also sounding very concerned, "and Mystic said she was worried that we were in danger."

"And I made that awful joke" murmured Jules, feeling even more guilty now. "I wonder if Mystic knows that something has happened."

"I don't know" replied Jerry, "I am sure she does, she tends to know about all sorts of things before they happen doesn't she?"

Jules did not know; she was still watching the television with a look of concern all over her face.

"Ah, here is a police spokesman" said the news reporter as someone emerged from the entrance and walked under the police cordon. "Inspector Jones, Inspector Jones, Claire Smith from Local News here, can you make a comment and update the nation on what has happened?"

Inspector Jones had heard her calls. He seemed reluctant, but came anyway over to the television camera. Jules and Jerry, and the entire nation, watched and listened in eager anticipation.

"Good afternoon Miss Smith" started Inspector Jones. "Police were called to the scene at twenty minutes past twelve this afternoon, by members of staff who were not able to get back into their place of work after their lunch break. It seemed that they had an early lunch break today, and that there was very few staff on duty inside at this time, which is very strange in itself. We shall of course be talking to all the staff, and also later to all clients who visited the depository today, and in the last week" he added.

Jerry and Jules turned and just looked at each other, their eyes wide open, and their previous looks of concern had now changed to looks of total fear, which spread right across their faces.

"One person was found dead when we arrived at the scene. It appeared also that there has been much damage done inside the building, but it seems that only one of the deposit boxes has been opened" continued the Inspector. "The box is empty, but of course we don't know if anything was in it."

"Was there anyone else hurt?"

"Not that we know of at the moment" answered Inspector Jones. "We are searching the building and..."

But what was to follow they never found out, for a uniformed policeman had tapped Inspector Jones on his shoulder and had whispered something in his ear."

"I am sorry Ms Smith" said the Inspector, "but I must return into the building. Please excuse me" and with that he hurried away, almost running back into the building with the officer.

"Wow, what do you make of that?" asked the reporter to the entire nation.

"Well that was extremely fishy" said the TV News Anchor, "have you heard anything else Claire?"

"No I am afraid that's it for the moment" she replied. "I will obviously remain here at the scene and update you the moment we hear anything. This is Claire Smith reporting for local news in Mayfair, London" and with that the picture faded and returned to the news anchor in the studio.

"Oh Jerry" said Jules, sounding rather scared. "Who do you think was killed?"

Jerry did not answer, but he somehow felt he knew what the answer was. He did not want to say anything though, for he was not certain enough.

"I feel that this is bad" he said to her. "What do you think we should do?"

"What should we do?" replied Jules, now with a look of astonishment on her face. "Why should we do anything? I mean we haven't done anything wrong have we?" she added, looking at Jerry as if he was a policeman and she was practicing her alibi.

"I know we haven't" he said. "Oh what would Mystic do now?"

"Well, let's ask her; she said you could speak to her didn't she?"

"Yes, I had forgotten that" he replied, feeling a tad stupid to forget something so important. He then shifted a bit away from Jules on the settee, put his closed hands over his eyes, and looked down at the floor. He then called inside his mind. "Mystic! Mystic! Hear me!"

As he did this he felt that he could see the inside of his living room within his mind, and he was moving, he was moving towards the window, out of the window, across the street and then straight into Castle Street and towards the sign post outside the Dog and Bone pub. As he moved closer to the signpost, he saw Mystic sitting at her normal place. She immediately turned to look at him.

"Yes Jerry" she said, or at least he thought she said; he could hear her voice within his mind, it was as clear as if she was standing next to him.

"Something terrible has happened at the depository."

"Yes, I know" replied Mystic. "It is Guardian Three; he has been killed by the Evil Lord; he was after the Verse."

"Was it the man we met on Tuesday?" asked Jerry.

"Yes."

"What should I do?"

"You shall do nothing" replied Mystic. "Stay where you are. I will visit you tonight. Do not go out unless you have to."

"I need to get some shopping at the local supermarket. Is that ok?" he asked, feeling a little stupid as he asked it. "It's fairly close, so it won't be for long?" He felt like he was a young child again asking permission from his parents.

"Yes, that should be ok" replied Mystic. "I will of course be close by. When are you leaving?"

"Oh, in about ten minutes I think. Is it ok if Jules come with me?"

"Yes of course" replied Mystic. "I will be watching you from a distance, just in case. Behave normally as if nothing has happened; you do not want to draw any attention to yourselves."

"Ok" he replied.

"Oh and Jerry" she added. "Make sure that you finish getting dressed first."

Jerry felt himself blushing slightly, but decided not to further comment on the state of his current attire.

"See you later then" he said, and with that last message he lifted his head up, took his hands away from his eyes, turned his head and looked at Jules, who had been watching him with admiration, but also a touch of concern, wondering whether he was ok or not.

"What did she say?"

"A Guardian has been killed" said Jerry.

"What… who?"

"It was that Mr de Gaunt, the owner of the Depository. He was a Guardian and the Evil Lord has killed him. Mystic thinks that he was after the clue in the box."

"Oh my dear" replied Jules, "he was such a nice man."

"Mystic said that we should stay here and do nothing" he added, looking at Jules in a strange way. "But it is ok for us to first get some shopping."

With that, Jerry then went back into the bedroom to finish getting dressed. Jules sat back down staring at the television. The news had continued onto other items, but Jules still watched closely, for she was sure that they would go back to the scene before the bulletin finished.

Jerry walked back into the living room, now fully dressed. "Shall we go then?" he asked.

"No, let's wait a moment; it's nearly finished" answered Jules. "I am sure they will go back to the depository before the end."

"Ok" replied Jerry and they both sat there watching the last few minutes of the news bulletin.

"And finally" said the news anchor, "we now go back to Claire Smith who is ready to give us an update from Mayfair. Claire, what's the latest?"

"Yes, hello John, hello everyone, this is Claire Smith reporting live from Mayfair in London, where police earlier this afternoon forced their way into the depository. One person is dead, and his body removed from the scene, but the police have not yet published the name of the person. Inspector Jones has just left the scene but he refused to talk further to us. He did not look in a good mood; that's two people murdered in mysterious circumstances within two weeks, and both in the heart of London."

"Ok Claire, thank you. We must stop now as we have run out of time" and with that the news bulletin ended.

"Come on then" said Jerry, turning his head to look at Jules; "We should go now."

With that, they stood up, put their shoes on, and went down together to the local supermarket.

On the way, Jerry looked around for Mystic, but he could not see her anywhere. He felt however that she was close by. He did not know how he could feel this, but he just knew. They arrived at the supermarket without any problems, did their shopping – Jerry getting a new stock of plonk, and they went back to his apartment to wait for Pete, and later Mystic, to arrive.

When they got back to the apartment, Jules sat down and started reading the Book of Gred, while Jerry put away the shopping. It was now four o'clock. Pete had telephoned Jerry while they were shopping and had agreed to meet them at Jerry's at five. After putting the entire shopping away, Jerry made some tea for Jules and himself, and then went to sit down in the living room, together with Jules who was, by now, half way through the book.

"This is very interesting" she said to him, as Jerry handed her a cup of steaming hot tea. "I mean, he was so young" she added, sounding very impressed.

Jerry sat in his favourite armchair. He felt tired, yet he had not done that much today so he did not really understand how he could be so tired. He concluded that he must be getting out of shape; normally a couple of hours in the shower would not have had this much effect on him, even if it was the best couple of hours he had spent in a bathroom in a long time. Yet, he was now feeling very tired, and while sitting in his favourite, most comfortable, armchair he quickly drifted off into a deep sleep as Jules read away in peace and quiet.

As Jerry fell asleep, he started to dream. It was a strange dream and he suddenly realised that he had been there before, just the previous night in fact. This was now the second time that he had dreamt that he was in a hospital. However, was he ill? Was he injured? No, he did not think so, for he was walking in a corridor, and he was looking for someone. There was blood on the wall. There was a fight going on outside, someone was injured, but he did not know who. Then he heard a voice. It was a woman's voice. Was it Jules? Was she with him? Was she injured? He called out to her. She did not answer. Was she dead? No, that cannot be. He would call again, but still she did not answer. What was going on? Then he felt something hit him across his face. It hurt. He could not see what it was. It hit him again, and then again, and then he heard the voice call out "Jerry." It was Jules' voice, and she was calling his name. Again and again she called him, and then he suddenly woke up to find Jules leaning over him, looking terrified and getting ready to land another whopping great slap right across his face.

"Whoa" he called out, "what is it? What's the matter?"

"Are you ok?" she asked, trembling and almost crying with fear. "You were in some kind of nightmare; you were having a fight in your dream. It was scary."

"I'm fine" he replied. "Did you hit me?"

"Yes. Sorry, but I had to wake you up. People can die in their dreams you know."

"No problem" said Jerry, who was quite glad that he now knew who had hit him, and more importantly, the next time that he went into a hospital he would not have to worry about someone hitting him across the face.

"What were you dreaming about?" she asked.

"Oh some weird dream about a hospital" he started to say, then after realising who he was talking to, he decided not to say any more, for fear of having to be interrogated for several hours.

"It was nothing" he added, "how long was I asleep?"

"Oh only for an hour" she replied, "I'll go and make us some tea" and with that she disappeared into the kitchen.

Jerry remained sitting in his armchair trying to recap the dream that he had just been having. He had been in a hospital and was looking for someone, or something, but he did not know who, or what. There was also a fight going on, but had Jules been there, or not? He was not sure anymore.

Pete arrived shortly afterwards. He had his laptop with him. As he needed a power connection for the laptop, they decided to work in the Den, on Jerry's desk. Jules wanted to finish reading the Book of Gred as she only had a few pages left.

"Is it Christmas already?" asked Pete, with a mischievous smile developing across his face.

"Of course not" replied Jerry, "why do you ask?"

"Well" began Pete, "I thought it must be; it seems as though you have been doing some tidying up; this desk is normally full of papers and the waste paper basket empty. Now the desk is clear and the bin is half full."

"Oh, ha, ha" replied Jerry, as he walked out and left Pete to set up, while he went to put the kettle on.

As he went into the kitchen, he saw Mystic at the window. He of course opened it and she flew in. "Mystic is here" he called out to Jules, who was still in the living room.

Jules got up and walked into the kitchen; she would read the last page later. Pete also walked in from the Den.

"Hello Pete" said Mystic.

"Hello" replied Pete, who then instantly froze and stared straight at the raven.

"You can hear her?" said Jules, looking astonished towards Pete, and then turning her head to look at Mystic.

"Of course he can" replied Mystic, "otherwise, why else would I have said hello to him?"

"But, why, how?" asked Pete, still apparently in an advanced state of shock.

"It is now time" replied Mystic, who then went on to ask them all to sit down, where she started updating them all on the events of the day. By the end of the meeting, Jerry and Jules had not learnt much new, but Pete was fascinated by the story and by the fact that he was now having a real conversation with a raven.

"What about the police?" asked Jules, "will they come and visit us?"

"No, it is not likely. I mean they will, but not because of the depository. But when they do Jerry, be careful not to say anything about the depository" said Mystic, who then wished them a good night and flew off into the clear blue sky.

"Wow" said Pete, "that was really weird."

"I wonder what she meant about the police?" said Jerry, appearing to be thinking his thoughts out aloud. "I mean, why would they visit us if it was not to do with the depository?"

"I've no idea" replied Jules, who generally was feeling that so many things were happening that it was difficult to keep track. In addition, this whole adventure had all started like a challenging treasure hunt. Now people were dead, killed in fact, and magic was being performed all over the place. It scared her.

Jerry turned to Pete. "How is the code breaking going?" he asked.

"Slowly" replied Pete. "It is quite difficult you know. It's not only about breaking the code; it's also about understanding that riddle."

"Can I see what you have done so far?" she asked.

"Yes of course" replied Pete, and they all got up and went into the Den.

In the Den, Pete had set up his laptop and had a spreadsheet open. Pete had obviously typed in the coded letters and was applying various transformations to them in order to try to decode the message.

"How do you know when you have got it right?" asked Jules.

"Well, it's a bit of trial and error really" he replied, "but when the words start to make sense then you know you are on the right track. When it all makes sense then you have most probably solved it. The thing with codes is that they must always follow a set of basic rules; otherwise, you can never decode the message. The problem is to find out what the rules are, and in some codes they are almost impossible to work out."

"What have you found out so far?" asked Jerry.

"Well I am sure that the secret to the code is hidden in the riddle" replied Pete, and went on to read back the riddle to them.

A used computer is what you need in order for this code to read. Key in the letters on the board, and work it out for your reward. But one decipher does not do, a Chinese rule is needed to. And then add on the four answers from five, repeating to keep your Quest alive. But then again to keep your Quest alive, the rule is back to Jackson Five. So now I've told you a bit too much, but this is how I made it such.

"The secret" he continued, "is to correctly convert the letters into numbers, and then to apply numerical operations onto the numbers, which then when translated back into letters make no sense. If you then apply the same mathematical operations to the coded letter, but in reverse, then you will find the original message." He then began to write down on a piece of blank paper.

"For example, if we assume the letter 'A' equals one, and I add five to it, then it is turned into the letter associated with six, which is 'F'. Then if I have 'F' which I know is six, and then take five away from it, then I am left with the number one, which represents 'A'."

"But that is easy" said Jules.

"Yes, yes of course" said Pete, "but that was just an example" he added looking at Jules who seemed to think that he was making fun of her. "For Jerry" he quickly added, causing them all to laugh.

"What does the first line mean?" she asked.

"Well that got me for a bit" replied Pete, "I mean what would be the difference between a new or a second hand computer. Obviously, the operating system on an older computer would not necessarily be the latest, but that did not make sense, as the newer PC's are normally the faster. But then it hit me" he continued. "It does not mean a used computer, it meant a..." and he re-wrote the word on the piece of paper.

US'ed

"What does that mean?" asked Jerry, obviously none the wiser.

"Well" said Pete, "it means that you need an American, U.S, configured computer."

"Why?" asked Jules.

"Each country" said Pete, "has a normal default configuration, and they are all different" he continued. "In the second line it talks about 'keying in the letters on the board,' which is obviously referring to the keyboard. Each country has a different keyboard and some of the letters are in different positions."

"Are they?" said Jules, "I never knew that."

"Well, how many times have you used French or German keyboards?" asked Pete.

"Well, never" she replied. "In fact I have only ever used a computer in England."

"That is the same with most people" continued Pete. "They only use computers in their own country which are all normally configured the same. The default is the English version, or most often known as the US-English or 'QWERTY' keyboard. It's called 'QWERTY' because these are the first six letters that appear on the top row."

Pete then ran his fingers across his keypad, where the letters appeared according to the traditional QWERTY keyboard.

$$Q \ W \ E \ R \ T \ Y \ U \ I \ O \ P$$
$$A \ S \ D \ F \ G \ H \ J \ K \ L$$
$$Z \ X \ C \ V \ B \ N \ M$$

"This originates from the very first IBM personal computers that came out many years ago, which were also based on the original typewriter keypads that existed before that, since the main use for personal computers in the beginning was for word processing, which was mainly used by secretaries. This to me" continued Pete, "is a clue indicating that the first cipher is something to do with the order of the keys, meaning that maybe the letter 'Q' has the value one, 'W' two, etcetera all the way up to 'M' what has the value twenty-six."

"Does that work?" asked Jules.

"Well it's a bit trickier than just that" he replied. "If you read the third line it says that 'one decipher is not enough', and it goes on to talk about needing a 'Chinese rule' as well."

"What does that mean?" asked Jerry.

"I am not sure" replied Pete. "In computers the word 'rule' has different meanings. It could be referring to the keyboard layout of a Chinese computer keyboard, but I checked those out, and they are the same as the US one, at least the main letters are in the same place. So it must mean something else, but I don't know what" he finished, looking stumped.

"It could mean" said Jules slowly, as if she was thinking as she was saying it.

"What?" asked Jerry, after several seconds had passed with her just looking into blank space.

"Sorry" she said, "it could be something to do with the fact that the Chinese read from right to left."

"You mean backwards" said Jerry, looking confused.

"Well it's not backwards to them" said Jules, "I mean they were reading and writing before we even dreamt about it."

"Oh" said Jerry, not realising what he had said.

"It could be that" said Pete, and he immediately started adding a conversion table into his spreadsheet.

"What are you doing?" asked Jerry.

"Well the spreadsheet" said Pete "has lookup features which allow me to look-up a value and convert it into another value. That is how I converted the letter 'A' into the value one and so on."

"Then what are you adding now?" asked Jules.

"Now I am adding a reverse 'QWERTY' code/decode" said Pete. "In this table the value 'Q' has twenty-six, down to the letter 'M' which has one'.

"Ah I see" said Jules. "Does it work?"

"Well the table works" he replied, "as long as I put the letters in the correct alphabetical order, but it still doesn't give an answer that makes sense" he continued, looking rather frustrated.

"What does the next line mean?" she asked.

"That also stumped me a bit" said Pete "and it could also be where I am going wrong. It talks about the 'four answers from five'. I mean what five? However, then I suddenly realised. The previous clue was called Verse Five, and it had four numerical answers, so they must be the four answers from Verse Five." He then paused looking a bit depressed, "at least we think we have got the answers right, but if the decode makes no sense, then it could mean that we were wrong somewhere."

"Oh no, not that test again" said Jerry. "Let's assume that it's right for now."

"Yes, that's all we can do" said Pete "and I hope that we are right. The four answers we got were twelve, nine, three, and seven. We must obviously have to add these to the previous result to get the next cipher."

Jules then thought of something. "But remember" she said as Pete listened intently. "We got the same answer with four different numbers in the beginning didn't we?"

"Yes" he replied, although this time he did not appear to be downhearted by her comment. "That could also be a double check though, since maybe if you got the original answer right, but the steps wrong, then the steps would not work in the next clue."

Jules and Jerry were both starting to look a bit lost, but they did not want to admit it, not yet anyway.

"And the fifth line" asked Jules, "what does that mean?"

"Ah" said Pete, "yes, that bloody song, I had forgotten how much I hated it when I was younger."

"What song?"

"Well I didn't remember it at first" he continued, "but then I was listening to the radio and they were playing oldies from the seventies. Didn't you ever see that cartoon program about the singing group 'The Jackson Five'?"

Jerry cast his mind back to his childhood. He had seen quite a few cartoons in his youth and now he remembered the one about the young American black boy band that were huge in America.

"Yes, I remember" he said, with a smile spreading across his face and he started humming to himself the signature tune.

"YES!" shouted Pete, "exactly, that song; It used to drive me mad."

"I liked it," said Jerry, "it was great."

"What Song?" cried Jules in frustration.

"A, B, C" sang Pete, trying to line up with Jerry's humming.

"It's easy as 1, 2, 3" added Jerry, "A, B, C, … 1, 2, 3."

"Ok, ok" said Pete. "You can stop now Michael" he called out laughing. "That's exactly it; it is telling us that the code is changed and it is now that 'A' has the value one, 'B' two and 'C' three, all the way up to 'Z' having twenty-six."

"Ah" said Jules, with a deep sigh, "and the last line?"

"The last line" continued Pete. "The last line is just telling us, that that's all we need to know. But it still doesn't make sense" he concluded, sitting there arms folded and looking frustrated.

Jules looked at the spreadsheet and looked at the Verse Five. After several moments of doing this, she turned to Pete and looked at him, smiling.

"What?" asked Pete, "have I made a mistake?"

"The last line" said Jules, "it tells us that this is how he made it, not how to break it."

"What do you mean?" he asked again.

"You have followed the instructions in the code, in the order that they were written" said Jules, "but the Verse says 'this is how I made it such'. This to me means that to decode it you have to do it backwards. Start with line five and then work your way back through the Verse."

"Brilliant!" screamed Pete, realising that Jules had obviously just experienced another eureka moment. "How could I have been so stupid to miss that?"

"Oh, you idiot" said Jerry laughing, as he went to make some more tea while Jules stayed and watched Pete frantically changing his spreadsheet to do everything, but in the opposite order.

He finally finished the formulas and pressed the magic 'F9' to recalculate, and it still did not make any sense. "Shit" he muttered under his breath.

Jerry walked back in with the tea. "What, it still doesn't work?" he asked.

"No" said Pete, looking dejected and starting to drink the tea, forgetting that it was a little too hot.

"Let's run through it to make sure you have not made any mistakes" said Jules and they both went through it together.

But then again to keep your Quest alive, the rule is back to Jackson Five.

"So, the first step is to convert the coded letters into numerical values according to the rule that A=1, B=2, C=3" said Jules.

"Yes" said Pete, "and that's exactly what I have done."

"Let me see the formulas for the first three letters" said Jules checking the formulas. "Yes, that's right" she concluded, making Pete feel like he was having his work checked by his teacher. "We'll copy them across to the other letters later once we checked the whole thing."

"Fine" said Pete, "that gives us H=8, T=20, A=1."

They both read the next, meaning the previous sentence from the Verse.

And then add on the four answers from five, repeating to keep your Quest alive.

"The four answers we got were twelve, nine, three, and seven" said Pete. "We need to now subtract those from the sequential letters. Twelve from the first, nine from the second, three from the third, seven from the fourth, and then repeating we continue with twelve from the fifth etcetera" he concluded.

"Yes, but wait" said Jules. "If you subtract twelve from eight then you get a negative number. What does that mean?"

"In that case" answered Pete, "if the result is less than one then I just add twenty-six, which means that the code just continually repeats itself. This means that previously I had the results eight, twenty, and one. Subtracting twelve, nine, and three, gives me then twenty-two, eleven, and twenty-four" he concluded.

"Yes, I agree" said Jules. "Now, the next line" and they both read out aloud:

But one decipher does not do, a Chinese rule is needed to.

"Now" said Pete, "I need to convert the numbers back into their equivalent letters, and then apply a transformation based on their position in the QWERTY keyboard, but back to front."

"How do you do that?" asked Jules looking puzzled.

"Oh it's quite easy actually" said Pete. "First I just convert the number into its equivalent QWERTY position; that is 1-Q, 2-W, 3-E etc, but then I need to apply the Chinese rule and convert it backwards so that Q gives 26, W-25, E-24 etc. I have to do this in two steps. First convert the current values we have twenty-two, eleven, and twenty-four, into their letters, and then convert these letters into the new code" and he showed her the two lines on the spreadsheet that did this.

Jules looked slightly puzzled. "Why are you using QWERTY?" she asked.

"Because that is taken from the first and second lines" replied Pete.

"But we haven't got to those lines yet" stated Jules. "According to the order we have now read the text, we are still applying the Jackson Five rule."

"What?" said Pete, and he grabbed the text from her hand and started looking very closely at it and at the formulas in his spreadsheet.

After several moments he sat back, sipped his tea, turned to Jules, and said, "you're right; I missed that" and he immediately set about changing his translation table such that it used the normal code.

"Now" said Pete, a bit more relaxed. "We had the values twenty-two, eleven, and twenty-four, they convert into the letters 'V', 'K' and 'X', and converting them back into numbers, using the rule now that A=26, B=25, C=24, down to Z=1, then we get the new numbers five, sixteen and three."

"Yes" said Jules, "I agree."

"Now the final lines" said Pete.

Key in the letters on the board, and work it out for your reward. A used computer is what you need in order for this code to read.

216

"Now" said Pete, "we need to convert the numbers five, sixteen, and three, back into letters, according to a US QWERTY keyboard. This gives us" he concluded, "the letters 'T', 'H' and 'E'."

"THE" shouted Jules, "Pete, its working!"

"Maybe" he said, but he was now also getting excited. "I need to copy all the formulas across to all the other letters" which he immediately did. He then placed his finger over the F9 key, closed his eyes tightly, and then pressed down on the magic 'F9' recalculate key, and the following text appeared on his screen.

THECODEDNUMBERISFOURANDITGOESI NPOSITIONTWO

"What does it say?" asked Jerry, as he stood up in excitement and almost knocked the tea over the computer.

Pete still had his eyes closed; he could not look. Jules was busy writing it down. She then sat back, turned and smiled at Jerry. "It says" she said. "The code number is four and it goes in position two."

"HOORAAY" shouted Pete, "it works!"

"BRILLIANT" shouted Jerry, and he jumped up in the air as if starting to celebrate when he had just scored a goal.

"Steady" said Jules, who was cowering slightly, scared that Jerry was going to jump onto her shoulders.

Jerry opened the draw of his desk and pulled out his piece of paper that he was using to save the results. He added the result of Verse Four. Now he had four numbers.

Verse	Position	Number
5	ONE	FOUR
4	TWO	FOUR
3	THREE	THREE
1	FIVE	FIVE

"All that is left now" continued Jerry, "is the last number in position four."

He was so excited. "Pete" he said, "send me the original email back with the solution attached will you; I want to keep this one forever."

"Ok" replied Pete, "I'll do it when I get home tonight and log in to the network."

Jerry was so happy; he now had four of the numbers and only one more to go. He of course had no idea where to find the last number; he had not yet even found the clue that would lead to the location of the last Verse. Nevertheless, even that did not bother him now; he had four numbers.

"Let's celebrate" said Jerry.

"What, more plonk?" asked Pete.

"No" he replied; "this calls for a super slap-up meal. I am going to treat you all to an evening out at a restaurant."

"Wow" said the others together. This was special; Jerry did not often delve into his wallet.

"Pete," continued Jerry "as you mostly solved it, you can decide."

"Well I was lost without Jules" he replied, smiling. "And I don't really mind where we go, as long as you're paying of course" he added. "Jules, what do you think?"

"Let's go to The Grid" suggested Jules. "You know the one which was owned by that guy who got killed in the museum."

Pete let out a yelp of agreement, but Jerry was not that sure. It was a bit expensive he thought, but what the hell; now was not the time to be stingy; he had four numbers.

"Ok" said Jerry, "The Grid it is then, and I guess we don't need to get changed. I will give them a call and make a reservation for eight o'clock. Can you check the number Jules in the phone book?"

Jules got the number from the phone book and Jerry made a reservation for eight o'clock, which meant that they only had half an hour before they were due to arrive. This caused a slight panic for Jules; even though she did not have to change, she still had to get ready. The boys therefore waited in the living room while Jules went into Jerry's bedroom to put on her make-up.

The Grid

Mystic was sitting on her usual signpost outside the Dog and Bone pub, and was feeling very worried; she was thinking to herself, trying to determine the best course of action to take. Mystic had been gazing into the future, something she did whenever she felt that something in the present was not looking good, and she was now even more worried. She had been on full alert ever since her recent trip with Jerry and Jules to London; she knew of course that the Evil Lord had detected their presence whilst they were in London, but now he had killed Guardian Three. She had warned Jerry to stay at home, but in the thrill of solving the code he had decided to go out, and not only that, he had decided to go to the only place in Cambridge that the Evil Lord knew of; the restaurant that was owned by Gavin du Faire, the Guardian he killed first. Mystic decided that she must call for assistance; it was a matter of life and death. She closed her eyes and looked down to the ground.

"Four, hear me" she called from deep inside her mind, and then followed her thoughts towards the city of Birmingham, in the midlands of England.

"Four, hear me, it is urgent."

"Yes Mystic" replied Guardian Four, "I hear you. What is it?"

"I told them to stay at home" she started, sounding very desperate, "but they are going out this evening. I am afraid that I will not be enough. You need to get here fast; I fear that he is coming."

"I'll be there straight away" she replied, and they both immediately stopped communicating.

Mystic however was still worried; if he was indeed coming to the restaurant then she would most likely need even more help; Guardian Four and herself would not be enough. There was only one course of action; she had to check with the Good Lord himself.

"Yes Mystic" replied the White Horse, in answer to her hail.

"My Lord" she said, trembling now with fear as she continued as fast as possible to tell him the latest status.

"You did well to call me Mystic" he answered, after listening to her whole story. "I will immediately travel with One and we will get closer to you. My powers are still strong enough to hide you all from him, if I am close enough. I need not come into the centre of Cambridge, but I will remain on the outskirts. If you need our help, then we can come in closer. One will stay with me Mystic. Good Luck!"

With that, they broke off their communication and Mystic then flew away towards the Grid Restaurant.

Jules was finally ready about ten to eight. The boys obviously did not appreciate that this short time qualified for an entry into the Guinness Book of Records as the fastest time ever to get ready for a restaurant, at least by Jules. The boys of course had been ready the moment the decision had been made, although truth be told, Pete looked as though he had been ready two days earlier. They walked out of the apartment and out onto the street, towards the restaurant.

The Grid restaurant was not that far away from Jerry's apartment. It was in fact just around the corner. Even so, it still took at least five minutes to get there.

The joining of two small typical old-fashioned local high-street shops formed the modern styled The Grid restaurant. It had two large shop windows at its front, each displaying several strategically placed tables with clear views out onto the main street. The sign over the front was hand painted with the words 'The Grid' in a dark crimson red, against a grey background. The entrance was a grand old affair; a sort of mixture between an old fashioned castle with a gleaming twenty-first century solid glass door, which was positioned between the two large windows facing the main street. Jerry, Jules, and Pete walked in and were met by the Maitre de who invited them to the bar area to take some refreshment before their meal.

The inside of the restaurant was very cosy; there were many tables, each covered with pure white table cloths, decorated with dark red napkins, thick red candles, and solid comfy chairs, each with red velvet cushions and backs. The dimmed lighting together with a central water feature, which gently trickled its contents onto a lower basin, accompanied by some soft background romantic music, set the tone of the whole restaurant.

Jerry, Jules, and Pete sat at the small bar and ordered some aperitifs, or to be correct, Jules ordered an aperitif while Jerry and Pete each had a small lager. After a few minutes, the Maitre de showed them to their table.

They had a nice table; that is to say that the table was the same as all the others, but it was in a nice position towards the far corner of the restaurant, away from the windows and the walls; a place where they could have some privacy. The restaurant was busy; with the people in the bar, and the people already sitting at their tables, Jerry reckoned that it was about eighty percent full.

Jerry had his jacket with him. It was not the done thing to keep your jacket on, or to put it on the back of the chair. Jerry therefore stood up and went to hang it up on one of the coat stands that were strategically positioned around the restaurant. This particular one was quite close to a table, occupied by a beautiful thirty-five year old woman, with long black hair, brown eyes, perfect teeth, wonderful succulent lips, and a pair of breasts that Jerry would have happily got lost in for a few hours, before he had been going out with Jules of course. The woman was sitting together with a similarly aged young man, who was expressing the deep felt emotions that he had for her.

"I love you Fiona" he said as his eyes gazed into hers, "and I want to spend the rest of my days with you."

"But you know I can't" she replied, "I am married" and with that the young woman, obviously named Fiona, looked up and saw Jerry. She felt a tad embarrassed; she had not seen Jerry approaching, but she guessed that he had most likely heard their every word. She looked at Jerry and her whole face immediately went the same colour as the napkins. Jerry however just simply smiled and winked at the young lady, hung up his coat, and then returned back to his table with the intention of taking her secret to his grave. This behaviour from Jerry was indeed an improvement from his earlier adult days; in those days he would not only have taken her secret with him, but most likely her telephone number as well.

The waiter brought three menus to their table and asked if they would like some more drinks. Pete obviously felt that it was an excellent opportunity, especially as Jerry was paying, to educate Jerry on the delights of French white wine, so he immediately asked for the wine list, which the waiter had with him of course, and handed to him straight away.

The menu was amazing. Jules just did not know what to have, as everything just sounded delicious. There was a mixture of Italian, Asian, English, Irish and Indian dishes, all brought together in a way only the French could do. It was mouth watering just reading it.

"What do you fancy for starter?" asked Jules, as she looked deep into Jerry's eyes.

The whole menu of course bemused Jerry. Normally the biggest choice he had to make was choosing whether or not to have cheese in his burger, or which type of curry to eat after his normal twelve pints following the day's football match. Running through the list of choices on this menu was quite a daunting task.

"I think that I am going to have the shrimps" said Pete, "they go excellent with this Chablis I have just chosen."

Menu

Starters

Tomato Bisque
Creamy tomato based soup, with a hint of Chicken.

Hot and Cold Noodles
*Ribbon noodles and pasta
served with vegetables and scallions.*

Eggplant Parmesan
*Oven baked eggplant in breadcrumbs, served in a
tomato sauce, topped with cheese.*

Roasted Shrimp
*Shrimps, Roasted on a pan,
and served with a mayonaise dressing.*

Sea Food

English style Fish & Chips
*Succulent Cod, fried
in breadcrumbs and served together with Chips.*

Italian Seafood Pasta
*Italian mixture of Shrimp, Lobster & Squid, served
in a tomato pasta, topped with cheese.*

Stuffed Lobster
*Thyme, Rosemary and Parsley are stuffed into
a prime Lobster, served with Lemon, Onions and Scallions.*

Asian Grilled Salmon
*Oriental style Salmon, cooked on
Charcoal, in a sauce of Dijon Mustard, Soya and Garlic.*

Japanese Unagi
*Unagi no kaba-jaki. Unagi is an eel, skewered and grilled in kabayaki
sauce, served with plain rice together with kimo-sui (unagi liver) soup on the side.
Only available in summer.*

Meat Dishes

Oven fried Chicken
Tender Chicken coated in
breadcrumbs and served on a bed of rice.

Korean Style Beef
Thin and long skirt steak,
served on a bed of Noodles.

English Steak Sandwich
Old fashioned English Entrecoute Steak in a sandwich,
served together with chips and side salad.

Red Beef Chilli
Ground Beef cooked
with Red Chillis and served on a bed of rice.

Irish Stew
Extra Guinness stout added to a Traditional Lamb based Irish Stew
cooked with vegetables, to give a wonderful taste.

New Delhi Curry
Tangy hot Chicken Curry
with vegetables, served with special Indian rice.

Tenderloin of Beef
Oven roasted Tenderloin of Beef,
served with vegetables and a red wine sauce.

Deserts

Hot Chocolate Tart
Naked chocolate tart, served hot,
sprinkled with powdered sugar and cocoa powder, and served with Whipped Cream.

Eclairs
Three Chocolate Eclairs,
served with Whipped Cream.

Pavlova
Raspberry Pavlova meringue,
topped with forest fruits and served with Vanilla Ice Cream.

Apple pie
A home made Apple Pie,
served together with Vanilla Ice Cream.

Cheesecake
Creamy Cheesecake,
served with strawberrys and whipped cream.

Knight Sakatini
Knight cocktail of Sake,
Chocolate and Hazlenut Liquers, with some special added ingrediants.

"What's bisque?" asked Jerry.

"It's a soup dearest" said Jules, suggesting that he read the details underneath the title of each dish.

"Oh" said Jerry, "then why don't they just say tomato soup then?" he frowned.

Pete and Jules smiled at each other but chose to say nothing.

"I think that I am going to have the eggplant parmesan" concluded Jules, after a long debate with Pete. Jerry stuck with the soup.

"What about main meal?" she asked. "I am going to have the 'Japanese Unagi'. I had that once before in another restaurant, it was really great" she added. "Apparently they are only nice in the summer."

"Steak sandwich for me" said Jerry, "and I hope they have some ketchup with it."

Pete turned the menu over to look at the other side, but there was nothing on it. He therefore decided to stay with the fish; obviously wanting to enjoy the Chablis, although he had seriously considered taking the Irish stew with extra Guinness.

"I am going to have the 'Asian grilled salmon'" he concluded; "I can't wait to taste that oriental style salmon, cooked on the charcoal grill. And I bet that Dijon, soya, and garlic are just superb."

They gave their orders to the waiter as he brought over the wine that Pete had selected. Jules suggested that Pete sample the wine, as she did not want to risk Jerry saying that he did not like it, and asking for lager instead. As it turned out Jerry liked it a lot, and after ten minutes, the first bottle looked as though it would not last much longer.

Meanwhile over by the entrance, three men had just arrived and were having detailed discussions with the Maitre de over where they should sit. Jules looked over at the three of them. One seemed healthy and fit looking, like Jerry but a bit older. One of the others was shorter and stockier. The middle one however also looked good. He was middle aged, with short blond hair, and was thin. He had a pale white skin, and his eyes were Jules' favourite colour, blue. She was not sure why, but the man in the middle looked vaguely familiar. The three men sat at the side of the restaurant that was furthest away from Jerry, Jules, and Pete. They did not go to the bar; otherwise Jules might have been able to see them a bit clearer. The waiter went straight to their table and gave them their menus.

Jerry ordered another bottle of the same wine; he had really liked it and was already talking about looking for it the next time he went to his local supermarket. The waiter brought them their starters and, as expected, they were magnificent; the food just melted in their mouths, each with rich flavours that just erupted like an explosion of taste onto the pallet. Jerry was clearly not used to this style of eating; nevertheless he was also clearly enjoying it. Jules of course wondered if his enjoyment would last when he got the bill, but she would also offer to pay some of it, since it really was not fair to let him pay for everything. Pete however did not seem bothered one bit by the prospect of allowing Jerry to foot the whole, and nothing but the whole, bill.

The waiter collected their empty plates; there was not a scrap of food left on any of them.

"Was everything ok, Sir, Madam?" he asked.

"It was excellent" they all replied, and they could not wait for the main meal.

Jerry noticed that the young couple; Fiona and her friend, were still deep in discussion. He also noticed however that she, every now and then, looked over at him and smiled. 'Still got it then' he thought to himself, mentally slapping himself on the back.

Their third bottle of wine arrived shortly before the main meal. Jerry was now in full flow and kept thanking the two of them for all the help they had given him. He knew that he had only progressed so far, thanks to the two of them.

The main meal arrived and it was again mouth watering. Jerry did not regret his steak sandwich one bit; it was the most delicious sandwich he had ever eaten. Jules loved her eel and Pete enjoyed his salmon enormously. After the main meal, they again consulted the menu to decide what they were going to have for desert.

Jules noticed that one of the three men that had earlier entered the restaurant together, the blonde one, was now walking around the restaurant, saying hello and generally greeting some of the other guests.

"He must be famous" whispered Jules, whilst nodding her head over in the direction of the blonde man.

"He does look familiar" replied Pete, as he looked over in his general direction.

"Yes, I think that I have also seen his face somewhere before" added Jerry, although he could not think where. "He'll be over here soon if he carries on like that" he muttered as he sat back in his chair. As he did so, he noticed again the loving couple sitting in the corner; she also had seen the blonde man and was now watching him and not really paying any attention to her dinner guest.

'He must be really bad' Jerry thought to himself as he looked at her dinner guest. He felt this because he was sure that he had not seen any wedding ring on the woman's finger, even though he had clearly heard her say that she was married when her dinner guest had expressed his love for her. In addition, she had been eyeing Jerry all evening, and now she was looking at the blonde guy.

Suddenly there was a brilliant flash of light, which lit up the whole restaurant, followed almost immediately by an ear-blasting sound of a large explosion, which had just erupted outside in the main street. The sheer force of the blast had rocked the whole restaurant, but curiously none of the windows appeared broken. Some of the guests had automatically covered their faces, or ducked behind their chairs, and some had even dived under their tables. The force of the explosion had even knocked some guests off their chairs. The blonde man however, had just turned to his two colleagues and then all three of them rushed over to the door to take a look outside.

Lord Dell, Johnson, and Smith got to the door of the restaurant and ran outside into the main street, looking for the source of the commotion. There was a fire over by one of the shops and smoke was pouring out of the broken window. Lord Dell looked around at all the devastation, and then he saw her, the black raven he knew was Mystic, she flew off before he had a chance to do anything about it. People were now also coming out of the restaurant and from some of the other buildings in the street, so he could not risk using his powers here.

"So fortune teller" whispered Lord Dell, "where now has your Chosen One run off to?" and with that he ordered Johnson and Smith to check the neighbourhood and look for anyone acting suspiciously. He also went further outside onto the main street and decided to search in the opposite direction.

Inside the restaurant there was much commotion; people were discussing the explosion and fantasising about why it had happened. It seemed that no one was really hurt inside the restaurant and even the restaurant itself was undamaged.

Within very short time, the emergency services started arriving on the scene and the fire brigade quickly put out the fire in the shop. Several ambulances had also arrived, but no one appeared to need them, and the police had started interviewing people in the streets and also inside the restaurant.

"Look" said Jules, "there is that Inspector Jones. He was the one on the television news the other day, at the depositary."

"Was he?" said Pete.

"He was also at the museum" added Jerry.

"And don't forget" whispered Jules, "this is the restaurant of the murdered man from the museum."

"Do you think the two murders are linked in some way?" suggested Pete.

"Maybe he was a Guardian as well?" whispered Jules, making sure that no one else could overhear her speculation.

Jerry was sure that she was right, but he did not say anything as he did not want her to worry, plus it would look suspicious if they were whispering together when the police came over, which he suspected they would, for Mystic had already predicted it.

The Inspector walked into the restaurant and looked around the room. He pointed to each of his assistants and assigned them a section of the restaurant.

"Ladies and Gentlemen" he called out. "My name is Inspector Jones from the police. We need to take your names and addresses so that we can make contact with you later to discuss if you saw anything suspicious upon your arrival or while you were here this evening. If you noticed anything, then please let one of the officers know, and we will then make urgent contact with you. Thank you for your cooperation everyone" and with that he turned to the officers and told them to get going.

The Maitre de also then spoke. "Ladies and Gentlemen, as no one was hurt during the explosion, and the restaurant is not in any way damaged, I have asked the police if they are ok with us continuing to serve you your meals. They have agreed, so normal service will resume immediately" he concluded.

"Good" said Jerry, as several of the guests started to applaud the decision. "I was looking forward to that cheesecake."

"Me to" added Jules, licking her lips; "all this excitement has made me even hungrier."

Within ten minutes the waiter had delivered their deserts and they had started eating. Pete had ordered the raspberry Pavlova and it looked, and tasted, delicious.

As they were half way through their desert, the officer assigned to their section of the restaurant came over to them and asked if he could have their names, which they duly gave.

"Did you see anything suspicious?" he asked.

Pete and Jules both said no, but Jerry added that the blonde man was no longer here and he had dashed out just after the explosion.

"Yes" said the officer, "several other guests made that comment as well; thank you Sir. Is there anything else?"

"Yes" said Jerry, "why is Inspector Jones here? Isn't he the one who is leading the investigation into the murder in Mayfair and the murder in the Natural History Museum?"

The officer paused; he was not expecting people to start questioning him.

"Are the two murders in any way linked together? Did Mr de Gaunt know Mr du Faire?" continued Jerry, but even he now knew that he had just gone a step too far.

"Thank you sir" said the officer, "I am afraid I am not at liberty to answer those questions as of now, but I am sure that Inspector Jones will be making contact with you shortly" and with that he left to go over to talk to the young couple sitting in the corner.

"Why did you ask all that, Jerry?" asked Jules; "remember what Mystic told us."

Jerry had remembered, albeit rather too late.

"Sorry" he muttered, "it just all came out. Come on, shall we finish up here, pay and get home. We can have tea at my place."

The others agreed and they finished up as fast as they could, still enjoying the taste sensations as they passed through their mouths.

The waiter brought over the bill, which did not even seem to shock Jerry, who paid with his credit card. Jerry then got up and fetched his jacket from the coat stand and they all left, saying goodbye to the police as they walked out the door.

"That's the one" said the officer to Inspector Jones, as they were standing a few yards away from the entrance. "He was asking all those questions; even knew the name of the deceased at the depositary."

"Did he now, Williams" replied Inspector Jones, thinking hard and looking at Jerry as he left the building, "what is his name?"

"Jeremy Dumbarton" said Officer Williams.

"Dumbarton" said Inspector Jones, "Dumbarton" and he immediately got onto his mobile phone and called the police station as the officer watched Jerry, Jules, and Pete leave the building.

"I thought so" said Inspector Jones, after he had finished the call; "he was at the depositary a few days before the incident. We shall have to speak with Mr Dumbarton. Make sure you note down his address Williams, and plan him in for first thing in the morning."

"Yes Sir" replied Williams, who duly proceeded to call up the station and make the arrangements.

When Jerry, Jules, and Pete arrived home, they went straight into the kitchen where Jerry put the kettle on to make some tea. Jules and Pete had already started an intense discussion about the evening's entertainment, so Jerry decided to go and put his jacket on his bed before he rejoined his colleagues in the kitchen.

"That meal was lovely" said Jules, changing the subject as Jerry returned, "we must do that again some time, Jerry" thinking that although Pete was great company, next time they would do it together, alone.

"Yeah it was very nice" said Jerry, "what did you think Pete?"

"The wine was great" he replied, "and the food even better; I haven't eaten so well in years. I will definitely go back there again."

They sat around the table discussing the events of the evening and drinking their tea. Around eleven, Pete decided that it was time that he left for home, and so he thanked Jerry once again, said farewell to Jules, and then left, taking his laptop with him.

"Don't forget the email mate" called out Jerry, as Pete walked out the door.

Jules decided to stay the night with Jerry and so they went straight to bed.

The Police

When Pete awoke the next morning, he decided that he would send the email and the spreadsheet to Jerry, before he got dressed. He got up and walked over to his PC, which was always on and connected to the Internet, and started-up his email application. Pete searched all through his Inbox and in several mail folders as well, but he could not find the original email that Jerry had sent to him anywhere, and therefore concluded that he must have deleted it earlier by mistake. Whilst Pete did not generally delete emails, he had done so in the past, so it could quite easily have happened again. He did still however have the spreadsheet that he had used to decipher the coded message, and as it was now getting late, he decided that he would quickly just send that to Jerry, and then look again for the original email later on. Pete therefore created a new email, attached the spreadsheet to it, and then sent it off to Jerry, before hurriedly getting dressed and dashing off to work.

Jerry awoke about half past nine and then proceeded to take a shower, trying not to waken Jules as he slipped out of bed. At a quarter to ten however, he heard her enter the bathroom. She walked over to the shower and opened the door. Jerry was ready for her; he was now fully refreshed after his few minutes under the tingling hot water, but Jules was not; she was standing there, wearing his dressing gown, and looking at him with a concerned look on her face.

"Jerry, the police are here; they want to talk to you. It's that Inspector Jones."

"What?" he replied from under the hot jet of water that was gushing all over his body, "can't he come back later when we're dressed?"

"No, that's what I suggested as well. He said it was no problem; they would wait in the living room until we were ready" she replied as she started to close the shower door to avoid getting wet.

"Ok babe" said Jerry, and he turned the shower off, got out, and started to dry himself.

Jules in the mean time had gone back into the living room to tell the Inspector that Jerry was just getting dressed and would be with them shortly. She then went into the kitchen to make some tea.

When Jerry had fully dried himself, he put on a clean pair of shorts and a t-shirt from the cupboard, and then went into the living room to greet the Inspector.

"Good morning Inspector" he said to him, as he extended out his hand.

"Good morning Sir" replied Jones, gripping Jerry's hand firmly and giving it a good hard shake. Both men now knew from this that the other was not going to be a pushover. He introduced himself, and his assistant, Officer Williams.

"Would you like a cup of tea while I finished getting dressed?" asked Jerry.

"That's fine sir" said the Inspector, "I think your lady friend…" because he had already noticed, being one of London's finest, that neither Jerry or Jules were exhibiting the wearing of a wedding ring, "…has already put the kettle on."

"Oh good" replied Jerry, who suddenly got the urge to explain himself a bit. "Normally I would be dressed by now, but we are on vacation this week."

"That's perfectly fine, Sir" replied Inspector Jones, "we have no problem in waiting for you, after all we were in the neighbourhood and we wanted to speak with you first. We will just wait here, Sir" he concluded, and they both sat back down while Jerry went into the kitchen where he found that Jules had indeed already put the kettle on.

Jules gave Jerry a quick cuddle. Jerry could tell that she was slightly nervous and he gripped her body firmly in return.

"It'll be ok babe" he said to her, in his reassuring and comforting voice.

Jules looked at him, smiled, and gave him a kiss, after which she picked up her clothes and went into the bathroom to take a quick shower, to make sure that she would be fully awake when the police started questioning her.

Jerry then went into his bedroom where he quickly finished getting dressed. He then dashed back into the kitchen, before returning a few moments later to the living room, carrying four steaming hot mugs of fresh milky tea.

Jules joined them shortly after, fully dressed and refreshed after her quick shower.

"We are sorry Sir, and Madam, to get you up so early" began Inspector Jones.

"Oh, no problem" replied Jerry, "I was just getting up anyway, and Jules no doubt" and he reached over and hugged her, "would have been up within a few minutes as well. What can we do for you Inspector? Is it about last night?"

"I wonder what you can tell me Sir, about Mr de Gaunt?" said Inspector Jones.

"The depositary manager?" asked Jerry.

"Yes Sir" said Inspector Jones, who liked to try to catch out his suspects by going straight to the point, catching them off-guard and then watching how they struggled to give their replies. This often gave a very clear indication as to whether or not the person was lying.

"Well" began Jerry, who had not been expecting that particular question, but also had nothing to hide, looked straight into the Inspector's eyes and started to reply. "We met him for the first time on Tuesday when we went there to view the contents of a deposit box."

"Which box was it Sir?" asked Inspector Jones.

"Well that is confidential" replied Jerry, still looking hard into Inspector Jones' eyes; "I mean when we left, Mr de Gaunt was still fully alive and kicking so it, and we, clearly had nothing to do with his murder."

Inspector Jones did not look pleased. Jerry was of course correct, but something was suspicious. He, Jerry, had looked at the contents of the box that they found open at the time of Mr de Gaunt's death.

"The box you looked at Sir" continued Inspector Jones "was the same one that was opened in the vault by the person, or persons, who broke in on Thursday."

"Oh, I see" mumbled Jerry, who had indeed suspected as much from what Mystic had already told him. He now also realised why Inspector Jones was pursuing this line of questioning. "Well all I can tell you Inspector" he continued, "is that we removed nothing from the box when we were there, and when we left, the box was returned to the vault still full."

"Yes Sir, we know that" said Inspector Jones. "The security staff provided us with back-up copies of the surveillance tapes and we checked them this morning before coming here. We could see two people, which we now assume were you two, receiving the box, which appeared to be full and heavy, and returning the box within five minutes also appearing to be full and heavy. Although we cannot tell exactly, Sir, if you removed anything, we can clearly see that the box still had some contents in it, and it seemed as heavy when the Guards returned it to the vault as when they removed it from the vault. However Sir" he continued, also looking straight into Jerry's eyes, "when we found the box on Thursday it had been emptied."

"Oh" answered Jerry, "I am very sorry to hear that Inspector, but there is nothing I can do about that, is there?"

"How did you know Sir, that Mr de Gaunt was the person killed?"

Now Jerry had a problem; he could not tell the police that a raven had told him, else they would have thought he was mad. He knew also that the police had not yet released the name of the victim, so the fact that he knew the name of the victim did seem suspicious.

"I called the depositary in the afternoon" began Jerry, trying to think up his story as he went along. "I asked to speak to Mr de Gaunt as I was suspicious" he continued; "for when I got through to the receptionist she just broke down in tears and said to me that Mr de Gaunt was not available and she did not know when he would be back. That was obviously a lie and she was clearly distressed, and in addition" added Jerry, now flowing at full speed, "you guys had not yet released the name of the victim. If it had been just some guard then it would not have been a problem to release his name, so it had to be someone important. I just put one and one together and came up with two" he concluded, feeling slightly proud of himself.

Now it was the turn of Inspector Jones to have a problem. The story seemed plausible, but he would have to check later if a call actually came into the reception, as a log was made of all calls. He now decided to change tact.

"Did you know Mr du Faire?" asked the Inspector.

"No" said Jerry, "I had never met him, had you Jules?"

"No" she responded.

"We obviously have heard about him on the news" added Jerry, "I mean, I read all about him in the newspaper on the Sunday following the museum incident, but apart from that I had never heard of him."

Inspector Jones was now starting to lose some of his normal confidence; Jerry had seemed such a hot suspect before he had met him, but now he seemed a likeable kind of person who just happened to have been in the wrong place at the wrong time. After all, he was nowhere near the depositary on Thursday; the last time a camera recorded his presence at the depositary was on Tuesday.

"Is there anything, Sir, that you can tell us that you think might help us in this enquiry?" asked Inspector Jones, completely changing his tactics again in his line of questioning. This however was also a well practiced technique; and gave the impression that the person being interviewed had won the round. This often led them into a false sense of security, which meant that they said one or two things that they would not have said if they had still been as alert as they were at the beginning of the interview.

"Well not that I know of" replied Jerry. "We told your colleague yesterday evening about the blonde gentleman."

"Ah yes, Lord Dell."

"So that's who he was" added Jules, this had been bugging her ever since she first saw him in the restaurant. "I knew I had seen his picture somewhere before, and I knew he must have been famous."

"Yes Miss" said Inspector Jones, "several people reported that he had been in the restaurant, introducing himself to them, and that he'd vanished from the scene almost immediately after the explosion."

"Yes" said Jerry, "I mean he looked ok, but he was the only one I spotted who left the scene fairly quickly; most of us were still there in the restaurant, getting up from off the floor."

"Yes indeed" said the Inspector, "it is suspicious that he did not stay, but then these sorts do not like to be around when there are reporters about."

"Did you spot anything Miss" he said, turning to Jules.

"No, it's just as Jerry said" she replied, "we were just sitting down and suddenly there was a loud explosion. I was surprised that the windows did not smash, and that nothing inside the restaurant was even broken."

"Did anyone get hurt?" asked Jerry.

"No Sir, no one at all, and we cannot find any proof of foul play. It looks like this one will go down as some kind of accident in the shop where the explosion occurred" concluded Inspector Jones, who was wearing an expression on his face of utmost despair, almost like a hunter robbed of the kill, as the hunted had disappeared into the shadows. At this point Inspector Jones finished his tea and turned to his colleague.

"Ok Williams" he said, "I think we have taken up enough of this couples' time this morning, we can cross them off our list for now and look elsewhere. Thank you Sir, Madam, for your time, we are sorry to have disturbed you" and with that they all shook hands and Jerry escorted them to the door, where they left the apartment.

"What do you think then Williams?" said Jones, as they left the apartment block and started to walk back to their unmarked police car.

"I am not sure" pondered Williams, who gave the impression that he was in deep thought mode, "I mean he is hiding something, that appears to be obvious, but he does not look like the sort who could commit murder."

"Yes, I tend to agree" surmised Jones, "but nevertheless, he has now turned up twice on our radar screen. If he turns up again then it will not be a coincidence" and with that they both got into their car and drove off towards their next suspect.

"Did you really call the depositary?" asked Jules as Jerry returned into the living room.

"No" he replied, "but I could hardly tell them that Mystic told me, could I?"

"Well no" agreed Jules, the concerned look reappearing across her face. "But I think you took a big risk," she continued, "I mean if they do check, and they find out that you lied to them, they will really pull you in and ask you all sorts of questions. Let's hope that they do not check."

"We'll see" said Jerry, "let's play it by ear and see what happens."

"Ok" she muttered, still looking rather worried. "Did you get the email from Pete" she then asked, trying to change the subject.

"I'll go and check" he replied and went off into his Den whilst Jules started to clear-up the mugs from the living room.

"Hey Jules" called out Jerry several minutes later from within his Den, "I got the email from Pete, but I can't open it. Can you help me?"

"Ok" she replied, "I'll be there in a moment."

Jerry was not an advanced computer user by any stretch of the imagination, and had concluded himself that he was more likely to damage or delete something by mistake if he continued trying different things. He had obviously tried to open the email but it seemed to have not worked. Now he decided to wait for Jules to come and help him, before he tried anything else. Jerry looked around his bedroom. It was rather a mess, with clothes spread out everywhere. He started picking them up from the floor and putting them on the back of the chair. He picked up his jacket. It smelt, but not the normal beer smell it regularly had from the Dog and Bone, this time it smelt nice, tasty even, as fond memories from the previous evenings food at the restaurant came flooding back to him. The jacket however seemed to look a bit worse for ware, so Jerry decided that he would take it later to the dry cleaners, and so started to empty out the pockets. In his outer pocket there was just an old napkin from the restaurant, but in the inside pocket he found a menu card, also from the restaurant. He wondered how that had got there; he had not picked it up. He pulled it out and looked at it. Again the fond memories came back to him as he turned it over and looked at the reverse side, where he got the shock of his life, for on the back side of the menu was Verse Two, and it was a Grid.

"JULES!" he called out rather excitedly.

"What is it?" she quickly replied as she came running into the bedroom, the worried look back again all over her face.

"It's Verse Two" he said as he looked at her, smiling. "It was here inside my jacket pocket. Someone must have put it there while we were in the restaurant; I mean there was nothing on the other side of the menu's we saw, was there?"

"No, I don't think so" she said, calming down. "Let me see" and she walked over to him and looked at the clue.

"It looks like one of those grids which you have to make words from" she muttered.

"Oh yeah" agreed Jerry, "I used to do those when I was younger."

"Yes, but this looks different. It says that the instructions are hidden around the edge. Quick Jerry, make some copies, maybe we can do this one before Pete even sees it."

"Yeah right" said Jerry with a touch of sarcasm in his voice. Nevertheless, he walked over to his desk, picked up his mobile phone, took a picture of the backside of the menu, and then radioed it over to his printer where he ran off several copies.

Verse Two

E	E	R	H	T	H	E	T	E	N	F	T	E	N	R
N	E	V	E	S	V	I	R	H	O	O	H	I	E	E
I	N	I	T	I	E	G	E	U	R	N	R	G	V	B
N	O	H	F	X	E	H	R	N	O	E	E	H	E	M
E	W	A	X	T	R	T	N	E	T	F	E	T	S	U
R	T	E	I	G	H	T	W	O	H	U	E	N	I	N
F	U	N	S	R	T	G	R	O	G	R	I	F	J	F
E	S	O	E	I	A	T	I	N	I	N	E	I	I	F
V	E	E	F	D	T	H	R	E	E	N	S	V	S	I
I	S	E	V	E	N	G	U	T	O	S	E	F	E	V
F	O	U	R	E	I	I	O	R	R	N	T	V	V	E
I	N	N	T	H	N	E	F	U	O	W	T	E	E	I
V	S	I	E	I	E	I	C	O	O	W	V	A	N	S
N	I	N	N	N	V	C	U	F	O	E	I	G	H	T
E	X	E	O	E	O	L	E	A	S	T	W	O	Y	W

**Around the edge are the instructions for you.
To tell you how to find the clue.**

They both then grabbed a pencil from the desk, Jerry putting the original menu card inside his desk draw, and went into the living room where they started immediately to try to crack it.

"Let's look for words" said Jules, "and see what we can find."

"Ok" said Jerry and they both set about trying to circle as many words as possible. "Are we allowed backwards words?"

"Normally" she replied, "any word is allowed as long as it is in a straight line and spelled correctly, either forwards or backwards, left or right, up or down, or diagonally" she added, as if she had been reading direct from the rule book.

They sat there together for around ten minutes or so, circling words.

"There are a lot of numbers here" said Jules.

"Yes" said Jerry, "I was wondering that."

"Have you found the instructions yet?"

"I am not sure" he replied, "I have found several words around the edge, but they don't make any sense yet."

"Let's compare notes" suggested Jules, and they sat together to see what they had each found.

They had both found many words, but mostly numbers. They agreed to look first for what appeared to be instructions.

"Look, there is the word 'THE'" said Jerry, "in the top row."

"Yes and the letters that spell the word 'NUMBER' appear in the right hand column, spelt backwards finishing in the top right corner."

"Oh yeah" said Jerry, "I didn't spot that."

"So now we have 'The Number'" said Jules. "What's next I wonder?"

They searched further. "There's the word 'WHAT'" said Jerry, as he pointed to the bottom right corner where a 'W' was, and the word continued diagonally upwards to the left.

"And there is the word 'OCCURS'" said Jules, pointing to the second 'O' from the bottom left and then going diagonally upwards to the right. "And the word 'LEAST'" she added, pointing to the 'L' next to the second 'O' from the left and the word going sideways to the right. "So, now have 'The Number what least occurs', I wonder if there are any other words?"

"Look" said Jerry, "there is the word 'IS' spelt backwards; look at the 'I' underneath the word 'number' that we just found."

"Oh Yeah" she said, "and it's the fourth number that we are looking for isn't it Jerry?"

"Yup."

"And there is the word 'FOURTH'. I didn't see it at first; I just thought it was 'FOUR' but it has a 'TH' on the end" and she pointed to the 'F' on the top row, and the word 'fourth' went down diagonally to the left. "Now we have the instructions Jerry" and she wrote them down:

THE FOURTH NUMBER IS WHAT LEAST OCCURS

"Great" proclaimed Jerry, "now all we have to do is find how many numbers we can find in the grid, and it is the one which occurs least that is the number, which then goes into position four."

"Yes, it certainly looks like that" agreed Jules, with a big smile on her face. "This should be easy; we should be able to crack this before Pete gets here."

They both then immediately set about circling all the spelt numbers that they could find in the grid. Ten minutes passed, then twenty, and then thirty before one of them spoke again.

"How many one's have you found?" asked Jules.

"Six" replied Jerry.

"I found eight."

"FIB!"

Jules laughed. "How many two's?"

"Six" said Jerry, although really he had only found five.

"Oh, I only found five so far" she replied. "Show me."

"No" he stated, "that would be cheating" and he quickly began scanning the grid for another 'two', one that he had not found yet. Luckily he found one, circled it, and then added. "Oh ok then, here, see."

Jules was impressed, for she was sure that he had been lying. However, he had indeed found six occurrences of the word 'TWO'.

In the end, they compared notes and summarised their totals. They were as follows:

ONE   *10*

TWO	*7*
THREE	*6*
FOUR	*6*
FIVE	*5*
SIX	*3*
SEVEN	*6*
EIGHT	*7*
NINE	*7*
TEN	*9*

"So" said Jules, "six was clearly the number that least occurred, with only three occurrences of the number."

"Let's, to be on the safe side" started Jerry, "just double check and scan for as many occurrences of the word 'SIX' as we can find."

Jules thought that was a good idea and they spent another fifteen minutes looking for the word 'SIX'. Afterwards they concluded that they could not find any more six's and so the number with the least occurrences had to be the number six.

"Finally" said Jerry, "The fourth number is six" and with that, he fell backwards onto the settee.

"Do you think that we should get Pete to check it?" asked Jules, as she walked into the kitchen to put the kettle on to make some tea.

"Yes, I was just thinking the same" remarked Jerry as he got up and followed her, "I mean it was a bit easy wasn't it."

"Why don't you call him and find out what time he is coming over?"

"Ok" he said, and picked up his mobile phone and called Pete, who said that he would be over between five-thirty and six o'clock. He also asked if Jerry had received the email, which Jerry replied that he had but that he had not been able to open it yet.

"Shall we take a look at the email now" he asked Jules, after he had hung-up the phone.

"Oh yes, fine, I had forgotten that" she remarked, and they both went into the Den.

Jules opened the email without any problem, but she could not open the spreadsheet that Pete had attached to it; it seemed to be of 'zero' size, so obviously something had become corrupted within the file. Jerry also had no copy of the email that he had forwarded to Pete, so he hoped that Pete had not deleted it; they would check with him later when he arrived.

It was now three o'clock. Pete would not be round for another three hours, and since Jerry and Jules had been interrupted this morning by the police, they decided to go back to bed for a few hours.

Evil Interview

Lord Dell was sitting in his study, thinking about the previous night's events. As ever, Johnson and Smith were not far away from him.

Lord Dell was trying to decide if he had actually seen or met the Chosen One whilst at the restaurant. He had not sensed anything there, he had not even sensed Mystic when he went outside, but he had seen her for sure. This intrigued him; if he had not sensed Mystic, then the power of the Good Lord must have been very strong at that location in order to hide her and whoever else that were around.

The previous owner of the restaurant was of course Gavin du Faire, whom he had killed in the museum. He had not known that Gavin du Faire owned a restaurant before he killed him; he had learnt that fact by reading the newspaper articles that came out after the event.

It was now the second time since the museum that he had been to the restaurant, but this was the first time that anything of significance had actually occurred there. The three of them, Lord Dell, Smith and Johnson had scoured the surrounding area after the explosion, but had not found anything which seemed out of place. Lord Dell had discovered a few students acting strangely, which was hardly abnormal, but none of them found traces of any Guardian activity.

'Maybe he had escaped' thought Lord Dell to himself, 'or maybe the explosion was a diversion; maybe he was still in the restaurant, maybe I had not yet met him, maybe I was getting too close?'

"I think it was a diversion" declared Lord Dell to his two sidekicks, who immediately both stopped looking through their newspapers and paid absolute and total attention to what he was saying. "It's the only answer that makes any real sense."

"Why do you think that Sir?" asked Smith.

"Well several reasons really. Firstly, we found nothing outside the restaurant. Secondly, I sensed nothing outside the restaurant, and thirdly…" He paused slightly and scowled as he thought about it. "Thirdly" he continued, "that bloody fortune teller was outside; I saw her."

"But what was it a diversion for?" asked Johnson.

Lord Dell looked towards Johnson. 'Why did evil villains always have such stupid assistants?' was the thought running through his mind. Johnson had his uses of course, but his ability to think before he spoke was clearly not one of them.

"I was obviously getting too close to someone that they did not want me to meet" he answered.

"You think *he* was in the restaurant My Lord?" said Smith, who clearly did have the ability to think.

"Who hadn't we yet met?" asked Lord Dell.

"Well there were still quite a few" continued Smith. "The restaurant was almost full, that meant about twenty tables, and to my recollection you had only met eight of them at the point when the explosion occurred."

"Yes, true" said Lord Dell, apparently impressed by Smith's recollections. "But" he then added, "I did meet two more couples at the bar, so that means that I didn't meet the people at ten tables."

Johnson and Smith just looked at him in admiration. They definitely did not want to interrupt him at this most important of moments.

"Quickly you two" commanded Lord Dell. "Come over here and help me remember who was sitting where, and bring the list of names you got from the Maitre de."

They both immediately jumped up and went over to his desk, where Lord Dell had placed a blank piece of paper on his writing pad and was now busy sketching out the layout of the restaurant and especially the positions of all the tables.

"Now, who was sitting where?" asked Lord Dell aloud, speaking to himself and to his two sidekicks.

"Major Prewett was sitting here Sir" said Smith, as he got the list of names out of his pocket, and pointed to the table closest to the window by the door, "with his wife and daughter."

"Yes" replied Lord Dell, who immediately wrote down the name 'Prewett' in the circle that represented the table at which the Prewetts were sitting. "And over here was Saunders. We were sitting here. There was that vicar chap, and at these two tables were that awful Faversham woman and her husband and that dentist with his wife. That makes six tables covered so far" he continued, as he wrote their names also onto the paper.

"Over here" said Johnson "was that gorgeous blond girl, with those two men. You hadn't met them yet Sir, had you?"

"No, I hadn't met them yet" replied Lord Dell, "but none of those two men looked as if they had an ounce of intelligence between them. The girl looked nice though, I must agree."

Within half an hour, they had made a pretty-accurate layout of the restaurant and placed all the people correctly at their tables.

"Now" said Lord Dell, "let's cross out the ones that I had already met" and he put large thick black 'X's covering over ten of the tables, including his own. "Now" he started again, "we will go through each of the tables that I had not met and try and remember what they looked like, and we will start with this one" he said, pointing to the table where the young man and girl had been sitting next to the coat stand.

"Ah, the one with the big boobies" said Johnson, licking his lips as he reminisced.

Smith burst out laughing, but Lord Dell just looked at them both in amusement. "Yes Johnson" he said, "the one who was heavily loaded up front. However, I doubt if she is destined to become the Good Lord. What about her man?"

"He was fairly young" said Smith, "does that matter?" he asked.

"No" replied Lord Dell. "The first Good Lord was that ridiculous eleven year old, Greg or something was his name. No Smith, age does not matter; although since the first one there has never been a Chosen One who was under thirty, and most of them had been fairly older. The current one was over fifty when he was selected."

"Oh" said Smith, "sorry my Lord."

"You do not need to apologise for that" said Lord Dell as he looked at him. "You could never have known that."

That cheered up Smith, for it was not often that Lord Dell was kind to him.

"Do you think it might be him then my Lord?" asked Johnson.

"Well, I don't know. It might be; I shall mark him down as a candidate" concluded Lord Dell.

They moved on to the other tables, slowly working there way around to Jerry's table.

"Now" said Lord Dell, "the last two tables. Let's start with this one" and he pointed to the table where Jerry, Jules, and Pete had been sitting. At that same instant in time however, the front door bell sounded, which startled them all.

Lord Dell immediately looked at his security monitor. It was Inspector Jones. He knew this because he had also seen him on the television news and had seen him arriving at the depositary when they were driving away.

"Quick, tidy-up everything here, and make out that we have been reading the newspapers all afternoon" he said, to his two sidekicks.

Within a few moments, Jensen had announced to Lord Dell that the police were here and that they wanted to interview him about the events at the restaurant yesterday evening. Lord Dell asked Jensen to show them into the study, which he promptly did.

Jensen arrived at the study door, knocked and entered. Lord Dell rose from his chair and walked over towards the door to welcome them. Lord Dell did not seem bothered at all by the police being in his study. Inspector Jones however seemed to be embarrassed for being there in the first place and was certainly impressed, and a tad overawed, by the surroundings. They asked Jensen to bring some tea and biscuits, which he saw to at once.

"Good afternoon your Lordship" said Inspector Jones, as he sort of bowed his head and addressed Lord Dell. "I am very sorry to disturb you my Lord, but we are talking to everyone who was at The Grid restaurant yesterday evening."

"Yes, of course" replied Lord Dell, as he walked his guests over towards the desk. "How can I help Inspector?" he asked as he clicked his fingers towards Johnson and Smith, triggering them to immediately get up and let Inspector Jones and his colleague sit in the chairs facing the desk. Lord Dell remained the same side of the desk for the moment, surveying the two of them.

Williams did not seem at all embarrassed by being in Lord Dell's study, and was not impressed in any way, shape, or form, by the surroundings or the trappings of wealth and power that were all over the mansion; he seemed more disgusted than anything and definitely did not hold Lord Dell in any sort of esteem.

"Well, Sir" continued the Inspector, who seemed to be behaving as if he was addressing God himself, the nickname they had all in the office given to the chief constable. "Should I first take it that these two gentlemen" he looked over at Johnson and Smith, who were now standing to one side of the desk, "are the two gentlemen who were with you at the restaurant yesterday evening?"

Lord Dell quickly thought to himself; he had no point in lying, and nothing to gain by it either, so he decided to confirm. "Yes, these were the *gentlemen* that were with me" he replied, looking rather amused when he actually said the word 'gentlemen' since neither of them in his opinion would qualify for that definition.

"Thank you Sir" continued the Inspector, who now seemed slightly relieved that he had succeeded in asking his first question. "Several of the guests remarked that you three left the restaurant immediately after the explosion occurred.

Can you please explain to me what you were doing and where you went?"

"Certainly Inspector" started Lord Dell; he was already prepared to answer this question as it was so obvious that it was going to be asked. "Hold on one moment please Inspector" he continued, as he walked over to the door and opened it for Jensen, who he had heard walking down the corridor.

"Thank you my Lord" remarked Jensen, as he passed through the open door.

"Over here Jensen" said Lord Dell, and he pointed to the coffee table that was in front of the fire, in the middle of the study, in between the other two armchairs.

"Please come and join me at the table" he said, to his two guests. "Johnson, Smith, please bring the chairs over, and we can all sit down, Jensen will see to my chair."

"Yes, my Lord" replied Jensen, who had just finished pouring the tea.

They rearranged the furniture and all settled down to drink their tea and help themselves to the delicious biscuits that Jensen had bought with him.

"Now Inspector" continued Lord Dell, "you were asking me where we went. Well firstly, we rushed outside to see if there were any people injured. It was clearly obvious that no one was hurt in the restaurant because not even one of the windows was broken, although I still don't know why" he added. "I expected to see quite a lot of people injured; I mean it was a fairly loud explosion so I thought it had been fairly large, but when we went outside there seemed also to be no casualties, quite miraculous really" he smirked.

"Yes Sir" replied Inspector Jones, "we also could not really believe it."

"Yes indeed" added Lord Dell. "Well, after looking around and ensuring that no one was hurt, I decided that I did not really want to hang around and wait for the reporters. It was obvious, at least to me" he continued, "that had I stayed, then it would be reported that I was in the restaurant, since I am such a well-known person, and I had introduced myself and said hello to at least half of the guests. I will however have to make sure that I pay my bill as well" he laughed, "because I left before the bill came to me, but I am sure that the Maitre de will trust me."

"Yes Sir" said Inspector Jones. "Did you see anything suspicious inside the restaurant, or outside when you arrived or when you left the building?"

"No, I can't say that I did" remarked Lord Dell, trying to look as though he was thinking back to the time. "Did you Mr Johnson or Mr Smith remember seeing anything, eh suspicious?" he enquired, looking at them both.

"No" said Smith, who then, together with everyone else, looked at Johnson.

"Well" said Johnson, which immediately caused Lord Dell's eyes to contract slightly, probably starting the worrying process over what he was about to say. "I did see a bird fly off from the scene."

"A bird?" asked Inspector Jones.

"Yes, Sir" said Johnson, "A raven, Sir" he concluded.

"How is that suspicious?" asked Inspector Jones. "Do you think the raven could have set off the explosion?"

"Eh, no Sir" answered Jonson, "it just seemed odd at the time; it seemed as though the bird flew right out from the shop which exploded and also did not seem to be hurt in any way either."

"Strange indeed" muttered Lord Dell, with a look of pity in his eyes.

The Inspector seemed a little perplexed. Was Johnson a bit soft in the head? "Eh, ok Mr Johnson, thank you for that" he mumbled, and then turned to his colleague Officer Williams. "Do you have any questions for these gentlemen?" he asked.

Williams sat thinking for a moment. He was not sure, but then he thought it would be no problem to ask anyway. He turned to Johnson.

"Have you recently been to the Natural History Museum, Sir?" he enquired.

Now Lord Dell was shocked; he definitely had not expected that question. He wondered how on earth the officer had even come up with it. Inspector Jones also looked rather shocked, but nowhere near as much as Johnson was.

"Sorry" replied Johnson, "the what?"

"The Natural History Museum" replied Officer Williams.

"HA!" shouted out Lord Dell, as he laughed aloud. "I am sorry" he said to the officer who looked puzzled as to why he had laughed. "I mean, Johnson, go to a museum; he probably couldn't even spell the word."

Johnson smiled, not really understanding that Lord Dell was making fun of him.

Officer Williams continued, "I am sorry Sir" he said as he stared at Lord Dell, "but I was not asking if he could spell the word; one doesn't need to spell murder to be able to commit one."

Now Inspector Jones chimed in. "Thank you, Sir" he said to Lord Dell, "thank you for your hospitality, but I am afraid that we have to leave now."

"Oh dear" said Lord Dell, actually quite relieved that they were not going to pursue the line of questioning any further.

"But Sir" protested the younger Officer Williams.

"Later Williams" said the Inspector, "not now" and he steered his young protégé towards the three, now standing hosts, to shake their hands.

"Nice to meet you sir" said Officer Williams, as he shook Lord Dell's hand.

"Likewise" replied Lord Dell, and he then walked them, followed behind by Johnson and Smith, to the door where they got into their unmarked police car and drove off.

Lord Dell closed the door. "That was a bit close" he muttered as he turned to face Johnson and Smith, "why do you think he asked that last question?"

Johnson did a shrug of the shoulders, but Smith was thinking.

"I think he was the one at the museum, leading the police up the steps" he suggested. "It looked like him anyway, although it was getting dark and we were in the shadows trying not to be seen."

"And not doing a very good job of it" sneered Lord Dell. "Let's go back to the study; we have some unfinished business with the restaurant."

The three of them walked back to the study. Jensen came to tidy up the tea cups and asked what time Lord Dell wished dinner to be served. Lord Dell felt that six thirty was a good time; that gave them an hour more to think about the restaurant.

Inspector Jones was furious with his young colleague Williams. "You can't go and accuse someone like Lord Dell of committing murder" he shouted at him, "and without even discussing it with me first. Have you any idea how many lawyers that guy has; we'll be lucky if he doesn't sue us for several million."

"I am sorry Sir" said Williams, not really realising what he had done. "I did not accuse him of committing murder, Sir."

"Damn well near as good as said it plainly if you ask me" spluttered Jones, "what was it? Oh yes – you don't need to be able to spell murder to commit it, Sir" he said trying to mimic a child's voice.

Williams felt embarrassed and his face started to show it. It was true that he had not talked about asking the question beforehand to Inspector Jones, and this was a cardinal sin, for the policemen normally conducting an interview always knew which way they were going to go with the line, or lines, of questioning, and who would say what and do what."

"What on earth made you ask the question?" asked Jones.

"Well Sir" started Williams, "when I was running up the steps into the museum, I swore blind that I could see two men. I could not see their faces. A third one then joined them. Then they sort of huddled together, turned a bit towards me, and then just disappeared."

"They did what" said Jones.

"They disappeared sir, that is to say when I got to the top of the stairs I could not find them. Apparently, no one else saw them either, so I just assumed that I had imagined it. However, tonight, when I saw that Mr Johnson in the light, I recognised his face. As the three of them turned, before they disappeared, the light from the streetlamp fell onto the face of the one nearest me, and I caught a glimpse of him. I could swear it was Johnson."

"Well Williams, you're an idiot" said Jones. "Firstly, if it wasn't Johnson then you have just almost accused the aide of one of the most influential persons in the country of committing murder, and secondly, if it was him, then you have just tipped him off that we suspect him, which we don't at the moment do we?"

"No Sir" replied Williams, feeling embarrassed.

"I don't remember reading anything about this in your report" continued Jones, still raving at him.

"Well I didn't include it Sir" said Williams, realising that this statement itself was perhaps the most alarming.

"YOU DIDN'T WHAT!" screamed Jones.

"I didn't include it, Sir" repeated Williams, "sorry."

Sorry was not enough to calm down Jones; he was livid with his young partner. "When you get back to the office Williams" he yelled to him, "I want you to go through every bit of evidence from the crime scene, including all the reports from the forensics, and see if they found anything of interest on the insides of the doors, and let's hope for your sake that they did."

"Yes Sir" replied Williams and with that, they both sat in complete silence all the way back to New Scotland Yard.

Pete arrived at Jerry's just after six. Jerry and Jules were all ready waiting for him, and were feeling happy about their progress during the day.

"We found Verse Two" said Jerry.

"And we solved it" added Jules, "at least we think we have" she then also added, just in case.

Pete was thrilled. "Well done" he said, "can I see it?"

They immediately showed him the back of the menu card.

"Wow" he said, "this was not on the back of my menu in the restaurant."

"Wasn't it?" asked Jerry. "How do you know, I mean are you sure?"

"Well I looked while choosing my main course" said Pete, "there was absolutely nothing on mine, and I could see the backs of yours, and they were empty as well."

"Great" exclaimed Jerry.

"What were the instructions?" asked Pete.

Jules picked up the paper that she had written on, and showed Pete the words circled on the printout that Jerry had made. Pete studied them both.

"Well it looks good" he said, "and you counted all the words that made numbers?"

"Yup" said Jerry, feeling even more proud now.

Pete looked further at the words circled and studied them for several minutes. "Well I can't see any other numbers" he said. "Yes it looks as though you have solved it. Well done!"

"BRILLIANT!" shouted Jerry; he really was pleased. He ran into his Den and opened the top drawer of his desk. He was of course looking for his piece of paper, the one on which he had written the other answers. He moved the old plastic coated text from Verse Three out of the way and then…

"Got it" he yelled, and ran back into the living room where he promptly added the answer to the last Verse.

Verse	Position	Number
5	ONE	FOUR
4	TWO	FOUR
3	THREE	THREE
2	FOUR	SIX
1	FIVE	FIVE

He now had all the numbers and their positions.

"Great" he said again, as he danced a sort of jig around the coffee table. "Even losing that email doesn't matter now" he added.

"What email?" asked Pete.

"The one you sent him" replied Jules. "He tried to open it this morning and it was blank. The spreadsheet had corrupted or something."

"Oh Shit" said Pete, "I thought it would be ok, but it was damaged on my PC as well. Now we have lost it completely."

"Never mind" said Jerry, "we don't need it any more."

"Fine" said Pete, although he felt a bit disappointed, especially after all that hard work.

What Now?

Jerry went straight to the fridge to fetch a bottle of wine to toast their success. However, after tasting the fine Chablis at the restaurant the previous night, his wine did not taste that good. Nevertheless, it was cold, wet, and alcoholic, and that was all they needed at this stage of the evening.

Jerry and Jules updated Pete on their visit from the police. They had not been at Pete's work to interview him, so Pete guessed they would maybe make contact with him later. Anyway, he was quite relieved as he did not like the police much; he had never trusted them since they wrongly arrested him once when he was younger, and was completely innocent. They of course let him go soon afterwards and apologised, but nonetheless, Pete did not really trust them any more.

"So, what now?" asked Pete.

"What do you mean?" replied Jules, who was really in a party mood.

"Yeah, what mate?" chirped Jerry.

"Well" continued Pete, rather pensively. "I don't want to be a party pooper" which by the way was exactly what he was going to be when he had finished asking the question. "But, what do we do now with the numbers?"

The atmosphere changed in an instant; it was as if someone had opened a window in an arctic weather station; the chilled wind blew out all the candles, sucked out all the heat, and froze Jerry and Jules to the spots on the floor where they stood.

"Sorry" muttered Pete, "I just wondered."

Jules looked at Jerry, who looked back at her, who then, followed by Jerry, looked straight at Pete.

"You plonker!" declared Jerry. "Why did you have to go and ask that question now for? We were having such a great time."

"Sorry" said Pete again, but it did not help any better than the first time.

"He's right you know" said Jules.

"I know he's right" mumbled Jerry, "he's always right. He's just lousy at timing."

They sat there in silence for a few moments.

"Well" said Pete, "do you have any ideas?"

"Not the faintest clue" replied Jerry. "Satisfied?"

"Don't take it out on him Jerry" said Jules, "he only asked."

"Sorry" grumbled Jerry, who now not only felt completely downhearted, but a bit guilty for taking it out on Pete, who had after all helped so much. In reality of course, and Jerry knew it, he would not have been able to solve any of the clues by himself, except maybe the last one.

"I tell you what" said Pete. "Let's forget about it for the moment and go down the Dog & Bone."

"No, I don't feel like it any more" said Jerry, and to be honest none of them did either.

"Ok" said Pete. "Look guys, I am sorry; I didn't mean to spoil the fun."

"We know you didn't Pete" confirmed Jules.

"Yeah, it's no problem mate" added Jerry, who then stood-up and roughed-up the hair on Pete's head. "I guess it's just that we are all a bit stressed and tired, I mean we have been at this for three weeks now" he said as he plonked himself back down on the settee, sitting next to Jules.

"Yeah" said Pete, "I could do with an early night myself" and he stood up, stretched, and looked at the two of them sitting together on the settee. "You two really make a good couple" he remarked; "you are right for each other you know."

"That's a really nice thing to say Pete" said Jules, "thank you."

"Have you both read that book already?" asked Pete, "You know, that book you got from the old horse."

"Yeah" said Jerry; "Jules finished it this morning."

Jules did not comment.

"Do you mind if I take it with me and read it tonight?" he asked.

"Sure mate" said Jerry, "don't lose it mind."

"No, of course I won't" he replied, "I'll guard it with my life" and with that he picked up the book, ready to go back home to his apartment. However, as he did so, he felt a rather strange sensation in his spine; he had obviously bent down rather too quickly, so he slowly straightened himself, up and rather gingerly walked out, massaging his back as he went.

"What do you reckon?" asked Jerry.

"About what?" she replied.

"About us making a good couple" he said, with that furtive look developing across his face.

"I think he's right" Jules murmured, smiling also as she said it. "We do make a good couple" and with that she poked him in the stomach, turned and ran into the bedroom with Jerry hot on her heels.

It was now Saturday and the White Horse was, as usual, in his field. It was again a glorious day; well at least the weather was glorious.

"What's the matter my Lord?" asked Annie, as she stroked his mane.

"I am worried about Jerry" he replied. "It has been almost three weeks and he has not yet found the Prize."

"Oh give him a chance" she said, "I mean, those clues are not easy are they?"

"No, they are not easy to solve correctly" he replied, "but time is running out; my powers are weakening and transferring to the Evil Lord; he is gaining strength and I am losing it. It can only be a matter of a few days now before the date of the replenishment, and if he has not found the Prize by then..."

He paused slightly, sighed, and looked at Annie, "Then it is lost for a thousand years at least."

"Not definitely" she replied, "I mean the Evil Lord still has to find it, doesn't he?"

"Yes, he does, that is true" murmured the White Horse, nodding his head in agreement. "But without a Good Lord he can take as long as he likes, and in the mean time spread evil and hatred amongst the race of man."

"I am sure Jerry will find it in time" concluded Annie.

"You like him don't you?" replied the White Horse; he had seen the look in her eyes.

"Oh it's not that" she replied. "Yes, I liked him, he was very nice when we were together, but my heart is with Jose now; I look forward to the replenishment, for my future is now clear."

"Ah yes" mumbled the White Horse, as he diverted his eyes towards the ground. "I only hope that you get the chance."

"Me to" she added, looking away in the direction of the pub.

They stood together for a few moments contemplating what the future had in store for them both.

"What do you want to do?" asked Annie.

"We must meet again" he replied. "Can you contact Mystic and set everything up. We must all meet this evening, at seven."

"Yes, I'll do that" replied Annie, "and I'll come back later this afternoon for your daily exercise. Is that ok?"

"Fine" he replied, "I look forward to it" and with that, Annie left him with some carrots to chew on and walked back to the pub into Jose's waiting arms.

Pete had started reading the Book of Gred from the moment he got home the previous evening. It fascinated him. When he awoke the next morning, Saturday morning, he decided to read it again. Come lunchtime he had read it three times. It was a fascinating story that captured his imagination. He wondered if Jerry would have all the powers that Gred had. He also was very fascinated by the references to Stonehenge. Was this really the original use of Stonehenge? Scientists and Archaeologists had been baffled and even arguing for years as to what its purpose really was, but here in front of his very eyes was a book that was thousands of years old, stating exactly why it had been erected.

Pete could just not put the book down; he read it again, and then he focussed in on one line.

When all five are solved the pathway to the Prize can be found. Consult this sacred text to find enlightenment and the pathway to the Prize…

'Jerry had the five numbers' he thought to himself. 'So now he should consult this sacred text to find enlightenment and the pathway to the Prize. But what did that mean? There was no map in this Book of Gred. It did not make any sense'.

Pete was stuck, stumped; he could not fathom it out. Somewhere in the book was supposed to be the pathway to the Prize. Pete had always assumed that the numbers opened up some kind of combination lock, like in a safe, but maybe this was not the case. 'But what else could they open up?' he thought to himself.

Pete read the book again. Luckily for him it was not so long and he was a quick reader. It would soon be lunchtime and he needed to get some shopping, but he also wanted to check his computer; he needed to look again into the deletion of the email and check the spreadsheet corruption, but he decided that he would do that later.

Annie had contacted Mystic and told her that the Good Lord wanted to meet with all the Guardians at seven o'clock that evening. Mystic said that she would see to it and make contact with each of the remaining Guardians. Annie had not heard about the death of Harrie de Gaunt, so she was quite upset when she returned to Jose.

"What is it my dear?" he asked her.

"Another is dead" she replied, tears falling from her eyes, "Three was killed the other day, in Mayfair; you know that item on the news."

"He was one of you?" said Jose, and he hugged his wife tightly. "We will get through this together" he declared, trying to comfort her by running his fingers through her hair and stroking her head while he was talking.

Nevertheless, Annie was not sure anymore; yes, she hoped that he was right, but now two were dead and only three remained. Mystic was also worried; she did not say so but Annie could tell by the tone of her voice, and by the fact that she was continually nowadays wiping away tears from her eyes.

Jerry and Jules awoke around ten after a good long sleep. They showered together and then had some lunch.

"When shall we start to look at the numbers?" asked Jules.

"Haven't got the faintest" replied Jerry, looking slightly concerned. "The numbers themselves do not make any sense. We need to know how to use them, and until we find that out then we can't get any further" was his conclusion.

Jerry was right; they both knew that the numbers opened something, like a combination lock, but they had no idea what. Jerry also knew that it was pointless asking Mystic since she was not allowed to help him. If he asked her, then she would only reply something about being worthy, and at this exact moment in time, that was the last thing that Jerry felt.

"What time is Pete coming over?" asked Jules.

"We didn't agree a time. I'll call him later" he replied. "I best speak with him anyway; I was a bit short with him yesterday."

"I'll tidy-up a bit" she suggested, and then went to the cupboard and got out the, rather dusty looking, vacuum cleaner.

Jerry was in the kitchen emptying the dishwasher; that was his weekly chore as otherwise his cupboards would get too empty. He also put the kettle on to make them both some fresh tea. It had been a hectic last three weeks and it had all started from the advert in the newspaper about finding a Prize. Since then he had met a raven that could speak and turn into a woman, the White Horse that could speak and was in fact the Good Lord. He had learnt about Gred and the history of the Good Lords and about the origins and meaning of Stonehenge. He had even learnt that he was the Chosen One and was destined to become the next Good Lord, assuming that he proved himself worthy by finding the Prize. He wondered what the Prize was. What could it possibly be? What was the thing that would bring love and happiness to the race of man? He had learnt about the Guardians, how they protected the Good Lord, and the clues that led to the location of the Prize. All through the journey so far, he had had Jules and Pete with him, they had been invaluable; without their support, encouragement, and just their basic help, he would definitely have failed at the first hurdle. They were already helping and protecting him, they were his mortal Guardians. Jerry wondered how he would feel watching Jules die as he lived on for a thousand years. The thought was not pleasant.

Jules called out from the Den; she had obviously finished cleaning in the living room and had moved on to the third messiest room, the Den.

"I put all those old papers we were using yesterday into the waste paper basket under your desk. It's now almost full, shall I empty it for you?" she asked.

"No leave it" he replied to her, she had done enough; it was his turn to do something. "I've made some tea, I'll do that later, haven't done it for months."

"Great" she said, walking into the kitchen, "I'm really thirsty. When was the last time you vacuumed?"

"Oh I don't remember" he replied laughing.

Jerry then grabbed hold of her as she came up to him and hugged her tightly. It really felt good. He was sure now; Jules was the one for him; worthy or not worthy.

"What's up?" she asked.

"Oh I was just thinking. What if I am not worthy?"

"You will always be worthy to me" she replied, hugging him tightly in return.

Jerry looked down at the woman he wanted to be with for the rest of his life.

"I love you" he whispered to her, as he gazed into her glistening eyes.

Jules listened and felt a warm sensation inside of her; she could not remember Jerry ever saying that to her the last time they had been together, albeit that time was only for a few months in total, but now they had been 'together' for just over a week. This Quest for the Prize had brought them closer together than ever before. Even if Jerry did not become the Chosen One, he was for sure her Chosen One. She looked up at him and gazed into his gorgeous blue eyes.

"I love you to" she replied, and kissed him long and slowly on the lips.

Pete had given up reading the book by now and had gone to the local supermarket to get some stores. He was running a bit low; the Quest had also taken up a lot of his time these past three weeks. He did not mind that at all; the challenge of solving the clues had been fun, and Pete was never one to refuse an intellectual challenge. Solving the clues was what he was good at, far better than Jerry. This was the type of thing that he could beat Jerry at; not sports or anything physical, but a good old-fashioned intellectual challenge. Pete had solved the code, albeit with a little help from Jules, and he had been the key person in finding out most of the other clues. Pete however did not want either fame or glory; all he wanted was the respect of his peers, as that meant the world to him.

When he returned from the shops, and after putting all his food away in their relevant places, Pete set about reading the book one more time. Something was in there; some little snippet of information that he had missed, and he, Pete Potts, was determined to find it.

Lord Dell was in his study. It was late afternoon and he had finished making the list of the key suspects from the restaurant, the list of who could be the Chosen One. Luckily, for Jerry, his name was not on the list. Lord Dell had decided that he would delve, one by one, deep into the minds of the suspects to see what they had been doing the last few weeks. When he found something interesting, then he would stay and look around for a bit, to see if he could find anything else. Normally such intrusions would go undetected; the unsuspecting person who was having his mind read like a book, might just feel a minor headache coming on, and would most likely put that down to something like not taking the right vitamins, or maybe drinking too much the night before. However, Lord Dell had to be careful, for if he stayed too long or got too intrusive then he could cause real damage and real pain inside his victim's head.

He decided to start with the man known as Mark; he was the friend of the beautiful woman sitting next to the coat stand. Lord Dell sat with his hands over his eyes and looked down onto his desk. He imagined the face of the man in his mind, and then reached out his thoughts to try and find him. It was a tricky process that had taken many thousands of years to perfect, but the Evil Lord could pinpoint any specific person within a one thousand mile radius, just as long as he had the person's name and a picture. If he had their address then it would be even quicker for he would know where to start looking.

Lord Dell started, watched on by Johnson and Smith.

"Mark, Mark" called out the Evil Lord, as he searched in his mind across the towns and cities that he had come to know so well. Then, after a few minutes, he stopped calling; he had found him. Now he homed in on the city of Birmingham and started delving deep into the mind of his victim, trying to make sense of what he had found.

"It's not him" said Lord Dell, opening his eyes several moments later and removing his hands from the map, thus breaking the magical connection that existed between them.

266

"This guy is an idiot" he continued; "all he wants is just to be with her for the rest of his life. Unbelievable!"

Johnson and Smith smirked at each other for both of them new exactly why Mark wanted to be with that woman for the rest of his life.

"Now, who is next?" muttered Lord Dell, and he got ready to start the whole process again, but with his next victim.

It was getting late, already close to six-thirty. Pete had now read the book in total ten times, and yet still he did not understand anything that he had not already understood after reading it the first time. Yet he remained convinced that something was hidden in there.

Pete was now getting frustrated and needed to calm down a bit. He decided to put on the television and try to sit back and relax. There was one of those detective series on television. This was one of those programmes where the detective solved the murder by putting together a series of randomly related clues that suddenly made sense, and only to him, just five minutes before the end.

'As if such things actually occurred in real life' he thought to himself.

This particular episode was about a jealous sister who had been sending a series of poison pen letters to her sister's friends. She had made the poison pen letters from cut out words from different pages of books, magazines, and newspapers, which meant that the reader would not be able to tell whom the letter had come from. It was clearly quite ridiculous, for nowadays you could just type each letter or word in a different font if you wanted to create such a letter; why bother with cutting out a word here and a word there, it was just not needed.

Suddenly however, as if someone had just switched on a light inside his brain, Pete jumped up.

"THAT'S IT!" he screamed as he immediately put his shoes back on, picked up the book, dashed out of his apartment, and started calling Jerry on his mobile phone.

It was now seven o'clock in the evening and the Guardians were assembling in the old barn to meet with the White Horse. They were one fewer than last time, which came again as a deep shock to Two and Four, who had not yet heard about it. Both of the men were now down. That left three women, Mystic, and the Good Lord himself.

Mystic however had not yet arrived; she had informed the Good Lord that she would be arriving slightly late as she was closely watching someone.

Harrie de Gaunt had been the longest serving Guardian; he had served for seven hundred years. Gavin had been the second longest; he had served for six hundred years. Diana had only served for two hundred, and she looked worried.

"How on earth am I expected to beat the Evil Lord?" she said looking depressed.

"Youth, agility, boldness, are but to name a few reasons" replied the White Horse.

She smiled back at him.

"Yes, maybe" she mumbled.

Mystic flew in, landed in the circle, and immediately transformed into herself.

"I am sorry I am delayed" she said to the meeting, "but I have good and bad news."

"Aha" said the White Horse as he smiled at her. "So Mystic my dear, which shall you tell us first?"

"The good news" she replied, nodding her head vigorously, indicating that the debate raging inside her head had concluded with the decision that it was best to say the good news first. "Yes, the good news is that he is not on the list."

"Oh" muttered the White Horse, starting to look concerned, "and the bad news is."

"He is not on the list" repeated Mystic.

The Guardians looked confused, but the White Horse just smiled.

"When will he be on the list?" he asked.

"At about a quarter past nine tonight" replied Mystic, with a deep troubled look now stretched right across her face.

"Oh dear" he groaned, in a concerned manner. "This is bad news indeed."

The Guardians had absolutely no idea what they were talking about so Mystic explained a bit further.

"The replenishment approaches" she started. "The truth is nearly exposed. The Evil Lord has worked out that the Chosen One was in the restaurant and that he had not yet met him when the explosion occurred. He currently does not suspect Jerry. He is invading the minds of all the people he suspects. Soon he will realise that he suspects the wrong persons, so he will go back to his list and work through the remaining people who were at the restaurant and he will come to Jerry. He will invade his mind. The truth will be exposed."

"What truth?" asked Guardian Four.

"Pete has just worked out how to use the code to find the pathway to the Prize and he is now approaching the apartment of the Chosen One. It is only a matter of time now before the code is broken. If the mind of the Chosen One is invaded after the code is broken, then the truth will be exposed and the Evil Lord will know the pathway to the Prize."

"We must not let that happen" said the White Horse, and with that he walked over to his drinking trough. "Come here my friends" he said to them all, "we will watch together."

They all walked over to the drinking trough. The White Horse lowered his head towards the trough, and through the water an image started to appear. It was the image of Jerry and Jules sitting together in Jerry's apartment. Jerry was looking very excited.

"What is it?" asked Jules.

"It's Pete" replied Jerry, "he just called me. He is on his way over. He says he thinks he's cracked it. He told me to get the numbers and some paper and be ready. He'll be here as fast as he can."

"He's cracked it?" said Jules, feeling as though someone had just lifted an enormous weight off from her shoulders.

"He thinks he has" said Jerry, who was also hoping beyond hope that Pete really had cracked it. "Oh I do hope so" he added.

"Quick, get your piece of paper with the numbers on it" said Jules, "and I'll put the kettle on."

"Put the kettle on?" said Jerry, with an expression of disbelief in his face.

"Yeah, didn't you know" said Jules, "Pete always thinks best after a cup of tea; it stimulates his brain you know."

Jerry decided that now was not the time to discuss this.

"Ok" he said to her as he dashed towards the Den. "Make a large pot then."

Jerry went straight to his desk in the Den, to get his piece of paper from the desk drawer. He returned within five seconds and laid the paper on the coffee table.

Verse	Position	Number
5	ONE	FOUR
4	TWO	FOUR
3	THREE	THREE
2	FOUR	SIX
1	FIVE	FIVE

Jules had gone into the kitchen to make the tea. They were both really getting nervous now. Where was Pete?

After a minute of Jerry walking around the coffee table and Jules spilling half the milk in the kitchen sink, Jerry heard Pete running up the stairs towards his front door. Before Pete even had a chance to ring the doorbell, Jerry had dashed to the door and opened it.

"What took you so long" they both said to each other, laughing a nervous laugh as they spoke.

Pete walked in carrying the Book of Gred under his arm, while Jerry slammed the door shut behind him, and they then both dashed into the living room where Jules came in with the tea.

"Great, tea" said Pete, which caused Jules to smile and develop an 'I told you so' expression across her face as she looked towards Jerry, who just ignored it.

"You've cracked it then?" asked Jerry.

"I think so" Pete replied nervously, "but I don't know for sure."

"Well" said Jules, almost exploding with anticipation, "tell us; what is it?"

"It's in the book" said Pete, "I knew it all along, but I just didn't see it."

"WHAT IS?" screamed Jules and Jerry together.

Pete was thoroughly enjoying the moment; he had the two of them in the palm of his hands, desperate to know the answer. He only hoped that he was right.

Pete opened the book of Gred. "There are three clues" he said, and he read out the three parts of the text that intrigued him:

To find the pathway to the Prize, he must find and correctly solve the five clues that lead to the location of the Prize. Consult this sacred text to find enlightenment and the pathway to the Prize.

Once the Prize is found, and the Good Lord replenished, then new clues and the Prize must be hidden anew.

This has since become a tradition; after the replenishment, the Good Lord's first task is to update the Book of Gred.

Jules and Jerry looked at each other dumbfounded.

"What?" they both said.

Pete started to explain.

"Basically, it says that to find the pathway to the Prize you must consult the sacred text. It then says that every time a

Good Lord is replenished then new clues must be made and the Prize hidden anew. It also says that the text is then, updated. This basically implies that the sacred text is the updated part of the book."

Jerry and Jules just looked at each other and wondered what-on-earth Pete was talking about; it did not make any sense. Pete however, continued.

"The majority of the text is talking about the life of Gred, and how he found the Prize. This cannot contain the code, since if this changed every thousand years, then it would not make any sense and would lose the whole meaning. Also, the text which is deemed to be the most sacred is" and he paused.

"The Testament of Gred" finished Jerry.

"The what?" replied Jules, who had not read that part.

"That last written page" said Pete, "where the testament of Gred is written. These are supposed to be his words, but how could they be? He talks about 'the old central park', how can a park exist today which was supposed to exist 6000 years ago? The only conclusion is that this text must be coded."

"The book even said" reminisced Jerry, "that the words did not make total sense, something about him being close to dying."

"That must have been a trick, to get us to just assume that" concluded Pete.

"I never read that part" muttered Jules, feeling as she had been deprived an opportunity to crack it herself, "Jerry gave you the book before I had finished. But anyway, how can a code be in a piece of text?"

"I didn't think about it" said Pete, "until I saw that detective film on the television late this afternoon. The sister cut out words from the book and pasted them to make a new message. That is what triggered me; I believe that the code tells us which words to take from the Testament of Gred to form a new message."

"Quick" said Jerry, as he motioned to Pete to open the book and put it on the coffee table. He already had the piece of paper there with the code words on it.

"What's the sequence" said Pete.

"Four-four-three-six-five" said Jules, fascinated.

"Fourth Word" said Jerry.

"THE" said Pete.

Jules wrote it down immediately on the piece of paper.

"Fourth Word" said Jerry

Pete counted four words further along. "PRIZE" he said, "the Prize."

"Shit" said Jules, "its working"

"Third word" said Jerry, holding his finger on the third number on the list, trying to make sure that he did not make any mistake.

"YOU" said Pete.

"Sixth word" said Jerry, almost constipated now with tension.

"SEEK" said Pete, "'The Prize you seek', Jesus, it is working."

"Fifth word" said Jerry

"THE" said Pete.

"Now what?" asked Jerry.

"Repeat the sequence" said Pete, "until we run out of text."

They continued this process for a period of ten minutes until they had indeed run out of text. Jules then showed them what she had written on the paper.

THE PRIZE YOU SEEK THE PLACE AN ILLNESS DRAWS YOU TO YOU MUST GO TO THE KINGS END CENTRAL WHERE PRIZE WAITING IN OR EIGHT LOOK WHERE PATIENT LIES SHOWS DIRECTION TO BACK UNDER WHERE FIND PRIZE BLOOD STAIN MARKS PLACE WHERE QUEST ENDS ONLY INHERIT WHEN FIND MISSING WORDS GOOD LORD SERVES FOR YOU

They looked at the text. Parts of it made sense, but there was no punctuation.

"It's obviously not one long sentence" said Pete. "I think that we have to work out where each sentence ends and the next one begins, then we can work out the true meaning of the message."

The others agreed and they immediately set to work on it. After half an hour, they got to the following message:

THE PRIZE YOU SEEK, THE PLACE AN ILLNESS DRAWS YOU TO.

YOU MUST GO TO THE KINGS END CENTRAL WHERE PRIZE WAITING IN OR EIGHT.

LOOK WHERE PATIENT LIES, SHOWS DIRECTION TO BACK, UNDER WHERE FIND PRIZE.

BLOOD STAIN MARKS PLACE WHERE QUEST ENDS.

ONLY INHERIT WHEN FIND MISSING WORDS, GOOD LORD SERVES FOR YOU

"What does it mean?" asked Jules.

"I think" said Pete, "that the first line is telling us that the Prize is in a hospital. The second line tells us the name of the hospital is the 'Kings End Central'. The third line tells us that the Prize waits in 'or eight'. What does that mean?"

Jules smiled, "'O' 'R' doesn't mean 'or' it means 'operating room'. The Prize waits in operating room eight" she said, still smiling.

"Brilliant" said Jerry.

"Yeah, great" added Pete. "So the Prize waits in O.R. Eight. The fourth line then tells us to look where the patient lies. That must be referring to the operating table. It says that it shows direction to back. I guess that means it points to the back wall."

"Under which" added Jerry, "you'll find the Prize."

"A blood stain marks the place where the Quest ends" read out Jules.

"What about the last bit?" said Pete, "that is a bit cryptic?"

"Only inherit when find missing words, Good Lord serves for you" repeated Jerry, starting to ponder.

"I think" said Jules, "that it is telling us that once you have found the Prize, you have to say some special word in order to be able to inherit it, and that word is the word which is missing from the sentence 'Good Lord serves for you'. So we have to find what the missing word is" she concluded.

"And we can work that out tomorrow" said Jerry who, like the others, was so happy now that the message had been decoded that he dashed in to the kitchen get some wine to celebrate.

Mystic wiped her eyes; she had been crying again, but this time it was with happiness.

"They have solved it, I am so happy for them" she said, but then she suddenly stopped, and a look of fear spread across her face. "I must go now" she continued, "for the Evil Lord will soon invade his mind."

"You must all go" added the White Horse. "Jerry is now in mortal danger. We cannot afford now for the truth to be exposed. Bring him here for only here can I protect him now. One, you must prepare rooms for them, for all of them."

"Yes my Lord" replied Annie, and she dashed off, back to the pub.

"Two and Four" he said, looking at Diana and Fiona, "You must go with Mystic and hurry; protect him at whatever cost."

"Yes my Lord" they all said, and then Diana and Fiona turned instantly into two white Doves, at the same time as Mystic turned into her raven form, and they all flew off as fast as they could, towards Jerry's apartment, leaving behind the White Horse, who wished them well as they sped away.

Battle Lines

Jerry, Jules, and Pete were still in a state of euphoria. They had deciphered the code and now had the pathway to the Prize in their hands. There was only one part remaining to solve, and that was the missing word. They decided that they would go to the Kings End Central hospital in the morning; that was Sunday morning, as the hospital would not be so busy, and then they could sneak in and take a look around without fear of interruption.

The Kings End Central was in London, so they would get the train to Kings Cross and walk the short way to the hospital. They had also decided not to work on the missing word any further that evening; instead they would start that tomorrow on the train journey to London. For now, all they would do was relax, celebrate, and drink some wine, and for security, Jerry decided to hide the book of Gred in a safe place, under his bed.

Lord Dell was still in his study, accompanied as always by Johnson and Smith. He had now gone through his list of suspects and not had any success, but he still had enough energy inside himself to continue. They had previously selected six names from the tables that they had not visited when they were in the restaurant, and the Chosen One was not amongst them. Lord Dell called over his two sidekicks.

"We have missed him" he muttered to them, "we must look anew, for I am sure that he is here somewhere."

The trio re-scanned the tables. Lord Dell had not yet selected any woman; the Good Lord up until now had never been a female, but in today's modern world such distinctions were nonsense as women were just as able as men, as they were in days gone by as well. However, Lord Dell felt that he would follow tradition, and first check the remaining men before moving on to the women.

"There are three men remaining" he concluded. "Two were sitting at the table with the good looking blonde woman and one sitting with what looked like his mother next to the window."

Smith wrote down the names for his master:

MICHAEL STELLIOS
JEREMY DUMBARTON
PETER POTTS

"So" said Lord Dell, "it is down to these three then. The Chosen One must be one of these three. I will start at the top and work my way down the list."

Johnson and Smith went back to their armchairs, sat, and watched their master slowly prepare. It looked as though going through the first list of names had weakened him, but he still had the resolve to go on, he had to, for finding the Prize was now the most important thing in his existence.

Jerry fetched the second bottle of wine and returned to sit down together with Jules and Pete in the living room. "Here's to our success tomorrow" he declared, raising his refilled glass towards them.

They both immediately raised their glasses towards him and joined in the toast.

"Here's to your success tomorrow, Jerry" said Pete, "I hope you find it."

"Yes, I second that" added Jules.

"Look" said Jerry, "I mean, I haven't found anything yet, and I might not even find anything tomorrow, but whatever I find, I wouldn't have been able to find it without you guys."

"If you carry on like that" said Pete, "I am going to need to borrow Jules' tissues."

The atmosphere was very happy in the room; it was as if nothing could spoil their mood; the next few minutes would certainly change all that.

Lord Dell had now found Michael Stellios, and had very quickly concluded that he was not the one. Michael, of course, had not felt anything and was none the wiser that the single most evil being ever to roam the planet Earth, had just invaded his mind. Now Lord Dell moved onto Jerry.

Jerry was just about to refill his glass again, when the window in the kitchen flew open, smashing against the inside wall and making an almighty racket. Jerry turned around to look towards the noise, when he saw three birds fly into his living room. Of course he knew the first one; that was Mystic, but before he could say anything Mystic had transformed into, what Jerry assumed was, her normal form as it was now the second time she had done this. The other two doves then immediately transformed into Diana Tugrow, the librarian, and Fiona Davis, the beautiful woman from the restaurant.

Jerry, Jules, and Diana all immediately put their glasses down and stared at the three women now standing in front of them.

"What's up?" asked Jerry, very quickly understanding, of course, that something was wrong.

"You are in great mortal danger" replied Mystic, "all three of you."

"We must take you and hide you immediately" added Diana, "no time to waste. Quick, get your shoes on."

"Not you Jerry" said Mystic quickly. "Pete, get his shoes for him" and she immediately went and stood right next to Jerry and placed her hand on to the top of his head.

"Jeremy Dumbarton. Jeremy Dumbarton, where are you?" called the Evil Lord from inside his mind, as it stretched out from his body and started scanning the country. "Ah Cambridge, yes, I should have guessed" he muttered, as he focused towards the town in the middle of England. "Let me find you Jeremy, let me into your mind."

He had found Jerry in an apartment in Cambridge, off Castle Street, but something was wrong; he could not get into his mind.

"This must be him" he muttered as he concentrated harder. "Someone is protecting him. I must increase my power."

Jerry was starting to feel hot, especially inside his head. Mystic's hand was firmly on his head, but it had started to tremble, as if some force was trying to remove it, to push it off.

Jules re-entered the living room holding her shoes in her hands, and suddenly froze as she watched Mystic trying with all her might to keep her hand on Jerry's head. Jules' face was now completely white with fear; she looked scared to death as something was clearly wrong.

"What are you doing to him?" she asked Mystic.

"I am" struggled Mystic; whatever she was doing was taking much effort from her and she could barely speak. "I am trying to protect him from the..."

They never heard the next words, for Mystic pulled her hand away as if it was burning in a fire. She looked shocked towards Jerry.

"NO!" she shrieked, her face also turning white with fear as she looked over to Diana and Fiona.

The effect on Jerry was immediate. He grabbed both sides of his head and screamed in agony as he rolled around on the sofa. The pain was unbearable; all he could do was scream, he could not even speak. It was pain beyond pain; something he had never felt in his life before.

"Quick" called out Mystic to the two Guardians, "help me."

Diana and Fiona immediately joined Mystic, where they formed a circle around Jerry, who was now rolling about on the floor, screaming. They stretched out their arms towards him and raised their hands, such that their palms were facing him, and let loose three powerful bolts of pure white energy, which shot straight into his still squirming body.

Jules, her face still pale, grabbed Pete's arm and squeezed it tight. There were now tears in her eyes; she was petrified with fright, concerned for her lover who was on the floor in absolute agony, and for whom she could do nothing.

Jerry's face had turned bright red, and his whole body was shaking as if he was having a fit. The red colour was now also starting to spread out through his entire body, beginning from his head, and then moving slowly in the direction of his toes. The beams of white light, emanating from the Guardians and Mystic, were also starting to turn red at the place where they connected with Jerry's body. The red stain was even beginning to work its way up their beams of power, towards their originators; it was as if another force, the force of the Evil Lord, was repelling their defence.

"Stronger" called out Mystic, as the three of them increased their level of concentration, and their white beams glowed even brighter.

Slowly but surely the red colour at the base of the beams of white energy were receding back into Jerry's body. They were winning; the evil influence was retreating and now his chest and even his face was going back to its normal colour. Then finally, he stopped shivering and just laid there, flat on his back, his body limp.

"NO!" screamed Jules; obviously fearing the worst.

The Guardians stopped their beams of white energy and immediately bent down over him.

"Revive him" commanded Mystic, who appeared now severely weakened herself, and had fallen to her knees. Diana leaned over Jerry's face and kissed him on the lips.

Jerry sprang back to life with a great shiver and immediately started looking around. The first person he saw was Jules, she was crying.

"Lay still" said Diana, "you must lie still for a few moments; we need to make sure that he is gone."

Lord Dell was now on the floor of his study. The force of the combined defence of the Guardians had thrown him up in the air and away from his desk. He had hit the back wall of his study with such a force, that the impact had crushed some of the shelves, causing many books to fall to the floor, and sent reverberations all around the room. Even some of the glass windows and cabinets had shattered due to the force of the impact. Johnson and Smith immediately went to his aid to make sure that he was all right. He was, but he was now also very weak; the battle, coming so soon after the many searches that had already weakened him, had weakened him even further. Nevertheless, he was still alive, he was still the Evil Lord, and he was still a very powerful force to deal with.

"Quick" he said. "I cannot do it from here; we need to get closer. Get the car; we are going to Cambridge, hurry!"

Johnson ran out of the room to tell Jensen to get the car, which he immediately did. He then ran back to his master.

"Help me up" said Lord Dell to his two aides. "I am weak, but I am not done yet; I will recover soon. Help me to the car."

Jensen was now waiting outside the front door with the car ready to go. Johnson and Smith helped Lord Dell into the back seat, where Smith sat next to him. Johnson sat in the front.

"Cambridge, and quickly" ordered Lord Dell, and Jensen immediately took off at high speed.

Jerry had remained laying on the carpet for several moments.

"What happened?" he asked, to the crowd that were now around him.

"The Evil Lord found you" said Mystic. "He invaded your mind. I tried to protect you but he was too strong. He forced me off, and then started to take over your whole body. Diana and Fiona helped me repel him from you. It was a tough battle, but the three of us overcame him. He was obviously far away so we had the advantage, but it was still a very close call."

"Are you ok, Jerry?" asked Jules.

"Yeah I'm fine babe" he replied, smiling at her, "why?"

"You were rolling about and screaming" she said to him, "it was terrifying."

Jerry got up and walked over to her and they hugged. Pete did not know whether to hug him as well or just pat him on the back. Nevertheless, he was equally as well relieved as Jules.

"I'm fine babe" he repeated.

"Fine you may be" said Mystic, "but if we stay here you will not be for much longer. The Evil Lord is without doubt now on his way here. The closer he gets to you the more power he will have over you. I can only hope that his attack has weakened him sufficiently such that he won't be able to do anything more tonight."

"What shall we do?" asked Jules.

"You must come with us" said Diana. Guardian One, Annie, has prepared rooms for you all at the pub. We must get close now to the Good Lord for he can still protect us while we are close to him. Let us go now, immediately."

They put on their shoes and Jerry grabbed his keys. Diana would travel in the car with Pete, Jules, and Jerry. Jerry would drive as he did not trust anyone else driving his pride and joy, and Jules would sit in the front with him. Mystic and Fiona would fly above them, watching out for any trouble, but Mystic was sure that they would be safe now, at least for tonight.

"Sir" said Jensen, as his master rested in the back seat.

"Yes, what is it?" he replied.

"Sir, I think we are being followed. That blue car has been behind us ever since we left the mansion."

"It's probably that stupid sergeant police officer" said Lord Dell who then closed his eyes and stretched out his mind. Yes it was. Williams was in the car behind them, obviously trying to follow him.

"Lose him" commanded Lord Dell.

Jensen immediately put his foot down. Their black Jaguar would far out perform the estate car that Williams was driving. Lord Dell knew that Williams would have to call in back-up to catch him, and he would not do that for fear of harassment charges coming from Lord Dell's lawyers.

"What happened, Sir?" asked Smith. "What happened in the Study?"

"I managed to break into the mind of that Jeremy Dumbarton" started Lord Dell. "He is the Chosen One; he was being protected by that weak fortune teller. She was no match for me, even over a hundred miles away. However, two Guardians assisted her; but even so, I still managed to get in. I saw inside his mind; he has all five clues, and he has now found the pathway to the Prize. It ends in London. He must be stopped else the Evil Lord will be thwarted again and sentenced to another thousand years of subservience, leaving those pitiful humans to live in peace."

"Him" muttered Johnson, "the Chosen One?"

Johnson clearly could not see what qualities Jerry had, at least not compared to him. Lord Dell merely laughed.

"Yes, him" he added, with a tinge of disgust also in his voice.

"Did you find out the pathway to the Prize my Lord?" asked Smith.

"No" replied Lord Dell, "I was not there long enough, and I was distracted by the attack from the Guardians. All I saw was that he will go there tomorrow and it is somewhere in London. We must get to him and follow him; else I will be too late."

Jerry drove as fast as was legally allowed in order to get to the White Horse pub as quickly as possible. The journey was uneventful, although you could classify almost anything as uneventful after what had just happened in his apartment. They arrived at the pub and were immediately greeted by Annie and Jose. They had already made a steaming hot pot of tea for them, which they immediately served.

Jules and Pete updated them on the events in the apartment. Jerry listened intently for he remembered none of it, not even the pain. Nevertheless, the story was frightening and sounded as if he had actually died.

"When are we going to sort out the missing word?" asked Jerry, trying to lighten the situation a little, and change the subject.

They all looked at him, obviously thinking that he was mad talking about solving the clues right now. Jerry however did not want to talk about the attack; he wanted to forget that it had ever happened, and the best way of doing that was to try to concentrate on something else.

Pete, sensing that this might be the reason, suggested that they could spend a couple of hours on it before turning in for the evening. After all, he thought to himself, now they were safe, tomorrow might be a different story.

"Good" said Jerry, "let's sit over there and start thinking about it" and the three of them, for the Guardians and Mystic could still not help him, went over to a table by one of the windows and sat down.

Jensen had broken every speed limit imaginable in order to get to Cambridge as fast as he could. However, when they arrived they found the apartment empty.

"Damn!" shouted Lord Dell, although he was not at all surprised. The Guardians and Mystic, despite being a pain, were not stupid. They would have guessed that he was on his way and would have made sure to move the Chosen One closer to the Good Lord. Despite being a little disappointed, he was also a little excited, for this made the challenge slightly greater, which made the battle more worth winning. Lord Dell walked around the apartment as if trying to picture Jerry, his habits, and his life.

"What are you doing Sir?" asked Smith.

"I am trying to understand my new adversary" replied Lord Dell. "You can learn a lot from how a man lives. Is he structured? Does he act impulsively? Does he store things?

Does he remember well? Or does he leave notes reminding him of things all over the place?"

Smith just looked on in admiration of his master.

Lord Dell walked into the Den.

"See" he said, "nice and tidy. This man is someone who does things deliberately. He tidies up after himself" and he pointed over to the full waste paper basket.

"I see" said Smith.

"I need to know who I will be dealing with" continued Lord Dell, "if he is to become the new Good Lord then understanding him, finding his weaknesses, will be a key to the final battle."

"The final battle my Lord?" asked Smith, not really understanding to what his master was referring.

"Yes, Smith" he replied slowly, "no other knows about the final battle, not even the current Good Lord; it is a secret from the dawn of time, written that the seventh shall be the last. So even if he beats me to the Prize, then I will still get my chance to defeat him forever."

"Wow" said Johnson, who was listening intently.

"Come" said Lord Dell. "We shall go now; I need to rest this night for a hectic day awaits us tomorrow" and with that they left, making sure that they left no traces of their presence in the apartment.

Jerry, Jules, and Pete had spent some time going through the possible missing words to the sentence:

GOOD LORD SERVES FOR YOU

They currently had worked out the following possibilities.

The GOOD LORD SERVES FOR YOU
GOOD LORD SERVES just FOR YOU
GOOD LORD SERVES always FOR YOU
GOOD LORD SERVES FOR YOU always

It was tough going. Not many words made sense, but even so, there were still many possibilities. They wondered if they would ever come to the right one, or how they would know which one was indeed the right one.

"The first thing" said Jules, "is to find the Prize; we can worry how to inherit it later."

This sounded an excellent strategy, at least for the moment, as they were all now starting to feel tired.

"You need rest" said Annie to Jerry. "Let me show you all to your rooms. Jules, do you want to sleep with Jerry?"

Jules of course said that she would and Annie completely understood why. Pete had his own room. Fiona and Annie would guard Jules and Jerry, and Diana would take care of Pete.

Annie showed them to their rooms. She and Fiona then sat in the corridor outside Jerry and Jules' room. There was not sufficient room in the corridor for Diana as well, so she waited for Pete to get undressed and into bed, and then she went inside to sit in his room.

Mystic was now also feeling tired and still felt weak from her exertions earlier in the evening, but she had one more duty to do this night before she could get some rest. She bade the others good night, walked out and towards the field next to the pub, to talk with the White Horse.

"Hello Mystic" he said to her, as she approached close to him. "I trust everything is well."

"Yes, my Lord" she replied. "He is safe now; the Guardians are with them, and you are close by. They will not be harmed tonight."

"Good" he said, "but something is troubling you my dear Mystic?"

"I fear for tomorrow" she continued. "I fear that not all of us shall return from the journey, although it is not clear."

"Not clear?"

"No" she replied. "The future is clouded; there is much that will be determined tomorrow."

"Much indeed" added the Good Lord; lowering his head and looking down to the ground.

"You know?" asked Mystic, somewhat surprised, "for I cannot see."

"I do not know" he replied to her, while deep in thought. "But things are already less clear than they were a few hours ago. The balance approaches equilibrium, but soon the forces of dark will take over."

Mystic opened her handbag, pulled out a clean handkerchief and began to wipe her eyes.

The old, wise, White Horse turned his head and looked at her. "It is time" he whispered.

Mystic looked back at him and nodded.

"Yes my Lord" she muttered, and then immediately started wiping her eyes more vigorously.

"What is wrong" he asked, "for you have known this time would come?"

"Yes, my Lord" she again replied. "But it has been so long in coming, and now it is here it seems that it is far too soon."

"Our time is near" he continued. "The battle lines have been drawn. Tomorrow, in London, at the Kings End Central Hospital, in operating room eight, we shall see what is in store for the race of man."

"Yes, my Lord" she replied, still crying and still wiping her now red eyes.

"Come, Mystic. Walk with me."

Mystic walked with the White Horse towards the barn. She held her arm around his neck, as if cuddling him as they went. The only sound was that of her soft whimpering tears. Within a few moments they arrived at the barn and then continued on together until they were inside. Mystic then closed the doors behind them; now even the sounds of her tears were gone. Then, after a few more moments of silence, a brilliant white light emerged from every possible open crevice in the walls, roof, and through the windows of the barn, spreading a bright white light far, wide, and high up into the night sky. Then, just as quickly as it had begun, it stopped. The light had gone, everywhere was dark, and the White Horse was no more.

Battle at Eight

It was seven o'clock in the morning, and Lord Dell had awoken slightly earlier but decided to remain lying in bed, wondering what was going to happen later in the day. There were many imponderables, many different avenues and options, huge amounts of variables, such that no one could predict the outcome. He doubted if even Mystic could foretell what would happen this day.

He decided to get up and take breakfast, so he got dressed in his most flexible suit and covered it with his finest evil cloak. Today was a special day; he knew that at least. Lord Dell walked downstairs and into the dining room where Johnson and Smith were waiting for him. Jensen came in with the toast and a special full breakfast; he knew that his master needed lots of good old-fashioned energy for the day ahead.

"Sir" enquired Smith, "any specific plans for the day?"

Lord Dell laughed to himself; for sure, he had plans for the day, but whether or not they would actually materialise the way he hoped, that was the sixty-four million dollar question.

"Yes, I have plans Smith" he replied, "if I get the chance to put them into action."

"What do you mean Sir?" he asked again, looking slightly puzzled by the uncertainty expressed by his master.

"Sorry Smith" he replied, "I was playing with you. There are so many unknowns that will after today become known's. None however are certain; if it goes my way then my plans will have worked, and if it does not go my way, well then I will not have been able to implement my plans."

Smith looked content with the answer. Johnson however looked completely baffled.

"What I mean is" continued Lord Dell, after looking at Johnson, "if I get my way then I will find the Prize, kill all the remaining Guardians and that damn fortune teller, and be rid of them all forever. The Good Lord will then fail to be replenished which will leave me alone in control of the destiny of the race of man. If I do not get my way then I will not find the Prize. I may however still kill a few Guardians, so the day may not be a complete loss after all. If I do not find the Prize and do not even get to kill any Guardians, then today will be a disaster. Do you get it now?"

Even Johnson understood that description and he nodded towards his master.

A knocking on the door awoke Jerry; it was Mystic saying that he should quickly get dressed. Jerry and Jules had slept well, despite the previous evenings escapades, and with Jules in his arms Jerry had slept like a log.

The morning was delightful. The sun was already shining and the temperature outside would soon be reaching twenty degrees, and would most likely rise to the mid thirties before the afternoon was out.

In their haste to depart the previous evening, they had not brought any fresh clothes with them, so they just washed and put the same things on as the day before. When they got downstairs they met Pete and Diana who were already waiting for them in the kitchen.

"Did you sleep well?" asked Jules.

Pete grinned and said that he was fine, even though he still looked tired, but his face did seem to have brightened-up somewhat. Jerry looked at Pete and grinned in return; today was going to be a day they would remember for the rest of their lives, and for many reasons.

Annie brought in their breakfasts. They were, what people in the trade called, 'full English' breakfasts, and were more like evening meals. Jose had done the pub proud, although Jerry and Jules could not eat everything. Pete however finished his whole plate.

Mystic walked into the kitchen.

"We will have to move quickly" she said to Jerry, "for you are still in grave danger. The Evil Lord knows of you now, and he has detected that you have solved all five clues, and that you now have the pathway to the Prize in your possession. He will now stop at nothing to get to the Prize before you."

Jerry, Jules, and Pete looked at each other. They were worried; Jules and Pete were not Guardians; they had no magic powers, and if the Evil Lord came after them, then they were dead.

Mystic knew of course what they were all thinking and so she answered the question before any of them dared to ask it.

"Pete and Jules must stay here for they will be safe with Jose. As long as they do not get in the Evil Lords way, then they will not be harmed, not today anyway."

The three of them looked at each other. None of them liked what Mystic had just said, but they all knew that it just had to be that way. It was down to Jerry now, down to him alone to take the final steps. Jules and Pete had been great so far; without them by his side Jerry's Quest would have never really begun, let alone finished with the pathway to the Prize in his hands. They all three stood up and hugged each other.

Jules had tears now streaming down her face. Was this the last time she would ever see Jerry alive? Of course she hoped not. Pete also had tears in his eyes; he was scared for Jerry, but now Jerry needed them to be strong.

"Guardians Two and Four are waiting outside" said Mystic. "We must go now. We will come straight back here when we are done and tell you about everything that happened."

Annie gave Jose a kiss and a big hug. He to was worried for Annie, but he knew that she had to do this; otherwise, they would never be together. Annie gave Jules and Pete a hug.

"He'll be ok with us" she said to them both, "that Evil Lord won't stand a chance against the four of us together" and she punched Pete on the arm. He hoped that she was right.

As they walked outside Annie decided that she would drive. Jerry was not so sure about this, but Mystic explained. "There must always be one of us on either side of you, and front and back" she said. "That way we form a kind of circle around you and can protect you from attack from all angles. With our combined powers the Evil Lord will not be able to take over your body like he did at the apartment."

That was enough to convince Jerry; he did not want anyone inside his mind ever again. They got into the car. Annie and Mystic sat in the front, with Diana and Fiona in the back. Jerry was sort of in the middle of the car, half way between the front and back seats. It was not comfortable, but they only had a short drive to the train station. The train was a much safer form of transport, especially as the electrical connectors interfered with the Evil Lord's magical powers, thus making it impossible for him to locate them whilst they were on the train.

Lord Dell had finished breakfast and he, Johnson, and Smith were now all sitting in the study around Lord Dell's desk. Lord Dell was about to start to track where Jerry was.

"Are you fully recovered from yesterday, my Lord?" asked Smith.

"No" replied Lord Dell, as he pondered on the answer. "I am not fully recovered, but I am back to at least eighty percent. Which is still enough to do away with three Guardians" he added, smiling.

Johnson and Smith both grinned back at him.

Lord Dell adjusted himself in his all black leather directors chair so that he was comfortable to start the pursuit. "Make sure that the car is ready to go at a moments notice" he said to Johnson, who then immediately dashed outside to inform Jensen, who brought it straight around to the front door.

'Jeremy Dumbarton! Jeremy Dumbarton, where are you?' called the Evil Lord from inside his mind; and then, as before, he extended his mind out from the confines of his body, where it started searching the country, looking for Jerry.

He was not in Cambridge, which of course he already knew, but he had to check. He was not in London. The search spanned outwards. He could not find him. He stopped searching and looked up at his two aides.

"What is it Sir?" asked Smith.

"I cannot see him" answered Lord Dell.

"Why not Sir?" asked Smith, for this had never happened before; Lord Dell could always find someone in the past if he wanted to.

"He is still being protected by them" he said, "and they are too far away from me at the moment, so I can't find them."

This was bad news indeed, but all was not lost for Lord Dell; he had learnt yesterday that their destination would be London. He also knew that London was in his radar, so if they arrived in London he would be able to find them. In addition, he had guessed that they would travel by train, since that interfered with his powers, and if he was now too far away for detection then he had to be in the midlands or northern part of the country. That meant that all he had to do was get close to the main line stations that served the midlands and the north and he would be able to find them. That meant Euston, St Pancras, and Kings Cross, and those three were all very close together.

"Right" said Lord Dell, "we are going to London" and with that they left the mansion and set off to London, to the main line train stations.

Jerry and his protectors rode without incident to the train station, although Jerry might have commented on the claim of 'without incident' as it had been very bumpy sitting in the middle and not actually on a seat. Next Good Lord or not, he still bruised like any other man.

Jerry bought the tickets and the train came in almost immediately. This was either very well planned, or extremely lucky, since the next one was not for another two hours. Jerry trusted that it was the former, although he did not dare to ask. They all got on board, found an empty compartment, and settled down for the journey to Kings Cross.

The journey was solemn; no one really spoke because everyone was preparing for what lay ahead. Jerry had his copy of the pathway with him; he knew that he had to get to the hospital and find operating room number eight. Once he was in there then he could start to look for the Prize, although he had no tools with him to dig anything. He also imagined that the floor of the operating room would be made of concrete, so how he could get through that he had no idea. His whole head was starting to fill with doubts; he even wondered why he was sitting on the train; it was so obvious that he was going to fail.

Mystic held his hand.

"You will do fine, Jerry" she said to him, in a comforting tone. "You will find what is hidden in the operating room. You will not need anything to dig with."

Jerry just looked at her. If only he had her confidence, if only he could see what she could see.

Lord Dell arrived outside Kings Cross and St Pancras stations. He tried again to make contact with Jerry, but failed. Even though Jerry was moving closer and closer to him, his powers were still not yet strong enough to detect him on the train with the electrical interference and the Guardians shielding him.

Lord Dell sent Johnson and Smith to Euston, and he would wait in the car with Jensen outside Kings Cross and St Pancras stations. If Johnson and Smith spotted Jerry then they were to call Lord Dell instantly on his mobile, although Lord Dell would most likely have already sensed them by that point anyway. Johnson and Smith agreed and went hot foot to Euston Station.

The train carrying Jerry, Mystic, Fiona, Annie, and Diana started to slow down on its approach to Kings Cross. Mystic and the Guardians stood up. Jerry naturally followed.

"Are we there already?" he asked Mystic.

"Nearly, but we will be using a different route" she replied. "Hold on to my shoulders Jerry."

Jerry instantly obeyed. Mystic then turned gently on the spot, and they both vanished, followed instantly by the three Guardians.

This was the first time that Jerry had vanished and then reappeared somewhere. Mystic called it transporting, and it was a strange feeling; one minute you were standing looking at a specific view, then you turned as if walking through a plate of water, and you instantly saw a completely different view. No time had elapsed and no sense of pain was experienced in any way; it was just that you were there and then you were here. He felt however that this would be a very useful mode of transport for the future.

"Where are we?" he asked Mystic.

"We are in a side road running adjacent to the tracks leading into Kings Cross station" she replied. "Lord Dell is waiting for us at the main entrance so we couldn't possibly just walk out for he would see us. Remember he does not know where we are going in London."

"Why did we not just travel that method from the pub?" asked Jerry.

"We, that is, the Guardians and I, can only do this over short distances" replied Mystic, "a maximum of about a few kilometres. The Good Lord can travel much further of course. It is very useful, but you need to know where you are going to. I checked this place out the last time we were here; thought it might come in useful later."

"Are we safe?" asked Annie.

"Only for a few moments more" replied Mystic. "The Evil Lord will detect us shortly. Quick we must go, the hospital is just up this street."

They dashed up the side street and could see a large building up ahead, which was the hospital. They were now moving away from the electric cables that were around the tracks.

Lord Dell froze in his car. He was sniffing the air; he could not detect Jerry, but he could sense a Guardian. "They're here" he shouted. "It's Kings Cross" and he got out of the car. Jensen immediately dialled Smith and told him and Johnson to come back here immediately.

Lord Dell was trying to sense the magical shadow of the Guardians; it was not in the station itself, but it was down to the side of it.

Johnson and Smith came running up to him, clearly out of breath.

"Where?" they both asked.

"Follow me" replied Lord Dell, and he set off along the side street. Johnson and Smith were immediately behind him, and Jensen was following a short distance behind them in the car. Lord Dell was sniffing as he walked and then he took a big sniff and started running towards the spot where Jerry and the Guardians had appeared after leaving the train.

"They were here" he muttered, "three Guardians, the fortune teller and the Chosen One." He turned to his two aides. "You will need to keep the mortals away. Do what ever you need to, kill if needed; I cannot lose the Prize again."

"Yes Boss" they both replied, and felt the insides of their jackets; making sure that their pistols were ready to use if needed.

"Only if absolutely needed" said Lord Dell, "understand?"

"Yes Boss" they again both replied.

"Follow me" he commanded and he dashed off up the street towards the hospital.

Jerry and his entourage arrived at the hospital entrance. As Mystic had predicted it was not busy. Sunday visiting was in the morning as well as in the afternoon and evenings, so it felt normal for them to walk into the main building.

"Fred Perkins" whispered Mystic, into Jerry's ear.

"What?"

"Tell them we have come to visit Fred Perkins" she said to him. "They will then let us all in."

"Oh" he replied, suddenly understanding.

The inside of the hospital was nothing special; the walls were of course all white, as were the ceilings. Notices had been strategically placed at various empty spaces on the walls alerting everyone to the dangers of doing virtually anything, and advising them on special help lines that were available to call if they ever needed them. The entrance was a kind of reception and waiting area. There were a couple of ill looking people sitting on two of the chairs, a drunk in the corner was sleeping off a severe hangover and a young lad had been brought in by his harassed looking mother with his left knee and ankle heavily bandaged. All were being watched over by a series of security cameras. Jerry and his entourage walked over to the reception desk.

"Hello Sir" said the pretty nurse on duty, "can I help you?"

"Yes" said Jerry, not at all in his usual style. "We have come to see Fred" and he paused slightly.

"Fred, Sir?" enquired the Nurse, looking a bit disappointed that Jerry did not appear to be as cool as she had imagined.

"Ah Sorry" said Jerry reverting back a bit to his more normal style, "I meant Fred Perkins of course; mind is miles away babe."

She smiled at him, "yes Sir, he is on floor two. You will have to sign in here."

"Ok" said Jerry and he signed his name in the book, along with indicating that he had four others with him."

"Thank you sir" replied the Nurse smiling at him. "Have a nice day."

They then all left the reception area and headed through the double green doors towards the lifts.

"Well done" whispered Mystic.

The doors closed behind them just as Lord Dell approached the hospital.

"It's in a hospital" he said to himself; "strange choice, but why not?" and he walked in together with Johnson and Smith and approached the reception desk.

"Fred Perkins" he said to the Nurse.

"What, oh Fred is popular today isn't he?" she muttered, as she asked him also to sign the visitors book. Lord Dell however just looked at the Nurse, waved his hand past her face, and said to her that he did not need to sign the book.

"Oh I am sorry, Sir" she replied. "My mistake, you do not need to sign the book. Fred is in the ward on floor two" and she pointed over to the same green doors that Jerry had just walked through, which led to the elevators.

"Of course he has to sign the book" called out an official looking person from behind the young nurse.

"Oh, I am sorry Matron" said the young nurse. "Sir you must please sign the book."

Lord Dell did not have time to argue, and he could not risk doing magic again with so many people around. He reluctantly signed the book and then moved with haste over towards the doors, followed immediately by Johnson and Smith. He looked through one of the two small glass circular windows in the door and he saw Mystic, walking into the elevator.

"Quick" he called to Johnson and Smith, as they followed him through the doors. Lord Dell pointed his finger and shot a bolt of bright red energy directly towards the lift doors. However, he was just a fraction too late; the lift doors had closed, the lift had started moving, and the bolt of energy just hit the outer doors leaving a big black scorching mark, and a little cloud of smoke. The lift had gone, but they stood outside watching the indicator to see where it would stop.

Mystic already knew that the Evil Lord was close behind them, and had already pushed the sub-basement button on the elevator the moment she had entered. She had also heard the bolt of energy hit the doors as they closed.

"He is getting closer" she said to the Guardians. "We must be prepared. If we stop the two sidekicks first, then that will protect Jerry and give him enough time to let him find the Prize. We will try and stop them entering operating room eight by diverting them in the main O.R. admittance area."

"Yes" the three of them replied, as the lift descended the three levels to take them to the sub-basement and the admittance area for all of the operating theatres.

Jerry was feeling very nervous at this stage; he kept taking out the piece of paper on which they had written down the pathway to the Prize. He had to get to O.R. eight, and then look at the operating table; the head showed the direction to the back wall, where underneath the Prize would be, most likely buried. He knew it all, but he just had to do it.

The elevator stopped, the doors opened and they stepped out into a round, large, white, sterile area, which had a reception desk in the middle and three corridors going off towards different groups of operating rooms.

"Quick, hurry" said Mystic, as she dashed towards the empty receptionist desk, followed by the others.

"Jerry" she commanded. "Quickly, go down there towards O.R. eight, and go quietly" she added, as she pointed over towards the middle corridor.

Jerry dashed down the corridor as quietly and as fast as he could.

"Sub-Basement" said Lord Dell, to his two aides, "quick, hold on to my shoulders."

Johnson and Smith knew exactly what was now about to happen; they would all disappear and instantly reappear a short distance away, this time however in a vertical downwards direction. The each grabbed hold of one of their Master's shoulders.

"Take out your pistols" said Lord Dell, "just in case."

They immediately followed their Masters orders and as they held their pistols, Lord Dell turned briefly on the spot and they instantly disappeared from the lift area in the main entrance.

It was as if they had suddenly arrived in the middle of a lightening storm; they were being continually bombarded from the moment they appeared in front of the lift doors in the O.R. theatre reception area by four bolts of pure white energy coming from Mystic and her three companions. Within a few moments they were being repelled backwards by the sheer force of the bolts hitting them straight in their midriffs. It was even too much for Lord Dell, as he cowered and backed away towards an identical set of doors that they had just passed through upstairs by the reception. The doors led to a staircase.

"He'll be back" said Mystic, as she called the Guardians over to follow her into one of the corridors. Strangely enough, it was the corridor towards operating rooms one to five.

"What about Jerry?" asked Annie, "will he be all right on his own?"

"He will be alright" replied Mystic, "but he is not alone."

The three Guardians looked at each other, wondering what Mystic could be meaning with 'not alone'. For Jerry had indeed gone off towards operating room eight, and they were all heading down the corridor for operating rooms one to five.

Jerry had found O.R.-8. He had to keep now very quiet so no one could hear him. He did not know how much time he had, but he knew that the sooner he found it, the better. He opened the door and walked in.

Lord Dell, Johnson, and Smith had all recovered and were now ready to launch their counter attack. Lord Dell would go first and put a shield in front of him to protect them all. Then he could start attacking the Guardians and Mystic, and if Johnson or Smith saw Jerry then they should shoot him.

Lord Dell pushed open the door and stood firm in front of it. The Guardians were no longer there. He sniffed the air; it was so easy they had all gone down the corridor towards operating rooms one to five, so that was now where they were going.

They shot off down the corridor, which was not very long, but it was narrow. When it ended it opened up into another slight smaller circular area, which had five doors, each one leading to one of the actual operating rooms. There were a couple of chairs outside each door, and in the middle of the circular area was a small metallic spiral staircase that led up to what was a viewing gallery above the operating rooms, with a view looking down into each room.

Lord Dell, Johnson, and Smith walked around the circular area, keeping a close eye out for anything that moved, but nothing did. They reached O.R.-1. The door was closed shut, like all the others. Lord Dell tried opening it, but it was locked tight. He then sniffed the air.

"They have split up" he whispered to his aides, who then both just looked at each other, not knowing what to do next.

"Divided they shall fall" laughed Lord Dell as he unlocked the door with a few mumbled words and walked into the operating room. "Nothing" he grunted, starting to get a bit agitated. "How long shall we play these games?" he called out to the Guardians.

As he finished, one of the Guardians responded; a bolt of pure white energy flashed down from the gallery above heading straight towards Johnson. Lord Dell was quick and repelled it away, where it headed to and hit an innocent looking cupboard, hanging on a side wall. The cupboard instantaneously exploded, sending dozens of small surgical instruments crashing to the floor.

"The Gallery" commanded Lord Dell, and they all three turned and ran back out of the operating room, towards the spiral staircase, and up to the gallery. As they reached the top of the staircase, they slowed; Lord Dell sensed a trap.

Jerry in the mean time had walked into O.R.-8. It was rather dimly lit, but he could still see the operating table in the middle of the room. Everything seemed to be prepared for the next day's operations, as there was equipment all over the place, all with different size tubes, coloured knobs, and video displays.

Jerry walked over to the table and stood facing the end where the patient's feet would normally lay. He could see clearly along the whole of the table towards where the head would rest. He looked straight up, and towards the back wall, trying not to move his head to the side. There seemed to be no specific markings on the wall; it was clean and sterile just as every other part. Nevertheless, Jerry marked the spot in his mind and very carefully walked over to it, making sure that he did not disturb any items of equipment that now lay in his path.

When he arrived at the wall, he looked back towards the table, just to reconfirm that he was in the right place. He started to feel the wall, searching for any hidden cavities, or just anything unusual. He felt from the top, right down to the bottom, but there was nothing.

Lord Dell sniffed the air; there were Guardians in the Gallery, he was right to suspect a trap.

"Wait here" he commanded to Johnson and Smith, who both gulped. Lord Dell raised his head slightly just as a bolt of white light went flashing past it. He immediately sprang out and took cover under one of the empty tables.

The gallery was just like a large canteen would be, but without any kitchen. It was a large circular open area with windows all around, each looking down into one of the operating rooms. Tables and chairs were scattered throughout the gallery so that people could obviously sit and discuss the goings-on in the rooms below. Over on one side there was a coffee machine.

Lord Dell tried to sense where the Guardians were; there were clearly more than one here with him. He felt that his best plan would be to immediately counter attack, and to try and catch them off-guard. With that thought in his mind he immediately sprang himself upwards and let out an enormous burst of energy such that the table covering him, and several of the tables nearby, all exploded in small pieces, which then all flew towards the windows overlooking the operating rooms. As the fragments of broken tables and chairs collided with the windows, several of them shattered into pieces, resulting in glass and other debris falling onto the pristine floors below.

Mystic turned, vanished, and immediately reappeared behind the Evil Lord and then sent a bolt of energy heading straight for his back. At the same time, Annie sent one towards his left side and Diana to his front. Lord Dell just laughed a cold cruel merciless laugh.

"Is that the best you can do, Guardians?" he called to them.

Fiona was now recovering down on the floor in OR-2; she had fallen through the broken window, after one of the exploding tables had hit her. She was not hurt, well apart from her slightly dented pride, but no physical damage. She instantly reappeared in the Gallery to assist her comrades.

Lord Dell fired a shot of Evil Energy straight at Diana, who met it in mid air with a bolt of white such that the two exploded when they made contact. Lord Dell looked astonished; no Guardian had ever done that to one of his power bolts before.

Jerry had now reached the floor. An enormous racket had erupted somewhere else in the hospital; smashing glass and falling debris; obviously the Guardians were now doing battle with the Evil Lord. Jerry however could not be distracted; he had his job to do. The pathway had said that the Prize lay under the back wall. Jerry was kneeling on the ground and feeling around on the floor. The lights were still dim, but there was just sufficient for him to see.

'It must be under the floor' he thought to himself; 'that's the only way it can be under the wall' but he could not feel anything loose. Mystic had said to him that he would not need anything to dig with, but the floor did seem to be of solid concrete. How could he do this?

Lord Dell turned and fired a bolt at Annie, who moved just in time. The bolt however hit the wall next to a window and subsequently exploded causing the window to smash into thousands of tiny fragments of glass.

Bolts of red and white light were being sent all over the place, it was almost like a laser show, but far more sinister. No one however was actually winning, and Lord Dell specifically was starting to notice this and get suspicious.

'They are trying to divert my attention from the Chosen One' he thought to himself, but he had no idea where Jerry was, and he could not stop concentrating long enough on the battle in order to locate him. The only solution therefore was to bring this battle to a swift and complete conclusion.

Lord Dell joined his hands together high above his head; he was forming some kind of shield since bolts of white light from the Guardians and Mystic were heading straight for his body but were being diverted away just before the reached him. He seemed impervious to their attack.

Then, over by the coffee machine, there was a sudden brilliant flash of bright white light. It was so bright and so powerful that it lit up the entire complex of operating rooms. Everyone stopped, including the Evil Lord; no one could look at the light for it was far too intense.

Lord Dell looked worried. The Guardians looked puzzled. Mystic was smiling.

Lord Dell summoned up all his energy and directed a huge bolt of red power straight towards the fifty-year-old man who was now standing at the point where the white light had emerged. The man was wearing a white tunic from head to toe, had long silver hair, a silvery beard, and was holding a white stave in his left hand, which he instantly thumped hard on the ground, resulting in several bolts of equally powerful white energy charging down the red bolt and dispersing it harmlessly into the air.

The Guardians by now had realised who had joined them, and they were now kneeling down where they had previously stood. Mystic had also done the same. The only one remaining standing was Lord Dell, who turned to look into the eyes of the silvery haired man.

"So" he said to him disdainfully, "fed up with eating straw, are we now?"

"I guess I shall never now tire of that, Ivor" replied the Good Lord. "It was just time for me to return to my original form in preparation for the replenishment" he added, still looking quite happy with his old self. "I had forgotten what flexibility I had."

"DIE" shouted the Evil Lord, as red bolts of power emanated from all over his body and headed straight for the Good Lord, where they merely bounced off and hit the ground.

"You cannot destroy me" he replied, "just like we cannot let you keep what is not rightfully yours."

Now it was the Evil Lord's turn to look puzzled, as he wondered what the Good Lord was referring to; he had had so much in the past that was not rightfully his.

The Guardians and Mystic stood up and moved slightly closer towards the Evil Lord, surrounding him in a circle. They each held out their hands and began sending huge powerful bolts of energy towards him. More and more, longer and longer, stronger and stronger, the bolts of energy left the palms of their hands and hit the Evil Lord's body, but nothing appeared to be happening. Then after a few more moments, the Evil Lord started to weaken; he fell to his knees and started screaming, as if being burnt by red-hot beams of white light. Then, after a few moments more, as the most evil of beings ever to roam the planet knelt on the ground in agony, white light started to emanate from his body. It was energy, and it was forming itself into a shape. It was the shape of a man; it was the shape of Harrie de Gaunt, the dead third Guardian, the one killed at the depositary. The figure of Mr de Gaunt extracted itself from the Evil Lord's cowering body and slowly glided over to where the Good Lord stood, where it then peacefully melted into his body, causing as it did the brilliance of the aura surrounding him to intensify.

However, it had not finished; another shape was now emerging and it was that of Gavin du Faire, the fifth Guardian, the one killed first in the museum. He also extracted himself from the now quivering body that was the Evil Lord, glided peacefully over to where the Good Lord stood, and like the one before melted into his body, causing the brilliance of the aura around him to intensify yet further.

The Guardians stopped. Lord Dell was now very weak and collapsed in a heap on the ground. The Good Lord was now brighter and even looked slightly younger. The power that he was emanating was indeed stronger.

"You two" called out the Good Lord, as he looked towards Johnson and Smith who were still hiding at the top of the spiral staircase. "Come here and collect your master; it is time for him to go home."

The two came running, gently picked up Lord Dell, and then carried him back down the spiral staircase and towards the lift. The Guardians followed them just in case they got any bright ideas, like going to find Jerry.

Jerry meanwhile had given up looking around the wall; that was obviously wrong as there was nothing there. Jerry was now looking at the operating table. The pathway said, 'look where patient lies, shows direction to back, under where find Prize'. This must mean something like look at where the patients back lies, and then under that you'll find the Prize. Jerry was trying to look under the operating table, which was quite difficult since there was a lot of equipment around the table. Jerry however had managed to crawl under the table and was feeling around, about in line with where the back of the patient would be. And then he felt something. It was definitely metallic; it felt something like a metal cigarette box. Jerry pulled it free from the table and moved quietly over to where the light was brighter.

Was this it? Was this the result of what he had been looking for these past three weeks? Was everything now coming down to this one monumental life defining moment?

Jerry looked at the small cigarette box; it was no more than 10cm long, 4 cm wide and 1cm deep and looked as though it was made from silver. There was a metal catch which kept the lid closed. The box looked very old. Jerry tried to open the catch but it was very stiff. Some of the edges were sharp as well and Jerry cut his right thumb while feeling around them. Eventually however the catch came loose and Jerry prized the box open.

Extra Time

"He has found it" said Mystic to the Good Lord, as they waited in the gallery for the Guardians to return.

"Oh" he replied, looking slightly disappointed; a look that Mystic did not understand.

"You had best go to him, he will need support now, and he will have many questions. Bring him to me."

Mystic bowed and walked away towards the central staircase where she descended into the circular room below, and set off to find Jerry. She felt a tad disturbed by the expression on the Good Lord's face; why had he looked disappointed? Was he not looking forward to spending the rest of his mortal life with her?

A short moment later the three Guardians returned from seeing off the Evil Lord, and they walked over to where the Good Lord was still standing, purveying over the destruction that had occurred in the bowels of the hospital.

"Welcome back my Lord" said Annie, as she bowed to him.

"Why thank you, One" he replied. "It has been a long time since I have used this form."

"They have left the building, my Lord, and are on their way back to Lord Dell's mansion."

"Very good" he replied, and smiled at her.

"What do you require from us now?" she asked.

"You shall all go home now" he answered. "Your job here is done for this evening. Jerry is safe now; the Evil Lord is far too week and will require many months to recover back to his normal self. He will also have to re-hide himself back into society as his disguise is quite useless now."

He smiled at the three Guardians standing before him.

"I calculate" he continued, "that with the return of the power of Gavin and Harrie that I, Albert, have been granted an extra year before the replenishment."

He looked at them all; they were all smiling back at him.

"What of Jerry?" asked Annie.

"Mystic has gone to him. She will take him back to the pub in a few minutes, but first I need to speak with him before he leaves here."

"Is he all right?" asked Diana.

"He is fine" replied Albert. "He is just a little confused at the moment."

"Is he the Chosen One?" asked Fiona.

"Oh, of that there is no doubt" he replied, his expression becoming much more serious. "But he still has much to do before he can become the next Good Lord."

They all looked at him; this did not really make sense. Sensing their confusion he merely relaxed slightly and smiled back at them.

"Until next time" he said, and they all took that as their instructions to go, and all three turned on the spot and disappeared, leaving him surveying the mess left behind after the recent battle.

Jerry was devastated; the box was empty. He had turned it upside down, had vigorously shaken it to see if anything fell out, but nothing did. He did not understand; he had followed the instructions, he had found the box in exactly the place where the pathway had described it, but it was empty. It did not make sense.

Mystic approached him.

"Jerry" she called out softly, as he looked around and met her eyes.

"It's empty" he said to her. "I don't understand?"

"Come with me" she replied, as she held out her hand.

Jerry grabbed her hand and instantly felt a warm sensation, like a child holding on to his mother.

"I don't understand?" he repeated.

Mystic, as if walking a young schoolchild up to meet his headmaster, escorted Jerry back to the viewing gallery. They climbed the stairs into the gallery area where the Good Lord was standing and waiting for them.

"Hello Jerry" he said, "we meet again."

"Have we met before, Sir?" asked Jerry.

"Yes" he replied. "I told you when we met in the field that that occasion would be the last time you saw me in the form of the White Horse."

"You said" interrupted Jerry, "that the next time I saw you would be when I had found the Prize and had proven that I was the worthy one."

"And have you found the Prize?" he asked.

"I found a box" replied Jerry, "but it is empty."

Albert stretched out his hand and Jerry placed the box in his open palm. The inside of the box was made of a red velvet material, and it looked empty. Albert however, merely drew the box closer to his face and peered into it.

"Fascinating" he muttered, as if he was reading something written all over it. But Jerry had seen nothing, and further more could not see anything.

"What does it say?" he asked.

"It says" started Albert, "that this is not the Prize, and that you have misread some of the clues and must now go back and retrace your steps. For only then will you be able to prove that you are worthy.

"I am not worthy" said Jerry, "I can't do it any more."

"Doubts and uncertainty are always present when something does not go the way you expect" added Albert. "This is part of the test to prove that you really are worthy. I should point out that since Gred no new Good Lord has ever gone straight to the Prize in their first go, why even I needed two attempts."

"You needed two attempts?" said Jerry, in a disbelieving voice.

"Two attempts" he repeated, looking deep into Jerry's eyes.

Jerry's heart lifted slightly, although he was still confused.

"What shall I do with the box?" he asked.

"You shall keep hold of it" replied Albert, "for you never know when you might need it."

"Yes, Sir" replied Jerry, and he took the box back and placed it in his trouser pocket.

"Now Mystic will take you back to the station, and travel back with you to the pub. You will be safe for now" he continued. "The Evil Lord is very weak and needs time to recover. You must continue your Quest for the Prize, as the replenishment has only been delayed, it has not been cancelled. You must still find the Prize before the Evil Lord, and be ready to replenish me. Good luck Jerry" he concluded, and then turned on the spot and vanished.

Jerry just stood for a moment. This had not been how he imagined the day turning out. He had imagined two alternatives, one being that he found the Prize, and the other being that he had not. Now he had found something exactly where the Prize should have been, but it was not the Prize, and even worse he had been told that he had misread some of the clues and would have to re-read them. This meant the whole three weeks had been a waste of time, well not completely a waste of time; he had found Jules again and a happiness that he had never had before. But even so, it was still very disappointing.

Mystic walked with Jerry back to the elevator where they ascended, said good-bye to the receptionist, and walked out of the hospital and back towards Kings Cross station. When they arrived they found that there was a train leaving within 20 minutes so they did not have to wait very long in the same old waiting room. Even so, Mystic still felt captivated by the painting of the old Queen Mary that was hanging on the wall next to the tourist clock. Jerry still had no time for either; he was holding on to the metal box that was now in his pocket, wondering what he would be using it for in the future.

The journey back to the pub was very quiet and sombre. When Jerry and Mystic pulled up outside the White Horse pub, Jules, who had obviously been waiting for him to return, ran out to greet him with a hug. She had tears in her eyes: she had been so worried the whole day. Annie had, of course, told them about the battle but even she did not know what Jerry had found.

Jules pulled him and Mystic inside, and made him tell them the whole story of what happened. Jerry started; explaining about both the walls and floors being solid, and how he had worked out that the text must have meant something else. He told them also about how he had found the metal box, cut his thumb on opening it, and how he found that it was empty.

Jerry went on to tell them about the Good Lord's change of appearance, and what he had said about the little cigarette box. Pete and Jules could not believe that they had any of the clues wrong, but that was what the Good Lord had said to Jerry, and they had no reason to doubt him.

"When we get back" said Pete, we will look again at the clues, double check them, and look for other answers.

"You will all have to find new places to live" said Mystic, "for the Evil Lord knows where Jerry lives now, so it will not be safe to stay there any longer."

None of them were worried about that, as the thought of moving was not really a concern for them. Jules wondered where they would go, but Mystic assured her that they would find something suitable.

"But now you must eat" said Jose, and he prepared them a slap-up meal which was a wondrous feast. When they had finished they were completely full.

"Where is the Good Lord now?" asked Jules, as she looked at Mystic.

"Oh, he will be around" she replied. "He now has some extra time and I am sure that with the unexpected weakness of the Evil Lord over the coming months, he will take the opportunity to spread more love and happiness around the world before his replenishment approaches."

"Will he come back as the White Horse?" asked Jules.

"I don't think so" answered Mystic.

"I will miss our daily riding session" muttered Annie, as she tidied-up and put the plates into the dishwasher.

"Will I have to be a white horse?" asked Jerry, also looking towards Mystic.

"That is completely up to you, Jerry" she answered. "The White Horse was a disguise. No one really notices if a horse stays alive for a thousand years, but if you are a person then you need to be registered and have ID cards and passports and all that" she continued.

"But that's not impossible to manage is it?" he asked.

"No, of course not" she replied. "You can be whatever you want to be. The Guardians are people and they have been around for many hundreds of years."

Jerry felt much happier now. The process of being able to talk about it and the way that Pete and Jules had reacted were a big comfort to him. The three of them said goodbye to Annie, Mystic, and Jose, and set off back to Cambridge.

Annie and Jose also said goodnight to Mystic as they returned into the pub, leaving Mystic to walk over to the old barn.

"Hello dear, sweet, Mystic" called out the soft voice of the Good Lord, as she entered the barn.

Mystic ran to him and hugged him tightly.

"We have been granted an extra year together" he said to her, cuddling her tightly in his arms.

"Yes, my dear Albert" replied Mystic, wiping her eyes. "Isn't it wonderful?"

"Yes" he whispered, as he continued holding on to her.

"Where shall you go?" she asked him. "I mean you can't live in the barn anymore can you, and there is no room on my street sign for a fifty year old man" she added, laughing slightly.

"Oh, we will find something together my dear" he replied. "Somewhere out in the countryside, where no one asks any questions and where the long arm of the establishment has not yet reached."

"And what of Jerry?" she asked.

"Well," he continued. "He is the Chosen One and he has done very well to get as far as he has. But he needs more help and I just hope that there is someone out there who can help him find the Prize because he has all the clues he needs to be successful in his Quest".

With that he grabbed hold of Mystic and cuddled her again.

"Do you think he will succeed in inheriting the Prize?" she asked.

"Oh yes" he replied, "of that I have absolutely no doubts. I am sure there is at least one out there who can help him. There must be at least one who can successfully decipher the clues, solve them correctly and determine where, and even what, is the Prize" and with that he suddenly froze. It was as if he had sensed something. It was a strange feeling, one that he had not experienced before. It was as if someone, at that very moment in time, was looking down on him and reading his very thoughts as if they were words printed in a book. The Good Lord raised his head, looked up from the printed words and extended his mind out and towards the face that was now staring down upon them.

"Is it you?" he whispered. "Can you find the Prize?"

A NOTE FROM THE AUTHOR

Dear Reader, I would firstly like to thank you for reading this book, and I sincerely hope that you enjoyed the story, and were not too disappointed by the little twist at the end, but more inspired by it. As you no doubt guessed, it was not really the end, but more a pause in the story, an opportunity for you to take stock, and decide how you want to go forward.

Book two, "The Replenishment" will be out soon, or maybe is even out now depending upon when you are reading this. In the second book Jerry will correctly solve each of the five clues and find the pathway to the Prize, so if you want, you can just sit back, relax, get on with your life, and wait until you get hold of book two, to find out where the Prize is, and what it is.

However, if you cannot wait, or if you just fancy yourself as a bit of a smart-arse, you might like to try and work out what the Prize actually is, and where it is hiding, for as Albert said, "Jerry has all the clues."

Yes, dear reader, all the clues are actually in the storyline, hidden away of course, teasing you, tempting you, tricking you, and maybe even testing you as well, but I assure you, they are there, waiting to be found.

For those who take the challenge, here is what you need to do. First determine which of the clues are wrong; you can work that out if you read carefully. Once you have done that, you can set about correctly solving them and then the pathway will be at your mercy. However, beware; there are a few tricks to overcome before you can get to the Prize . . .

Good luck . . .   Keith Dyne.

316

Printed in the United Kingdom
by Lightning Source UK Ltd.
135861UK00001BB/79/P